TIM RICHARDS

APPROXIMATE LIFE

THE PRINCE AND OTHER STORIES

CONTENTS

INTRODUCTION

Approximate Life is a trilogy that consists of three books that Tim Richards published in the 1990s: *Letters to Francesca* (1996), *The Prince* (1997), and *Duckness* (1998). Despite being separated into three parts, *Approximate Life* was always meant to be read as a complete work in itself. This new edition is thus notable for the way it brings together these pieces into a single volume, making it possible for Richards's literary masterpiece to be read as it was originally conceived.

The shifting nuances of 'approximate life' are key to understanding what Richards is exploring in this book. In the opening story 'Days Without Violence', for instance, a brilliant but unstable mother teaches her two sons the importance of confronting life's inherent uncertainty. 'You can't live with someone who lives in fear of approximates and approximation,' she insists. Like many of the stories in *Approximate Life*, these observations lead the reader into a hall of mirrors that causes us to wonder: is the narrator's eccentric mother a madwoman, or is she a genius?

Similarly, 'The Leisure Society' recounts how a German billionaire, Klaus Obermeier, becomes consumed with recreating the 408 photos lost after a memorable trip to Australia. 'To begin with, Klaus contented himself with rough approximations,' but the penchant for precision that made him such a successful businessman eventually wins out. 'He is ruthless in his pursuit of authentically re-created perfections,' a fixation that quickly descends into nihilism and absurdity. Klaus's behaviour provides a template for many of Richards's characters, whose inability to cope with the approximations of life transforms desire into obsession.

The most important nuance of approximation in the trilogy concerns the fraught relationship between fiction and reality. In *The Prince*, for example, the protagonist Richard Thompson opines that '[e]very reality is a flawed approximation of the ideas that brought it into being'. This willingness to concede that perfection is impossible becomes the mark of a healthy and creative human being. 'To approximate is to assert your inability to arrive at the Truth,' Thompson continues. 'You fashion a poetry that hovers in the vicinity of the truth.' Nonetheless, Thompson's position as the communal executioner—a morally questionable role that brings material prosperity and a sense of community to Hampton, at the cost of seven random killings each year—leaves the sincerity of his words endlessly open to doubt.

Richards repeatedly deploys the name 'Richard Thompson' in *Approximate Life* as a fictional caricature of himself, employing this self-mockery as a mode to question and critique the world around him. He makes the Melbourne suburb of Hampton into the centre of his fictional universe, for instance, so that in 'Our Swimmer' and *The Prince* this unassuming area, in a satirical twist, becomes a place of global importance. 'Prickly Heat' and 'Criminal History' draw on his experiences as a junior bureaucrat working in the police records office, each story satirically transforming this soul-crushing job into a biting fable about modern life. Richards also imbues his literary doubles with other aspects of himself: Tim, the narrator of 'A Letter to Francesca', finishes reading Cortez's life-changing novel *Melbourne* at 4:40 am on June 3rd, the exact hour at which the author named Tim Richards was born. The date is repeated in *The Prince*, so that 'large crowds gather in Hampton to celebrate Thompson's birthday'. *Approximate Life* is not only an approximation of life in general, therefore: it is also a literary approximation of Richards's own life, 'a poetry that hovers in the vicinity of the truth'.

In this sense, *Approximate Life* is both a work of literary fiction *and* an experimental new form of autobiography. This mode of autobiography does not seek to assemble the mundane facts of its author's life, but instead imaginatively creates a fictional approximation of his identity. 'Only in fiction do you get the most accurate approximations of true identity,' ruminates Thompson in *The Prince*. 'If I were to write my autobiography most truthfully, it would need to take the form of an expressionistic fiction.' The point where these two genres fuse is driven by a logic that Richards borrows explicitly from Alfred Hitchcock's film *Vertigo*: 'desire fashions reality', so that what is expressed as 'truth' is an emotional rather than a factual interpretation of life.

The result is an approach to literature grounded in the modernist style known as expressionism, which privileges the subjective emotions of the artist over objective reality. 'Distance Education', for instance, unfolds as a series of letters between a teacher, another Richard Thompson, and Sarah, a young woman enrolled in a correspondence course who, in place of her academic assignments, submits disturbing stories about being impregnated by an alien that Thompson describes as 'expressionistic autobiography'. Julia Cortez, in 'A Letter to Francesca', justifies the wild inaccuracies in her novel *Melbourne*, which also features a protagonist named Richard Thompson, by insisting that they are 'indispensable to the mode of fiction I choose to call 'Theoretical Expressionism''. The Richard Thompson who narrates 'The Fiction Consultant', in turn, has written a story called 'The Summer Festival of Kissing' using 'a new form of prose called 'autobiographical expressionism', where outrageous distortions and extrapolations are used to communicate interior truths'. This story acts as an implicit counterpart to *The Prince*, which features yet another permutation of Richard Thompson, the officially-appointed Killer at the annual Hampton Festival of Killing (the exchange of a single letter shifts the entire premise of the second narrative) who, in his journal, articulates a similar theory of autobiography as 'expressionistic fiction' as his namesake in 'The Fiction Consultant'.

While these self-caricatures ruthlessly mock the anxieties

and bad faith that mark the modern individual, this approach also provides an equally powerful critique of the ethical limits of community. This dynamic is most obvious in *The Prince*, which examines how the legacies of the competing political philosophies of Jean-Jacques Rousseau's *The Social Contract*, Thomas Hobbes's *Leviathan*, and Niccolò Machiavelli's *The Prince* converge to create the independent city-state of Hampton. Through this satirical glimpse of 'the most curious social experiment in Australia's history', Richards depicts a utilitarian, neo-liberal dystopia that, in the years since the novel's original publication, has proven to be depressingly prophetic.

Richards is particularly attuned to the inconsistencies that keep society, especially Australian society, together. The mother in 'Days Without Violence' instils in her sons a robust suspicion of established authority that metamorphoses into her own form of emotional tyranny. Her rebellion against conventional notions of time, for instance, is coupled with an attempt 'to engage the specificity of spatio-temporal relations the way the Aborigines had', as she unleashes a whirlwind of contradictory ideas culminating in her conclusion that 'nature, as an intellectual construct, was itself unnatural'. For all their mother's apparent paranoia, the boys come to realize that there is an underlying truth to her warnings, exemplified by the heavy-handed intervention of the state in their lives.

These themes culminate in the book's final story, 'Still Life with Lamingtons', in which Richard (presumably Thompson) and his brother Jack travel to the Greek island of Meskos to meet a young woman named Elizabeth Colley. Before this journey, Richard's obsession with the loss of his ex-girlfriend, Miranda, had landed him in a psychiatric hospital. Upon his release, his mother insists that Elizabeth may be the woman who can deliver him from unhappiness. What ensues is an allegory in which the Colley family represents a comically hyperbolic version of the Australia of a generation earlier. Elizabeth's father Max, for instance, reminisces about playing tennis with Lew Hoad and

Ken Rosewall, keeps a large photograph of the Queen on his wall, and praises conservative politicians like Robert Menzies and John Howard. Elizabeth is cast from the same mould, with a feminine twist: she disdains modern literature, is blithely ignorant of her own sexuality, and spends much of her time baking large batches of lamingtons. Despite living in Greece, she affirms: 'It's only Australia that I know about'. Richards thus enacts a satirical confrontation between old and new Australia that ponders, with humour and insight, how society has changed, and how it continues to change.

For many readers, Richards's work will recall the fiction of Jorge Luis Borges, especially their shared fascination with irony and paradox, and the use of fiction as a tool for philosophical contemplation. Richards's writings, however, are warmer, more emotionally engaging than Borges's, thanks largely to the mode of 'autobiographical expressionism' that distinguishes his work. Also like Borges, Richards is a writer whose fiction simultaneously reflects and transcends its immediate context. You do not have to have lived in Hampton, or Melbourne, or even Australia to appreciate the depth and brilliance of these stories, a truth that I have witnessed firsthand in university classrooms ranging from New Jersey to Seoul. This new publication of *Approximate Life* is a joyful event, the resurrection of an overlooked literary classic that a whole new generation of readers can now enjoy.

Peter D. Mathews
Professor of English Literature
Hanyang University
June 3rd, 2021 at 4:40 am

I

LETTERS TO FRANCESCA

OCTOBER, 1984–OCTOBER, 1994

Leave everything
Leave Dada
Leave your wife leave your mistress
Leave your hopes and your fears
Sew your children in the corner of a wood
Leave the substance for the shadow ...
Set out on the road.

—André Breton, *The Surrealist Manifesto*

DAYS WITHOUT VIOLENCE

Because people believe what they read in trashy magazines, they expect me to resent my mother. Nothing could be further from the truth. If there is one thing in my life I resent, it's the pernicious influence of clichés like 'the wisdom of hindsight'.

Where is hindsight's wisdom? Hindsight is arrogance worn like a miner's lamp, a narrow beam of light directed for a specific purpose. Why should that view be considered authoritative? Hindsight should set itself the task of providing accurate weather predictions instead of trespassing on the privacy of lost moments.

When the merchants of hindsight invite me to join the condemnation of my mother, I upset them by refusing to alter the facts to suit their preconceptions. I insist that their theories don't interest me. I will describe the events of my childhood only as they are impressed upon my memory.

Inevitably, I picture Mother waltzing between the kitchen and her study, swaying like someone dribbling an imaginary basketball, baulking phantom opponents, never two steps in a straight line. Her head is full of inspirations, wild ideas that need to be danced out. She can dance for hours at a time, unreachable, sweat streaming down her face, her mouth twisting as she spews out song lyrics, numbers, or incomprehensible phrases. She could be in tears. All this, she told us, was the hallmark of her genius. She could only create when caught up in pure joy, and she tried to organize her world so that nothing would interfere with these eruptions. She never doubted that what she was giving us was the secret of exaltation.

Standing in the entrance hall at Netherby was a blackboard

that was central to Mother's experiment in behavioral modification. A sign written in sky-blue chalk pronounced DAYS WITHOUT VIOLENCE, and the total below was adjusted each day so that it might read '36 (Previous Record: 82)'. Mother had based this experiment on the DAYS WITHOUT INJURY signs she remembered outside industrial plants, and her scoreboard operated on a roughly similar principle.

If Johnny and I went fifty days without wrestling, kicking or punching each other, we were rewarded with a new book. It was a ploy. Mother didn't care about the harm we did to each other. Her sign was meant to discourage us from *reporting* harmful acts. She didn't want her work interrupted by calls to adjudicate.

Hair had a special importance. Mother had long raven locks, the most gorgeous hair I've ever seen. During the day she tied it up in a bun, with just a ringlet or two allowed to dangle enticingly beside her ears. At night, she let her hair fall. She brushed and brushed, the most wonderful repetition, and our greatest thrill was to be allowed to brush her hair.

For all her vanity, Mother was brutally unpredictable with our hair. A sudden shriek announced that a haircut was in progress. I might wake to find her above my pillow, scissors in hand, or else I'd peer through the kitchen doorway to see Johnny's wild protests as Mother used his sandy locks as a means to explore some radical new geometry. If you had seen her cutting our hair, you might have thought her cruel, and I'll admit to being shaken by Mother's ambushes, but her peculiar sense of hair design never bothered us. We had been conditioned to accept untidiness and unpredictability. Certainty or reliability would have terrified us.

Mother told us that she earned money writing articles for mathematical and philosophical journals. Because our father had sabotaged her career, she couldn't get her work published in Australia unless she submitted under a pseudonym. But mostly she translated the articles into French or Spanish to facilitate their publication in European or Latin American journals. Mother was always writing, elbows tucked in, guardedly looking over her shoulder, frightened that a masked scholar would burst through the door and steal her theory of existential ahistoricality.

I don't recall her saying that she had inherited money. Only the house. Her father built Netherby, and she lived in the house when she was a girl. She told us that Netherby had been left to her when her parents were killed in a light plane crash in Kenya. Mother hardly ever mentioned money. We probably assumed that everyone had gardeners and cleaners as a matter of course.

During the morning, she would instruct us in mathematics, philosophy, and literature. After completing our study tasks, we were free to do as we liked: to draw, read, or play in the vast grounds of the property. We would look up to see Mother sitting on the balcony, staring out over the bay, shaping some new definition or aphorism. We never thought ourselves prisoners or captives. We were only captive to the extent that we were Australian.

Australia is a captive nation, Mother told us, ransomed off from the Brits to the Yanks. After a time, hostages forget their status, which is precisely the point when they begin to think like hostages. This house is a republic. The slavery of mind stops at the front gate.

I remember wanting to play with other children. Sometimes we heard them call to us from over the fence, and we called back, but to play with them was out of the question. We knew they would contaminate us.

My brother Johnny gave up sleep after a run of bad dreams. Just eleven, he decided that sleep was more trouble than it was worth. For several weeks, he suffered dreadful fatigue, but after that his metabolism seemed to adjust. Johnny used to say that insomnia was a muscle, the less he slept, the less he needed to sleep.

At night he read, gazed at the stars, or painted. Sometimes I'd wake to hear him discussing things with Mother, talking into the early hours. Johnny would talk with her, and brush her hair, thousands of long, smooth strokes. I'm sure it was the time he spent with her while I slept, brushing her hair and talking, that made Johnny Mother's favourite.

Mother detested all institutions and institutionalized practices. She warned us against physicians, hospitals, psychiatrists, banks, insurance companies, churches, and government. More than anything, she loathed schools.

Schools were established to set limits on possibility, and to restrain sexuality. She said that the primary business of a school is to infect the world of knowledge with the knowledge of mediocrity. The secondary business of a school is to contaminate the outer world with the mediocrity that passes as knowledge. She said that schools were red carpets rolled out to honour the unexceptional.

Neither Johnny nor I ever thought to question the definition of terms like captivity, deprivation, intellectual freedom, genius, or madness as they related to our predicament. Mother made sure she had defined them in ways that championed her seismic intelligence. She thrived on paradox. Contradiction only became problematic if she needed to explain the necessity or usefulness of contradictory utterances. On the one hand, she wanted to live in relaxed coalition with contradictory assertions. On the other, she needed to obliterate contradiction to support her denial of mysticism. If we had been more independent we might have asked what dance, poetry, and the refutation of time were if not a form of mystical engagement. But we didn't ask. We were too accustomed to her amazing capacity for reversals and revisions. She was a master of *ad hoc* rationalization.

Everyone asks about the eggs. It never occurred to us that Mother only knew how to cook eggs. Typically, she turned her deficiency into a theory which gave eggs pre-eminence in the diet of an intellectual. Poached eggs for analytical thought. Fried eggs for creativity. Hard-boiled eggs for persuasive argument. Scrambled-eggs to assist the cross-fertilization of disciplinary fields. If we ate bread or toast, it was only to diffuse the dangerous potency of the eggs. We ate serials and fruit to give the eggs something to operate on. Any slowing in our intellectual activity was attributed to an inferior strain of egg.

Not so long ago, a doctor told me that Mother fed us eggs because she had a paranoid fear that someone would try to poison her. I can't recall Mother being concerned about poisoned food. What worried her was that someone might try to poison our thoughts and memories.

We were taught to be wary of the gardener, the cleaning woman, the woman who ran errands, the milkman, the baker, the postwoman, the meter reader, Mormon missionaries, scouts, and insurance salesmen. They were agents, opportunistic purveyors of mediocrity. Mother said that she left our father when he revealed himself to be an agent.

Your father, she told us, was an apologist for institutions. When they made him Professor, he straight-away turned into one of those old Greeks who were terrified of the irrational. Some of those Greek mathematicians were driven to murder and suicide by their inability to rationalize the square-root of 2. You can't live with someone who lives in fear of approximates and approximation.

We had no television or telephone, no clocks or calendars. Time was an enemy. Of all the agents, time was the most malevolent. We were taught that death and decay weren't the work of time, but the consciousness of time.

Mother's disdain for chronologicality was behind her encouragement of our most sensuous activity, dance. We danced so that we might hover oblivious to a history constructed out of events, presences and crucialities. Mother taught us that dance

and sex were the only points where mind and body met in pure
exchange. But I don't recall her explaining sex so thoroughly as
she explained dance, or the pure poetry signified by the square-
root of 2.

A new grammar displaced the new geometry that superseded
the most recent algebra. None of Mother's innovations made
much sense, but it was the beauty of their senselessness that
we clung to. On one day we could be entirely committed to a
version of English where numbers replaced nouns. This, Mother argued, would enable us to embrace the specificity of spatio-temporal relations the way the Aborigines had. A few days
later we would be told to be suspicious of numbers, that numbers (implying that more than one instance could exist of the
one thing) were an anathema to nature. Numbers and nouns
could only exist where specific details had been overlooked or
distorted. Yet numbers were restored to favour when Mother
adopted the idea that nature, as an intellectual construct, was
itself unnatural.

I remember spending the latter portion of my teenage years as a
case study, a human inkblot. I was entirely cut off from Mother,
and rarely saw Johnny or my father. All the stories and poems I
had written were sent to be dissected by forensic psychiatrists.
If every absence implied an absent father, every downbeat signified the heavy-footed presence of an egg-eating Queen Lear.
My childhood was made and unmade in front of me. My memories were corrected like school history assignments.

Several times since I've tried to read my poems as poems, to
ignore their 'coded intimations of tyranny', yet I am unable to
reinstate their stolen innocence. The doctors' incessant question, Did you love your mother? runs through my head on a
loop. When my replies didn't suit them, they would answer,
sagely, Of course, you knew no better.

I remember the warm summer evenings when the windows were thrown wide open so that the breeze carried the sound of trains or traffic or children splashing aimlessly in their back-yard pools. That's when we would play board games where the object was to land on a square which directed you forward to a square which directed you back to the original square, and so on, *ad indefinitum. Ad indefinitum* was a favourite phrase of mother's. When one of us grew tired of shifting our piece back and forth between the two squares, she reminded us that the idea of infinity has its basis in a binary opposition which is essentially mystical.

We lived in a world made meaningful by definite action and commitment. Mention of the infinite was to be treated with contempt. When my deprogrammers referred to these games as a Sisyphean cruelty, I tried to convince them that Johnny and I never tired of the games. We would often seek them out during Mother's phases.

Mother's worst phase came not long before the final crisis. She became fixated with the idea of a champagne cork halted in flight, and took to whirling around the library in fast-decreasing circles, trying to fuel the formation of a theory. She soon got so dizzy that she slammed into a wall and knocked out a tooth.

Not long after, I saw her sitting at a table making minute notations on a large sheet of paper. From what I could see, they were more like hieroglyphs than mathematical symbols. She wrote furiously, and when she finished writing she gazed at the page for more than an hour. I left the room. When I came back, Mother was staring out the window, and her notes were gone. Later, Johnny told me that he'd watched her tear the sheet into long strips. She rolled each strip into a thick scroll. There were ten or eleven of these scrolls. She made a mark on the outside of each and sealed the end down with glue, before arranging them into some kind of order. Then, one after the other, she placed each scroll in her mouth, chewed, and swallowed.

Besides books and intellectual journals, our only knowledge of the world outside Netherby came from postcards sent by my mother's sister Madeleine. My aunt had married an American journalist and settled in Baltimore. Although they had three children, it seemed to us that my aunt and uncle did little but travel. She sent us postcards of ruined Inca cities, gondolas in Venice, paintings by Edvard Munch, and photographs of film stars like Marlon Brando.

Aunt Madeleine wrote of cinema and television, orchestras and jet travel, and Mother loved to read her sister's letters out loud so that she could provide a vehement critique as she went. My aunt would tell us how beautiful her blonde daughter Catherine was now that she was a young woman. She and Uncle Scott had spent fifteen thousand dollars on orthodontics to give Catherine the most perfect smile in Maryland. Johnny was very taken with the thought of his cousin. He would interrupt mother as she read Aunt Madeleine's description of a family trip to ask, Does it mention Catherine?

Once, when Johnny said that he would like to travel with his American cousins, Mother got furious and called him a fool, describing all these travels as a figment of her sister's imagination. She told us that Madeleine's marriage had collapsed, and she lived alone with her children in a godforsaken caravan park on the Gold Coast. Aunt Madeleine's real name was Judy. Her sister pretended to have all sorts of glamorous adventures, and perfect American children, but really she was just another victim of mediocre thought and ambition.

If I was stunned by this news, Johnny was devastated. He told me Mother was jealous of her sister, and that Aunt Madeleine's letters were too vivid not to be true. Why would Mother read and discuss the letters with us if she had known her sister was lying?

Early one morning, while I was asleep, Mother sent Johnny to fetch a favourite brush from her wardrobe. Misunderstanding her instruction, Johnny opened the wrong drawer. Inside, he saw a stack of unmarked European postcards, along with airmail envelopes of the type Aunt Madeleine used for her letters. Johnny would have been nearly seventeen then.

What I remember most vividly from the four days Johnny went missing was Mother's ceaseless agitated muttering. She would grasp my upper arm, Where did he go? Did you see him? And the only thing I could think of was that he had been taken by a gardener or baker, that he'd been claimed by one of Mother's agents, because it was unthinkable that Johnny would have left of his own volition, that he could just run away. Johnny was Mother's favourite. Why would he want to go? I was the one that didn't matter. I was the one that needed sleep.

I remember the doctor telling me to accept things that I couldn't accept. He told me my father had always loved us. My father had always searched for us.

To believe what the doctor said would have been the same as saying that my mother was bad, or that she didn't have our best interests at heart, and I knew my mother loved us.

I was told that I would be confused by a lot of things because wrong thoughts, and wrong patterns of thought had been placed in my head, and I would need to be taught to see the world the way that ordinary people saw it.

No one tried to understand me when I said that I didn't want to think like an ordinary person. I recall one doctor asking me to repeat something I'd said so she could make a note. I told her that ordinary people were hostages to the ordinary. Ordinary people are like the worst kind of Americans: the wannabe Americans, the pseudo-Americans.

For a long time I refused to speak to my father because he was American.

When I refused to speak to him, my father sent me a list of 'facts'. He'd done nothing to harm my mother's career. He had never been an academic, nor had he been employed by an Australian university. He was a journalist who lived in Baltimore.

He married my mother in Australia and took her back to the United States. I was born in the United States.

He told me that my mother hadn't lived at Netherby when she was a child. She hadn't even lived in Melbourne. When he met her she was living in suburban Brisbane. She took Johnny and me when she received her inheritance, having suffered a breakdown when her parents died. He told me I had an older sister named Catherine.

I sent back a letter saying that he was acting just like an agent would. I returned the American birth certificate ripped into fifty pieces. I accused my father of pretending to have an American family in order to further his career as a university professor.

Not many people my age can remember the first time they watched television, but I can. I was thirteen years old, and my mother was being interviewed. I remember her trying to convince the interviewer that there was a second spectrum of light, a set of colours imperceptible to ordinary vision. Past and future events were encoded within this spectrum. Access to the second spectrum would enable you to travel through time. My mother offered to supply the journalist with her knowledge of this spectrum if they would reunite her with Johnny.

I don't remember her brushing her hair, but that's what everyone else recalls. They will tell you how shocked they were to see a woman casually brush her hair while being interviewed about the abduction of her children. People focused on the hair brushing because they were envious of her beautiful hair, and needed to rationalize their mean, mediocre thinking.

No-one paid any attention to what Mother said. She told the judge that he wasn't entitled to judge her because he was a tool of the social apparatus she had rejected, but he judged her anyway. When the prosecutor asked what she hoped to achieve by holding her boys captive, she said she had achieved everything that she set out to. Her boys understood the awful power signified by the square-root of 2.

I wasn't permitted to see my mother until I turned eighteen, by which stage I was more confused than I had been as a child juggling contradictions at Netherby. She had stopped dancing, but she still made discoveries, and tried to convey their importance to the nurses. She called me Johnny, and after a time I stopped trying to correct her. She loved to reminisce about the nights when I brushed her hair till dawn. Her hair was still beautiful, and I knew the nurses loved to brush it for her just as we used to. She would badger me to recall her aphorisms.

But you've forgotten the one about creativity, she'd say.

Only creativity releases us from agency, I told her.

Three years ago, the French Government bestowed the Legion of Honour on a 'remarkable Australian philosopher and mathematician' named Christine Marker. We discovered that this was one of many pseudonyms my mother used when she contributed papers to academic journals in the early 1970s. After the award, the same universities Mother had always distrusted and despised offered her professorships and honorary doctorates. It was a pity she was so far beyond telling them what she thought of institutions and institutionalized thought.

For a long while, I felt lost without Johnny, and tried to keep in touch. But when Johnny left to live in America, I found it difficult to forgive him for an act that Mother would have considered base treachery. He did invite me to his wedding, and I could have gone, but chose not to. Other than one or two snippets of news sent by Father, I hadn't heard of Johnny till this commotion in the last couple of weeks.

Having gone to visit Mother, I found her in the company of three men. One was a Federal Police officer, while the other two were Americans, agents from the Federal Bureau of Investigation. One of the Americans was asking if she'd heard from Johnny, or if she knew his whereabouts. They were surprised when she pointed to me.

Here's Johnny now. Why don't you ask him yourself?

The Americans are here to follow enquiries into a kidnapping. They believe that my brother has taken his two American children and brought them to Australia. I couldn't tell them whether this would be consistent with Johnny's recent behaviour. I did tell them it was unlikely that Johnny would seek to make contact with either me or my mother.

Could you suggest where he might take the children? Is your brother a violent man? Would he be likely to harm them?

Though amused by the mention of violence in connection with Johnny, I told these agents that I couldn't imagine Johnny being violent to his children. But harm was a different question.

How do you mean? the taller of the Americans asked.

It depends what you mean by harm, I said, making sure to look at Mother as I answered. If you asked Johnny, he'd tell you that he had the happiest childhood imaginable.

If you told him that he meant to harm his kids, he'd tell you exactly what I'd say, that a few lousy haircuts and a diet of eggs never harmed anyone.

1986

MARLON BRANDO

Tell me what happened.

I was writing a short story. A kind of love story.

Yes?

Well, I'd got to the part where the hero, Tim, has a chance meeting with the girl of his dreams. Before he can appreciate the significance of the meeting, the girl is gone. Then he sees her in the distance and chases her. The girl is about to board a tram. Tim knows that if he loses her now, she is lost forever. That's when it happens.

What happens?... Tell me exactly what happens.

The girl, Catherine, is pushing through a crowd of people at the tram stop, and one of them turns out to be Marlon Brando.

Marlon Brando, the actor?

Yes.

At a tram stop in Melbourne?

Don't ask me why he's there, but it's definitely Marlon Brando. He's just wandered into the crowd of people waiting for a tram.

And?

And?... This is Marlon Brando! Do you know what it costs to have Brando appear in one of your stories?

But it's an accident, surely?

Accident or not, it costs the same. If Marlon Brando wanders into the foreground of your story, you're up for one million dollars. If Marlon actually says something, stops to ask someone the time, you're talking another ten million, at least.

But you're The Author?

[Pause] Yes.

Can't you control what's going on?

[Silence]

It is a matter of control, isn't it?

Stories aren't film sets. On sets they have security people controlling who comes and goes.

[Pause] *Tell me ... Are you a premature ejaculator?*

[Pause] Sometimes.

Often?

Sometimes.

You can see what I'm getting at, can't you?

[Silence]

Can't you just erase him?

He's there. He's part of the story now.

So what happens?

I could finish the story and sell it. If I sell the story, at best it will fetch me two hundred dollars. But it will cost me one million for having Brando in it. [Pause] What a bitch! Marlon Brando wanders into one of your stories and your literary career is over.

That's bad luck.

Yes.

Couldn't you ...?

What?

Couldn't you ...?

Couldn't I what?

Couldn't you just kill yourself?

[Pause] I wouldn't give Marlon the pleasure.

1984

A LETTER TO FRANCESCA

Three years ago, when I was a student at Melbourne University, my friend Catherine recommended to me the novel *Melbourne*, by the Brazilian writer Julia Cortez. Though my main interest was contemporary Australian fiction, I had read Cortez's previous collection, *Packing Death*. I found these stories to be affected and derivative, drawing heavily on the metaphysical ruminations of Borges and the so-called 'metafictive' games of recent American fiction. Still, I had no wish to question Catherine's judgement (I wanted to sleep with her), and the idea of a 'postmodern fantasy' set in the least fantastic of cities intrigued me.

Having since abandoned my PhD, I am now reading *Melbourne* for the twelfth time. The paperback Catherine gave me disintegrated under the pressure of my penciled notations. A second copy, in hardback, became so weighted with notes that the text was unreadable. I now read from a hardback first edition, and make my notes in a series of Spirax notebooks. This most recent copy of *Melbourne* is inscribed by the author with the message: *To Tim, the most diligent reader any author could imagine, best wishes, Julia Cortez.* We correspond now, Julia and I.

My fascination with *Melbourne* began when I discovered that its central character and narrator, Richard Thompson, lives at 19 Passchendaele Street in the Melbourne suburb of Hampton, which happens to be my own address. When you read a detail like this in a novel, it takes some time to sink in. I can't imagine anything more curious than having a South American writer—who has, according to the publisher's blurb, never travelled outside her country—create a fictive character who lives at your address.

Naturally, I called Catherine, hoping this coincidence would provide a good opportunity to test her affections.

Yes, I thought you'd be amazed, Catherine said. Julia Cortez is a wild writer. A lot of the coincidences are uncanny, don't you think? You and Richard for a start.

I've only read three pages so far, I said.

It gets better, believe me. But I don't want to ruin it for you. We should have a chat when you've finished.

That night I read the remaining 285 pages of *Melbourne*. A note on the title page of my paperback copy indicates that I finished reading at 4.40 AM on the third of June, so I suppose it must have taken five or six hours.

Looking back at it now, I can see that my earliest responses to the novel were neurotic and paranoid. Catherine must have thought that I would enjoy drawing parallels between myself and Richard. But I didn't like the implications of those parallels.

I could only think that Catherine had set out to hurt me by recommending a novel which would tell me, specifically and unreservedly, that I am a lunatic. In my confusion I began to hate Catherine. I now regret the letter I sent the next day, not only because it became a police matter, but also because it foreclosed all opportunity for sexual engagement. At the time I hated Julia Cortez also, for knowing so little, and presuming to know so much.

When I first read *Melbourne* it seemed obvious that the author knew nothing about the city in which the novel is set. At least, nothing beyond what Julia Cortez must have learnt from a street directory, probably *Melway*.

Most of the geographical references to suburban road and transport networks are accurate. The major public buildings, schools and parks are correctly named, but much of the information is bizarre if not ridiculous.

In charting the progress of the number 8 tram down Toorak Road, for instance, Cortez's narrator, Richard, locates gasworks on the corner of Toorak Road and Chapel Street, which is the heart of Melbourne's most expensive shopping precinct. Early in the novel, Richard rides a train on the Sandringham line, but the vehicle is a double-decker train of the kind generally used in Sydney. While making this journey, Richard reflects somewhat harshly on the pollution he observes rising from factories in Brighton, which is, in reality, Melbourne's oldest establishment suburb, and free of such industries.

With these errors and fabrications continuing throughout the novel, I began to compile a list headed 'Discrepancies and Variations in Julia Cortez's *Melbourne*'. The list fills 63 A4 pages, and notes, among other things, climatic errors, errors in currency, perspective errors, gross historical errors, cultural misrepresentations, socio-economic errors, geopolitical misinformation, and the extreme unlikelihood that Richard's father would be distraught at having 'backed his Dodge over a wallaby' when reversing from a driveway in Hampton.

Had I simply posted this list to Julia Cortez via her Brazilian publishers, I might have saved myself a second major embarrassment. (I must say with regard to the first that I had no intention of disembowelling Catherine, as my letter threatened, but it took some argument to persuade the magistrate of that.) Unfortunately, I included with the list a letter attacking Julia Cortez's characterization of Richard, and criticizing his erratic departures from reality.

Julia's reply (translated into English by Madeleine Elster, who translated *Melbourne* from the original Portuguese) is a model of patience and kindness.

August 17

Dear Tim,

Thank you for your letter and your interest in *Melbourne*. Yours is certainly the most passionate response my fiction has yet provoked.

No Tim, you are not Richard Thompson. Never imagining that my novel would be translated into

English, I did not anticipate that this problem might arise. I apologize for any embarrassment which may have been caused by abducting your address. I do not know any of your friends. No-one has 'put me up to this', as you say.

Nor do I accept that Richard is mad. It seems to me that most of his behaviour is as sane as you could expect from a sensitive individual living in the quantum world. What happens to Richard may be internal, external, or allegorical. This is part of the amusement of fiction, don't you think? I choose to think of Richard as a 'post-romantic hero'. (Excuse the pun.)

I also beg to differ regarding your criticism of *Melbourne*'s 'copious errors'. On the contrary, the novel is a masterpiece of careful research, and I might suggest that I know more about the true city of Melbourne than some of its inhabitants. Where factual distortions and fabrications occur, they are indispensable to the mode of fiction I choose to call 'Theoretical Expressionism'.

Once more, thank you for your interest, Tim. Rest assured, I had no wish to depict you (or any real person) as a 'hyperbolically neurotic sociopath'.

Yours Sincerely
Julia Cortez.

The pun in this 'post-romantic hero' business has to do with Thompson's obsessive letter-writing, which forms the core of *Melbourne*'s narrative.

Richard is a student of philosophy who lives at home with his parents in Hampton, just as I do. He finds it difficult to concentrate on his studies, distracted by the absence of his girlfriend, Francesca, who is travelling through Europe. Richard writes to

Francesca daily. He has so little to write about that he begins to create fantastic tales of the city and the suburbs to amuse her. He invents plays and pop stars, sporting events and national heroes, impossible public buildings, and mysterious sightings of celebrities like Marlon Brando. Richard writes only about Melbourne, believing his stories could only be appreciated by a like-minded Melburnian.

Francesca replies with humour and enthusiasm. encouraging the game, and hinting at the possibility of marriage when she returns. Then her correspondence stops.

Diplomatic enquiries reveal that Francesca has gone missing from a youth hostel on the outskirts of Copenhagen. As time passes, only Richard refuses to believe that she is dead. As a reader, I find it difficult to determine whether the situation has disturbed Richard's sense of reality, or whether an already disturbed sense of reality has been exacerbated by Richard's fears for Francesca. He re-reads Francesca's letters over and over, and takes them apart word by word, believing they hold a clue to her disappearance. He continues to write to her, hoping that one day Francesca will collect his letters.

After so many readings of *Melbourne*, I still fail to understand why Richard cannot accept Francesca's death.

I will grant that he is smitten with a woman who has in her absence become as crucial to his imaginative life as she had been to his lusts. But Richard is meant to be an intelligent, reflective man. I feel certain that I would be more fatalistic in those circumstances.

What could Richard hope to achieve by badgering authorities as he does? Foolishly, he rejects police advice and hires a Danish private detective, Andersen, an opportunist who sees the advantage in not reporting the obvious to him. Meanwhile Richard persists in writing letters which (he must surely realize) betray a weak grasp on reality. Yet he remains capable of noting in his diary, 'I worry that I am a cerebral person who feels that he must pretend to this passion.'

Last year I read a paper by a respected feminist critic who observed how frequently female characters go missing in Australian fiction. When their presence becomes too problematic or inconvenient for the (male) author, these women are murdered, disappeared, transformed into leopards, or revealed to be figments of the narrator's (libidinous) imagination.

The same critic wrote that Julia Cortez's *Melbourne* ought to be read as an elaborate feminist critique of the vanishing woman in Australian fiction. Richard has rendered himself vulnerable by allowing Francesca to authorize or define his fantasy life. In order to reclaim control of his fantasies, Richard must kill her and then reinvent her.

When I look at the photograph of Julia Cortez on the back flap of the hardback edition of *Melbourne*, I don't see her a woman with an agenda. Julia has soft, generous features, and seems ready to explode into a broad smile. I imagine her to be someone who would giggle, girlishly and unashamedly, when something amused her. Julia's eyes are not those of a revolutionary. She has the eyes of a storyteller.

As an author in the South American tradition, Julia Cortez has a multiplicity of intentions, yet I do not see her as a political hardliner, nor am I aware of evidence which would establish her acquaintance with recent Australian fiction. In my thoughts of Julia, I prefer to emphasize her mystery and complexity—her handwriting is an artwork—and these qualities would be diminished were she to be cast as an ideologue.

When I place this photograph next to the photograph of Julia Cortez on the cover of the paperback edition, it strikes me that she does not look Brazilian. At least, she does not resemble the mental impression I have of a Brazilian. Julia looks to me like a northern Italian, a wonderfully stylish woman who would turn heads—male and female—as she walked the streets of Florence and Milan.

It has occurred to me that when Richard describes his beautiful Italian-Australian girlfriend, Francesca, I have been picturing a young woman who resembles the photographs of Julia Cortez which appear on the various covers of *Melbourne*. 'No one who has the opportunity to know you,' Richard writes to Francesca, 'could fail to fall at least a little bit in love with you.'

By picturing Francesca as Julia, I gain some knowledge of the anguish that prompts Richard to behave so irrationally. But how is the reader of *Melbourne* to explain Francesca's postcards?

Several months after Francesca's disappearance a postcard arrives in the mail, addressed to Richard, but unsigned. Though the card carries an Australian stamp, and a Melbourne postmark, the message appears to have been written by Francesca. At least, Richard is satisfied that the message was written by Francesca. It says: *R, meet me under the spires of the Castillo at 6 PM on my birthday*. The police are not convinced, believing it to be a cruel hoax.

For the Melburnian reading *Melbourne*, the postcard is unusual in that it features the image of an ornate, Spanish-Gothic building known as the 'Castillo del Flinders'. A typed caption on the card describes the Castillo as 'Melbourne's most prominent late-eighteenth century building'. Given that most Australian readers of *Melbourne* would be aware that white settlement of the city dates from the 1830s, the assertion of this fantastic building is disturbing. An earlier reference to the Castillo in one of Richard's letters to Francesca locates the building 'opposite the Treasury Gardens on the corner of Spring and Flinders Streets'. Richard, as we recall, has fabricated tales of a fantastic Melbourne to amuse Francesca, but it remains unclear to me whether the Castillo, 'notable for golden corkscrew spires which can be seen from distant suburbs of Melbourne', is part of a reality that Julia Cortez has fabricated for Richard, or one of Richard's own fabrications.

Richard waits at the appointed place at the chosen hour, but his Francesca does not arrive. Nor does anyone contact Richard claiming to be the author of the card.

The Castillo card is the first of a succession of bizarre post-cards that arrive at Richard's home, each arranging an appointment never kept by the correspondent. Dismissing police opinions that the cards are a sadistic game, Richard waits in parks, restaurants, and under statues dedicated to the memory of historical figures whose names, deeds and existence make no sense to anyone who knows the real Melbourne.

Confused and desperate, Richard's narrative becomes painful to read. He begins to hate this Francesca who taunts him, and is tempted to suicide when he becomes ashamed of his own hostility.

Clearly Julia Cortez invites the reader to balance the surmise of Richard's madness against the likelihood of a conspiracy which may or may not involve him. Replying to one of my early letters, Julia dismissed the suggestion that enemies are conspiring against her narrator.

> Tim, you say that my novel is like Alfred Hitchcock's *Vertigo*, full of spiraling confusions and conspiring minds. You suggest that someone may be trying to discredit Richard by getting him to assert the existence of an imaginary, resurrected Francesca. But you must remember that Richard is a no-one. Who would want to discredit him? Richard is just a philosophy student who has scarcely been touched by the real world. He takes himself and his grief too seriously. *You* take him too seriously!

Like most authors, Julia plays down the significance of her own work. However, this novel fascinates critics more eminent than I. The noted American scholar Allen Doust argues that Francesca never actually leaves Melbourne. Doust reads Francesca's 'European trip' as a fantastic, intimate game played out with her lover. (In their letters, she and Richard speak of 'Europe' as a kind of Disneyworld, hypothesizing a network of elaborate film stages constructed on the northern outskirts of Melbourne.) According to Doust, their letters, and her 'disappearance in Copenhagen', take place within the framework of complex erotic invention.

We should recognise that Allen Doust is a member of a critical school that sees all literature as a game, or mirror-maze. If Professor Doust were to read of Francesca's kidnapping in the morning edition of *The New York Times*, her plight would be little more than a literary game to him. No-one has murdered the Professor's wife or girlfriend. Only someone who shares a Hampton address with Richard Thompson could appreciate the way that *Melbourne* connects with very real confusion and pain.

In her most recent letter Julia continues to berate me and ridicule my theories, but I know she does so because I am closing in on the truth, that I live in the emotional vicinity of the truth.

February 25th

Dear Tim,

I'm begging you to put down my novel and start something new. Your personality is not suited to academic enquiry. When you first wrote to me, you described my novel as a 'psycho-critique' of your own life, suggesting that I was in league with your friend Catherine.

Now you acknowledge you had it wrong, telling me that *Melbourne* is 'a celebration; an incitement to a divided man standing at the threshold of a new life'. I would like for you to retain this point of view, but you must dispense with the idea of 'prescription'.

Tim, *please understand*, I am not a kindred spirit prescribing a course of action for you (or your city, for that matter). You are confusing the fact my novel is set at your address with the idea that it is addressed to you.

I am particularly disturbed by what you say about the need for Catherine to vanish and be reinvented. I am concerned for you, and I am concerned for her. Catherine is not Francesca. She will not 'be made real by being reinvented'. Be sensible, Tim, and leave her alone.

I try not to tell people how to live, Tim. My novel touched you, but it does not seem to have enriched your understanding. I don't believe you will find happiness by reading yourself into my novel. You may find peace by leaving Melbourne.

My most recent novel will be published this Friday. The narrative is set in San Francisco, and I expect that its title will translate as *Approximate Life*. I hope that you will read it and experience it (only) as a grand entertainment.

Yours Sincerely
Julia Cortez

Of course, I had spoken of Catherine only by way of example, and Julia's overstated anxiety betrays her fear of my intuition. I can live without Catherine, just as I can live without plaudits from Julia, but I cannot leave *Melbourne* alone.

Richard is no madman. He is not a no-one. He has fervour and imagination. In fact, I am beginning to prefer Richard's Melbourne, with its gigantic edifices, to my own.

If nothing else, Richard is loyal to his vision ...

I trust that you will forgive the poverty of this tale, Francesca. Your continued silence dismays and unsettles me. The Youth Hostel in Copenhagen has asked me to send no more letters to their address. They say they will return the letters that I have sent. Consequently, I will post this to your bank in London. I long to hear from you, to kiss you again. Promise me you will be in Melbourne for your birthday. We will drink champagne under the great golden spires.

My love, always, R.

1990

THE LEISURE SOCIETY

Klaus and Heiki had a really good time ...

Klaus Obermeier has promised to buy me a new Audi and a three-bedroom apartment in Berlin if I continue to help him. His project can't be finished without me. I feel sorry for Klaus. For a rich man, he's not a bad bloke, and his wife Heiki is the most tolerant person I've met. When the Obermeiers tell me that my involvement is crucial, I say that I appreciate their difficulties, and would like to help, but I'm tired, and my dog is growing old. What's more, I suspect that Klaus is beyond assistance.

I'd never heard of Klaus Obermeier till four years ago. His brother Rudi moved into Passchendaele Street two years before that, and I often saw him with his three boys, kicking a soccer ball around the High School oval. I'd give a slight nod as Rudi's family drove past in their sky-blue Mercedes. Other than that, I had nothing to do with them. Rudi's English was good, but Anna and the boys spoke little English then. Later, someone told me that Rudi had come to Melbourne to manage the local subsidiary of Klaus' firm, Svekels, which has its headquarters in Bremen.

Even in retirement, Klaus is one of Europe's best known industrialists. His company developed digital timing mechanisms accurate to one millionth of a second, and sold the technologies to space agencies. By the time he retired, Klaus' personal fortune made him one of the wealthiest men in Germany. Not that you would have guessed at the family's wealth from Rudi and Anna's lifestyle. Though the local Obermeiers always looked comfortable enough, and drove the best car in Hampton, they bought an unpretentious weatherboard home, and sent their boys to state schools.

Retiring at sixty, Klaus was determined that he and Heiki would enjoy themselves. They would be as single-minded in their pursuit of pleasure as Klaus had been in building Svekels. Heiki collected paintings, and Klaus wished to indulge his passion for hiking and photography. Already well acquainted with Europe, Africa, and The Americas, they were eager to investigate Australia. As a devoted family man, Klaus looked forward to catching up with his youngest brother, Rudi.

Men who spend their lives dividing time into millionths of a second tend not to be frivolous, so Rudi drew up a ten-week itinerary for Klaus and Heiki which organised their movements in fine detail. And Rudi was surprised when his brother rejected this itinerary. During their many phone conversations, Rudi had often told Klaus of his enthusiasm for the relaxed way of life in Australia, and Klaus and Heiki liked the idea of being swallowed up by a great leisure society.

Though few of us knew it at the time, for several weeks in 1990, Hampton played host to a rotund billionaire and his vibrant wife. Klaus and Heiki used Rudi's home in Passchendaele Street as their base between trips to the farthest corners of the continent. They snorkeled, bushwalked, and climbed Uluru, they bought Australian paintings, ate barramundi and kangaroo, scoffed wine, and slept out under the stars, they sailed on Sydney Harbour, went caving, saw a football match at the Melbourne Cricket Ground, and attended the opera. Though the pair met with many dignitaries, including a brief lunch with the Prime Minister, they enjoyed the company of ordinary Australians too.

They would have met few Australians more ordinary than the Passchendaele Street neighbours Rudi invited to a special farewell barbeque. I didn't know Rudi well enough to score an invitation, but friends who attended spoke of Heiki's fabulous cakes, and Klaus drinking like a fish when he wasn't taking photographs. The couple told everyone they'd had the trip of a lifetime. Klaus would have retired five years earlier if he'd known how much fun it was to live hedonistically.

Maybe that euphoria would have worn off soon enough, I don't know. Klaus hugged the strangers he met at the barbeque. He told his brother that he was reluctant to leave. He even enthused about quiet, mundane Hampton. As he flew back to Germany, Klaus called his brother from every airport stopover to thank him for organising such a perfect holiday.

... but when they got back to Bremen, something terrible happened ...

Klaus and Heiki couldn't stop telling their German friends what a fabulous time they'd had staying with Rudi and travelling through Australia.

'Wait till you see the picture of the crocodile. You won't believe the size of it,' he'd say.

'The blue of the sky. The intense colours. You wouldn't credit the reds and blues in the centre of Australia,' Heiki said.

'The striped fish on the Barrier Reef.'

'Yes, the Reef was extraordinary,' Heiki agreed.

'Everything worked out so perfectly.'

Klaus sent seventeen rolls of colour film to be developed. No photographs were ever returned.

'We're terribly sorry, Mr Obermeier,' the manager told the billionaire. 'We can't account for your film.'

Klaus was devastated. He reminded the processing firm that he wasn't accustomed to error, and wouldn't accept their sloppiness. He initiated legal actions, and threatened them with corporate takeover. But, despite the pressure Klaus applied to the firm, nothing turned up. Seventeen rolls of film had vanished. Four hundred and eight lovingly composed shots taken with the most sophisticated photographic equipment available. Though Heiki could still admire the superb intricacy of her aboriginal paintings, the swirling blues of her three Brett Whiteleys, and the unsettling use of space in her massive Fred Williams, Klaus felt that his greatest moments had been stolen from him.

Taking out his notebook, he reminded Heiki of the unique brilliance of every one of the four hundred and eight photographs he had taken. The odd characters. The peculiar shifting light at Katajuta. The footballers' dynamism. Klaus swung between teary nostalgia and impotent fury.

'Don't fret. There's nothing to stop us going again,' Heiki said.

'You're damn right we'll be going again,' Klaus told her.

... and the horror of this loss sent Klaus on a voyage in search of authentic moments.

The fourteenth image on Klaus' sixteenth roll of film was a flukey shot by comparison with some of the more artful moments captured during his travels.

Rudi had been kicking the soccer ball with his fifteen year old son on the school oval. Klaus liked their total absorption in the game, but, more particularly, he liked the late afternoon light. Dark storm clouds had gathered over the buildings to the east, sharply contrasting a red-gold brilliance in the west. With the grass turning pinkish, the tall gums skirting the oval seemed to flame, and the two players cast long, mysterious shadows. It was one of those times you wish you had a camera with you, and Klaus always had a camera.

That's when I came into the picture.

I'd been running my cocker spaniel across the bottom end of the oval. When I tossed a tennis ball, Tuddy raced after it, leaping to catch it on the bounce. Though I nodded to Rudi and Michael, I wasn't aware Klaus was watching, or that my dog and I had made ourselves an essential element in the most perfect composition Klaus had ever seen.

I would not have become aware of my part in Klaus' perfect moment if he and Heiki hadn't returned to Australia determined to re-create every one of the four hundred and eight photographs Klaus had lost.

To begin with, Klaus contented himself with rough approximations. One blue-gold fish swimming above a pink stretch of coral was as good as another. He wasn't concerned that Heiki should wear the same dress in the same location, so long as the dress was similarly coloured, that she occupied the same position, and took a roughly similar attitude. But serious photographers aren't prepared to compromise with the light.

Klaus spent four weeks waiting for a sunset in Broome to match the sunset he photographed on his first night there. Never mind that he witnessed many more spectacular sunsets during his return stay, it had to be *the same one*. No bunch of footballers would do. They had to be the same three footballers, in a similar relation to each other, in a real game at the same venue. If just one of the three had been injured, or retired, Klaus would have spent a fortune to extend his career. He would have paid-off team selectors, just for the sake of a single image.

Klaus told people that he'd never known the relaxation, or disinhibition he'd experienced during those two perfect months, and he wasn't going to accept losing his images or their associations. A memory wasn't enough. If The Leaning Tower of Pisa collapsed, it would have to be rebuilt exactly. It would have to be rebuilt with the same propensity for collapse. And the idea of distortion horrifies Klaus. He is ruthless in his pursuit of authentically re-created perfections.

Somewhere along the line, Heiki lost interest. Everything's gone flat for her. She wants to see new galleries and do new things. Much as she understands her husband and his peculiar earnestness, she finds it hard to come at visiting the same restaurants, with the same people, all ordering the same meals, just for the sake of a photograph which seemed banal in the first instance. She hates waiting for it to start raining. And she hates being embarrassed.

When an aide told Klaus the Prime Minister was too busy to meet for the purpose of re-staging a photograph, Klaus threatened to exercise his influence on the Svekels' board. Klaus could persuade the company to withdraw its subsidiary operation in Melbourne. Facing the loss of three hundred jobs in a marginal electorate, the Prime Minister reconsidered. He then sent an aide on a four-hour round trip to fetch the tie he'd worn on the occasion of his luncheon with Klaus.

Everything about this exercise has been a misery for Klaus but he won't relent. When he first offered to pay me to walk my dog on the school oval at sunset, I told him I didn't want to be paid. I figured it was no big deal if it kept an important visitor happy.

That was eighteen months ago. When I told Klaus that I wouldn't be available to walk my dog at sunset *every* evening, he offered to pay me two hundred dollars a day. I would have refused, if Klaus hadn't already been sly enough to 'discuss matters' with my boss. After this discussion, my contract was revised to ensure that work wouldn't get in the way of my availability to model for wealthy Germans.

But it isn't just me being fickle. My dog has grown old. The arthritis in his back legs makes it hard to jump. And Tuddy's lost interest in chasing tennis balls.

I run in front of Tuddy, clicking my fingers.

'If he won't do it, threaten him!' Klaus shouts.

Klaus' nephew Michael is now a young man in his final year of secondary school, and he would prefer not to spend long hours playing soccer with his father, but he does so under threat of disinheritance. It's even harder for his father. Rudi had a heart-attack last year, and he shouldn't be chasing soccer balls each evening.

The real problem is the light, waiting for those same unique storm clouds. None of us will be real till we exist in an image which corresponds to the reality in Klaus' memory, and we will only be authentic when we are authentic in a photograph that re-captures the authenticity of a moment when we were truly authentic. The longer this process takes, the less likely it is that this authentic moment will be successfully re-staged.

I want to help Klaus, because I know he is feeling a loss which is beyond my understanding. And I feel sorry for Heiki. She wants to go home. And I'm certain that when she's back in Bremen, she will refuse to view Klaus' four hundred and eight photographs. But the more we wait, and the more I try to help, the more I begin to suspect Klaus has stirred something in me that won't go when he goes.

I have accepted Klaus' word that I was once accidentally part of a perfect moment, a time that I have no memory of. And if I am so oblivious to real perfection, can I have any real use in life other than to act as paid background for billionaires who need to substantiate their authenticity?

I fear that one day I may discover that my only purpose was to exist for a single moment in which the accident of my existence lent substance to the life of someone I neither knew nor cared for. I might find that I had no importance besides a single moment stolen from time to be lost forever by a German photo-processing firm.

1994

PRICKLY HEAT

1. The Men With The Nets

Every public servant has a slightly different version of the same dream. They will be working in a vast office, full of desks, filing cabinets, and computer terminals. The clerks seem edgy, consternated. They sense that something is about to happen. Someone drops a stack of files, or spills a cup of coffee. For some reason, the phones have stopped ringing. Filing clerks dart back and forth, unable to concentrate on their immediate task. Normally silent officials chatter nervously.

Suddenly, the glass door which leads to the lift-wells is flung open, and a superior dashes into the room, bellowing, They're coming! Take cover!

Intuitively, we know who he means. We've waited for them without knowing we've been waiting for them. The younger staff clamber up the filing cabinets, while senior officers take refuge under their desks, or in the toilets.

Then they appear, tall men decked out in SWAT-style polo-necked jumpers and peaked caps. Powerfully strong, agile men with dark moustaches. They move in slow motion. Even their speech sounds distorted, slowed down. Get that one! Get her! Two of them set after a young woman and corner her as she scurries into a dead end. She shrieks, No! No! as the net drops over her.

Other men go searching down the aisles between tall filing cabinets, net in hand. A terrified clerk dashes across the centre of the office, and two men with a net begin to pursue him, before a superior shouts, Leave him! We only want the talented ones!

When two or three public servants have been collected in their nets, the invaders leave to go about their business in offices elsewhere. No one tries to rescue the abducted officers. The incident is never spoken about. Soon, the office will be working as if nothing has happened.

Every public servant has a different version of a dream where the men with nets rush into their office, seize the talented people who ought not be there, and take them to a place where their talents will finally be put to proper use.

As a public servant, you consider yourself to be living in temporary exile from your true destiny. One day, you will be snatched from your too-safe world and dragged screaming into the spotlight that's always awaited you.

2. Prickly Heat

Sleep is everything, the central preoccupation of the shift worker. Your head turns on the pillow, you feel the beam of warm sunlight hit your face, and you try not to think, not even about moving the curtains, because thinking will take you further from sleep. But what you're thinking is that you'll be totally fucked at work if you can't get to sleep. You know that terrible sick-in-the-gut, tongue-dead feeling of sleep deprivation. Telling yourself, you *must* get some sleep, as if sleep, having slept, is something you can hold onto.

It's the caffeine paradox. Because you haven't slept, you belt back coffee to get you through a night at the office, and now you can't sleep due to the caffeine dancing through your bloodstream. You try to piss it away, to piss it all out of your system, but always you're left with that insistent prickly sensation, like an army of tiny spiders racing across your flesh. Two teams of prickle-footed spiders playing soccer on your skin. You can't rub them away. You can't piss them away. And before you know it, your eyes are wide open to the glare of the afternoon sun, thinking, Christ, what am I doing this for? Please, I'll do anything, just let me sleep.

And this, the caffeine poisoning, the spiders and the prickly-heated despair, is your punishment for murdering a Scottish King, for returning to the public service when you promised yourself you'd starve rather than work another lousy office job. You have to say it out loud, because otherwise you're in danger of not believing it: You say, I'm better than this.

3. Godzilla Versus The Manual Index

The Criminal Records section of the Police Department occupies one complete floor of a tall city office building. This building also houses the Fingerprint Division, the Missing Persons Office, the Fraud Squad, the Armed Robbers, Homicide, and Sexual Offences, along with an ordinary police station and a Criminal Intelligence Branch.

If there is one experience shared by the civilian clerks and uniformed police working in the Records section, it is that they have all, at some time, fronted a mirror and thought, I deserve better.

The police are elderly sergeants on the verge of retirement, or young sergeants and senior constables using the office as a stepping stone to seniority. The poorly paid clerical officers are students taking a break between studies, kids working their first job, or the tragedy cases at a port of last resort, all desperately hoping something better will turn up.

You are one of the tragedies. After teacher training, you'd decided that you didn't have the stomach to teach uncouth fourteen year olds, and now you tell yourself that you only need to stay at Criminal Records while you await the outcome of two job applications: the first to be an English teacher in Japan, the second to be a student at the National Film School in Sydney. Though you have worked in several other government offices, this is a Siberia like no other.

Because crime doesn't take holidays, the phones never stop

ringing. Criminal records checks. Security checks. Shooter's licence checks. Warrant checks. In order to serve officers on the beat, the section stays open twenty-four hours a day, and clerks are rostered in three eight-hour shifts.

After a time, the job begins to take hold of your body. When you aren't sleeping, or thinking of sleep, you are on the phone, or up to your wrists in the file cards which make up the near-infinite manual index of Victorians boasting a criminal record. Names, false names, and nicknames, millions of file cards jammed tight into the narrow draws of grey cabinets which circle a vast room. Persons frequently known to police have their records made up into comprehensive files known as dockets. Each year, four or five thousand new dockets are added to the collection.

You are engulfed by ignobility. This is the shadow history of Melbourne and Victoria. Halfway through a tough shift you get lost in all those cards and files so that your head spins with names and tattoos, dates and codes, protocols and prohibitions, the half-remembered list of corrupt officers who aren't to be given information, and the officers whose names are to be recorded if too much interest is shown in sensitive information. Juvenile criminals, druggies, Old School criminals, careerists and psychopaths, you live with them night and day.

There is a complete cabinet full of cards—thousands of cards—detailing criminals known to have tattoos on their penis.

One young prostitute has a cat and a mousetrap tattooed on her left inner thigh, a mouse and SOME CHEESE on her right groin, and a dog under her left breast. She is gradually transforming her body into a relief map of the food chain.

Another tall, flame-headed member of a bike gang has just one tattoo which takes up his entire chest: Donald Duck smoking a huge joint while sodomizing Mickey Mouse, accompanied by the speech balloon, 'It's grouse if you can get it!'

On the phone, you inform officers of priors and pendings, suspicions and outstanding warrants, the persons to be approached with caution, and the premises believed to house stashes of weapons. Always the swirl of names and birth-dates and spellings, possible spellings, and alternative spellings, till you find yourself riffling through the manual index at four in the morning, having lost all confidence in your ability to order the letters of the alphabet. You live in fear that a new letter has been added to the alphabet since your last shift.

This index of criminals infiltrates your consciousness. To your friends outside work you can talk of nothing but crime and criminals. And you can't get over how much recorded crime there is. You try to persuade yourself that it's natural a city of three million should have crime, but not this much crime surely. This much brutality, deception and indecency.

The Homicide detectives want information urgently. The police on the road want information now. If you fuck-up, if you flick past one index card in a tray of thousands, if you fail to consider an alternative spelling, or the possibility that two similarly named criminals may be one in the same, a superior will arrive to tear you to shreds. If you miss one crucial thread of information, someone might die. And all this time, you are sleepless, or else your sleep is polluted with images of the vast Manual Index.

When the interview for the teaching position in Japan finally comes up, you haven't slept for seventy-two hours. You sit opposite a panel of two Australian women and a Japanese man. Even the most predictable question no longer has an obvious answer. Why do you want to teach in Japan? You riffle through your mind, but your mind is filled with the names and descriptions of criminals.

Why do I want to teach in Japan? Getting desperate now. Why *do* I want to go to Japan? They are waiting for your answer. Think! *Think!*

Your answer, that you'd like to meet Godzilla, does not convince the Japanese Government to offer you a teaching position.

The Manual Index may yet prove to be your destiny.

4. The Unknown Criminal

A new filing cabinet is requested to accommodate the constantly expanding Manual Index. When the Stores Branch fuck up the order, two cabinets are delivered, the second standing empty next to the cabinet jammed thick with W to Z miscreants. After a time, one of the staff tapes an identikit photo of a criminal to the drawers of the empty cabinet, along with the label, *'Tomb of the Unknown Criminal'*.

It isn't such a big joke, and the photograph and label would have been removed soon enough if local detectives hadn't warmed to the idea. Detectives from the Homicide Squad, and the Sexual Offences Squad began to stand before The Tomb of The Unknown Criminal, hoping for inspiration as they continued to investigate an unsolved crime. Superstition soon becomes tradition among the superstitious. Within a matter of weeks, no one thought to question the idea of a detective paused head-bowed in front of an empty filing cabinet.

5. Distractions

There are quiet times. The cold, wet mornings when even the hardest criminals prefer bed. As soon as the phones stop ringing, we start organizing our competitions, and gather nominations for the Mongrel of the Month Award. Each month, the criminal who perpetrates the worst crime or crimes takes out The Mongrel, and remains in the running for nomination to The Hall of Shame. The Hall receives three new inductees each December. Hall of Shamers are mongrels *par excellence*. You know they would be proud of the honour if they could be notified. Our oath of confidentiality prevents us from informing recipients of their new status. Nevertheless, we write induction speeches on their behalf, and deliver them in their absence. The speeches are polite and grateful. Parents are thanked. Family and schoolteachers. Society at large. Invariably, the new Hall of Shamers promise not to let the honour distract them from their mission. They remain dedicated to a life of malevolence.

6. The Line-up

One morning a supervisor calls together the young male clerks. We are asked to go downstairs to the Victims of Crime section to take part in a line-up. Though it isn't irregular for office staff to make up numbers for a line-up, this is your first time. As a film buff, you imagine that the whole thing will be like Hollywood film noir. In movies, the victim stands anonymous behind double-plated glass as suspects are paraded under an intense lamp. This arrangement is designed to protect the victim from retribution or threats.

But that's Hollywood. Maybe that arrangement doesn't exist anywhere in reality. When we arrive downstairs, we are led into a large auditorium. Twenty men have been invited from different sections of the building. A detective asks us to form a line at one end of the room. We are told to remove police ID tags. You presume that their suspect is the thin, blond man who has no tag to remove.

Then a woman is escorted into the rear of the room by two detectives. She is a petite brunette. Pretty. She smokes a cigarette. Even from a distance, you see the cigarette trembling in her fingers.

The woman is brought to the front of the auditorium to stand no more than two or three metres from the line of men. She stands there, smoking, looking down at her feet, while one of the detectives reads out details of the circumstances in which the woman was raped.

As she walked along a street at night, she was dragged off the footpath into the back seat of a parked car, where she was violently assaulted. Unlawful sexual penetration is alleged to have taken place. While the detective reads, the woman smokes and looks down. There are twenty men listening to the details of the offence against her. She is the only woman in the room.

Then a detective asks the woman if her assailant is one of the men standing in the line-up. The woman looks closely at the first seven or eight men standing in the line before taking a cursory scan of the men further down the line. You don't remember if she ever looked directly into your face. You doubt that she looks down the line as far as the thin, blond man you presume to be the suspect.

The detective asks her again, formally, whether her assailant is in the line-up. The woman says, No.

After the woman has been escorted from the room, we are told that we can return to our sections. A detective thanks us for our participation.

As you go upstairs to the phones and The Manual Index, you consider the meaning of the verb to participate, and decide that you have participated. You had participated by allowing the detective to thank you for participating. And already your participation has left you feeling strangely unclean.

7. The Shades of Criminality

The year gets worse for you. The National Film School advise that they cannot offer a place in their one-year screenwriting course, and now your only hope of acceptance is to gain admission into the school's three-year Bachelor of Arts course. To succeed, you will need to be one of the anointed twelve from a field of seven hundred applicants nationwide. You have written just one short script, and you have never peered through the lens of a video camera. The worry makes you look at your clerical colleagues, and wonder whether, forty years from now, you will die with them at your side, surrounded by an ever vaster, ever dustier labyrinth of files, index cards, and cabinets.

During meal breaks, you talk about old hit records and television shows. One cartoon that often comes to mind is 'Tooter and The Wizard' from *Leonardo The Lion*.

Tooter was a kid who always thought the grass would be greener in another place at another time, and the kindly old wizard, a Viennese Freud caricature, assisted by transporting Tooter through time to the historical moment of his choice. Invariably, Tooter got himself into strife, being attacked by pirates, Indians and communists, and when things were at their most desperate, Tooter would fall to his knees and bellow, *Mr Wizard! Mr Wizard!* At which the know-it-all wizard waved his wand and incanted, *Teetle, tattle, tootle, tum, time for this one to come home*, so relieving Tooter from the misery of spatio-temporal dislocation.

There are times when every public servant would like to fall to his or her knees and scream, *Mr Wizard! Mr Wizard!*

This is a record-breaking year. There are twenty-five murders in six weeks even before the massacre at Hoddle Street, where a disgraced ex-soldier shoots motorists as they drive home late on a Sunday night. Several days later, there is a particularly brutal double-murder in Sandringham, and you find yourself sharing a lift with two Homicide detectives. They talk casually about football, and why Essendon has had such a poor season. One of them holds a sealed plastic bag which contains a blood-stained kitchen knife.

Murder seems to be closing in on you. You remind yourself that exile in the public service is your punishment for murdering a Scottish King, for not heeding the voice of reason. It may be that you will catch this murder virus.

8. Rare Passion

A police officer in Moorabbin calls to enquire about the record of a suspect, formerly resident in Western Australia. A telex is sent to the Criminal Records Office in Perth, and after twenty minutes you are able to inform the requesting officer that his suspect has a prior conviction for 'Attempted Carnal Knowledge of a Horse'.

This is the first time you've seen the offence referred to in this way. More commonly, it would be 'Gross Indecency', or 'Aggravated Cruelty to an Animal', or even, in some statutes, 'Bestiality'. Still, the sergeant takes it in his stride. You overhear him speaking to the suspect.

Had a bit of trouble with a nag out west, did we, mate? Never mind, he tells the offender, I know how it is. You're in the darkness of a crowded disco, and someone special takes your fancy. She might be fifteen, might be sixteen. A bloke in the throes of a rare passion can't stop to count her teeth.

9. The Persistence of Memory

You have two conflicting desires, to sleep, and to drink coffee, and these desires are locked in mortal combat. However much you beg for sleep, it eludes you. Coffee, on the other hand, is there when you need it, and you always need it.

A woman sits opposite you in a South Yarra cafe one lunchtime as you stop for a coffee on the way to an afternoon shift. Though you seem to remember her face, you can't place her. The longer you look at her, the more you are convinced she is someone you know. You could approach her and ask, Don't I know you? but you hate using lines that sound so much like lines.

The woman is petite and dark-haired, probably in her early thirties. She is pretty enough to be someone you might have seen on television, or in a magazine. Equally, she could be someone you worked with in the past. Mostly, you remember things, but lately you've found it difficult to situate your memories.

For just an instant, she makes eye contact. She realizes that you've been looking at her and shifts her gaze. She then gulps down the last of her coffee, and fumbles through her purse to find coins to cover the bill.

Sure that you know her from somewhere, you watch her hurry out of the cafe. She is half a block down Toorak Road before you realize she is the woman who once examined your face while you stood in a police line-up.

10. The Fuck-up

It's nearly December, and you've heard nothing from the Film School. There has been another insane massacre. This time a gunman has gone on the rampage in central Melbourne, terrorizing an office building in Queen Street. You're so twitchy that the slightest contact with another human being makes you jump.

It's Friday afternoon, and you're re-filing index cards when a highly agitated detective slams open the door which leads to the Manual Index. From behind a cabinet, you hear him yelling at one of your superiors. It's obvious that there's been a fuck-up. All the clerks fall silent and wait to see who is going to be scapegoated. The detective and the supervisor riffle through the inquiry sheets to see which clerk handled the record search in question. After a time, you see the pair striding in your direction.

You! the detective shouts. Did I speak to you on the phone about a crim named Cook?

You remember that you checked the files for a Cook earlier that afternoon. The detective is red in the face.

You told me that Alastair Cook wasn't recorded or wanted, didn't you? Then how the fuck is it that this Alastair Cook did time for grievous bodily harm? How come he's got an outstanding apprehension warrant for escape and attempted murder?

You look at the sheets, and the index card in front of you, and try to work out what happened, but the detective is prodding you in the chest with his index finger. Jabbing the place between your chest and your shoulder-blade. Jabbing hard enough to push you back against a filing cabinet. The supervisor tries to grab his arm, but the detective keeps jabbing you hard.

We had Cook, but because you're a lazy fuckwit, we let him go.

Your colleagues have put down their phones so they can circle your humiliation, so they can see you get punished for the fuck-up.

You are trying to explain that Cook's Christian name had been spelled out to you as Alistair, and that the Alistair Cooks and the Alastair Cooks ought to have been consolidated in the index, but in fact there were twenty Albert Cooks and Alfred Cooks separating Alistair from Alastair. You want to tell the detective that it's not your fault, that it's the fault of this impossible Manual Index. You want to say that there are bound to be errors when clerks are filing and re-filing millions of error-laden index cards. You'd say all this, but the detective is hitting you in the chest with his fist.

I'm not getting through to you, am I? A member could have got killed because you didn't warn him that he was dealing with a fiend. And this head is still out on the fucking street. He might kill someone yet.

You want to fall on your knees and beg. You want to scream out, *Mr Wizard! Mr Wizard!* But you know that cartoon wizards can't save you from real-life injustice. The detective is punching you, and your colleagues watch him punch you, too fearful to intervene. You are crying.

Then, just as the detective prepares to re-organize your face, someone picks him up, and heaves him onto the table in the middle of the room. You see the other staff scatter. You see a net descend over your head, and hear a slow, distorted voice pronounce, That's the one! Take him!

You are being carried away by two men at either end of a large black net.

When they see that no one else is to be taken, your stunned colleagues run to protest. They tell the men with the net that you're a no-talent who is not entitled to be rescued. Only just now you've caused a major fuck-up.

We're more talented than him, they say. Take us!

But everything is in motion now. You've never felt so

comfortable and safe as you feel embraced by that net. As your skin begins to relax, you feel the calm certainty of approaching sleep. You know that when you wake, you'll be five hundred miles from the Manual Index, a student at the National Film School in Sydney.

And much later, when you're safely making student films, when you've nearly forgotten the constant prickling sensation of caffeine overdose, you just might kid yourself that you live in a world where everyone gets their just desserts, and this is the only way your story could have turned out.

1993

MOTION SICKNESS

Leaving Central Station, the train travels in reverse for fifty minutes until it arrives at a Y-junction on the outer perimeter of the city. Disturbed by this unexpected reverse motion, many new travellers try to swap seats so they can travel forwards. Being accustomed to the peculiarities of the journey, I explain to confused passengers that the train will assume their favoured direction as soon as it leaves the suburbs.

As it happens, I prefer reverse motion. You can watch the suburbs peel away like cellophane packaging, and imagine that they feature in a film being screened incorrectly. You expect a point will arrive when the screen will go to black. Then, after frenzied activity in the projection room, the film will be re-screened as its director intended. Travelling backwards enables me to imagine that everything done might be undone.

The man who sat opposite was in his early-twenties, red-headed, a little scruffy, probably a student. He wanted to get the attention of the pretty brunette sitting next to me. At first, the girl seemed indifferent to his vacuous chat, and refused to return eye-contact. Then he realized, at about the same time I did, that the young woman was deaf. After that, we all communicated in a pigeon sign language which had the young woman in hysterics. Her exuberant smile reminded me of Christine, a girl I was fond of before I married. (I cannot go anywhere without seeing these resemblances.) My neighbour's speech was a monotonous mish-mash of sound, frequently impenetrable, but from what we made sense of, she was a well-educated person who worked as an animator for a foreign company.

I had mistaken the man's first approaches to be a brazen play for the young woman's affections. As it transpired, his sole aim had been to share his joy with anyone who cared to listen.

Only the previous evening, the man had become engaged to his first cousin, an arrangement postponed for several years owing to the displeasure of a mutual grandparent, now deceased. The young man was on his way to tidy up some business, then the cousins would marry as soon as he returned.

Alice is extraordinary, the man said. We knew that we would marry from the very first, from when we used to play together as kids.

From his wallet the man produced a snapshot of himself standing alongside a radiant, red-headed girl. My neighbour commented that the man's fiancée was very pretty, which was undeniable. With the man so unrestrained in his delight, I felt it imprudent to say that I could detect a strong family resemblance.

We each drank from the man's bottle of vodka, and the three of us continued to giggle over the imprecision of our signed gestures, joking a little bawdily as the train rumbled into the evening-pink countryside. The alcohol accentuated my tiredness, and not long after the compartment lights went down at eleven, I fell into a deep sleep.

That night I dreamt of something which may have taken place when I was eleven or twelve. I say may have taken place, because it is unclear to me whether the incidents I recall relate to an actual event, or to an unusually vivid dream from that time. My father was taking me by train into the city to buy my first adult cricket bat. As no one in our family owned a car, we rarely left our suburb, and the city seemed to me to be a confusion of dark laneways and backstreets. I was thankful my father knew the way.

At the sporting goods store, my father agreed to stretch his budget to enable me to buy the brand of bat endorsed by my idol. As I caressed the smooth willow blade with my open hand, the old salesman smiled with stained yellow teeth. He advised my father to purchase a bottle of linseed oil, instructing me how and when I should apply the oil.

I was remarkably happy to have the full attention of my father, and to be the owner of a new bat. But, as the train neared our station on the return journey, I realized that the bumping motion of the old red carriage had given me a very conspicuous erection. I became worried dad would notice and think me shameless, and I tried to bring to mind the most tedious things I could imagine. Yet my consciousness of the problem only seemed to accentuate it. I still hadn't deflated when we arrived at our destination. To preserve some modesty, I positioned the bat in front of me as we left the carriage.

On the platform at Hampton station my father met a man he knew, a superior at his office, and he told the man that we had been to the city to select my first bat. (In this most recent dream, the man looked less like the man I remember from the event, or the original dream, than he looked like Mr Sanders, who would have been my Maths teacher at the time.) When this man asked if he could inspect my bat, I made such a botch of passing it to him that I drew attention to my aroused condition. All three of us were embarrassed, and the bat was passed back to me without comment. Later, as we turned into a quiet street, my father pinched the flesh at the back of my arm, telling me, You're not to be trusted. I can't take you anywhere.

When I awoke from this dream, the train was thundering across a moonsilver plain, and the pretty deaf girl was asleep with her head resting on my shoulder, so that the perfume of her silky hair invaded my nostrils, and I was bone hard for the first time in many months.

I saw that the young man opposite was wide awake, staring into the luminous countryside. At intervals he took a swig from his nearly drained bottle of vodka. When he noticed that I had woken, he offered the bottle to me with a nod and a conspiratorial smile, as if to observe that both he and I were lucky with women. Then guessing I was offended by an inference that I was a man who might take advantage of an innocent situation, he tried to erase this hint of carnality by observing, She's very sweet. He spoke clearly, aware that sound would not disturb our sleeping companion.

It's a sad thing, isn't it? Such a pretty girl. Do you have children? I'm guessing from your ring that you're a married man.

When forced to consider the matter, I see my married life unveil like the suburbs of a city seen from a train travelling in reverse; a collection of pain-tainted vignettes that become less threatening as they retreat into the middle distance. I could extend the metaphor to incorporate the stations of my wife's infidelity, but when asked about my marriage, I generally choose to be vague and evasive, to assert that I am a traveller committed to the perspectives afforded by travel. I believe it's possible to remember everything, imagine anything, while I am aboard a train in motion.

I knew intuitively that none of this would interest my companion. He wanted to tell me that his father was dead, and he would inherit his father's wine-importing business. This inheritance would make him one of the wealthiest men in the country. He wanted to tell me that it wasn't his grandfather who disapproved of his love for a cousin, but his father who prohibited his love for an older sister. As he told me this, he examined my face, expecting it to register shock or outrage, but I wasn't shocked, because I have travelled, and I have known alcohol to facilitate confidences of this kind.

Now scarcely able to string a sentence together, the man declared that he had known his sister intimately since he was eleven and she thirteen, and his business at our destination was to arrange a change of identity so that he and she might marry and start a new life in the west.

If I cared more, I might have told the young drunk that nothing can distance a person from integral truths. Having decided that a truth is crucial, you give it licence to hunt you down. You will be hunted down by dead fathers, betrayed mothers, or by the thought of your wife naked beneath the motion of another man's buttocks.

I know we're going to be happy, he insisted. So happy, she and I, when we're husband and wife. Happy together.

Though he meant for me to endorse this comment, I refrained. I know more about the thoughts prompted by vehicles in motion than I could claim to know about happiness. Happiness is no more explicable than the rousing fragrance of the pretty deaf girl who chose that moment to shift her head on my shoulder.

Do you suppose she had an accident? the young man asked.

It's probably genetic, I said.

As the sun rises, the train will begin its descent from the mountains towards the distant corkscrew spires of the great city. There is nothing particularly dramatic about this elevation. Nevertheless, many first-time travellers are excited by the quality of the morning light, reaching for their cameras when they see the green-gold of rolling hills spotted with cows and sheep. Once I might have done likewise, but a real traveller knows that to capture a brief visual impression insults memory as much as it insults travel. There will always be a Y-junction on the outer perimeter of the city, and a pause before the train shifts into reverse. However you choose to situate yourself in relation to the vehicle's motion, you travel steadily and inexorably toward that place from which you hoped to have found refuge.

1992

DISTANCE EDUCATION

May 4th

Sarah,

once again you have displayed admirable style and technique. Your evocation of time and place is especially convincing. However, I can only give this piece a C, since you have responded with a work of imagination when you were instructed to submit an essay written in a personal (non-fictional) style. The Board guidelines are rigid in this matter, and I refer you to p. 31 of the Handbook. However skilled you may be as a creative writer, you mustn't imagine that your skills entitle you to operate outside the brief. If you resubmit by May 15th, I will consider an upgrade of no more than ten per cent.

May 8th

Mr Thompson, I was very disappointed by the comments (and mark!) on my recent story. I followed the instructions you supplied and wrote a personal essay—rather more personal than I usually present to strangers. Why did you offer no specific comment about the *content* of my essay? You are wrong to *presume* that it is a work of imagination. It may be that my suffering threatens or discomforts you in some way. I certainly will not re-write or re-submit till you are more precise in stating your objections to my story.

May 11th

Sarah,

following your correspondence of May 8, I re-read your story 'Koorook', and I remain of the opinion that it is a (not inconsiderable) work of imagination. I should put my cards on the table: I know Koorook quite well. I lived there for the first three years of my life. My parents left Koorook for Melbourne on the day that John F. Kennedy was assassinated. I still have friends and relations who live in the area. So far as I am aware, Koorook is not a drop-off zone for alien spacecraft. You say that the alien visitor from Zon-X closely resembled a Gas and Fuel plumber who once visited your house. If, as I suspect, you are writing a form of expressionistic autobiography, I think you need to be more cogent, or telling, in the parallels that you draw. Wild leaps of imagination diminish the credibility of your story. For instance, it's not obvious to me why your mother would 'slut off with' an alien simply because he shows an interest in patchworking, and shares her taste for Belgian chocolate. Nor am I convinced that knowledge of such a liaison—is it sexual or merely intimate?—would disturb your 'father' to the extent that he would explore hitherto latent homosexual desires. If your story is to be construed as an innovative form of non-fiction, you need to make it apparent how these metaphors operate as metaphors. As a reader, I need to have some cues which would enable me to decode or interpret your narrative. That said, even if you could persuade me that your mother's relationship with Gorb expresses a manifest yearning in her life, or that your father's misadventures after the football club pie night are the direct consequence of his failure to understand your mother's needs as you perceive them, I would still be inclined to say that 'Koorook' is a work of fiction. As such, it contravenes the specific guidelines for the sec-

*ond common assessment task set down in the Handbook.
I am prepared to extend your re-submission deadlines
to May 22nd, which would mean that it should be forwarded alongside your essay on* The Go Between*.*

May 15th

Mr Thompson, it seems to me that Koorook must
have changed quite a bit since you lived here.
Whether or not you believe in alien visitation
doesn't really bother me. I know the truth, and I
am looking forward to having Gorb's child. (I'm
less thrilled about having to tell my mother that we
share a lover.) I would ask you to be more discreet in
the notes you attach to my essays. My parents often
ask to read them. My mother isn't aware that my father knows of her affair. Nor does she know that he
sought solace with the junior football coach. I don't
understand what you mean about 'expressionistic
autobiography'. I write about my life as I experience it. I don't know how I could write more personally or truthfully. For me, the only real truth is
emotional truth. After all, if my memory of a dream
or a desire is more compelling than memories of an
actual experience, how can I say that one is more
'real' than the other? By giving reality to my most
truthful dreams, fears and desires, I am inventing a
more real, more compelling version of myself. What
could be more fictitious than the idea of a personality which is whole, discreet, and continuous? I would
insist on getting a second marker, but it makes no
difference now. I am going to have Gorb's child, and
any academic ambitions I had are now secondary
... I enclose my essay on The Go Between. I ended
up liking the book quite a lot. Marion's situation—

getting duffed-up by rustic Ted—isn't so different from my own. (Would you be my go-between, Mr Thompson? Would you help if my father insists on an abortion?)

May 18th

Sarah,

This is a fine essay. You write with great sensitivity about Leo's predicament, and the multi-dimensional aspects of moral decision making. I particularly enjoyed your illuminating discussion re. Hartley's use of cricket metaphors. This is definitely worth a High Distinction.

May 24th

Mr Thompson, pleased as I was to get a high grade on my <u>Go Between </u>essay, I was disappointed by your lack of care or compassion. Since Gorb and his colleagues left for Zon-X, my mother has been stuffing herself with sedatives. She refused to believe I'd had sex with Gorb until I described the mustard-coloured rings around his engorged penis. Now she can't decide whether to smack me or beg my forgiveness. My father goes off to the garage with his stick-mags. He pretends none of this has happened, but he'll piss off on us as soon as he's found work in the city. He has asked a specialist friend in Bendigo to 'attend to my problem'. I am dreadfully confused. I want my baby. Why have you chosen to ignore this matter entirely? Are you so frightened of being touched by reality?

May 27th

Sarah,

I don't think you realise how busy I am. I process fifty pieces of student correspondence every day. I simply don't have the time or energy to buy into your fantasies. You are an exceptional student, and it is always a great pleasure to read your work. (Unfortunately, I'm not a great fan of science fiction.) With the job market the way it is, every mark will be crucial to your future prospects. Please don't waste this opportunity. You have a rare talent, but talent alone doesn't count for much. I'll expect your <u>Sons and Lovers</u> essay on June 5th.

June 2nd

Mr Thompson, last Thursday my father forced me to have Gorb's child aborted. He drove me to an expensive clinic in Bendigo, where pock-faced Dr Pascoe sat me down and told me I mustn't be ashamed. Country girls tend to be adventurous, and these mistakes happen as a matter of course. Dr Pascoe wanted to know who the father was, and if I had his permission to abort. When I told him that Gorb was several light-years away and unable to be contacted, Dr Pascoe told his nurse I was a smartarse. But when their vacuum began to suck out crusty, green foetus, he and his nurse were sick all over the place. Total gut panic. I was still under a local, and it was all I could do to calm them down. I shouldn't have expected anyone to understand. I was probably too hard on you. It was a ninety-minute drive back to Koorook. There was a big squall and the rain belted against the screen so that the wipers could barely keep up, and all my father would say was, 'You know what you are, don't you?' My mother doesn't speak. I haven't been good for much these past few days. I've got a folio deadline for Australian History. I hope you'll understand if my <u>Sons and Lovers</u> essay is a couple of days late.

June 4th

Sarah,

<u>this has to stop</u>! You're spending more time fabricating these diversions than you are doing your work. Really, you seem to forget that I have information about you and your family on file. I know about your mother, Sarah. It's a terribly sad thing, but you can't go through life playing on people's sympathies. It doesn't do you any credit to concoct these stories about your father, or to make black jokes about abortion. Actually, I've had enough of this alien business. If I don't see your <u>Sons and Lovers</u> essay by June 11th, I'll be required to deduct marks.

June 8th

Mr Thompson, so you know about my mother, do you? Who are you to say that you know about my mum, or that you know anything about my life? Do you really believe the lies my father told for your shitty files? He's never once told the truth. You say you know Koorook, you <u>know</u> about my mother. What you know is FUCK ALL! Since you know so much, maybe you should tell me what you're doing there. I've heard that The Correspondence School is a sheltered workshop for damaged teachers, all the worst basket cases. (*I might have something about you here in my files. Let me see ... Ah yes, your mother. Don't think I don't know about your mother, Mr Thomp-*

son!) So what happened to you? Did a gang of boys gag you, and gaffer-tape you to the ceiling? Maybe you just dropped the chalk one day and stood there bawling your eyes out. Or else you went home early to find your wife giving slippery tuition to your star Lit. student. Why are you in that Ivory Cellar of yours? And how can you presume superiority when you're so obviously Mr Fucked-Up? (Just for your records, Mr Thompson, it was an abortion. You see, people have them ... No, girls have them, out here in the real world.)

June 12th

Sarah,

once again this is a fine essay that deserves an A. The observations that you make about Paul Morel and his inability to form mature relationships are most insightful. You would have benefitted from greater attention to detail when discussing Lawrence's use of sexual symbolism. (And I do like your observation that Lawrence's high-frequency repetition of the words dark, darkening, darkness etc. articulates a kind of emotional tunnel-vision. DH is the most emotion conscious of authors.) Speaking of emotions, I shouldn't have written what I did in the last note. It was out of line, and I'm sorry. Let's forget about it, and get on with the business of getting you a high mark in November.

June 14th

Dear Mr Thompson,

My daughter Sarah has asked me to write to you with regard to the feedback she has been getting on her assignments and stories.

As you will have gathered, Sarah is a high-strung, imaginative girl. She's suffered a great deal since her mother's death, and is given to dark moods and flights of fantasy. I know Sarah is talented, just as I am aware that she can be callous and manipulative.

I hope you will try to understand Sarah, and not allow her indiscretions to get under your skin. She needs your help, and she needs remarks on her submitted work that are less perfunctory than they have been in recent times.

Yours Sincerely

James Dickson

June 17th

Sarah,

I take your point. I was absolutely wrong to comment on matters that I knew nothing about. Yes, I ought to have written more extensively on your <u>Sons and Lovers</u> and <u>Go Between</u> essays. I suppose that I was troubled by your previous remarks and felt helpless ... Are you all right? ... If nothing else, you will have a long and glorious career as a swindler. (I doubt that your father would write so formally, or that he would type a short, personal request. I do know that he doesn't press quite so hard when making his signature!) I should have received your answers to <u>The French Lieutenant's Woman</u> questions by June 24th.

June 20th

Mr Thompson, yes I am all right, thank you. It gets so fucking boring here. It's just netball, the pub, the Young Farmers, or else you make your own fun.

I'm sure you know the old saying, When things are crook in Koorook, they're totally shithouse. I love <u>The French Lieutenant's Woman</u>. It's wonderful. If there weren't books, I'd go spare. Tell me the names of your favourite authors ... And I <u>would</u> like to know what you're doing at that school. As for my father's signature, and my version of it, personally, I don't see how you could tell the difference. Calligraphy's one of my favourite things. Calligraphy and sex ... There were lights in the sky again last night.

June 28th

Sarah,

These <u>TFLW</u> answers are excellent. You need to be this detailed when writing your essays. Always draw the most pertinent details from the text to support your arguments ... My favorite books? Too hard. <u>Dead Souls</u> by Gogol, <u>Gulliver's Travels</u> by Swift, <u>Lolita</u> by Nabokov, <u>Labyrinths</u> by Borges ... Kundera, Alice Munro, Ian McEwan, David Ireland, Eugene Ionesco, Beverley Farmer ... far too many to mention ... As for the school, you weren't that far wrong. The Correspondence School is a sheltered workshop for storm-damaged teachers. I wasn't cut out to be a classroom teacher, and, after I finished my diploma, I'd decided to give the profession a miss. But then I was offered a soft job in a boy's school, teaching English and Lit. to clever (mostly), well-motivated (mostly) boys. I thought I'd landed on my feet. They actually enjoyed Shakespeare, T.S. Eliot and Lowell ... One Sunday, one of my boys got upset, got drunk, got a rifle, and sat on a roof. He shot some people as they drove past, strangers, and then he shot dead (he said 'picked off ') the people who went to help the people he'd shot ... Look, I don't know. It might be just an excuse, *these things are complicated. Other things were going on at the time. Maybe my being here, with all the other basket-cases, has nothing to do with the shooting business. It's not a bad job though. I've always liked writing letters. I'm much better with people on paper.*

July 2nd

Mr Thompson, so sorry for yourself! You need to get out and have fun. How old are you? Are you married? Do something outrageous, get yourself a lover or an exercise bike. Anything.... I enclose the creative piece, 'The Stench of Recently Warped Time' for my folio.

July 6th

Sarah,

This time you were instructed to write an imaginative piece, and you have, indeed, responded with a powerfully disturbing work of imaginative fiction. I find it very difficult to comment on this story, or to predict how the examiners would respond if you were to produce a similar piece of work in the examination. The first criticism that I must make is that this story isn't sufficiently self-contained. Your stories tend to leak, one into another. Certain details concerning Gorb and his motivations demand some knowledge of your previous (science) 'fictions'. The violence is too confronting. So is your use of coarse sexual language and imagery. I'm tempted to call your story pornographic, but I can hardly be dismissive when it is so imaginative, and when so much of what is currently revered as 'art' plays with these same sado-masochistic themes. I can understand why the alien Gorb might want to punish the narrator for aborting his child, but why does Gorb force

*her father to watch? The description of the father mas-
turbating while Gorb rapes and brutalizes his daughter
is too horrible to contemplate. I'm sure you expect me to
be shocked, and I am shocked. You would probably expect
me to refer your story to a psychologist, but I'm not going
to allow you the pleasure of distraction, when distraction
seems to be what you want ... Sarah, you mustn't take lib-
erties with your talent. I'm going to give you an A here, in
spite of my puzzlement and revulsion. I think that you are
capable of better than this.*

July 9th

Mr Thompson, <u>Revulsion</u>! You hypocrite! First you
bawl me out for playing games, then you write,
'I'm giving you an A here, in spite of my revulsion'.
Who's living the fantasy now? I don't believe you
were revolted by my story. Otherwise, you would
have shown it to a shrink. I'm sure that an intelligent
man like you would know about Freudian denial.
You were revolted by the fact that it excited you. I'm
wise to you, Mr T. We're kindred spirits. I'm sure we
both enjoy the same games. Surely, you must have
guessed who Gorb is by now (?).

July 14th

Sarah,
*ENOUGH!!! No more Gorb! No more juvenile games!
I'm waiting for your essay on <u>The Crucible</u>. I'll be re-
quired to deduct marks if it doesn't arrive by July 20th.*

July 22nd

Sarah,

I haven't received any submissions since your correspondence on July 9th. I'm also advised that you failed to submit folio work for Australian History. If I don't hear from you by the end of the week, I'll have to notify the Principal.

July 25th

Dear Mr Thompson,

Don't you think it's strange that a teacher would fail to notify the Department, or his superiors when a troubled girl submits a story about being raped and humiliated by an alien while her father watches and masturbates? Don't you think it would be appropriate to bring that kind of thing to the attention of her parent? Why didn't you notify me when you suspected that my daughter had forged my signature? You worry me, Mr Thompson. What have you been playing at? Did Sarah's version of my signature look so different to this?

Yours Sincerely

James Dickson

P.S. It's my guess that you knew who Gorb was all along.

July 27th

Mr Dickson,

What have you done with Sarah? Why haven't I heard from her? Don't think that you can faze me with insinuated threats. I want proof that Sarah's all right.

Otherwise, I'll have to ask questions with the police in Koorook.

Yours
Richard Thompson

July 28th

Sarah,
I'm worried. Please contact me. If it's your father, we can help you. We'll do everything that we can.

July 31st

Mr Thompson, 'Sarah'? Really, you disappoint me. Still, it confirms what I've always heard, the Correspondence School is a sheltered workshop for damaged teachers, last refuge for the chronic basket-cases. Sure, come up and visit me here, by all means. Sgt. Watson could use a giggle, and boys like you need to get out and have some fun. Twenty years ago, I had a fabulous English teacher down there at the Correspondence School, Mrs Corcoran. She only gave me 74 for the same <u>Sons and Lovers</u> essay you went apeshit over. Have standards dropped that much? *Your standards couldn't drop any further, could they?* There are too many lights in your nightsky, Mr Thompson. Too much perversity, and not enough honest to goodness fun. Don't fret, Dick, 'Sarah' still sends you her wettest kisses.

Yours etc.

James

1993

OUR SWIMMER

Seeing films has corrupted the way we recall things. Our minds will now perform sophisticated technical operations. We can isolate the subject in the frame, we can enhance or colorize, we can edit our memories into dazzling montage sequences. Now, when I remember Marianne Topp, I see her moving in a stylised, filmic way, as if every second frame of memory has been extracted to create a more expressionistic version of my emotional attachment to her.

Marianne was an extraordinary looking girl, her dark hair so often pulled up in a bun that emphasized the curve of her neck, her cheeks, and her red-charged lips. Yet the essence of my attraction wasn't the way that she looked or moved. Her voice stole my heart—a low, carnal mutter, not so studied as Mae West's growl, but with the same coarse-textured depth. Marianne's voice had a natural insinuation that sent blood racing to vital outposts. And she understood the power of this weapon. Her speech was always so measured and deliberate. Everything about Marianne was perfectly composed.

I was browsing in Chapters' Bookshop, scanning the blurb of a paperback. The book was *Oranges Are Not The Only Fruit*, and she must have been looking over my shoulder.

'If you like Jeanette Winterson, you should read *The Passion*.'

I turned to tell the woman with the pulverizing voice that I'd read *The Passion* and adored it. Then I saw that the speaker was Marianne, whom I'd only ever worshipped from a distance, and her mouth broke into a soft, slightly embarrassed smile, and I was in love then, instantly. I was seventeen, and like everyone else, I was in love with Marianne Topp.

Marianne Topp kept so much to herself that people seldom associated her with her mother Beatrice, Hampton's most forceful presence. When Mrs Topp's newspaper was left to soak in the rain, she had the paperboy, Wayne Burgess, locked in stocks for two days. This punishment might have continued for a week, but the matriarch relented when the boys' doctor testified to his epilepsy.

I was playing cricket with Sam Morrissey the day that Beatrice Topp found Sam to be the author of obscene letters sent to her daughter at the Topp's Favril Street home. Two senior teachers ripped Sam off the field and took him to be interrogated by Mrs Topp. You didn't need to be Einstein to predict the outcome. My mother went to console Sam's mum, a friend she knew from tuckshop duty.

Having confessed to the crime, Sam was condemned to death. On the day of the execution, the Principal pulled six boys out of the final year geography class and took them to the school oval where they were told to construct a pyre out of old desks and chairs. Mrs Topp had decreed that Sam be taken up in a cherry-picker and lowered by rope onto the flaming pyre below.

All of Hampton gathered for the execution, scheduled just after sunset on March twenty-ninth. Mr Paterson the sports-master was assigned the task of restraining Sam. He was an unpleasant man well suited to the job. Sam's shrieks were so loud that Paterson was forced to gag him while Mrs Topp read a list of his offences to the crowd. She was wearing her favourite purple jumpsuit.

Mrs Topp said Sam had written anonymous letters in which her daughter—she didn't name her, but everyone knew she meant the eldest, Marianne—was described as a cheap slag who'd jazzed so many men her mother was forced to install a condom machine beside her bed. Few of us had ever heard such a vile attack against an innocent girl. When Beatrice Topp called for a volunteer to light the pyre, dozens of outraged

Hamptonians rushed forward.

Flames speared out into the night sky. As sparks and embers wafted over the orange-faced gathering, dramatic relief gave the yellow cherry picker the appearance of a sad mechanical giraffe. When Mrs Topp nodded, Mr Paterson eased Sam over the side of the bucket. For a few seconds, Sam looked like he was swimming across the sky. He flailed and shrieked as the rope was lowered toward the rising flames.

Finally, Mrs Topp raised an arm to halt the execution. Sam was reprieved. His death sentence was commuted to permanent banishment from Hampton, and from that evening he was never seen again. Not so long ago, someone told me that he'd gone on to do valuable research work in immunology. But we'd all got the message. Take Beatrice Topp lightly, and you'd live to regret it. But it's pointless for me to tell you this. You really can't conceive of such power unless you've experienced it first-hand.

Ruthless as she was, Mrs Topp was not a political leader. No-one elected her, and official authority resided with The Mayor. But Mrs Topp held sway in Hampton. She represented our suburb at Summits which detailed the latest advances.

I remember waiting impatiently for her to return with the New Knowledge from the International Geometrical Forum in New York. Everything we thought certain could be stood on its head by some astonishing development: the square triangle, or the refutation of Pythagoras.

That was the winter of unprecedented snows. The winds blasted up from the Antarctic and snap-froze birds in flight. Port Phillip Bay iced over for the first time in memory. Children skated across the rough surface and fishermen dropped lines through holes in the thick ice. You'd see vandals strip palings off fences to fuel the bonfires they lit on the beach. Old Ryan, who lived in the telephone box outside the Post Office, was taken in by church people who feared he'd freeze to death, but they were so chilled by his incessant prophesying they passed him on to the Community Welfare Officer.

Old Ryan bellowed that God was visiting us with the fruits of our sins. He didn't actually use the word Repent! but you knew what he was getting at. Not that we would have repented. We were too curious, too used to these astonishments to be fazed by them. So we waited for Beatrice Topp and did what we could to keep warm.

I often played squash with my friend Yuri at the fitness centre by Hampton railway station. After a match, we swam a few lengths, or sat by the pool and watched Marianne cruise through her 10,000 metre training regime. We were entranced by the rhythmic thrust of her muscular arms breaking the surface, and fixed our gaze on the dark locks she dragged through the blue water, the tufts of hair under her arms, and the sheer magnificence of the so-womanly body packed into a black one-piece swimsuit.

Like most of the students and staff at Hampton High, I worshipped the enigmatic Marianne Topp. What's more, we were expected to worship her.

At school assembly, the Principal detailed Marianne's latest achievements in the pool. He told us that she had swum nine seconds inside Janet Evans' official World Record for 800 meters freestyle. Even her final 400 meters was three seconds faster than Janet Evans' record for that distance.

'Marianne Topp,' the Principal told us, 'is a uniquely talented young woman who upholds the finest traditions of the school. Look closely at her performances, and you will see that Marianne is a negative splitter ... She's even stronger at the end of a race than she is at the beginning. In that,' he emphasized, 'there is a lesson for us all.'

After a spirited round of cheering, I heard the boy behind me say he'd give anything to be Marianne's bicycle seat, and when I turned to see who it was, I saw that Mr Simonescu, the woodwork teacher, had heard the remark, and was smiling lasciviously.

All the teachers were hot for her, the women as much as the men, but Marianne ignored their attentions. She did them a favour. Being on staff wouldn't have saved them from the cherry picker.

We all knew Marianne would have been an Olympic gold medalist if her mother had allowed her to represent Australia, but Mrs Topp was a fierce anti-nationalist. She would have had Hampton secede from Australia if it was possible for a suburb to secede.

'Australia is lazy and complacent,' Mrs Topp said, 'too satisfied with living vicariously through its sporting heroes. Hampton has to make itself a model for what's possible.'

For Marianne to have represented Australia would have been an unthinkable treachery.

Nevertheless, the school celebrated its negative splitter in very Australian fashion. The administration building was two storeys high, with a vast expanse of white wall facing west. The Principal instructed the senior art teacher to design a mural portrait of Marianne Topp. Each day, a group of fourth formers was sent out to bring the project to life. It took a full term to complete an immensely beautiful, eight-metre square portrait of our swimmer. Each of her lips was the size of a tall sixth form boy lying on his side, and at lunchtime you saw clusters of students gathered below Marianne's image. Swooning.

Marianne had one or two friends, but she wasn't part of a group. She didn't identify with heroes or pursuits the way that some kids identified with Nick Cave, football, or weekend alcoholism. She gave the impression that she was entirely self-sufficient, that she had all she needed emotionally, or thought she had. I don't mean to suggest that she was stuck-up or arrogant. She was guarded. Her smile, magnificent as it was, was a this-far-and-no-further smile.

'What happened to Mr Topp?' I asked my mother.
'She dispensed with him.'

'How could she get so much power without backing? What made her want to take over?'

'I don't think she planned to. She just seemed capable at a time when people needed someone capable. She was co-opted by our neediness.'

'What could we need so much that we were ready to be treated like shit?'

'I didn't say need. I said neediness. It's a different thing.'

The ice began to crack and melt. The skies turned a darker, cloudless blue. A rumour plague broke out. The Geometrical Summit had collapsed, with participants devastated by the discovery of a previously unknown real number between sixteen and seventeen. The seventeen-year olds among us feared this would affect eligibility to take the driving test at eighteen.

Marianne was due to turn eighteen in October. When she broke her own unofficial world record for the 400 Freestyle in September, the Principal called a half-holiday. Students wishing to commemorate Marianne's achievement were encouraged to visit Ron Dorfmann, the tattooist in Hampton Village.

I remember a proud Jane Nelson unbuttoning her blouse to show us where Ron had etched the letters M.T. above the nipple on her perfectly shaped left breast. Poor Jane was mortified when we explained the double-entendre.

But Marianne-madness was like that. Someone discovered her taste for expensive Belgian chocolate, and within days Hampton Post Office was jammed with parcels of chocolate addressed to Ms. M. Topp. At times, she seemed to be the only person in Hampton not affected by Marianne-madness. We were all hopelessly distracted, waiting for her mother to return, and waiting for Marianne to betray just a hint of vulnerability, a vacuum of neediness that we could be sucked into.

I told Yuri he was crazy to spend his savings buying chocolate for Marianne. He was inviting her contempt. But I never told him that I slipped $200 to a waitress at Coriander's Deli for a white coffee cup that still had Marianne's lipstick print on its rim. A perfect smear of Black Tulip.

Looking back at my chance meeting with Marianne in Chapters' Bookshop, I see things that self-consciousness prevented me from seeing at the time. In flickery, stylised motion I see the fraction of a second when Marianne forgot about the impression she was making and became someone capable of speaking her adoration for literature. She put her emotions on the line.

I hold that moment in freeze-frame. We are connected, perhaps ridiculously, by our mutual feeling for the work of an author neither of us will meet. We are as powerless before this feeling as any character in a fiction by Jeanette Winterson. How is it that I can now find the audacity to call this sentiment love?

A few days later, I was standing in the shaded quadrangle between school buildings, hanging out with friends, when Marianne Topp strode between groups of gawping students to present me with a novel, *Love in the Time of Cholera* by Gabriel Garcia Marquez. No particular sign of affection, or eye-contact, just, 'You might like this,' before she disappeared through the crowd.

'Thanks ... Marianne,' I called after her, scarcely able to believe I'd spoken her name out loud. My friends had lost the power of speech entirely.

Inside the front cover of the hardback novel was a note written on a slip of paper. Marianne's handwriting was as stylish as she was, and equally impenetrable. I spent the best part of that afternoon deciphering her short message. *'After Hours is playing at the Colosseum on Saturday night. You can meet me in the foyer. M'*

The Colosseum was a grand name for a fleapit cinema which used to stand opposite the Post Office, where the supermarket is now. The pavement outside the cinema was a favourite hang-out for warring philosophers. If you were short of entertainment on a Saturday night, you could practically guarantee a stoush between the followers of Quine and the Wittgenstein loyalists.

One old woman would sit in the doorway of the cinema holding a placard, DEFEND COPERNICUS!

If someone teased her, she let out a machine-gun blurt, 'The New Knowledge is a farce! The New Knowledge is a lie! Topp must be stopped!'

My nerves were shocking. I was back and forth to the toilet. What on earth was I doing having a date with Marianne? With stomach buckling, I tried to calm myself by singing. I love singing, but the only songs which came to mind were songs about panic, apprehension, and death. Who the fuck was I to be meeting Marianne Topp at the cinema? I brushed my teeth a dozen times and brushed my tongue as often.

Outside class, Marianne nearly always wore black, very occasionally a bright red jacket, but mostly shades of black to match her hair. Which is not to forget the deep, lascivious red of her lips.

'Hi, Richard. Have you been waiting long?'

I didn't want to admit that I'd been in the foyer since the manager unbolted the doors. I might have grown a beard while I'd been waiting.

I remember little about *After Hours*. We hardly spoke before the film. Marianne saw a woman she knew and spoke to her for ten minutes, while I smiled an idiot smile, and shifted my weight from foot to foot. I've never been a student of body language, but I knew enough to realize that this engagement wasn't about tit-feeling in the dark, or even hand-holding, which was just as well, since someone had installed a sprinkler system in my palms.

What I do remember is that Marianne wore a subtle perfume which activated with the rise of her body temperature. Two-thirds of the way through the feature, my nose got hooked on an updraught of irresistible scent, and I was so far lost in Swoonsville that she had to send out a search party when the film ended.

She must have known what she was doing to me, but what did she want? Not a kiss, though I would have sold my parents into slavery to kiss Marianne's full red lips. I thought then that my neediness, my undisguised adoration, might have been a quaint joke to her, that she was drawing strength or resolve from my own obvious weakness. But now I'm inclined to believe she wanted someone to trust but didn't dare cross the line to enter a zone where her fears and desires would be exposed.

I walked her home. We said little. A few comments about books we'd read, and films we'd seen.

'I see you at the pool,' she said.

'Well, yes. Actually, I'm a drowner.'

There was the slightest hint of a smile. 'I know,' she said. 'You ought to get some coaching.'

When I asked if she knew when her mother would come home, she became uncomfortable, and didn't answer.

I certainly wasn't going to interrogate her, to ask what it was like to be Beatrice Topp's daughter, or to be so often home alone with her two sisters. Instead, I asked what she'd do when she left school.

'I have to get out of Hampton. I'm suffocating here.'

'C'mon,' I joked, 'where in the world would you find somewhere more exciting than Hampton? I never cease to be amazed by this place.'

'It's possible to have too much imagination,' she said.

We were at her front gate then. Her German shepherd was barking. Marianne moved her hand so that it briefly touched the back of my hand.

'Thanks, that was nice,' she said.

I reconstruct this scene in my mind. I doubt that I could have played it differently, even if I'd known it would be the last time I'd see Marianne.

Shortly before dawn, two days later, a light plane flew into Hampton, using a four-lane stretch of Ludstone Street as a landing strip. When it took-off thirty minutes later the plane struggled to squeeze through a gap between overhead power lines. Among its passengers were Marianne Topp and her two younger sisters, Beth and Cicely.

The Topp girls left in a big rush. Their house was a mess. Though Hampton people speculated that they may have been taken by force, it was impossible to compare the scene they left behind with how they lived ordinarily because the Topps invited no-one into their home.

Their moonlight departure became widely known when Federal Police disclosed that they had been monitoring the activities of Beatrice Topp. They alleged she had been in Hong Kong conducting unauthorized land deals. At a time when she ought to have been gleaning The New Knowledge from the International Geometrical Summit, Beatrice Topp had been flogging pockets of Hampton to Asian and American developers. No one knew what had been sold, or the legal status of her transactions, but one thing was certain, Hamptonians could no longer imagine they lived at the centre of their own small world.

A friend with access to police intelligence said that Mrs Topp had fled to Switzerland or Kenya and had arranged for her daughters to be brought to her. That was as close as police ever got to locating the family.

In her absence, Hampton's matriarch was tried by criminal courts, being prosecuted first for fraud, then for various misappropriations. As hostility grew, new charges were brought. Soon, Beatrice Topp was being tried for crimes that hadn't seemed like crimes at the time: abuse of public trust, conspiracy, and false imprisonment. Each week, another charge went through the court, and Mrs Topp was sentenced to a further term of imprisonment. And so it went on, till Hampton had satisfied its need to purge itself.

If anything, the airbrushing of Marianne was crueler than the vilification of her mother. It was possible to speak your outrage at Mrs Topp's treachery, but Marianne's name could not be spoken. It was as if she had been a collaborationist entertainer in Vichy France. Marianne's name was removed from the school's honour boards, her photographs taken down from corridor walls, and the same students who produced the superb mural portrait of Marianne were sent up the scaffolds to slather it with garish yellow paint.

It is a difficult period for me to speak about. Shock and confusion kept me at one step remove from feelings which might have been totally destructive. I seem to have lived in a permanent dream, a festival of imagined departures and passionate reunions.

My most frequent dream was the one where Marianne taps on my window late at night and tells me that she has to go. I am so overwhelmed by this that I can't question why, or express my feelings for her, or say any of the proper things. There is no kiss. But in the dream it seems enough that she's chosen to tell me.

She is rushing for the plane when I remember that I still have her book. 'What about your Marquez?' I call.

She turns, and there is the miraculous coalition of the two gestures that I least expect from Marianne: a relaxed, unrestrained smile, and a single tear. A moment where everything is exposed entirely. 'I want you to have it,' she tells me, before rushing to her appointment at the makeshift airstrip.

I *did* have Marianne's book, and I've read it many times in the intervening years. *Love in The Time of Cholera* turned out to be a novel about the postponement of fated love. The two lovers reunite, gloriously and miraculously, when it seems least possible. How many times have I read Marianne and I into that scenario? I want more than anything to believe she left that Marquez novel because it articulated her most fervent hopes for our relationship. In spite of everything, we would one day be reunited.

But I'm not such a fool that I can't admit the possibility of coincidence. Who can say that she gave even a moment's thought to how I might construe or misconstrue a subtext? Maybe it was just an accident that I had her book when she was forced to leave.

Six years have passed. I often wonder whether Marianne kept swimming. I keep a close eye on major swimming championships. Only in the last eighteen months have swimmers begun to approach the unofficial world records that Marianne swam when she was Hampton's darling.

After much procrastination, the Federal Government decided to compensate the business people who had been stung by Beatrice Topp's illegal transactions. Though this spared Hampton from foreign ownership, the suburb couldn't insulate itself against changes brought by market forces. The cinema was forced to close, and the High School that was so much the heart of our community was sold to developers. The school buildings were demolished, to be replaced by gauche but costly residential dwellings.

During the demolition of the administration block, I befriended Josef, a plump, black-bearded Romanian who operated a massive bulldozer. I managed to persuade Josef to gently tilt a portion of west wall so that it could be recovered with its yellow-coated brickwork intact. The retrieved expanse of wall, one and a half metres high, and three metres wide, stands on my back patio, leaning against the garage.

After receiving advice from conservators at the State Museum, I began to excavate a portion of the Marianne Topp mural. It's a laborious process, scouring away the thick coat of yellow plastic paint, while trying to keep the submerged level of portrait undamaged. Friends joke about my enterprise and refer to the wall as The Hampton Shroud.

Gradually, the outline of Marianne's fabulous red lips has begun to emerge. When they are finally retrieved, I might use them in photo-composites or treatments, but just now it is enough that they will be retrieved. A romantic side of me wants to believe everything worth retrieving can be retrieved.

Still, my cynicism reminds me that it's not a Michelangelo I toil on, but the rushed work of spotty fourth form art students. In many ways, my quest is pathetic as it is heroic.

The air got terribly cold as I worked on Marianne's upper lip last Sunday. I could barely flex my fingers to operate the spatula. Feeling something brush my ear, I looked up from my work to see a brief, majestic flurry of snowflakes. My heart almost seized with joy. This was the first snow I'd seen in Hampton since that extraordinary winter when the Bay iced over and small birds snap-froze in flight.

1992

THE EXERCYCLE

Midway through last year, I made a discovery. I was in the family room, riding my exercycle, when sentences began to flood into my brain. Phrases flowed seamlessly, one into another, and these were brilliant sentences, insights dramatic as they were unexpected. However, when I leapt off the bike to record the lines which had come to me, my inspiration failed. I still had my narrative voice and situation, dazzling phrases that I could save, but my stream had dried up.

Not long after, when seated on the cycle completing my twenty-kilometer daily regime, the sentences again stole into my head, prescient and majestic, taking up where they left off. They came at such a rate that I was at once trying to remember them and allow them to flow. I asked my partner Catherine to fetch a pen and paper, and, while still cycling, I began to transcribe the paragraphs that were being mysteriously dictated. During this process, I noticed something striking. If my peddling slowed below a certain speed, the quality of the language deteriorated. If I increased pace, the narrative lost sense and logic. So long as I maintained a speed which was precise to a decimal point, I was on the road to literary fame.

Quite apart from the awkwardness of needing to write while peddling, there was the problem of maintaining speed. I feared I lacked the fitness to become a great writer. But this was my uncorked genie. Just as some artists find inspiration in opium, and others find it in the texture of a half-dunked Madeleine, the most creative regions of my brain activated when peddling my exercycle at a precise speed.

This sense of breakthrough was endorsed when a publisher offered me a five-figure advance on the basis of fifty pages I sent her after my first epiphany.

Had I stumbled upon a secret already well known to the great writers? Perhaps this was how Toni Morrison, Milan Kundera, and Alice Munro composed all along. But the thing was, and I say this with due regard for modesty, the fiction I wrote while cycling at the literary limit was far more astonishing than anything these heroes could have written. I was awestruck by the power of my prose. My publisher must have felt likewise. She volunteered to raise my advance even before receiving a second installment.

Just when the future couldn't have been brighter, my discovery struck a hitch.

You are waiting for me to say that thieves stole my exercycle, that the chain slipped, I had a heart attack, or that the speedo began to malfunction, but this hitch belonged to the class of conceptual oversights.

Having taken note of the exact speed to optimize literary production, I assumed this speed brought about a mysterious chemical change within my brain. What I failed to consider was that I'd accidentally stumbled on something of even greater significance—a universal law of *masterpiece* production.

This unhappy extrapolation revealed itself one evening as I sat listening to the stereo: it might have been Ed Kuepper or R.E.M., I don't remember which. What matters is that I was pondering things unliterary as Catherine did her bit on the exercycle.

With so much money and praise coming into the household, Catherine was curious about the optimal speed, and set about maintaining that speed for a kilometer or two. She had barely cycled more than 500 meters at the required pace when she asked me to bring a pad and pen. Cath likes taking the piss, and I love to give her the chance, because that playfulness adds resonance to our sex-life. So, standing to one side while Catherine cycled and scribbled, I was smugly confident that she would have written 'Fuck you, Richard!' five hundred times by the end of her epic journey.

I might have been happier with five hundred 'Fuck yous!'.

What Catherine had written was incredible. Her prose left my own nascent masterpiece in the shade. And the worst thing was, Cath's never wanted to be a writer. She's a forensic pathologist: a technician, and a remarkably skilled one. She realised even before I did that her confirmation of the cycling speed to maximize literary consciousness had effectively undermined thousands of years of courage, toil, and talent. What we've just done, she told me—and only a forensic pathologist would describe it thus—is sodomize Charles Dickens' corpse.

You look at your bike differently once someone's told you that.

Educationists have it wrong when they warn the young about the danger of drugs. They depict drug users as dehumanized desperados, and imply that a drug like heroin will automatically give users the appearance of a sick panda. The real problem with smack is that the sensations it offers are too good for the world we live in. The drug induces a sublime sense of wellbeing which doesn't correspond with ordinary experience, effectively mangling perspective. The sad truth is that our pissy lives aren't good enough for the mind-altering substances that we use to enliven them. Our efforts to incorporate two realities too frequently result in corporate takeover.

My point is this, it's the duty of artists to supply a middle-ground, to chip away, to offer new ways of seeing. While relishing the margins, artists should be *of* the world, occasionally tossing the pink streamer which makes our drab, meaninglessness bearable.

Once I realised that my discovery would devalue all literature, I had no choice but to do the honourable thing. I withdrew my novel and returned the advance. Catherine and I destroyed the passages we had written, and made a pact to never disclose the optimal cycling speed for literary production. To do so would be the modern equivalent of putting a torch to the

Library of Alexandria. By allowing any fool to be Shakespeare, you murder Shakespeare.

Let the vapid telling of this tale demonstrate that whatever genius I possess belongs to the creative endorphines released when cycling at the optimal speed.

If anything, my literary career has withered since making this great discovery. I now perceive with acute clarity how banal my unenhanced works are. Still, I'm lucky to have Cath's support, and seek no praise for acting selflessly. However, should you read this story and consider yourself a more talented writer than I, you might wish to send some token of your appreciation to the publisher. If nothing else, my sacrifice has added value to your labours. And that generosity will receive due reciprocation. When I read your true works of art, I'll read them while cycling at a speed that optimizes literary appreciation.

1992

THE VIENNESE SCHOLAR

1. Fathers and Sons

At the beginning of *The Great Gatsby,* Fitzgerald's narrator recalls his father advising him to beware of criticizing people, because few people were as advantaged in life as Nick Carraway had been. This was a period in American fiction when fathers gave lots of fatherly advice. William Faulkner's great novel *The Sound and The Fury* becomes coherent at the beginning of the second section, when Quentin Compson recalls being given a watch by his father, along with the advice that he should use the watch not to remember time, but to remember the futility of trying to conquer time.

So far as I recall, dad has never offered me philosophical advice of the kind that I could begin a great novel with. I think of my father as a peculiarly happy man, as gentle and good-natured as anyone you could meet, and I would treat his advice with respect. But my father thinks like a scientist, and I'm sure he feels that I can work things out for myself. So, in the modern way of inverting things, this story begins with a specific piece of advice I gave to my father. It takes a certain dickheadedness to instruct someone so in touch with the world as Dad, but I can be cocky, and besides, I stand by the advice I gave. I told him to beware of Joseph Pauli.

2. My Father Was a Teenage Expressionist

Though my sister Eliena is nineteen years old, she looks younger, and with her black hair cut short, she could pass for fifteen. This sometimes makes it difficult to take Lenni seriously. I was writing when she pushed open my bedroom door.

Whose room is he going to have?

Whose room is *who* going to have?

The Austrian student, Joseph Someone. He wrote to dad ... Turns out that dad's art teacher at Grammar was a famous painter, and this Austrian bod wants to interview dad for his PhD.

Because no one tells me anything, no one had told me I was likely to be uprooted to accommodate a foreign guest. I tried to straighten things out with my parents while they were reading in the lounge.

Ah yes, Herr Pauli, dad said, looking up over the rim of his glasses. He wants me to be a footnote in his thesis.

Dad passed me the letter in which Joseph Pauli introduced himself as a doctoral student at the Vienna Institute of Art. Pauli was writing a thesis on the Bauhaus movement, and his researches indicated that my father had been taught by Frederik Berg. Before Berg fled Europe in the thirties, he'd worked with Gropius, Klee and Kandinsky at the forefront of the Bauhaus school. Pauli was coming to Melbourne to further his researches, and he would like to have the opportunity to discuss my father's recollections of Frederik Berg.

I spoke with this Pauli on the phone a night or two back, my father said. Chap sounded more like a Yank than an Austrian, but that's how it is in Europe now, I expect. He's going to stay here a couple of nights.

I found the whole picture very confusing. My father was a professor of physics, just a month or two away from retirement. Before slipping into academia, he had been the number two man at Defence Sciences. He wasn't an artist. He didn't even paint our house.

Berg presented your father with the art prize at Grammar, my mother announced. Your father was a teenage expressionist, even before they'd invented teenagers.

I dabbled, dad said.

Mum was much less modest on his behalf. She said Berg gave my father an original oil painting as first prize in the senior art exhibition. This Berg original was gathering dust somewhere in the garage.

It's probably worth a fortune now, dad said, but it's a God-awful thing. Trees in blue and black. I prefer the really abstract stuff. I'm more of a Rothko man.

Meeting me must have stifled your father's creativity, my mother said as she lit a cigarette.

What about Berg?

Decent chap, dad said. Stiff, but knowledgeable.

He's dead now?

Yes ... Well, he must be, dad said, pausing to make some mental calculations. Yes ... Heard nothing of him for years, and he'd be kicking on for ninety. He must have died.

That night, I did a few mental calculations of my own. I thought about my father, and his relationship to Berg and Pauli. I was puzzled about what information the Austrian student could expect to get from my father, information useful enough for Pauli to justify the expense of flying from Canberra, where he had been studying the Berg paintings held by the National Gallery.

I'm always the first person to admit that I have an overdeveloped imagination, but as I lay in bed, my mind ran wild with considerations:

1. Pauli knew of my father's Berg painting and wanted to steal it.

2. Pauli wanted to trick dad into selling the painting at a steal.

3. Frederik Berg had been a Nazi, or a Nazi spy, and Pauli was a Jewish Nazi-hunter seeking out Berg, or information concerning his associates.

4. Berg was a Jew or a Communist, maybe both, involved in a network of ex-patriot Austrians opposed to the Nazis, and Pauli was a new model fascist trying to track down and discredit prominent anti-Nazis.

When I put these speculations to the family at breakfast, Eliena looked at me as if I'd been dropping acid.

All I wanted to tell them was that dad should be careful about what information he gave to this stranger, that Pauli's motives might not be scholarly.

I think you're finding it difficult to accept that your father was a talented artist, mum said, crunching her toast. You mustn't think you possess the only creative mind in the family.

Someone has to question these things, I said.

Someone has to be an idiot to remind us what sanity means, my sister added.

You wait and see, I told them. Pauli will be bad news.

Mum always has the last word. Oh, for goodness sake, Richard. You're carrying on like the witch scene from *Macbeth*.

3. The Distractions of Youth.

I had been at a production meeting when Joseph Pauli arrived. Eliena met me at the front door. She was highly excited, whispering so that she couldn't be heard in the family room.

He has a friend with him ... a *woman* friend.

I couldn't see why Lenni was making such a fuss about it. I left my briefcase in the hall, before opening the door to the family room, where I saw Joseph Pauli sitting alongside dad as they looked over old photographs set out on the breakfast table. They turned as I entered, my father rising to introduce me, quickly followed by the scholar from Vienna.

Pleased to meet you, Richard, Joseph said as he lent forward to shake my hand.

I was surprised to find that he was a man of my age, only twenty-three or twenty-four, but formally dressed in a black suit, white shirt, and sky blue tie. Pauli had narrow cheeks, and circular glasses that rested on a long, thin nose. His black hair was greased, and combed straight back, so that he might have stepped out of a Christopher Isherwood novel.

Of course, you've already met my daughter, Eliena, dad continued.

Ah yes. It's an unusual name, Eliena, the Austrian observed.

Dad's fond of Russian classics, my sister told him.

He learnt Russian so he could read the great writers in the original. Eliena's a character from Turgenev.

Eliena is a charming name, he said.

So, is dad changing the course of thought on Frederik Berg? I asked.

We've only just started, but his recollections are very interesting.

I was about to ask him why Berg chose to come to Australia when our conversation was interrupted by my mother opening the sliding door that led into the garden. Accompanying her was a tall blonde woman.

Oh, it's such a beautiful garden, the young woman enthused in forced English. Joseph, you must see the garden with torch-light. We saw squirrels with thin, white tails.

Possums, my mother suggested.

Oh, I'm sorry, possums, the blonde corrected, blushing as if she had made a terrible error. Joseph, such beautiful possums.

Eva, my mother said, this is Richard ... Eva is travelling with Joseph.

My eyes hadn't left Eva since she entered the room. This Eva was, in my estimation, a run of the mill Teutonic goddess: high pink cheeks, sea-blue eyes, blonde curls that cascaded over her broad shoulders, and breasts that were unavoidably large, however much I tried not to gawp at them.

I understood then why Eliena was so excited. She'd been trying to warn me about the danger of flying too close to the sun.

Eva is an actress, Lenni told me. She and Joseph met at a theatre in Berlin.

Heidelberg actually, Joseph said.

Eva took a seat next to Joseph. The two of them made an odd couple: Joseph so measured, and Eva vivacious, bursting with energy, and very nearly bursting out of her white blouse. I couldn't imagine how a poseur like Joe had managed to win Eva's heart. Joseph reached inside his coat to produce an antique silver cigarette case.

What do you do, Richard? Eva asked.

I write comedy sketches for television.

That's wonderful.

Television, Joseph said, pulling a cigarette out of the silver case.

We satirize politicians and institutions, I told them.

It's not a great show, but it's better than most.

Yes, Joseph said, pausing to light his cigarette, I've seen television.

Joseph blew a thin trail of smoke out over the table and looked at me as if I'd confessed to molesting children.

Eva then got up to assist my mother, who was pulling a roll of beef from the oven in the kitchen that adjoined the family room.

How was your flight from Europe, Joseph? Lenni asked. It's such a disgustingly long trip.

Oh, I slept, Joseph said.

It was a *fabulous* adventure, Eva said, with dramatic emphasis. I'd never flown before. And such a distance! You picture the earth and the oceans all spread out below you, and you know that down there people are shepherding goats, or going to banquets, or searching for food. They are learning to read, or wanting to cry.

While I sleep, Eva dreams, Joseph said.

No, you mustn't say it like that, she objected. You make out there is something wrong with me for not ignoring things ... When you fly, you fly over the whole tapestry of human experience. All the people down there who just might be having their first kiss.

And all the men who make unnecessary trips to the dentist, my mother added while stirring the gravy.

Yes, yes, Eva enthused. You fly over people who might be re-reading love-letters. The millions of people who have never heard of Freud. A young girl hearing the piano for the first time. People who have never owned a toothbrush.

How about a couple just starting a relationship that will be made into a famous movie? Lenni asked, eager to keep the game in motion. Eva needed no encouragement.

People who look in the mirror and smile. People who look in the mirror and remember the fragrance of the breeze when they first fell in love. People who are too frightened to look in a mirror.

I looked at Eva and imagined her imagining the ordinary miracles happening on the planet below her. It seemed to me she wouldn't have needed a jet to soar above the earth.

And Eva might have gone on, but she caught Joseph giving her a look which said, Enough. He was thin-lipped then. He fetched another cigarette and stood. I think I will look around your garden now, he said. To see your possums.

During dinner, Eva told the story of how she met Joseph. She had been playing Kate in a travelling student production of The Taming of the Shrew. There was a scene where Petruchio had to fling her to one side, but Eva hit a patch of water on the stage, skidded, and landed heavily in the front row of the audience.

She broke my nose, Joseph said.

With my elbow, Eva added, raising the elbow in question.

After the show, I went to see how I would be compensated, Joseph continued.

And I thought it would be cheaper to become his mistress, Eva said, beaming. And she placed her hand on Joseph's hand, and he smiled for a moment, before pulling the hand away so he could return to his beef.

Since Joseph planned to spend the evening discussing Berg with Dad, Lenni suggested that she and I should take Eva to a movie in the city. I was thrilled when Eva agreed.

I parked the car some distance from the cinema, and as we walked through town we were caught in a sudden shower of rain. Though I cursed not having an umbrella, Eva couldn't have been more delighted. She put one arm around my waist, and the other around Eliena. She pulled us close, and squealed with joy, pushing her face into the shower. How wonderful, she said. Spring rain in Melbourne.

Caught up in Eva's joy, the three of us danced and skipped our way to the cinema, drawing odd glares from other pedestrians. Eva insisted on holding our hands through the film, and only released her grasp when she visited the toilet after the film ended.

What do you think of Joe? I asked Lenni while Eva was gone.

He's cute. Sort of.

Cute! He looks like an anal retentive to me.

Cut the crap, Lenni said.

Yes, exactly. He's a crap-cutter.

And what about Eva? Lenni asked.

She's unbelievable.

I'm in love with her, Lenni declared, calmly.

Well, if you're going to chase girls, I told her, you'd be wise to stick with girls from our planet. But how could I expect my sister to heed a warning I wouldn't have heeded myself?

It was an indelible evening. When Eva returned, she kissed each of us on the cheek like intimate friends she hadn't seen for years. She was intoxicating. The smile only left Eva's face once, when we were driving home.

Your father has beautiful eyes, Eva observed. Artist's eyes.

They're scientist's eyes, I corrected. He's a physicist.

He used to work with the Defence Department, Lenni added. He did weird acoustic experiments. They were looking for ways to disable nuclear submarines.

A nuclear scientist! Eva said, horrified. Your father one of those criminals who'd destroy the planet.

No, no, he was trying to disable nuclear submarines, I said. It was all theoretical. He's never seen a submarine.

Hitler never visited the death camps either.

No, you're misunderstanding us, and it's all a non-issue anyway. Dad left Defence Sciences years ago.

There was a silence then before Lenni changed the subject. Do you like Berg's paintings? she asked.

Not much, Eva said, but I'm no fan of Bauhaus art. You should ask Joseph about the paintings.

As it turned out, Joseph had already gone to bed when we got home at midnight. My father was drinking port and looking over the Berg paraphernalia he'd shown to Joseph. I remembered the Berg painting when I saw it and had to agree with Dad's view that it was a dreary thing.

So, are we sitting on a fortune? I asked.

Apparently not. It seems I should have asked for one of Berg's drawings. Or one of his Kandinskys even better.

Are they still in Australia, Berg's Kandinskys?

No, he left for America in the fifties. I dare say that Peggy Guggenheim got her claws on them ... You might be pleased to know that Mr. Berg died in 1970, in New York, so your speculations were off the mark.

But dad didn't seem pleased with his victory over my imagination. In fact, he looked quite disconsolate. I began to think something must have happened while we were gone.

Dad said he hadn't been much help to Joseph. He'd been able to suggest a couple of addresses, lend him some photos of Berg at Grammar, and that's all. He hadn't been able to recall anything worthy of a quotation.

I spent that night on the couch in the family room. It wouldn't be true to say I slept there. I thought a lot about Eva and Joseph sharing my single bed, about Eva's warmth, and her arm tight around my waist. I heard sharp, thumping noises, and imagined for a moment that it was Joe fucking Eva in my bed, but it turned out to be a couple of heavy-footed brushtails entertaining themselves on the roof.

It must have been after four when the fluorescent light flicked on in the kitchen. I heard someone pour a glass of water, then saw Eva step back from the sink. She was naked, but for a pair of skimpy white underpants, long blonde hair falling over her magnificent breasts. She was as startled to see me as I was to see her.

I'm so sorry. I didn't know you were sleeping here. I thought there was another room.

She was more embarrassed about having woken me than she was about her nakedness.

It's all right, I said, eyes tracking every quiver of her breasts, I wasn't asleep.

Eva came toward where I was on the couch, and just for a moment I thought reality and fantasy might be about to merge.

Do you think the world will end in a nuclear holocaust? she asked me.

The question took me by surprise. I said that I am a pessimist in most things, that there might be a catastrophe, but I didn't think it would obliterate everything. Somehow, life would go on mutating and re-generating, no matter what.

But our lives, the destruction of everything we've created and valued. Doesn't that matter? What would you do to save human civilization? Would you kill yourself for the sake of the earth?

I was caught off guard by Eva's morbid interrogation. If my wits were working, I might have reminded her that I am a comedy writer. Any comedy writer would happily kill himself if it would get a laugh. But I stammered, and anyway, Eva had her hand resting on my arm, so the proximity of her naked flesh was all I could think of.

Never mind, she said.

Just at that moment, the door opened, and Joseph entered. He was wearing a pair of black jockey shorts. His hair was ruffled, and he was without his glasses. Joseph seemed remarkably unsurprised that Eva should have engaged me in conversation while being almost totally undressed.

Please forgive Eva, Joseph said. She wanders at night.

I was asking Richard what that noise was.

Just possums, brushtails, I said quickly.

When I came to next morning, it was past eight, and the family was rattling breakfast plates around me. There was no sign of Joe or Eva.

When do you think they'll get up? I asked. I need to get the computer from my room.

Joseph and Eva have gone, dad said. There was a phone-call early this morning. Something urgent.

I hope you've checked to see that we still have our original Berg.

Don't let your imagination cloud the truth, dad said.

I was only asking.

You're such a fuckwit, Lenni said. She was annoyed that she hadn't been able to say goodbye to Eva.

I'm sure she wanted to tell Eva that she loved her.

4. A Dagger of the Mind

Though Eva still wanders in and out of my fantasies, I haven't heard anything of Eva or Joseph since then. Dad said Joseph promised to return the photographs and send him a copy of the book when it appeared, but of course, there was no guarantee Joe's thesis on Berg would be published. For a day or two after Joseph and Eva's departure, Berg's painting was given a prominent place in the lounge. Then it was relegated to the garage. I'm sure it isn't a piece of work that Frederik Berg would want to be remembered by.

Unfortunately, we're not always remembered for our best works.

A short time after Joseph and Eva left, I came home to find a note to the effect that my parents had flown to Sydney, and would be away for three nights. One of Dad's old bosses had died, and they were taking the opportunity to catch up with some Sydney friends after the funeral. I mightn't have thought any more about it if I hadn't seen a short item on that evening's news bulletin.

A man described as a senior public servant had been shot dead in his Mosman home some time on the previous weekend. Police believed that Peter Sandford had disturbed an intruder, but they hadn't determined whether anything was stolen. The news report highlighted a black and white photograph of the victim shaking hands with the former Prime Minister, Gough Whitlam.

I remembered Peter Sandford well. He visited our home many times when he and dad worked together in Melbourne. He was a tall, affable man with a ruddy complexion. He loved to drink and tell stories about the politicians and dignitaries he had met. He was dad's superior at Defence Sciences, and my father liked him very much, though he often criticized Peter's political expedience.

It disturbed me that someone I'd known had died so violently, and I knew dad would be feeling Peter's death dreadfully. Lenni spoke to mum on the phone the next afternoon. Mum was OK. Dad had got drunk at Peter's wake. The two of them were staying with cousins at Bronte.

Because a murder in Sydney is deemed to be Sydney news, there was no follow-up report on television that evening, but a radio bulletin reported the funeral of the murdered department head Peter Sandford, along with the news that Federal Police wanted to speak to a young German couple who met with Sandford on the evening of his death.

Now, I warned you earlier that I have an overdeveloped imagination.

My mind exaggerates things, sees motives and conspiracies

that aren't there. My imagination often gets me into trouble. But I also make a fair income writing comedy sketches from the bizarre things which travel through my mind. While it's easy to disparage overcooked thought, you need to remember that the truth broadcasts on many different frequencies.

That said, I wasn't going to expose these new concerns to ridicule from Lenni or mum, and I wasn't sure how I should raise them with my father.

Dad was depressed when he got home. He said it was a terrible thing for someone to die like that. Police felt certain it was a burglary, that some cash would be missing. Dad spent most of the three days in Sydney drinking, and reminiscing about Peter, and he wanted me to keep him company through a whisky bottle. At the half-way mark, I asked whether Peter had been doing classified work.

Not that I know of, dad said. We don't have real secrets anymore. Just commercial secrets. Science is commerce these days.

Peter wouldn't have been trading in information then?

A spy! Who on earth would he be spying for?

All that acoustic stuff. There are still submarines. I'm sure someone could use it.

I asked Dad if he and Peter were on the same side, expecting the question to annoy him, but he was more unsettled than irritated, and chose to give an ambiguous answer.

I'm sure we'd both say we were on the right side.

I wasn't asking what side you thought you were on.

I was *always* on the right side.

Then I tossed him my googly. I said I hadn't known that he and Peter were at school together.

We weren't. He went to school in Adelaide. What gave you the idea that we were school friends?

I don't know. I just thought he might have been another protege of Berg, that you and Peter were the teenage expressionists at Grammar. The three of you might have been part of a circle.

Dad put his whisky glass down on the coffee table. We were

both very drunk.

Look, I only know one thing for sure, dad said. The world's a complicated place. Best to avoid complications that can't be uncomplicated. You hope the truth will win out, but in the long run, you end up believing what you want to believe.

Always avoid complications that can't be uncomplicated. Is that the fatherly advice to start a novel with, or has the world got too complicated for fatherly advice to be useful?

Whether or not he takes his own advice, my father has always been an unusually happy man. He plays his old records by Tom Lehrer and Barry Humphries, and he can still recite favourite passages from Gogol and Lermontov. He sings Gilbert and Sullivan in the shower. If I choose to believe in my father, it's not just that I want to believe in him. I need to believe in fixture, and a capital-G Goodness which goes beyond good intentions.

Let me ask you this, could anyone who believed he was accomplice to an evil or treacherous act sing so wholeheartedly as my father sings under the shower?

1993

THE FICTION CONSULTANT

I doubt that it is possible for someone who has never written fiction, or had a work of fiction rejected, to fully understand the heartbreak of watching a postman deliver to your address an envelope addressed in your own hand, when you know the envelope contains a returned work of fiction. If I could distance myself from the experience, I might find a metaphor telling enough to convey to non-writers the distress of such a moment. The closest thing that comes to mind is a teacher confiding that one of your children will never amount to anything. But that won't do. The anguish of literary rejection is more specific.

It shouldn't surprise you that I don't recall any of those moments in detail. Literary rejection is a disappointment you hide in the least accessible folds of memory. The truth is not so much I can't remember, but I don't want to. I don't wish to recall where I was when I opened the self-addressed envelope containing the manuscript of *A Summer Festival of Kissing*. Nor do I wish to recall whether I stood or sat while I read the editor's polite note, and her fiction consultant's comments. I do know that two months passed before I had my emotions sufficiently under control to be able to re-read the opening section of my rejected story.

The Kiss List

Ever since my first romantic kiss at the age of seventeen, I have recorded and filed all my kisses on a numbered sequence of index cards, cross-referencing the kisses where necessary. With the introduction of a new kiss measurement formulation, enabling an expanded profile and analysis of the individual kiss,

I may find it necessary to transfer my records onto a computer-based file. Even if this eventuates, I doubt that I will destroy the neatly written cards which detail my first, tentative explorations of the kiss.

My practical interest in kissing began during October in my final year at High School. Even though Georgina Christianson was my friend Yuri's girlfriend, she used to laugh at my weak puns, and I fancied her with an intensity that was new to me. I had gone with Georgina to study at her house, but we had only walked halfway before we were caught in a sudden violent cloudburst. We began to run, Georgina grabbing my arm as we crossed the street, wanting to lead me to shelter on the veranda of a nearby home. Shy about entering a stranger's property, I steered her back under a large gumtree. The air was warm, and we were both ridiculously wet. Catching a hint in Georgina's eye, I pulled her to me, and we kissed as the rain bucketed down.

You can whistle and jeer as much as you like, roll Jaffas down the aisle, but I'm not going to apologize for the energetic incompetence of that first kiss, for the wet hair sticking to my forehead, or the heart thumping at the back of my rib-cage. That's the way it happened.

In the card index it appears as

    No 1.   Georgina CHRISTIANSON
              May St. Hampton 12/10/77
              Approx 10 seconds. Slight dizzy sensation.
              Loss of feeling knee region.
              Strong tumescent reaction.

The Fiction Consultant's comments at the end of this section informed me that my narrator's description of this first kiss, a kiss that I considered to be a precious moment of spontaneous desire, might be read as a clichéd episode betraying a debt to Hollywood cinema of the 40's and 50's.

If you didn't know he was one of Australia's most important writers, you might be tempted to say that Bernard O'Connell was an ordinary man who leads a life of dazzling mundanity. Far from being the Artist fired by uncontrollable creative passions, Bernard O'Connell is fixated with order and regularity. He is widely known as an author whose interest is to explore the specific, specifically interior, dimensions of individuals who lead outwardly quiet suburban lives. Few readers would guess the extent to which Bernard O'Connell's life enacts his literary vision.

But for an apparently deliberate imprecision when shaving the tufts of hair beneath his nostrils, Bernard's life is based on exactness. Each morning he rises at precisely 6.15 to commence a day divided into compartments and regimes. After making a cup of coffee, he will write for seventy-five minutes between 6.30 and 7.45. Following breakfast, he drives his thirteen-year-old Corolla to the university, where his day is divided between his lectures on fiction, seeing students, and attending to the business of being a well-known literary figure. At exactly 5.15 every evening, he picks up Kaye, the younger of his two daughters. She will be waiting for him outside a friend's house, where she spends ninety minutes after school. Bernard will dine with his family, and discuss matters with his wife, Annette, before retiring to his office at 8.30. Sometimes he types and corrects his morning's work. Mostly, he researches form-guides, and familiarizes himself with racehorses, jockeys, and trainers. At weekends, Bernard takes any opportunity he can to attend race meetings at Flemington. He is, from what I've observed, a moderately unsuccessful gambler.

If you were to peer through the window into the O'Connells' kitchen, you might see Bernard eating in the way of a pleasure-postponer, attending to his orange vegetables, green vegetables, roast potatoes and meat in that order. He is not unaware of these eccentricities, nor proud to be so fastidious. Quite the contrary. As a highly-regarded author, Bernard is embarrassed by his compulsion to act in a way which draws attention to himself. He is ashamed to still fear that his life will collapse should he abandon his regimes. Obsessive fears are unbecoming for a public figure recently turned fifty years of age.

In the past five years, Bernard has supplemented his income by acting as the Fiction Consultant to the prestigious intellectual journal *Approximate Life*. He takes these duties seriously. Keen to encourage young literary talents, Bernard often returns manuscripts with as many notes written in green ink as there are typewritten words on the page. He appreciates the dangers in being so forthcoming. Talented young writers can be sensitive to criticism, however constructive. Bernard often describes his position at the journal as The F ...... C ..., since he imagines that's how many aspiring writers refer to him.

The mistake I made was to trust Bernard O'Connell's judgement. I wanted to believe that O'Connell would understand my work, because he knows what it is to cultivate a challenging, idiosyncratic style. I wanted him to recognise me as a fellow traveller, a writer of distinctive vision. And I expected Bernard O'Connell to recommend my story to the editor of Approximate Life. He did not.

I failed in my earlier attempt to communicate the shock of receiving a returned manuscript covered in Bernard O'Connell's green scrawl. I know this will sound overdramatic to those who haven't experienced rejection or acute disappointment, but I felt like O'Connell had lowered his trousers and defecated on my soul.

Had the criticisms come from anyone else but O'Connell, I would have written them off as envy and thought no more about it. After all, it's not as if one expects justice, or to have originality recognised in this uninspired climate. But Bernard O'Connell knows how lethal a green pen can be. It's well documented that you can kill a man with a biro. You sneak into your adversary's room while he is sleeping, push the pen into his mouth, and shove it up through the soft palate so that it penetrates the base of the brain. Someone as central to the Australian literary scene as Bernard O'Connell would know that an astutely used green pen can kill off a rival even before that rivalry has been signaled.

My story, *A Summer Festival of Kissing* is a peculiar, disjointed narrative about my own obsession with kissing and the desire to kiss. It is a story about a lifelong determination to understand the allure of kissing. I don't believe in disguising the autobiographical centre of my narratives. Though the stories incorporate attitudes and events that aren't factual, I am reluctant to call them fictions. I prefer to believe that I am advancing a new form of prose called 'autobiographical expressionism', where distortions and extrapolations are used to communicate interior truths.

Any true version of a person's life would not discriminate between that person's actions, desires, dreams, memories, fears and fantasies by creating or presuming a hierarchy of importance. No true version of the same would fall prey to a false opposition of the real and the imagined.

I detest the word authenticity. So much autobiographical writing, or fictionalized autobiography, is disabled by its adherence to these absurd hierarchies.

You can't tell me that consciousness is perfectly regular and compartmentalised. The moment you describe an experience as fantasy or daydream or phobia, the moment you fix it with a mundane term or cue, you give the reader licence to disregard its cogency, to treat it as something of lesser importance, as unreal or irrational. This despite the reality that our lives are lived as much in the past or future, or speculative pasts and futures, as they are in anything so 'concrete' or 'real' as the present moment.

I give my own name, Richard Thompson, to the person who narrates my story. Thompson's narrative mingles anecdotes about the most crucial kisses and near kisses in his/my life with statements concerning his mock socio-scientific ambition to optimise the efficiency of kissing as a form of human expression. He is determined to eliminate confusing or confusable kisses. Like me, he sees ambiguous kisses as a major source of human misunderstanding. My intention is to represent this extrapolated version of a man's search for understanding as no more bizarre than my troubled and confused personal experience of kissing.

Yet my shifts from hard reality to expressionistic invention seem to defy Bernard O'Connell's comprehension. The Fiction Consultant is particularly unhappy with my decision to have my narrator share the same name as the story's author. Later, he goes on to dismiss a whole strand of my story with the pejorative 'whimsy'. Having witnessed some of O'Connell's behaviour, I find it difficult to imagine that he has ever been whimsical.

Why can't O'Connell realise that I have no choice in this matter? I am writing truthfully and honestly about myself, endeavouring to chart the often bizarre paths taken by my consciousness. If my narratives are silly, unconvincing, or distracted by conventional terms, it is precisely because I am seeking the truths contained by silliness, distraction, and avoidance in order to re-define the understanding of the essential, or truthful.

So much autobiographical writing is tokenistic in its inclusion of embarrassing desires or incidents in order to suggest the integrity of an author who can rise above shame. I do not wish to rise above shame and abjection. My life *is* its conceits and embarrassments. The sum of a life is not much more than ignorance, discarded certainties, and irony.

The fantasy or whimsy Bernard O'Connell derides as 'froth' is central to a wider project of replacement myth. Because Richard Thompson cannot explain his passion for the banal, middle-class suburb of Hampton, he reconstitutes Hampton in a way that makes it possible to communicate those feelings. *A Summer Festival of Kissing* features the exaggerated operations of a scientific institution where Thompson furthers his investigation into the kiss. Bernard O'Connell doesn't seem to think that you can distort the world without needing to use those distortions as the basis for a Swiftian satire on institutions or pseudo-sciences.

Why do I need to read about Thompson's work at The Doisneau Institute, and his comic book equations and formulations, when his memories, fears, and daydreams are so much more compelling?

The Fiction Consultant would have me dispense with Thompson's mock-theoretical enquiries. He suggests that I construct a new story by cutting and pasting Thomson's recollection of crucial kisses, and detailing the circumstances which re-activate those memories in his mind. The Fiction Consultant is encouraging me to gather my material into a readily comprehensible story of the kind he would write, as if there were a version of my life which could be turned into the kind of life Bernard O'Connell might lead. He uses his ticks, asterisks, and circled asterisks to coax me to betray my vision. He seeks to deflect me from my truths toward his.

Ambiguous Kisses

Analysing my career to this point, I would say that, of all kisses I have experienced, one kiss from Francesca was most instrumental in determining that I turn my fascination with kissing into a life of scientific enquiry.

Francesca and I kissed at Melbourne Airport when I was leaving to spend five months travelling through Europe. I had already shared farewell kisses with two other close friends, Catherine and Elizabeth, but the unexpected intensity of Francesca's kiss nearly persuaded me to tear up my ticket.

When does a pile become a heap? When does a farewell kiss become more than a farewell kiss? Are the elements which might redefine a friendly or chaste kiss as a passionate kiss capable of being isolated and quantified?

I knew that if I could find a means of clarifying confusable kisses, I could eradicate a major source of human tension.

During the five months that I travelled, my lips retraced the path of Francesca's disconcerting kiss, and my mind pursued the theoretical questions aroused by that kiss. I was thinking about Francesca's kiss as I stood at the base of Glastonbury Tor, remembering her kiss as I walked by the river Seine in flood, mentally recreating her kiss as I sipped Pilsener from a tall glass in a gloomy East Berlin bar. When I looked at the other men sitting alone in that bar, all peering into the gloom, I believed that each of them was trying to re-capture the essence of a lost kiss.

Approximate Life's Fiction Consultant would have me speak to him only with truths which correspond to or ignite the half-formed truths in his own mind, truths which open the door to emotions he has been unable to articulate. What he doesn't want is for a writer to challenge his intelligence by insisting he pursue the more difficult questions raised by the incongruities of my narrative. So it is to be expected that O'Connell would enjoy this discussion of Francesca's ambiguous kiss, because it calls to mind certain troubling kisses from his own past. He would argue that it is the business of true fiction to investigate the precise meaning of persistent memories in this way. In turn, I would argue that it is equally the business of literature to propose, prescribe, and redefine, to offer truths found within the unfamiliar quite as much as it is to present the familiar made new.

I haven't been able to satisfy O'Connell that Thompson and I are psychologically indistinguishable, that Thompson's preoccupations are a near equivalent of my own manias. The Fiction Consultant is determined to read my unhinged scientist as invention, fancifully distinct from the world his author knows most intimately. I can only suspect that O'Connell needs to read Thompson this way because he is loathe to accept that my strangeness belongs to the world he needs to regiment.

My scientist is nothing more than the expressionistic projection of my own more unsettling impulses. If I could convince O'Connell that the scientist Thompson's extreme obsessiveness is a reasonable approximation of my own, he might then be forced to acknowledge the cogency of my artistic vision. When I re-read O'Connell's comments, I see him demanding a demonstration of mental instability sufficient to prove that my truths are certifiable truths.

But he's not *a scientist conducting research into kissing, is he? ... These fanciful passages bring to mind the silly speculations of journalists trying to fill daily columns ... This does not interest me.*

Why must he obsess about the authentic, or the convincing? I don't live in order to be convincing. I don't dream in order to become more authentic. An autobiographical expressionist does not write about the man he ought to be, or the dreams and fears he ought to have, but the ones which actually dictate his thoughts. I write from the multiple intersection of fear and desire, hope and disappointment, knowledge and uncertainty, memory and forgetting, optimism and pessimism, dream and reality. No point within those intersections is more crucial or authentic than any other.

Though Bernard O'Connell has often expressed his contempt for the seldom-challenged truths and jargon of psychoanalysis, he would have me bring false coherence to my narrative by invoking the spirit of Freud. He wants me to look beyond the immediate so that I might offer the suggestion of suppressed or ulterior desire.

The Kisses of The Enemy Are Deadly

Sometimes, mid-kiss, I need to tell myself to suspend analysis of the situation. I keep a typed statement blue-tacked to the wall above my bed, underneath my framed print of Edvard Munch's *Shriek!*

Relax. You are a kisser, not an air-traffic controller.

No one will perish if the kiss goes wrong.

I may decide to remove this statement. More often than not, it acts to remind me of a gratuitous observation made by Tracey H's habitually indiscreet sister, Jellybean.

I can't imagine you kissing a girl, Richard.

You've seen me kiss Tracey.

Oh, is that what you call it? In that case, always keep a dentist's number close to the phone.

I tell myself to relax because I tend to worry about things which shouldn't concern me. Does it matter that a kiss might not be perfect? Does it matter that I know more about kissing than I know about women? I don't imagine that Einstein or Rutherford knew any more about women than I do.

This section seems close to the real story. When I read these pages, the bits about The International Summit of Kissing in Atlanta, and the formulas and ratios fall away like husks. I've seldom read a story which has so insisted that I ask, 'Why do you need to write this story?' Surely, this is a story about someone who is so preoccupied with kissing that he has lost sight of the women he kisses, lost the natural connection between kissing and fucking. I'm deeply interested in the subjects of kissing and fucking, but your scientist is a passive blockhead unworthy of the consideration you give him.

Bernard O'Connell can call my narrator a passive blockhead, but he is not *just* a passive blockhead. O'Connell may regard my use of mock-science as disingenuous, yet I suspect that he is transferring his own feelings of evasion onto me.

Maybe the Fiction Consultant uses words like fuck and fucking in front of friends at the racetrack, but I'd bet that he wouldn't use those words in front of his children's teachers. O'Connell doesn't want to recognise that I am writing with a unique honesty, that the deficiencies and limitations of my narrator are *my* limitations. He is so keen to dismiss my narrative in terms of competent or accomplished literary fiction (according to his own narrow definition), that he is unable to see that I am capturing the integral personality at the point of its disintegration.

Would pretending to be other than I am give my narrative greater truth or integrity? Would using the word fuck when I mean kiss make my story more earthy, or more readily comprehensible? The truly eccentric threatens our sense of ourselves and our place in *the scheme*. I expected Bernard O'Connell to understand that.

What gives the Fiction Consultant the right to place asterisks against crucial episodes from my life and say that they are unbelievable, incredible, or contrived? Or even to judge, as he does in the section *Vampire's Kiss*, that they are 'interesting'?

Vampire's Kiss

In the film, *Vampire's Kiss*, the actor Nicholas Cage plays a disturbed publishing executive who forms the mistaken belief that he is a vampire, making life a misery for his temporary secretary. On his desk sits a framed portrait of Franz Kafka, and when my friend Gabriella saw this, she made an involuntary shriek, 'Kafka!', much to the amusement of the audience in the Valhalla Cinema. Since Kafka's portrait is seldom seen in films, I consider it reasonable that a viewer might choose to honour his appearance with a commemorative shriek. When I saw *Vampire's Kiss* at another cinema nearly twelve months later, a dozen people yelled 'Kafka!' when the portrait appeared, so the cult has acquired a following.

I saw quite a few vampire films in the company of Gabriella, who is the sister of my friend Yuri. Her pale, bloodless beauty always seemed to make the choice of a vampire film obvious enough. On one particular evening, we were at Gabriella's house, watching Max Schreck star as the vampire in the silent classic *Nosferatu*. I'd been wanting to kiss the delicate Gabriella for some time, but we were both shy, and extremely conscious of my long friendship with her brother.

When the film finished, I contrived to sneak up on Gabriella as she reclined on the floor, placing a soft vampire bite on her neck. I might have feared a shriek, but Gabriella remained impassive. I advanced to her lips. Gabriella is a slender, mysterious girl, a subject stolen from Modigliani, but her lips were unyielding.

What's the matter? Don't you want to kiss me?

It's not that. We've known each other since I was eleven. It would be like incest.

What was the use of arguing that we had no blood relation, or that incest is a legal prohibition, not a psychological one? Gabriella was a lost cause. However desirable, the passions she had were reserved for Kafka.

The Fiction Consultant's interest in this section is not his interest in my kiss, or my frustration, but his interest in Kafka. (Perhaps this explains why he gave his daughter an outdated name like Kaye.) Bernard O'Connell is just another reader drawn to cyphers and allusions.

But why did you need to write this story?

I needed to write a story about kissing because I cannot in my heart believe there is anything more fascinating or urgent than the desire to kiss, or anything so painful as the frustrated desire to kiss.

I realise that my views are extreme, but they are no more extreme or unpalatable than the impulse to contaminate a young writer's precious recollections with notions of 'interest', with indiscreetly expressed preference or indifference, or even to suggest, as O'Connell does in one instance, that my paradoxes are insufficiently paradoxical.

When you pass judgment on a work of autobiographical expressionism, you pass judgment on the veracity of the author's intersections with the reality. Bernard O'Connell would wish to believe that judgments of this kind are his entitlement.

What's to stop me reading this as the sort of story that I've told you earlier that I would like to read—the story about a solitary maniac, scribbling about an imaginary institute and remembered kisses? I assure you that I am not trying to do more than report my honest reactions when I say that your whimsical pretexts do not interest me.

O'Connell goads me by insisting that a truly convincing maniac is someone who lives and breathes mania.

I could campaign against O'Connell's reputation. I could subvert him. My surveillances have given me information that would damage him both professionally and within his family. But I'd like to believe that he respects my imagination, that he would expect more from me than second-rate subversion. And the Fiction Consultant deserves an imaginative response. After all, he's taken fragments of my memory, and contaminated them with base jealousies. He's spoken to me as if I were an idiot.

I have been foolish, but I'm not a fool. I was once foolish enough to trust a literary journal with my precious kisses, and O'Connell betrayed that trust. His only concern was to rid himself of someone who might rise to challenge his authority. His conspicuous malice betrays a wariness. And the Fiction Consultant is right to be wary.

You need to focus your energies, to strip away everything that isn't vital ... It's not enough to tell me about the urgency of Thompson's quest, I need to experience that urgency ...

Yes. A jaded man needs to experience urgency.

Everything about Bernard O'Connell's life is predictable. He drives down the same streets at the same time each weekday. At 5.15 every evening, his young daughter Kaye sits on the red fire hydrant cover outside number three Sterling Street and waits for her father to arrive. She puts her arms around his neck. He smiles and gives her a chaste kiss. Despite his absolute punctuality, he asks if she has been waiting long, and she always says, Too long, but in truth she waits no more than five minutes, and he would have her wait no longer because he knows of the many troubled people who live in a vast metropolis like Melbourne.

1993

You seem to be obsessed with mysterious external forces …

External forces?

You feel as if you're not in control of your own destiny …

I used to believe I could influence things, that I was imaginative enough to create relationships, that I could invent a version of the world where I could be happy …

Used to?

Well … It goes back to when Catherine and I were in partnership as literary agents. We were handling a dozen or so writers, all topnotch, and we'd got involved with a Californian producer, Ray Bennett. Ray was keen to option some treatments that were kicking around … It got touchy. We thought that we were dealing with a money man, an executive producer, but it turned out that he was an intermediary employed by a third party …

He was trying to shaft you?

Not really. They were good deals. It's just that we didn't know who we were dealing with … If anyone was being deceitful, it was Catherine. She'd been keeping me in the dark.

Doing deals behind your back?

She was negotiating the sale of material which wasn't for sale.

Screwing you?

You have aggressive turns of phrase … Cath *thought* she was doing me a favour. She'd got onto a colossal deal, and she figured it would be best if she handled it herself. It wasn't as if she meant to tear-off with the money.

I'm sorry. You've lost me.

It came to a head one Friday night ... We had tickets for the theatre, and Catherine got home ridiculously late. I was angry enough already, but she made me furious by refusing to take my anger seriously. She said she'd been caught up with something really big at the office. A fax had come in from Hollywood. She said Steven Spielberg was ready to make a deal.

The *Steven Spielberg?*

Absolutely ... Spielberg was the silent party. The money.

That's fantastic!

That's what I said. But then Cath told me I should sit down, because the deal wasn't about what I thought it was ... She told me that Steven Spielberg wanted to make a film about my life.

She'd been selling your life story?

She'd told Spielberg about my life, and he was very excited by it. She'd sent him a thirty page treatment. Spielberg was willing to pay two million for the rights.

You're kidding me!

That's what I said. I said, this is fantastic, Spielberg wants to make a film about *my* life ... He's going to pay *two million dollars* for the rights to make a film about my life! And Cath's rushing around the room saying how enthusiastic Steven is, that he's never been so excited. She's waving her arms saying that not even Schindler excited him so much.

But?

Well, yes ... *but ...*

But what?

She said Spielberg was *incredibly* enthusiastic about the project, but there was just one thing ...

... he wanted Richard Dreyfus to play the lead ...

Worse than that.

There's worse than that?

There was just one thing Spielberg wanted to change ...

Oh, no ...

I said, What do you mean, 'one thing he wants to change'?... And she said, it's just one little thing. And I said, *Like what?* And Catherine looked at me, and she stopped smiling then, and I could see her eyes getting wet, and she said, Richard, this is our chance of a lifetime ... Steven's happy to run with the obsessions and repetitions, the disappearing women and the pathos and the approximations. He might even fork-out for a computer-generated Brando.... And I said, *what* little thing?... And she said, Spielberg's *incredibly* enthusiastic about your life, and its commercial potential, but ... He wants to change the ending.

1993

2

THE PRINCE

THE PRINCE

EDITED BY THOMAS DIXON

INTRODUCTION

Is it possible to find an Australian who doesn't hold an opinion about the Hampton Festival of Killing? Only the Kelly Gang's siege at Glenrowan and Azaria Chamberlain's mysterious disappearance at Uluru come close to challenging Hampton's Festival for notoriety.

The six years since the collapse of the Festival have seen the publication of seventeen books, two stage dramatisations, an opera, two feature films, three feature-length documentaries, two cartoon series, and a television quiz show. At the time this volume went to press, two further films were in production, one to be shot in a Scottish village, and the other, *Backwater*, to be filmed at Tathra on the New South Wales coast.

As time passes, the Hampton myth feeds off itself and takes on a narrative life of its own. Following the pattern established by the Hollywood Western, writers have tended to use previous films and fictions about Hampton's Killer as source materials. The facts of the case become ever murkier. The 195 cm tall Swede, Daniel Lundquist, set a trend for casting tall athletic blondes to play Richard Thompson. Now we are shocked to see footage of the real Killer, just 170 cm tall with wavy dark hair, and seldom dressed so suavely as those who depict him on screen. We are also shocked to be reminded that 'the real Thompson' (a dangerous presumption, if ever there was one) never used a gun or a knife to dispose of his fellow Hamptonians. Screenwriters versed in the lore of the cinema apparently find it impossible to imagine a Killer who did not employ the screen killer's standard weaponry.

And producers seem unable to resist the temptation of devising a passionate love-interest for the Killer. Yet the one aspect of Thompson's personality that most fascinates scholars is his 'ability' to resist sexual temptations, while remaining conscious of that temptation. In his journal, the Killer refers to this semi-voluntary celibacy as his 'weird priesthood'.

Under the sway of post-Jungian theorists like Joseph Campbell, many scholars are determined to construct a version of Thompson which readily obeys classical heroic models: Hampton's Killer must be either hero or anti-hero, never a combination of both. His many complexities, contradictions and personal confusions are smoothed over to facilitate the creation of an easy to digest moral fable.

Sides must be taken.

Lately it has become accepted wisdom to deride Hampton's Killing Festival as barbarous social experiment, or mad folly. Many historians are keen to bracket Hampton with the former Soviet Union, and to view the Festival's ultimate failure as inevitable—a failure to recognise and accept the constants of human nature. Yet complacent, 20/20 hindsight only serves to obscure the discoveries still to be made through close analysis of Hampton's unique contract of association. The anthropologist Gabriella Rossi has gone so far as to suggest that the final demise of The Hampton Festival represents not a triumph of decency and common sense over evil but the death of romantic vision at the hands of cynical opportunism.

My first-hand knowledge of the Killer is slight. I met Richard Thompson just once, when I was a member of a delegation of Christian academics which visited Hampton to protest the depravity of the Festival. Though Thompson listened carefully to our arguments, he refused to debate them. Later, he sent me a short note.

> *I understand your views, but I cannot respect them. You are seeking to condemn the culture of my tribe without having sought to understand the specific circumstances and imperatives which gave rise to that culture. You condemn the citizens of Hampton on the basis of universal*

terms which simply do not apply.[1]

It is not my intention in this volume to rehearse arguments related to the morality or utility of the ideas which produced the Festival. Nor is this the occasion to rehash the legal questions related to accusations of criminality made against Hampton's Killer. Those matters, and matters related to the alleged conspiracy to implicate Richard Thompson, have been dealt with at great length in my previous books: *The Loaded Mirror* and *A Model Society*.

My hope is that this new source of primary materials will enable a more considered, scholarly analysis of Hampton's Festival. Following the judgement of the Witherspoon Commission, it is now possible to publish in full the hitherto suppressed 'October' segment of Richard Thompson's personal journal. These journal entries offer a fascinating insight into The Killer's notoriously enigmatic personality, and the circumstances leading to the Festival's demise. By publishing the crucial journal entries alongside Christine Marker's Channel 4 transcripts, the two letters of disputed origin, and a newly discovered letter written by Christine Marker to her sister, we may now find it possible to piece together a more complete picture of the most curious social experiment in Australia's history.

I am particularly indebted to my colleague and partner Miranda Murray for her assistance in indexing the small mountain of testimony and documentary evidence presented before the original Coronial Inquest, and the subsequent Elliot and Witherspoon Commissions. It is to her that I humbly dedicate this book.

Thomas J Dixon
Professor of Australian Studies
Calwell University

---

1   Honesty compels me to report that Thompson made brief reference to this delegation in his journal, wherein he chose to describe me as "a snivelling, morally superior shithead". See *If Looks Could Kill: The Diaries of Richard Thompson*, edited by Miranda Murray.

(i)

TRANSCRIPTS TO THE SOCIAL CONTRACT

The physical makeup of man is the handiwork of nature: the constitution of the State is the product of art. It is not in men's power to prolong their lives, but they can prolong the life of the State for as long as possible by devising the best possible form.

—*The Social Contract*, Jean-Jacques Rousseau, 1762

... that the object of mans desire is not to enjoy once onely, and for one instant of time; but to assure for ever, the way of his future desire. And therefore the voluntary actions, and inclinations of all men, tend, not onely to the procuring, but also to the assuring of a contented life; and differ onely in the way; which ariseth partly from the diversity of passions, in divers men; and partly from the difference in the knowledge, or opinion each one has of the causes which produce the effect desired ...

—*Leviathan*, Thomas Hobbes, 1651

Mid-way through July in the fifth year of Hampton's Festival, the renowned Anglo-French filmmaker Christine Marker began a feature length documentary on The Hampton Festival of Killing. At that stage, The Festival had already claimed thirty-two lives. Financed by Britain's Channel 4 in partnership with Amnesty International, Marker's film was intended to be the first documentary examination of the Festival to be made with the participation of Hampton Council.

Marker and her three-person crew (Michael Tynan on camera, Penny Donaldson on sound, and the researcher–production assistant Gillian Chatterton) arrived in Hampton in early October. During the next month, they taped something like thirty-nine interviews. Many of these are preserved in the transcripts which Christine Marker sent to Michael Ambrose, her Executive Producer in London, after Hampton police seized her video-tapes.

Apart from comments made in letters written by the film-crew, journal entries made by Richard Thompson, and the testimony of several interviewees, the transcripts are all that remain of the documentary that Marker proposed to call *The Social Contract*. The audiotapes, notebooks and diaries to which Marker refers in her correspondence vanished and are presumed destroyed.

The authenticity of the Marker transcripts remained a matter of legal dispute until the Witherspoon Commission overturned a ruling made by the previous Elliot Commission. Justice Witherspoon accepted that the documents are a complete and authentic representation of correspondence sent by Christine Marker to Michael Ambrose on November 10. Following this determination, Justice Witherspoon withdrew the order which had suppressed publication of the transcripts.

CHRISTINE MARKER
PASSCHENDAELE HILTON
HAMPTON
NOVEMBER 10

MICHAEL AMBROSE
EXECUTIVE PRODUCER
CHANNEL 4 FILMS
LONDON

Dear Michael,

As you'll be aware from the faxes sent to Sarah, things have taken a dramatic turn in the past few days, and the immediate future of the Festival is uncertain.

On Thursday, Thompson failed to appear for an interview with the Head of Internal Security, and a warrant was issued for his arrest.

At about the same time, a dozen police arrived at our hotel, ransacked our rooms, and confiscated my videotapes, computer and discs. They told us that they had reason to believe that the tapes held information pertaining to the murder of Keiko Morimoto, whom we had interviewed in the week prior to her murder. Though the Mayor and the Head of Internal Security have given an undertaking that the tapes and discs will be returned once they have been copied, they will not say when this duplication will take place. I am extremely concerned that the Council won't honour these assurances, and I urge you to make a representation to them on our behalf, preferably under an Amnesty International letterhead.

In the meantime, I have reconstructed most of the interviews from our audiotapes and continuity notes. I think it best that you hold a copy of the transcripts in case we are subjected to further confiscations. The local legal system is highly idiosyncratic. I am worried that material in the confiscated tapes might be used to compromise interviewees to whom we promised confidentiality.

Before the Morimoto tragedy, it seemed likely that the final killing of the year would take place sometime in early December.

At the moment, I doubt whether Richard Thompson would be permitted to continue to act as the Killer, and whether he would wish to execute the seventh killing of the year, even if permitted. Thompson is an enigma. He impresses as being forthright and deceptive at the same time. I couldn't offer an educated opinion about his possible involvement in Morimoto's murder.

I am sure that you will accept the necessity for us to stay on through the resolution of the current crisis. I'll fax through a revised budget in the next couple of days.

In the meantime, I would be very appreciative if you would seek the assistance of the Foreign Office to gain the speedy return of the tapes and computer. If police refuse to return the tapes, we will require legal assistance. Sarah has the originals of the contracts we entered with Hampton Council.

These transcripts represent a third of the interview material that we've shot, and I am very confident of the quality of the footage that we have. I'll keep you informed of further developments.

Yours
CHRISTINE MARKER

1. RICHARD THOMPSON, KILLER — OCTOBER 17

We filmed The Killer in an arranged interview at his unpretentious Fewster Road home, tracking through the front door past a security guard. Richard Thompson is a conservatively dressed, friendly man in his early thirties. We see him surrounded by bookcases full of paperback novels, biographies, philosophical works and film criticism. On one wall, there is a framed Kandinsky (possibly original), 'Street Scene in Murnau'. Beneath this is a framed photograph of Hampton Street, in the vicinity of Hampton Station, 1913. Though he was geared for criticism, Thompson remained calm, and sipped coffee throughout the interview.

When did you decide that you'd like to become Hampton's Killer?

THOMPSON: It was a combination of circumstances ... I was coming back to live in Hampton and needed work. The Council wanted a Hampton person who cared about the future of Hampton ... I grew up here, went to the local schools, church, scouts, that sort of thing.

You were a teacher?

THOMPSON: I taught high school English and Media studies.

Were you good at it?

THOMPSON: Not particularly. I liked aspects of teaching, working with the texts, seeing kids charged with new ideas and ways of thinking, but that didn't happen all that often. I wasn't good with the uncommitted kids, the ones filling in time. It disappointed me that so much of teaching was delimitation and control ...

Like killing?

THOMPSON: Different. With students, you have to restate and redefine roles and relationships. Here, people know what The Killer's role is. They accept that I have a job to do.

That you are a professional killer ...

THOMPSON: That I'm paid to kill seven people a year.

How many people have you killed?

THOMPSON: Thirty-three. This is the fifth year of the Festival.

Are you proud?

THOMPSON: Pride is a loaded term. I'm not sure it's the word I'd use ...

But you enjoy killing?

THOMPSON: There are two aspects to each kill. First, there's the planning and execution. I don't think anyone would say that they enjoy the kill. It's very solemn. You're trying to combine decency with efficiency ... It needs to be orderly, and you want to be sure in your own mind they understand and accept why you're killing them.

They?... The victim?

THOMPSON: Yes. You have to do things properly.

And the second aspect?

THOMPSON: Afterwards. When people seek you out in the street. The respect they give you. The Killer is the lifeblood of this community, someone special. And as the Festival draws near, there's a momentum, a tremendous anticipation that you're at the centre of.

Because you kill human beings ...

THOMPSON: Because I perform an essential social function which binds this community together, which allows Hampton to be prosperous, and to share its prosperity ... Before the Council took on the Festival concept, Hampton was finished ... Businesses were closing, churches were being pulled down, the high school was demolished, there was no sand on the beach ... You can't be a beach suburb without sand. The Festival gives Hampton a face, an identity. It allows Hampton to continue to be Hampton.

But, in the final analysis, it's all about money?

THOMPSON: No. *Community* is what it's all about. Common values and objectives. The prosperity comes from the strength and single-mindedness of the Hampton community. The Killer is the embodiment of that single-mindedness, and Hampton's prosperity is a bi-product of our success in shaping a genuine community.

<u>2. LORRAINE DI STASIO, HAMPTON MAYOR — OCTOBER 19</u>

The slightly cross-eyed Lorraine has been on the Hampton Council for nine years. She was instrumental in Hampton's successful campaign to gain the status of Independent Territory. This is her second term as Mayor. She is an enthusiastic woman in her mid-fifties. We see her seated in the Council chambers, dressed in her Mayoral robes.

How did the Killing Festival come about?

LORRAINE: The idea was first proposed seven or eight years ago. At the time, people thought it was outrageous. How could you sanction someone to kill seven residents each year? But Hampton was practically dead then. The businesses in the local shopping strip were being killed off by the massive shopping malls in nearby suburbs. The Victorian Government treated Hampton like a poor relation. We'd lost our school, our beach. There would have been nothing left of Hampton's character if we hadn't acted. State Government ministers were telling us that we should turn the suburb into exclusive golf courses for Japanese businessmen. Hampton people were prepared to do anything to keep golf out of the suburb. So we formed a breakaway Council, with sub-committees investigating a variety of financial strategies ... The Festival idea kept re-emerging, but there are so many festivals: arts festivals, comedy, food festivals, sporting carnivals ... Our festival had to be unique, something which would make Hampton a centre of national focus.

Now Hampton is internationally notorious.

LORRAINE: Yes, because we tapped into something that really interests people.

Murder.

LORRAINE: Not murder, killing. It's a Festival of Killing. When you say murder, it implies that something's done against a person's will. We were able to say to our people, Look, we have a strategy that will make Hampton the most comfortable, desirable suburb in Melbourne, something that will breathe life back into the place. To do that, we need to hire someone to kill seven residents each year, no more, no less. The killings will be at random. No one has to stay, but if you want to run a business here, you'll need to be a permanent resident. When the seventh killing takes place, we'll hold a week of festivities, a big, emotional thanksgiving. We said to the Hampton people, If you let us stage this Festival of Killing, we can save Hampton from dying ... At the beginning, I'm sure no-one anticipated how big the Festival would become. A lot of people left—thirty per cent of the population—but now people are voting with their feet. Real estate in Hampton has gone through the roof. We have a three-year waiting list. The Federal Government granted us Independent Territorial status. We're like an island within metropolitan Melbourne, and Hampton has community facilities which are unmatched by any community anywhere. The Festival has enabled us to build the finest art gallery in the southern hemisphere, and within ten years it will be the finest gallery of modern art in the world. There's a holiday atmosphere all year round, and the Festival itself is a joy beyond our wildest dreams.

But how do you reckon the value of a human life?

LORRAINE: How do you measure the worth of genuine community? Hampton people are bound together by this great adventure, they're successful, they know that anything worth accomplishing involves sacrifice.

Thirty-three lives so far ...

LORRAINE: Folk that died willingly, people who died happy in the knowledge that they've left joy, gratitude and prosperity behind them ... You've seen our Shrine of The Martyrs?

Yes.

LORRAINE: It's beautiful. It's very tasteful. The Shrine's one of Hampton's most popular attractions.

3. WENDY BILLINGSLEY — HAMPTON TOURIST COMMISSIONER — OCTOBER 20TH

Wendy is a young tyro who has lived in Hampton all her life. We filmed her at the Hampton Tourist Authority, in a luxurious office which overlooks both the Bay, and the Shrine of The Martyrs. Her office is part of a recently constructed 20-storey complex on Hampton Street which doubles as a set-down point for tourist buses.

What is the Festival worth to the local community?

WENDY: It's difficult to say exactly. Hampton has 15,000 residents. Festival Week will bring more than 300,000 people into Hampton. The all-round income generated from The Festival this year will be something in the order of thirty billion dollars. On average, we get fifty tour buses through every day of the year, to see the Shrine, to see the statue of the Killer. Of course, everyone wants to see the Killer in the flesh. The hotel where your crew is staying used to be an Italian restaurant, now it's a five-star international hotel with four hundred rooms that overlook the bay. We have new industries setting up ... You've seen The Killer's Beer. The merchandising is phenomenal. T-shirts, maps of the killing sites, project posters of the weapons used, photo-montages of the victims, board games, mugs, video-games, swap cards, snowdomes, Wedgwood plates. Then there's the betting ... Just five years ago, ninety per cent of Hampton people worked outside Hampton. Now you'll find

that the vast majority derive their income from
Festival-related business, even if it's only
renting out a bungalow in the weeks leading up to
the seventh killing ...

**So The Festival's gradually become more than just
one week of the year?**

WENDY: That's the whole beauty of having seven
killings. It's something we didn't anticipate. A
whole series of 'mini-events' have self-generated
around each killing. Of course, you've got the
funerals, and a week of mourning ... The first
killing of the new year has taken on a special
significance. It's known as The Profanity.
There's a very solemn parade where the community
celebrates the importance of the undertaking
which binds them. It's now traditional for the
Killer to stay out of public view for the week
following The Profanity. We even refuse to allow
an official betting market on the date of The
Profanity ... Like I said, there's a special
parade, and The Killer's effigy is burnt on the
steps of the Shrine of The Martyrs ... But after
that, each killing brings a rising level of
anticipation and excitement. The gambling begins
to escalate ... It's fantastic!

What about Richard Thompson?

WENDY: Another of our traditions is that the
Killer is never referred to by his given name ...
Out of deference to his public responsibility.

Could another person become the Killer?

WENDY: Sure. The Killer operates according
to yearly contracts, but this Killer's been

fantastic for Hampton.

He's an intelligent, thoughtful man.

He's terrific with the media. Some people
think that all he has to do is knock-off seven
residents each year—Actually, that *is* all he's
required to do according to the terms of his
contract. He could be totally reclusive if he
chose to be. But our Killer's civic-minded.
He deals with the press, with international
television. He gave one thousand interviews last
year. He speaks to tour groups, he appears at
non-Festival functions. He loves Hampton, and
the Hampton people feel the same for him. The
most important event of the Festival Week is the
Killer's Parade, when he's driven down Hampton
Street on the back of a massive float, being
kissed and hugged by the families of that year's
Martyrs, being cheered and showered with rose
petals. It's tremendously moving.

So what is happening in Hampton now?

WENDY: Right now we're waiting for the sixth
killing ... Once that's taken place, we can
start putting up the billboards and the banners,
organising the floats. The long-term tourists
come in, to wait for the last killing. That
might be ten or twelve weeks. All the time
the atmosphere is building up. The tension's
enormous. It's a sensational time.

You've lost a brother?

WENDY: Yes ... In the third year.

He used to work with you here at the Tourist
Authority?

WENDY: Johnny was terrific. I miss him so much.
Everyone does ... Cyanide poisoning. Very quick.

A shame.

WENDY: It's exactly how he would've wanted it.

4. DOUG & MAVIS SHRIMPTON, THE KILLER'S NEIGHBOURS — OCTOBER 20TH

We filmed the elderly Shrimptons in their front garden which overlooks The Killer's own front yard. One of his security guards wanders in and out of shot in the background.

MAVIS: When we heard that the Killer would be moving in next door, well, naturally we were quite apprehensive. I mean, we knew Richard from when he used to live in Hampton as a boy. He was a sweet, quiet lad, but he wasn't a killer then ... You don't know how being a killer might change someone, the sort of people he might associate with.

DOUG: He used to play cricket with our Joe ...

So you knew before he arrived that your neighbour would be the Killer?

MAVIS: Yes. The Council bought the house specifically to be the Killer's residence. That's why it's so well maintained.

DOUG: The security's something terrific.

MAVIS: Of course, we wanted assurances.

Assurances?

MAVIS: That he wouldn't be doing the killing next door. As you know, he uses a lot of different methods; electrocution, injections, cross-bows ... They say it's quick and clinical, but it's not the kind of thing you want happening over the side fence.

DOUG: Not on a regular basis.

MAVIS: You'd have the police and ambulances coming at all hours of the night.

DOUG: The Council assured us that the Killer wouldn't bring his business home.

What kind of neighbour is he?

DOUG: Friendly. He'll always smile and speak if he sees you in the street. But he's quiet. Keeps to himself.

Girlfriends?

MAVIS: Not as such ... Not that we know of. Quite a few girls drop by, their mothers send them by with cakes and casseroles and things. I suppose that they might have, what do you call them?

DOUG: Ulterior motives.

MAVIS: Well, he's a sensible lad ... I don't see him being swayed by cream sponges.

You're not bothered that your neighbour might decide to kill one or both of you?

DOUG: Not in the slightest. It'd be an honour. When you think of the good he's done for Hampton.

MAVIS: Of course, he wouldn't be allowed to kill the two of us at once, not since the Nguyens a couple of years back. That got the bookmakers in a helluva flap, wanting to know who went first, was it him or her? Then, Mr Nguyen was over 35, and she was under. It upset all their betting categories, so the Council changed the regulations so that the sequence of deaths had to be separated by at least the one week of mourning.

DOUG: Did we tell you that he painted our letterbox?

5. NICK PTSOURIS — CHIEF INSPECTOR, HAMPTON POLICE — OCTOBER 23RD

We filmed Inspector Ptsouris sitting on the bonnet of a police divisional van parked in the street. He waved and smiled as pedestrians went past. At one point, a small group of South Korean tourists stopped to photograph the interview.

How do you find out about each killing?

NICK: The Killer has a hotline. He contacts us immediately after each kill. There are code-words, that sort of thing.

Does he meet you at the scene?

NICK: No, there's a protocol. The Killer leaves the scene before we arrive. Then our responsibility is to determine what happened independent of any input from the Killer.

Why can't he just tell you what he's done, and how he did it?

NICK: There's the danger that he might accidentally reveal some part of his methodology—why he chose a certain person, or mode of killing—and then his position would be compromised.

But isn't his position compromised by everyone knowing who the Killer is?

NICK: When the Festival idea first came up, the suggestion was put that the Killer should be anonymous ... But then we felt we'd have amateur Columbos coming in from all over, prying into everyone's lives, as if Hampton was a giant

Cluedo board. Another suggestion was that there
should be Kill Roster, that each citizen would be
rostered to kill a person whose name was pulled
out of a barrel at a designated time, but that
mitigated against efficiency. Not everyone has
the skill to be an efficient killer, and you
don't want people wandering through the streets
with a crossbow bolt through their neck, y'know,
bleeding to death ... Finally, it was accepted
that the Killer would have to be someone widely
recognised, someone who could be celebrated for
doing a difficult job for the Hampton community.
We don't think of the Killer as an ordinary
citizen, we see him as the embodiment of the
community's will.

**So the police have no idea who he'll kill, or
when?**

NICK: None.

It could be you.

NICK: Yes, it could.

**Have you formed any theories on how he decides on
the next victim?**

NICK: Everyone has theories—Names out of a hat,
or some convoluted sociological distribution ...

**But there's no way to ensure that his method is
perfectly random, that some kind of favoritism
won't come into it. The Killer would be open to
corrupt approaches.**

NICK: Absolutely. That's where it becomes an act
of faith.

Faith?

NICK: Yes, I think so. Trust.

But there have been complaints, haven't there?

NICK: Of course. I mean, it's only natural that in the week after your wife, or father's been killed, a relative's going to complain that it's unfair, or too calculated. Hampton hasn't tried to legislate against grief. But people do come around. Finally, they accept the killing allows us to survive and prosper as a society ...

Do Richard Thompson's friends and family prosper?

NICK: It was agreed that they should leave Hampton prior to the first killing.

But he'd make new friends, be attracted to young women, offered entreaties ... I've heard it said that mothers have sent their young daughters to seduce him ...

NICK: I've heard it said that he's a homosexual. If you listen long enough, you'll hear every sort of rumour. This place is rife with gamblers and their gossip ... Look, you'd have to ask the Killer about entreaties. We're satisfied that there's been nothing improper about the killings ...

Nothing?... What about Angela Kaufmann?

NICK: What about her?

She was fifteen years old ... There were allegations that she'd been interfered with before the killing ...

NICK:(VERY ANGRY) That's a lie! I attended that scene. You'd have to look at the people making the allegations. None of the allegations ever come from within Hampton. Outsiders get niggly about our wealth. We live well, very well, in a close community, our kids are well clothed and well educated ... Envy is a shocking thing. Outside people resent the sacrifices that Hampton people have made and try to undermine the success of the Festival. I've heard every sort of lie. But the proof of the pudding is that right across Europe and Asia and America, you have small towns trying to emulate the Hampton experience ...

So Angela Kaufmann wasn't raped?

NICK: No. She was not interfered with in any way.

Would it have made any difference if she had been raped before she was killed?

NICK: Don't be ridiculous! What do you take us for? We'd never condone that ... If you're going to circulate allegations, let's see some proof ...

6. RICHARD THOMPSON, KILLER — PUBLIC PARK, OCTOBER 23RD

On this occasion we filmed Thompson in a small park while he gave a public demonstration of target shooting with a crossbow. Three security guards held back a large crowd of tourists and locals who applauded each accurate shot. We questioned Thompson while he was reloading.

Can you tell us about the Angela Kaufmann killing?

THOMPSON: Sure, that was two seasons back. I met her as she was coming home from school.

Was she with friends?

THOMPSON: No, killings have to be more discreet than that. There'd be a betting plunge if I was seen escorting someone away from a group.

What happened?

THOMPSON: I told Angie that I was going to kill her, and that it would be best if we did it at her place. She was very calm about it. In fact, she asked me if I was nervous. She also wanted to know if she'd have time to write some letters.

Did you let her write the letters?

THOMPSON: One, I think. It was a finely balanced kill time-wise. You can't afford to have other people on the scene distracting you. I figured that I had about ninety minutes before her parents got home. Generally, I like to make a kill, get off the scene, notify the police, and have them waiting when the victim's next of kin arrive. It would be too horrible if family had to discover the body.

Did you find Angela attractive?

THOMPSON: Don't think I don't know what you're getting at. Angie was a terrific kid. I had a job to do. She accepted that.

Did you find her attractive?

THOMPSON: She was a pretty girl.

You smothered her with a pillow.

THOMPSON: You'll find all that in the police report.

She was dressed in her nightie ...

THOMPSON:(CALM) That's not true. She was dressed in a windcheater and jeans. Check the report.

But you've heard the allegations?

THOMPSON: I take it you're repeating them? **(LONG PAUSE)** They're fictions. I hear all sorts of insinuations and sleazy innuendo. I've been spat on by outsiders. All that goes with the job. It's no rose garden. But you won't find the Kaufmann family making accusations. I can look Angie's family in the eye ... Speak to them yourself. They know I treated their daughter with care and decency.

You smothered her to death.

THOMPSON: I gave Angie the choice of being electrocuted, injected or smothered. Sometimes, when a kill has to be really quick, I can't offer a choice.

How do you choose an intended victim?

THOMPSON: I have a random method ...

What is that method?

THOMPSON: I can't divulge it.

You don't try to choose 'the deserving'?

THOMPSON: It's not my business to make moral judgements.

You don't play at being God?

THOMPSON: No. I kill seven people a year.

Do you believe in God?

THOMPSON: Well, I think God would do a better job than me if He or She was Hampton's Killer, but, things being what they are, and the community's expectations being what they are, I do a pretty fair job.

Do you have a killing schedule?

THOMPSON: Sometimes I decide a month in advance, sometimes I decide an hour or two before I make a kill ... It comes down to a judgement about when it will be most efficient.

Does it get messy?

THOMPSON: It can. I guarantee a quick kill, but that doesn't always mean it will be a clean kill.

You once made a claim on the Council for a new pair of shoes ...

THOMPSON: Yes, they were saturated in blood. Don't imagine that it's an easy thing being a killer.

But you are so well paid. Don't you think that was insensitive? You killed a mother of six, and then you hit the Council for the cost of new shoes ...

THOMPSON: That's not how it happened. There was a lot of blood at the scene. The police found my footprints everywhere ... Not unnaturally, they thought it would be better for them if I didn't track blood all through Hampton. When they took the shoes, they suggested that I claim for them. The Council also cleans my car and carpets from time to time. But you're right. I do make a lot of money from performing my duties. And I am aware of the need to be sensitive. You'll notice that I drive a rusty twenty-year-old Datsun. All of my investments are channeled back into Hampton companies.

Isn't it wrong to kill your fellow human beings?

THOMPSON: That's a big moral question ... I'm not sure that I have the time.

When will you have the time?

Just at that moment Thompson was besieged by kids looking for autographs.

When will you have time?

THOMPSON: I'm giving a public lecture about the morality of killing next Thursday ... But you'll have to get the Council's permission to film ...

BOY: (CHEEKY) Hey, can you autograph my bum?

THOMPSON: (FRIENDLY) How would you like me to kill your mother and eat her?

7. AMERICAN TOURISTS AT KILLER MURAL — OCTOBER 26TH

We filmed a group of mostly elderly Americans posing in front of the large mural portrait of Thompson engaged in various acts of killing on the outer wall of Hampton Primary School.

What brings you all to Hampton when it's not even Festival Week?

BEA: Well, you want to see the Killer in person, and the places where the killuns were done ... All the statues and museums.

STELLA: We saw the Shrine to the martyrs ... They have their photos, and information about their lives up to when they were killed.

MARK: We thought Hampton would be a town, but it's more like a suburb really—Hampton people talk the same as Melbourne people do.

Are you disappointed?

STELLA: Not me. Hampton's real pretty ... My husband Ernie had his photograph taken with the Killer.

RAY: Well, I am disappointed. Yes, ma'am. We thought we'd get to see a killun, that it was all ceremonial, kinda like them bullfights ... Well, you're Spanish, aren't ya?

No, I'm French.

RAY: Yeah, well we thought that, at very least, we'd get to see the dead folks. When the travel agent said there was a Shrine to The Martyrs, I expected to see embalmed bodies like how the old Egyptians did them mummies.

BEA:(LAUGHING) That's just you. You're stupid!

RAY: Who says?... These people in Hampton say they've got a killer, but no one gets to see no killuns. He steals out in the dark of night and he kills someone real polite. You don't get to see the blood, just some plaque that the Mayor puts up outside the victim's house. That's not killun'! You go t' Fort Worth, go to Austin ... Go t' Dallas. Your killers there are *real* killers. They don't squirrel around in the dark ... They kill cause they like killun'. This Killer doesn't look like no killer I've ever seen. He smiles, he plays with kids. What's the good of having a killer if you're not scared to the crapper of being killed by him?

STELLA: Ernie had his photograph taken with the Killer.

ERNIE: He put an apple on my head and aimed his crossbow at me.

You weren't worried?

ERNIE: Heck no. He's not allowed to kill tourists ... **(DISPLAYING APPLE)** Look, he even signed the apple for me.

RAY: Well, that's just it—If he don't kill tourists ... If he don't kill journalists from France ...

We're from Channel 4 in Britain ...

RAY: Well, if he don't kill you folks, how can he claim to be a killer? *How do we even know that he is a killer if you don't see the bodies?*

How do you mean?

RAY: One day someone's there, the next day they're gone. The Killer puts up his hand, and the cops say that he's killed someone. The museum people put another face up in the Shrine ... Shit, how do we know the whole thing's not a huge grift?

A hoax?

RAY: Sure it is. It's tourism! These so-called Martyrs are all sipping cocktails in the south of France. Heck, you probably know some of them.

JOANNE: Ray's just sour cause they don't have no Killin Festival in Texas ...

RAY: Don't talk crap!

MARK: That's the truth, Ray.

RAY: We got *real* killers in Texas! Mean sonsabitches. You don't get your picture took with no Texas killer. No, ma'am!

8. TRACEY HARNETT — FORMER GIRLFRIEND OF RICHARD THOMPSON — OCTOBER 27TH

Tracey Harnett, a former girlfriend of Hampton's Killer, does not live in Hampton. We filmed her at her flat in an inner suburb of Melbourne. A heavy smoker, she is a pretty woman with a high brow, and unusually large green eyes. She had been reluctant to speak to us because one of her sisters lives in Hampton, and she feared the consequences of any criticism she might make of Richard Thompson.

You and Richard Thompson were lovers?

TRACEY: Well, we went out together for a year or so more than a decade back. We were both studying.

What was he like then?

TRACEY: Nice. A bit soft, you know, wimpy. But he could be charming and smart. At his best, he's quite funny. He was just, I don't know, too sensitive ... Thommo was thoughtful in a self-conscious way. Shy, but it wasn't an endearing sort of shyness.

It surprised you then to see him become Hampton's Killer?

TRACEY: Yes, it did. But he seems to have come out of himself since I knew him. He couldn't have delivered a speech to a large group of people then. He was so anxious.

Why did the two of you fall out?

TRACEY: I knew other boys ... I wanted to have fun. Thommo was so serious minded. We used to argue.

What about sex?

TRACEY: Was the Killer a deviate, do you mean?

Was he?

TRACEY: He was no Lady Killer. He was nervous ... He was keen on me, but not always the most functional of lovers ... That was consistent with his personality then. Thommo was tense and panicky. But I don't think you could say that he kills people to sublimate his sexual tensions or anything like that.

Did he ever threaten you?

TRACEY: No. Richard's not violent. He's cerebral. He spends much too much time thinking. He's only ever been attracted to brilliant women ... He liked the challenge of brilliant women, but he never really rose to the challenge ...

You are aware of other girlfriends that he's had since?

TRACEY: Not girlfriends as such. He was always getting infatuated with someone or other. Richard's an obsessive man. He used to write hundreds of letters. He was keen on my sister Elizabeth for a time, was mad about a close friend of hers, Francesca Morricone. Catherine O'Shaunessy ... He was crazy about her.

Would he still write to any of them?

TRACEY: He fell out with Liz and Catherine ...
Francesca's dead.

When did she die?

TRACEY: She disappeared in Denmark. There was a
big investigation. She'd been staying at a Youth
Hostel in Copenhagen ... She just vanished.

What about Richard?

TRACEY: He was devastated, I think.

I heard from friends that he hired a private
detective to search for her ...

Had they been lovers?

TRACEY: God, no!... She liked him, and they were
close, but not close enough for him ... He was
crazy about her.

Crazy enough to have killed her?

TRACEY: Thommo can be stupid, and intense. But
he couldn't have killed her. I can't imagine him
hurting anyone.

You can't?

TRACEY:(LONG PAUSE) No, I can't. I know what you
are thinking, but there's a difference.

Between killing neighbours and murdering a friend?

TRACEY: Yes, I think so.

How so?

TRACEY: I know Richard pretty well. He's a big
schmuck for doing the shit he does, but he's not
a murderer.

9. KEN JANSZ — STATISTICIAN — OCTOBER 27TH

We filmed Ken in his small office. He's a native Sri Lankan in his mid-forties. Ken sat at his desk, surrounded by computer screens and filing cabinets.

You spend most of your time compiling statistical information concerning the killings ...

KEN: Yes, the whole thing fascinates me.

How can you justify the time commitment?

KEN: Well, I'm not an amateur. This is a lucrative business. I supply information to gamblers, bookmakers, interested parties. The Festival is a multi-billion dollar industry, and everything about it requires a totally professional approach.

What kind of statistics do you provide?

KEN: Everything. As you know, there have been thirty-three killings. We provide location breakdowns, time breakdowns, data related to the method of killing, whether or not the persons were known to the Killer socially.

Could you give some specific examples?

KEN: Well, there have been 18 male victims and 15 female, never more than four of one sex in succession ... All but six of the victims have been killed in their own homes, fourteen in daylight, thirteen at night. The crossbow has so far been the Killer's favoured weapon. He's used the crossbow to make seven killings. He hasn't used a gun, or a knife, or cutting weapons. You

could get odds of 50-1 on his next victim being
killed with a chainsaw ... Twelve of the victims
had never spoken to the Killer prior to the
killing, only eight could be said to have known
him well. The information I have breaks down into
hundreds of categories and cross-references. Age,
religion, race.

**How about non-Anglo-Celtic girls aged between
twelve and eighteen?**

KEN: Two.

Similarity of method?

KEN: None ... One smothered, one poisoned.

What's all this information leading to?

KEN: Predictability ... We don't hope to uncover
an exact method of selection. There's The Paradox
of Schrodinger's Cat for a start. The Killer's
actions won't be unaffected by the fact that
he's being scrutinised, and knows he's being
scrutinised. What I'd hope to offer my clients is
an increased probability ... I don't believe in
absolute, or pure randomness. That is, I don't
believe that the Killer could operate by a method
that's perfectly random. There's got to be an
imperfection somewhere, some fear or favour or
blindspot ... Eventually, I'll find a pattern,
whether it be initials of the victims' surnames,
or anagrams, or a numerical scheme related to
their telephone numbers. It's a game of guessing
and double-guessing.

The Killer has to be seen to be impartial?

KEN: Yes, that's his mandate.

**What if it's found that he's not totally
impartial?**

KEN: Well, that wouldn't worry me ... I'm
speaking personally now. I'd be much more worried
if the Killer really had found a random method
of victim selection, or a random application of
dissociated random methods.

Why?

KEN: Because it wouldn't be human. It's not even
God-like to be so perfectly disinterested or
indifferent. Don't get me wrong, I believe in
the Festival. I believe in the importance of the
Killer as an agent of the Hampton community's
will, but what are we left with if that agent is
inhuman?

**Statistics that don't indicate anything, random
numbers.**

KEN: Yes, and *that* concerns me. It would totally
destroy the gambling industry centered on The
Festival if it was accepted that the killings
were entirely unpredictable.

Do outsiders buy your information?

KEN: For gambling?

Gambling ... anything.

KEN: Certainly. There are people, outsiders
mostly, who question the morality of this
enterprise, whether it be the morality of the
killings themselves, or the morality of the
betting which surrounds the Festival. I imagine
that's what your film is about, questioning the

morality of the Festival. People hope to uncover the Killer's darkest secrets and prejudices through statistical analysis. They'd like to learn that he's a racist, or a misogynist, or an ageist. They'd like to discover that he plays favourites, or he's been seduced or corrupted. Some outsiders desperately need to believe their society is morally superior to Hampton's form of association.

Would you help outsiders gather information that might be used to subvert the Festival?

KEN: The Festival's about making Hampton people more prosperous ...

At any cost?

KEN: The cost is a matter of public knowledge. Seven lives a year.

But there is also a greater cost ... The justification of cold-blooded murder.

KEN: Only if you choose to see it that way. Hamptonians don't see it that way.

10. CHARLES AND DEBORAH KAUFMANN — PARENTS OF ANGELA — OCTOBER 29TH

I interviewed the Kaufmanns in the living room of their substantial Bolton Avenue home, a room lined with books and art works, and photographs of their two children. Charles is older, mid-fifties, while Deborah is in her mid-forties.

When was your daughter Angela killed?

CHARLES: Two years ago. Near the end of the third season ... She was fifteen. **(LOOKING AT PHOTOGRAPH)**

This is Angela?

DEBORAH: Yes, that's her with her older sister Sharon ... She was a very pretty girl.

CHARLES: And bright. She only ever got A's. She wanted to be a research scientist.

DEBORAH: Angela was a gifted pianist. We have a videotape of her playing, if you'd like.

Sure, that would be great.

DEBORAH: You couldn't get her to practice, but she had a gift ...

We pause to watch the video of Angela playing The Moonlight Sonata very competently, with feeling.

She plays beautifully ...

(LONG PAUSE)

Do you resent her death?

CHARLES: It's a terrible thing when anyone dies. Especially when they're young with so much to give.

DEBORAH: There's a grief, a hollowness, but you can't call it resentment ...

But she didn't have to die ...

DEBORAH: Angela was very aware of being part of the community, part of the social contract.

Can a girl of fifteen make that sort of decision?

DEBORAH: Children in Hampton are invited to contract every year from when they turn twelve. At eighteen, they're forced to decide. Contract, or leave Hampton. It's not like banishment. If they leave, they can visit whenever they like, and they are subject to the same protection as tourists. It's just that they can't study or work here.

Please forgive me for being blunt, but I find it incredible that the parents of a brilliant, beautiful fifteen-year old girl could accept that the community has the right to sanction her killing.

CHARLES: We are a community. We need each other to survive. The lives of individuals can't be seen as being distinct from the life of the community. Angela willingly volunteered to take on the responsibilities which go with being part of this community.

DEBORAH: We never saw it as a cold-blooded decision to kill Angela. It's a tragic event ... an impersonal tragedy. If a tree falls on a child and kills her, you don't cut down every tree in town. You don't ban lightning, or deep pools ...

But I don't see how you can call it impersonal? A man has entered your home and smothered your

daughter. You know who he is. You see your daughter's killer on the street.

CHARLES: Other people have been killed. Some are good people, some not so good. We know that it could have been us, or Sharon, that it still could be any of us ... The killings give value to our lives. Every day is like a glorious bonus. After the seventh killing of the year, when the Festival begins, there's an extraordinary release of joy. It's a heartfelt thanksgiving.

The Festival has made you prosperous.

DEBORAH: Yes, that's true. We run a gallery on the beach front. Business is excellent. We've recently purchased paintings by Kandinsky and Marc, and several erotic drawings by Gustav Klimt.

Have you become prosperous at the expense of your daughter's life?

CHARLES: (CONSIDERED PAUSE) I know that's what outsiders say. It's a very simplistic equation ... We're not the only ones who have prospered. Everyone has. Hampton's become a wonderful place. Hampton people are closer than people anywhere ... You should have seen what it was like before the Festival.

DEBORAH : Hampton people care about each other. They appreciate that all citizens are making a vital contribution ... They love each other.

But isn't that notion of love, gentleness and affection at odds with the rumours surrounding your daughter's death?

CHARLES: We don't listen to foul gossip. We know the truth.

The rumour is that Angela was raped before she was killed ...

CHARLES: That's a *pernicious* lie.

DEBORAH: We saw her body.

CHARLES: It's totally untrue.

If it became known that there was perversity associated with the killings, it would destroy tourism, it would end the Festival ...

CHARLES: Angela was smothered ... She died decently, she was treated with respect.

... and people made wealthy by the murders might be prepared to keep quiet about an outrage which would threaten their prosperity ...

CHARLES: (FURIOUS, GETTING UP TO PUSH THE CREW OUT OF THE HOUSE) Who are you to talk of outrage?... How can you speak to us like this?... These lies, they're cruel fabrications. The propaganda of foreign commercial interests. You people hate the idea that Hampton people might be content. You have to contaminate happiness wherever you see it, because you don't have the courage or imagination to find your own happiness. These accusations, they're lies invented by sick people ... Pathetic, envious perverts.

DEBORAH: Listen to me. We trust the Killer. You couldn't know him to spread those lies about him ...

**The people who'll watch this film only care about
the truth ...**

CHARLES: Do they?... You know them, do you? Do
you really know your audience well enough to say
what they care most about is the truth?

11. RICHARD THOMPSON — KILLER'S ANNUAL SPEECH — CONCERT HALL, HAMPTON CASINO — OCTOBER 29TH

Since the commencement of the Festival, an outstanding casino-conference centre has been built on the site of the former Hampton Community Hall. A sell-out audience of two thousand, most of them tourists, turned out to see an evening of entertainment by the local avant garde band Approximate Life, and the Killer's third annual lecture. He instituted the lecture as a means of explaining his various moral and political positions. Even as a former school teacher, Thompson is a poor speaker, given to reading nervously from a prepared text. Locals jokingly refer to these speeches as his 'sermons from the mount'.

THOMPSON: Some time ago, a friend who no longer lives here asked me to distinguish between my role here in Hampton and that of the State Executioner in societies where capital punishment still operates. From the tone of her enquiry, I had no doubt that she was unable to differentiate between the two functions. Those of you who have heard me speak before will know my attitude to this. I do not see the Killer as an operative who enforces the moral or legal judgements of this community. To the contrary, the Killer's agency *underpins* the contractual arrangements binding the community and its individual constituents.

Many people outside Hampton argue that all killing is immoral. To that, I say this community has decided that seven killings done at random each year—and those seven only—are morally justifiable. Our community is agreed that seven killings are essential to safe-guard the future well-being of Hampton. To put it more succinctly, No Festival, No Hampton.

The rejoinder is predictable enough. Critics insist that if one human life is deemed to be expendable, then all human life is devalued. The seven killings we have decided upon is an arbitrary nomination—the number might as easily be two or two thousand—that we are all expendable, and so forth ... Ultimately, I consider this to be a debate about diction and contradiction. It's a debate about a community's right to define itself, to decide upon its own laws and moral imperatives.

So often when visitors complain that killing is wrong, they assert that capital punishment is morally reprehensible, and even the most heinous criminals should be locked up for life. Superficially, I'd feel inclined to agree with them. Killing people is dirty work. It's entirely undesirable. I'm also quite happy with the argument that capital punishment won't deter capital offences, and that the elimination of criminals won't contribute to the community's sense of life having intrinsic value. But the alternative is locking the murderer or rapist away for what, thirty years, forty years, at thirty thousand dollars a year. You're talking a million dollars.

Now, I'm not saying it's indefensible for a community to spend one million dollars to sustain an imprisoned murderer. However, I would say that it may be immoral for a community or State to outlay that money on an imprisoned criminal

if it is a *choice* between the murderer and the
purchase of a humidicrib, or an intensive care
ambulance, or research into breast cancer or cot
death. *Every community* has to determine its life
or death priorities within the limits of its
financial resources.

What I'm saying here is that Hampton is not a
unique society, or even a particularly unusual
one. Every society has paid killers. They are
persons whose role it is to define and implement
life-or-death priorities. They determine who
lives and who dies, albeit at a greater distance
than I do in my operation.

Let's suppose you decide to commit your resources
to humidicribs. With the technology that we have
available now, you can save the lives of babies
born thirteen weeks premature. Most of these
babies are kids who would have died without
medical intervention ... That's terrific. A
society might even be prepared to wear the fact
that these highly premature kids have a much
higher probability of illness in later life
than your average punter. But where does your
benevolence stop? What if you could save the lives
of kids who are less than half-term? Somewhere
along the line these prem. kids will start
ringing-up very serious outlays for your health
system. Will you feel morally constrained to save
the little buggers because every human life is
uniquely valuable, that every prematurely born kid
might be Mozart? To save them whatever the cost?

While you're ploughing money into humidicribs
to save the kids nature would have sacrificed,

you've emptied your cash register of funds for
kidney research or liver research, or for the
cancer research which might save a 39 year-old
much-needed mother of four ... We're talking very
big equations here.

What I'm saying is that every society, every
administration, has a dozen or more of these
hired killers, but you won't ever see them with
a big 'K' stitched onto their blazers. The
difference here is that Hampton's Killer doesn't
hide away in the darkest recesses of a shadowy
institution, anonymous and removed.

In Hampton, you can be sure your age or sex or
wealth or race or political influence won't be a
determinant in your Killer's calculations. What's
more, the prosperity of our community enables
all Hamptonians to have access to the very finest
health care. This community donates tens of
millions of dollars for various forms of medical
research, both inside and outside Hampton. We have
a sense of purpose here. Since the inception of
the Festival, there hasn't been a single suicide
in Hampton. Let me repeat that, not one suicide
since the Festival started. In the five years
prior to the Festival, there were thirty suicides.
We believe that life *is* valuable, and we consider
that Hampton's Festival is a *celebration* of the
true value of life and association.

But this is no fairyland. Maybe this community is
alone in recognising the true relationship between
the cost of living, and the value of life.

The wealth and prosperity of our tribe offends
those who are not so wealthy, or those whose

wealth is built on a less equitable, less
democratic foundation. These people are most
offended by the unity of our community.

Many outsiders feel constrained to depict Hampton
as a dangerous and subversive 'other', a sinister
death cult. It suits some external interests to
portray Hamptonians as greedy hillbillies who
enjoy the fruits of a deep shame.

We don't compel people to be initiated into
our tribe, and we don't prevent them from
dissociating if they so choose. Nor do we send
out assassins to eliminate those who have left
us—many of whom seek to profit from defamations,
untruths and actions designed to subvert our
community.

When critics argue that Hampton prospers through
making killing an entertainment, they demonstrate
their failure to grasp the real achievement
of our Festival. Tourists don't come to see
the killings or the bodies—the killings take
place in private, and no bodies are displayed.
What visitors actually come to see—and all our
research supports this—is a working model of a
happy coherent society at ease with the forces of
life and death. People are tired of association
through fear and extortion, and they want to see
their innermost dreams enacted. They want to
experience harmony. True harmony.

Never fall into the error of calling Hampton a
suburb or a place. The Hampton that I care about—
the Hampton I'd kill for—exists at the intersection
of dream and desire, fear and fantasy.

12. GRACE JOHANNSEN — PSYCHIATRIST — OCTOBER 30TH

We filmed Grace, a young psychiatrist,in her large, luxuriously appointed office, which overlooks the Shrine of The Martyrs. She started her practice in Hampton three years ago. There are four practising psychiatrists in Hampton. Eight years ago there were none.

What struck you about Hampton when you first moved here?

GRACE: The distance between the myth and the reality. The outside world has this notion of Hampton as a kind of weird socialist cult. If you listen to the local government, or the residents, they hardly speak a sentence without using the big-C word: Community. The truth is somewhat removed from that—Hampton is a gambler's paradise. It's a mad bull-run. The Council presents the Festival as means of protecting and preserving the values that Hampton was losing. The Festival is supposed to establish a new tradition and continuity. After living here, and dealing with many clients, my feeling is that the Festival will ultimately produce the opposite. Hampton will have a high-turnover population. Sure, you have the old residents who will stay no matter what, but mostly you have a loose association of hit and run capitalists masquerading as community-minded citizens. Hampton has already become a haven for business adventurers who want maximum profit in the shortest possible term. If they weren't baring their arses at Death in Hampton, you'd find these people taking the most outrageous risks on the

stockmarket. The irony of the Killing Festival is
that just about *everyone* here is out to make a
killing. The Killer may be one of the few people
who actually believes in the sugar-coated myths
fed to the public.

What do you make of Richard Thompson?

GRACE: He's a curious character. I think he's
sincere when he says he's working for the greater
good ... But he's much more the pragmatist
than the glassy-eyed idealist. He's quite
Machiavellian, actually. The Killer believes that
the prosperity of Hampton justifies the means by
which it arrives at that prosperity. The truth
is, nobody knows a great deal about him. Except
that he's a likeable, apparently straight-forward
bloke. I doubt that anyone but Thompson could
convince the public to place their faith in the
Killer as an institution.

But why would someone choose to become the Killer?

GRACE: A desire for power. A sense of
powerlessness. A craving for notoriety ... It
could be any of a hundred things. I've heard
the Killer say that he took the job because he
wanted to save the Hampton he knew as a boy from
disappearing. That makes me wonder whether he
lives in the past, or an imaginary version of
his childhood, and whether he actually *sees* the
suburb he's living in now. Nothing has changed
Hampton more than the Festival. The Killer
seems unaware of the paradox. The success of
the Festival has ensured the disappearance of
the old Hampton. You'd be hard pressed to find
a community which has altered so drastically

as this one. I'm very curious to know how the Killer deals with that contradiction, whether it's something he could ever allow himself to be conscious of.

And what about the people who choose to live in Hampton, who volunteer to live in the line of fire?

GRACE: Many of them are people who are inordinately fearful of death. Hampton has a double-edged attraction for a certain kind of personality. It's easy to use the single-minded pursuit of personal fortune as a distraction from having to deal with your deepest, morbid anxieties. People treat material gain as insulation from death. The *process* of gaining in material terms gives people an excuse to postpone questions of meaning, or spirituality. You find that people here define themselves very much in terms of their material acquisitions, or their accumulated fortunes. Many of the highest flyers couldn't differentiate between the possibility of bankruptcy and the possibility of death. If you can cheat and scrounge and trade your way out of one, then you can do the same with the other.

You make Hampton sound like a panel by Hieronymous Bosch.

GRACE: You'll find some very medieval behaviour here. Some people have extraordinary superstitions — obsessive-compulsive behaviours only slightly removed from 'step on a crack, break your mother's back'. People who, for reasons best known to themselves, never walk northwards along Hampton Street on a Friday ... And bizarre rituals. People who *must* smile at the Killer whenever they see

him, and people who feel compelled to look away.
After a while, these lunacies become local custom
... You're right. A lot of the behaviour here is
very basic, very Bosch ...

So why are you here?

GRACE: There's good business to be done. Hampton
has an unusually wealthy clientele with an
unusual need for psychiatric services. And
Hampton also presents a unique opportunity for
research. I have two books in development which
analyse my experiences here.

**How much of your work involves counselling the
bereaved?**

GRACE: Surprisingly little. The bereaved tend to
buy into the mythology of the Festival. They need
to make an emotional investment in the idea of
a community made possible through sacrifice. In
their grief, Hampton people resist examination of
their real underlying motives.

Which are the same as your own, surely?

GRACE: I can't deny that. To get on. To advance a
career. To make money quickly. I won't apologise
for that. I don't see myself as morally superior
to the other people who have come here.

**But you are, as you say, "out to make a
killing"... Morally, your position's no different
from Richard Thompson's ...**

GRACE: That's an interesting question. On the
surface, I'd be inclined to agree. I'd have to
consider it more closely ... Just now, you must
excuse me. I've been keeping a client waiting.

13. NATALIE SHERRIN — BANK MANAGER — OCTOBER 30

We located Natalie in the extravagantly spacious foyer of The Hampton Bank ...

Was it opportunistic to establish a private bank in Hampton?

NATALIE: We were responding to a demand. It was a unique situation. In the early years of the Festival, there were lots of people from outside Hampton who wanted to invest in Hampton businesses, or wanted to set up business in Hampton to capitalise on the Festival ... Then you began to get a diametric shift. It only took twenty months for Hampton people to become so wealthy that they needed a bank which could respond to their specific investment needs.

There is a phenomenal amount of wealth here ...

NATALIE: Yes. It's like a small oil state, a Brunei or Kuwait, the only difference being that the wealth is more widely distributed here.

Can you put that wealth into some kind of perspective?

NATALIE: In ten years time, Hampton people will control ninety percent of the wealth in the State of Victoria ...

That would give Hampton an inordinate amount of political influence ...

NATALIE: Of course, small numbers of people have always exercised an inordinate amount of political and economic influence. It's the extreme convergence factor which makes this

situation distinct. If international tourism
to Hampton stopped, the State's finances would
collapse. There's an obvious imperative.

An imperative?

NATALIE: Hampton will have to extend its domain
to keep pace with its financial growth and
political influence.

**So you envisage that a suburban Festival of
Killing will eventually become a Melbourne
Festival of Killing as Hampton's investments come
to dominate the city?**

NATALIE: Dominate the State. Hampton will become
the seat of power. It's inevitable that Melbourne
will become as geographically subordinate to
Hampton as it is politically and economically
subordinate. A major realignment will take place.
Melburnians will fall under the extended control
of the Hampton administration, whether they
approve of the Festival or not.

**So it will become impossible for Melbourne people
to dissociate, even if they regard killing to be
morally indefensible?**

NATALIE: That's pretty much the case already.
Melbourne people depend on the killings as much
as the people in Hampton do. It's like living
in one of those cities on the Danube or the
Rhine. You cop the flow-on from what happens
upstream, whether you like it or not. When
you've got as much money as the Vatican, it's
virtually impossible not to invest in companies
which somewhere down the line produce weapons
and contraceptives ... You can't contain the

ramifications of something like the Hampton experiment. If you live in greater Melbourne, the Hampton Festival will change your life whether you approve of the killings or not ...

A Domino Principle ...

NATALIE: You want to be pure, but you can't insulate yourself from what's happening next door. Nation and contamination are two sides of the same coin.

But what would economic expansion or colonisation do to the unity of purpose in a small community like Hampton?

NATALIE: I'm a banker. My pragmatism inclines me to the view that community interests will always be subordinate to financial interests. There's so much myth-making that goes on here. When Hampton people rationalise the killings, they tell you that Hampton's no different to anywhere else ... And that's what I'd say too—Hampton's no different, except it's got this massive profit generating enterprise. And when that enterprise finally ceases to generate wealth, Hampton people will behave just like people everywhere else.

Early in the afternoon of October 30th, the sixth kill of the season took place. Marie Donkersloot, the mother of two school-aged children, was killed in her home, shot at close-range by a cross-bow bolt which penetrated her heart. Ironically, her husband Piers is a heart surgeon at Hampton's recently opened Community Hospital.

The conventions of the week-long period of mourning prevented us from interviewing Piers.

*He and his young family emigrated from South
Africa four years ago. The renovated and extended
weatherboard home in Mills Street which they
purchased for $812,000, had been sold at auction
for $288,000 just three years earlier.*

*Though allowed to film the funeral procession,
we were prevented from taking shots inside the
church or the cemetery. In order to keep faith
with the discretions which follow a killing,
Richard Thompson cancelled an interview which
had been arranged for November 3. Hampton people
also refused to be interviewed in the following
week. While schools close the day after each
killing, all businesses continue to operate,
reaping the benefit of money brought in by people
on pre-arranged package tours, and the thousands
of funeral junkies like the Englishwoman Rachel
Manzie ...*

14. RACHEL MANZIE—FUNERAL JUNKIE— NOVEMBER 4TH

We filmed Rachel, an Englishwoman in her late-fifties, in the street outside the Shrine of The Martyrs ...

You seem to enjoy the funerals?

RACHEL: This is my thirty-fourth. I've been to every funeral.

You fly in from Bath for each funeral?

RACHEL: They're extraordinary ... so moving. An unbelievable level of sacrifice. All thirty-four of these people bound together by their civic-mindedness.

And bound by a single killer?

RACHEL: Yes, that's right.

Are you a religious person?

RACHEL: Yes, very.

How can you reconcile your Christian convictions with this morbid celebration of killing ... with a man putting himself in the place of God?

RACHEL: Do you think that's what's happening?

What do you think is happening?

RACHEL: Something extraordinary, something magical. It's an appreciation. You'll feel it yourself when the preparations for the Festival begin ... In the next day or two, they'll start decorating the streets ... All the colour, the excitement and anticipation. It's like no place on earth. Your senses become rarefied,

appreciative. It's like the world must have been
at the outset. In Paradise. Euphoria occasionally
interrupted by the voice of God. It's a real
festival. It's very medieval. Where else would
you get a more powerful sense of God's presence
in the world?

**That's fine, so long as the autographed bolt of
lightning doesn't have your name on it ...**

RACHEL: I don't think you understand. I think you
have a problem with The Festival because you're
not a religious person ... You don't have a
cosmic intuition.

Why don't you come to live in Hampton?

RACHEL: I'm on the waiting list. But by the time
the opportunity comes around, I'll be sixty-five
or older, and beyond starting a business here.
It's business people they want in Hampton, not
potential Martyrs.

15. "MICHAEL" — PROFESSIONAL GAMBLER — NOVEMBER 5TH

Our meeting with 'Michael' was a breakthrough. Until then, we had only been able to find Hampton people who supported the Festival, or those who had mild reservations about the morality of the Festival. 'Michael' was able to lead us into the dark side of Hampton. Owing to his desire that his identity be kept secret, we promised that interview footage would not be released before the end of this year. The interview was filmed in a hotel room in Williamstown, a suburb across the bay from Hampton. Throughout the short session, 'Michael' wore a gorilla mask, and the audio quality was so poor that we will need to run subtitles over the footage.

How long have you been involved in gambling in Hampton?

"MICHAEL": I've had a casual interest since The Festival began, but in the last two years I've been pretty much full-time.

Do you make money?

"MICHAEL": I haven't cashed-in yet, but I make money. As a consultant mostly. I pass on my opinions and judgements. I make very few bets myself. You'll find that there are lots of people who'll bet on anything — The date of a killing. The hair colour of a victim. I prefer to observe and wait. The biggest part of a bet is choosing what to bet on. You have to keep things within your sphere of expertise. When I decide what it is I'm going to bet on, it's not a gamble anymore.

How do you do that?

"MICHAEL": I watch the Killer very carefully ...

Do you stalk him?

"MICHAEL": No. Of course, you have people who try
that. But they're kidding themselves. You've got
to read the Killer's personality. The important
thing is not to understand what he is or what he
does, but what he *thinks* he is, and how he wants
to be seen. He knows that he needs to be seen to
be impartial, but a question of nerve comes into
that. Even impartiality has a time-frame. You
ask yourself would he really be prepared to kill
three sixty year-olds, or three homosexuals in a
row, even if a random method told him he had to,
because by doing that he'd allow a *suspicion* of
partiality or prejudice sufficient to undermine
people's confidence in the Festival. Perception
is everything. He has to be constantly double-
guessing. The Killer has long-term considerations
and short-term ones, and there must be times when
these conflict. That's what I'm waiting for, the
moment of vulnerability, the loss of nerve or
self-belief. I'm slowly developing an intuition
with regard to his misgivings ... I keep a close
eye on what books and magazines he reads, and the
films he watches.

**I can imagine how you could find out what he's
buying, but how can you know what he reads, or
what he actually watches?**

"MICHAEL": There's always someone who has the
information you want, or someone who can get it
for you.

But how is it possible to regulate the gambling in Hampton if confidential information can be purchased?

"MICHAEL": It's not possible! The regulations are a fucking joke! I can't believe that people believe in a suburban council's capacity to regulate a gambling industry of this size. The whole Festival is corrupt. Hampton is owned by the crime bosses.

The Council?

"MICHAEL": Crime operates at every level. From the 'genuine' citizens who run shelter companies that expatriate profits to criminal organisations outside Hampton, to the councillors in the pay of developers ... Then there are the strictly illegal activities; protection rackets, money laundering, drug trafficking, prostitution ... It's all here. In a big way. The public want to see Hampton as a worthy social experiment, to see it as separate from the real world. The truth is, Hampton *is* the real world, only more so. Everything that's wrong and evil in the real world exists there in concentration ... Wherever you have big money, you will attract the interest of disreputable people who want a piece of the action.

How does organised crime corrupt The Festival?

"MICHAEL": Fear. Extortion. In hard dollar terms, tourism is just a piddle. The most lucrative part of the Festival is gambling, so that's also where Hampton is most vulnerable. As soon as the Festival proved itself to be a money-making concern, the Council found itself under threat

of terrorist attacks on the main tourist hotels.
What would you do?... You buy peace. And once
you've made a secret transaction to preserve the
integrity of your Festival, you set in motion
an endless series of extortions and pay-offs.
Not even the people who make the payments could
tell you how much of the income raised by the
Festival gets siphoned off to crime bosses in
other countries. It's like the island of Grenada
experimenting with socialism, and having its tiny
economy boycotted out of existence by the Yanks.
The Yanks couldn't afford the risk that socialism
might be seen to work, not at any level. Only a
naive community could imagine it would be able to
stand apart from the forces which infiltrate and
corrupt the world ... Look at the people on the
streets of Hampton. How many of them are locals,
how many are tourists, and how many are ghosts?

Ghosts?

"MICHAEL": Operatives, couriers, private
detectives, pimps, drivers, bodyguards, pushers,
bent detectives. The jolly suburb you see on the
surface is an illusion ... If Hampton ceases
to interest the big bosses, if the main game
moves elsewhere, then Hampton and its killing
spree will dissolve overnight ... How do you
think the legislation which allowed Hampton
to secede came into being? Not through demand
from the Australian public. Pockets were lined.
Inducements and advantages were made available to
Federal Politicians.

Why are you speaking to us?

"MICHAEL": I'm a gambler. I'm compulsive.

What are you going to bet on?

"MICHAEL": I'm betting that truth will catch up with the Killer.

Could you be more specific?

"MICHAEL": You might not know the truth when you're looking for it, but you'll always know the truth when you find it. Sooner or later, the Killer's going to see the gap between what he thinks he is, and what he is ...

And then what?

"MICHAEL": That's the question ... And then what?

16. "K" — PROSTITUTE — NOVEMBER 6TH

'Michael' put us into contact with 'K', a very articulate Japanese-American prostitute who has an Australian mother. We filmed her in the room of an expensive Hampton hotel where she conducts her business. Still in her early-twenties, she was very nervous and smoked throughout the interview. We shot 'K' in silhouette. Despite her Asian appearance, she has a pronounced American accent.

How long have you worked as a prostitute in Hampton?

"K": Three years.

Is prostitution common here?

"K": Officially, there's no prostitution in Hampton. Street prostitution's illegal and it's heavily policed.

Unofficially?

"K": It's rife. The brothels are highly organised. There's a trade-off between the crime bosses and the Hampton authorities. If you work for the right boss, the police look the other way.

The police have been corrupted?

"K": (LAUGHS LOUDLY) ... Everything here is bent! There's big money in Hampton. Rich tourists want girls. They expect to get whatever they're willing to pay for. Girls who have sex with you. Girls who will be filmed having sex with you. Girls that you can tie-up and torture ... Most of the girls are Asian. You get local girls, or girls from other parts of Australia trying to do business in Hampton, but it's dangerous if you're not tied to a big boss ... Girls just disappear.

Murdered?

"K": Sure.

By the crime gangs?

"K": By the police, by the gangs, same thing. Vice has to be kept concealed. Amateur prostitutes would draw people's attention to the possibility of corruption.

Have you been forced to work here?

"K": Not forced ... Coerced. I have expensive habits.

You could stop working if you wanted to?

"K": I wouldn't need to work if I didn't shoot smack. But I couldn't give up smack, give up work and expect to live. Girls are good business in Hampton. The people I work for don't like people messing with their revenue ... Hampton is supply and demand. There are plenty of people with lots of money to spend, and lots of them have exotic tastes. Young girls. Young boys. If you want something badly enough, there's someone here who can get it for you.

Drugs?

"K": Are you joking?... **(EMPHATIC)** The only reason they cover-up the prostitution's to mask the reality that the prostitutes are a cover for the crims who run drugs. Don't listen to what

people tell you ... You have no idea how much
money comes through this place. It's Fantasyland.
And your head has to be in Fantasyland to think
you can have this much money around and people
won't get bent. The Festival's about making money
by killing people. It's dirty money, so Hampton
people can hardly complain if there's dirty money
about.

So, everyone has a price?

"K": Well, yeah ... In my experience.

Could the Killer be bought off?

"K": Sure. But why would anyone want to? The
crime organisations don't *need* to buy the Killer.
They have everyone they need. Better to let
the Killer do his duty thinking that he's being
honourable. He kills all these people, but he
might be the most decent person in this town ...
Decent but dumb. Dumb enough to believe he's a
hero. That's all that matters to him.

17. RICHARD THOMPSON — MARIO'S RESTAURANT — NOVEMBER 7TH

We interviewed Thompson while he ate a large plate of fettuccini at Mario's, an elegant, old-fashioned Hampton restaurant. Thompson's personal assistant had told us that he had recently received bad news about the death of a friend overseas, but he displayed no sign of being distracted ...

Is it good?

THOMPSON: Mmm.

Are you a vegetarian?

THOMPSON: (MOUTH FULL) Not on your life.

We filmed your lecture ... This idea of tribalism ... Do you see yourself as the equivalent of a tribal witchdoctor?

THOMPSON: Well, I'm no anthropologist or sociologist. I'm more concerned with the kind of moral judgements which are made about the Killer's role, and this community, and the paradoxical situations of the people who make these judgements. I could understand people wanting to intervene if Hampton was in a constant state of civil conflict, or if Hampton people were crying out that they were being persecuted or coerced ... But where are the unhappy people? Think about it. Any Hampton person related to a Martyr could make a fortune by spilling their guts about the Killer or condemning the Festival ... Way more money than most could hope to gain commercially. So why don't they do it? We have a fixed set of laws that we as a society have agreed to. No community anywhere in the world has a greater sense of purpose of cohesion. The central tenet of our association is that seven citizens are killed each year. No one is forced to associate.

It's just that you raised the tribal thing, and I suppose that if you were looking to compare your tribe with an aboriginal tribe, you'd say that indigenous societies operated a system which was sustainable over a long period of time, but your system, killing for the entertainment of gamblers and tourists, it's much like the circus. Once the routine of The Festival becomes too familiar, or overexposed, the profitability of the operation must fall into decline. Already, you have the Hampton Festival being emulated in cities in Asia, and the former Eastern Bloc.

THOMPSON: I don't see the circus example as relevant. This is more a matter of ritual and tradition. Ceremony. To say that it's killing for entertainment is too reductive. Being the first Festival of Killing, we have every chance to outlast our imitators. **(PARODYING ADVERTISING SLOGAN)** Ours is the authentic Festival, recognised throughout the world.

I asked earlier if you thought that it was wrong to kill, and in your lecture you defended your role on pragmatic grounds, that every society has functionaries who make life or death decisions— What about your ideal philosophical position?

THOMPSON: I don't believe in black and white positions. Every situation is distinct. The rightness or wrongness is dictated by a specific context. We're nearly a century removed from Einstein, yet we're still struggling to deal with relativity. You won't find perfect resolution in Hampton, but you won't find it anywhere else either.

Could this relativism apply to a murder, to a crime of passion where a man murdered a lover who had disappointed or betrayed him?

THOMPSON: Your example's too vague. That's where the worst errors are made; categorisation, generalisation. Details are everything.

What happened to your friend Francesca Morricone?

THOMPSON: (MATTER OF FACT) Francesca vanished.

Was she murdered?

THOMPSON: Probably ... All I know is that she stopped writing to me.

Maybe she accidentally wandered into a communal society which permits the murder of seven strangers a year?

THOMPSON: (SOUR) What Freud says is true, a joke's only a joke when the audience laughs.

But that would be one of your paradoxical moral situations, wouldn't it, if the Killer, the white knight of society, turned out to be a base murderer ...?

THOMPSON: I didn't kill Francesca. I loved her. We had a falling out. She left for overseas. I expected her to write, but then the letters stopped. Something awful happened to her ...

Do you feel guilty?

THOMPSON: Yes, I do feel guilty. I might have said something, done something that drove her away. *Should* I feel guilty?... Being alive is a kind of complicity. We're all accomplices and collaborators in every foul deed.

Who are you?

THOMPSON: Who are you to ask?... Christine, you should tell me what distinguishes a journalist, a writer, a forensic pathologist, or an historian from a socially sanctioned killer. You've begun with the presumption that what I do is wrong. I could just as easily adopt a position which presumed that journalism, or pathology, or historical enquiry were morally abhorrent and unjustifiable. We're living in the quantum age. You've got to learn to love paradox.

It might be time for you to acknowledge what's going on around you ... We've spoken to people who've told us that the Hampton Festival is entirely corrupt; the Council and police are obedient to the interests of organised crime, Hampton businesses operate as fronts for drug and prostitution rackets, and Hampton traders are under the thumb of gangsters demanding protection money.

THOMPSON: Protection from me?

Protection from Mafia retribution ...

THOMPSON: Mafia! Yeah, right. Look, I don't know who you've been talking to, but, all this stuff ... It's puerile fabrication ... There've been

rumours of Mafia activity since Day One, but if
organised crime was here, I'd know about it. If
the Festival was known to be corrupt, the Killer
would be reviled, not celebrated. People would be
leaving in droves. It's all part of the game of
subversion. Outside business interests. Outside
pressure groups. They'll never leave us alone.
There are a tremendous number of people who want
to undermine the Hampton Festival. One of the
best ways for them to seize the moral high ground
is to employ agents of subversion. These people
slip out of the shadows to propagate the view
that Hampton is a secret Sodom and Gomorrah ruled
by fear, that Hampton folk are too frightened to
say what really goes on here. You'll end up being
very confused if you believe everything people
tell you in Hampton.

**Why wouldn't organised crime be attracted to
Hampton?**

THOMPSON: *You want to believe* that the Festival
could be corrupted or debased. That's been your
slant from the beginning ... Sure, there are
circumstances under which a Festival like this
could be corrupted. But what would that mean?...
Think about it ... It might mean that Hampton
people were too naive, that the Festival was ill-
conceived, or not worth the risk ... But it could
also mean that a good and harmonious society
is impossible to achieve, because corruption
and contamination are inevitable. That's what
you're saying. You're saying that evil and chaos
are irresistible forces in this universe ...
Of course, if you accept that, it follows that
you advocate a fatalistic policy of surrender,

that people shouldn't even *try* to construct a better version of society, because all your best intentions are sure to be foiled. Is that what you want, Christine?

I'm interested in the things that are actually happening here ...

As I began to make my point, there was a sequence of loud explosions in the street outside the restaurant ...

Jesus, what was that? A bomb?

The other restaurant patrons began to applaud wildly and burst into song ...

THOMPSON: No ...**(VERY AGITATED)** They're fireworks ...

Thompson moved away from the table, motioning for the maitre d', then requested that a telephone be brought to him.

What's going on?

THOMPSON: I don't know ... I'm sorry. I'll have to cut short the interview.

Is something wrong?

THOMPSON: The fireworks signal the seventh killing. It's the beginning of the Festival.

Has there been a seventh killing?

THOMPSON: Look, I'm sorry ...

We tried to follow Thompson as he was escorted away by the maitre d', but the kitchen door was closed on our camera.

Though it was eleven in the evening on a cool, wet night, crowds were flooding onto the streets, popping champagne corks, twirling brightly coloured umbrellas ... Bands were driven through the streets on the back of floats. People danced, and embraced, and drank. The night sky was filled with exploding fireworks and dueling laser lights.

Though we tried to follow Thompson's car, we lost him in the throng of people in the streets. Quite by accident, we came across a fleet of police and emergency vehicles in Chiselhurst Road, just as a body was being loaded into the back of an ambulance. We tried to approach the premises, only to be barred by police. From where I stood, I could see a pool of blood in the driveway of number fifteen. After several deflections, we were able to waylay Chief Inspector Ptsouris ...

18. INSPECTOR NICK PTSOURIS — SCENE OF KILLING — CHISELHURST ROAD, NOVEMBER 7TH

What's going on?

NICK: It appears that there has been a murder ... A young woman has been bludgeoned with an axe.

It's not the seventh killing?

NICK: No. We don't believe so ...

What about the fireworks?

NICK: A stuff-up. Our people were notified that the seventh killing had taken place.

Notified by the Killer?

NICK: Apparently not.

But there's a special phone. A code.

NICK: We'll have to look into that.

So someone's deliberately faked the seventh killing?

NICK: It appears that way.

As a practical joke? Sabotage?

NICK: Look, it could be any of a hundred things ... You'll have to excuse me. This is pretty deep shit.

You've spoken to Richard Thompson?

NICK: Briefly.

What did he say?

NICK: That he had nothing to do with any killing. It's too early for a start ... It's not even summer.

It has since come to light that the victim was the young prostitute Keiko Morimoto, daughter of the famous American performer Kohji Morimoto. She was murdered by a single killer, as yet unknown. The police believe that the murderer comes from outside Hampton. How the murderer obtained the Killer's codes has not yet been determined. There was no evidence of a break-in at Richard Thompson's home. Theoretically, the Killer's codes are known only to Thompson and the most senior police officials, though it is not inconceivable that they could have been obtained by security staff who guard Thompson's home.

Since no person or group has claimed responsibility for the murder as a deliberate attempt to sabotage the Festival, most speculation centres on the likelihood that the crime is connected to a betting plunge. It is widely rumoured that unusually large bets were placed on the day prior to the murder, and that many millions of dollars changed hands before the festivities were curtailed.

A more bizarre possibility is that the murder was the work of a psychotic copy-cat. The Hampton Police have since disclosed that an unpublicised murder took place in Orlando Street in March. At the time, they attributed the motive to burglary. Hampton residents have already set up a lobby group whose concern is to determine whether other crimes have been covered up as a concession to tourism and business.

For their own part, Hampton Council and its Tourist Authority are struggling to keep a lid

*on the ill-feeling engendered in Japan. Japanese
cancellations are said to be running at sixty per
cent. At the same time, Hampton officials need
to deal with feelings of bad faith among foreign
tour operators. The Hampton Tourism Authority
sells December as the most likely date for The
Festival. Even the possibility of a leakage into
November would be enough to make foreign operators
go cold on selling Hampton's Festival as a major
international event. Whatever the actual outcome,
this debacle has undermined confidence in the
ability of the current administration to organise
a multi-billion dollar event.*

*By far the most damaging rumour is that Richard
Thompson intends to resign as the Killer before
the seventh killing takes place. Thompson is
said to be dismayed either by revelations that
internal gambling interests were behind the
murder, or that a sequence of copy-cat murders
might jeopardise the social contract.*

*One cannot rule out the possibility Thompson was
behind the murder, using it as a shield to divert
our attention from the allegations of perversity
made against him.*

*Thompson failed to appear at an interview which
we had arranged for this morning.*

*His personal secretary indicated that Thompson
had been required to attend an urgent meeting
with The Mayor. We have rescheduled a meeting for
Tuesday.*

*I am trying to line-up interviews with the
Morimoto family. Kohji and Suzanne Morimoto will*

*arrive tomorrow to take Keiko's body back to San
Francisco.*

*Naturally, Michael, I will keep you informed of
any further developments.*

Christine Marker, November 10th.

The day after Christine Marker's transcripts were sent to London by International Courier, three members of her Channel 4 film-crew; Michael Tynan, Penny Donaldson, and Gillian Chatterton, were found murdered in their hotel rooms. Each had been bound with cord before having their throat cut. Christine Marker had vanished. Bloodstains in Marker's room were consistent with her having been executed in a manner similar to her colleagues.

The initial Inquest presided over by the Hampton Coroner, Helen O'Brien, determined that the crimes were highly likely to have involved Hampton's Killer, Richard Thompson. Forensic experts argued that bloody footprints found at the crime scene were produced by a pair of white Diadora sports shoes found in Richard Thompson's bedroom.

The subsequent Elliot Commission, while not absolving Thompson, found that there had been serious irregularities in the conduct of the coronial inquiry. Elliot criticised the failure to have the forensic evidence examined by an independent agency. Too much weight had been given to testimony that the letter written by the person purporting to be Morimoto's killer[2] was the product of Richard Thompson's desktop printer. That of itself was far from sufficient to establish Thompson's involvement in the conspiracy to kill Morimoto. In Elliot's view, the murders of the documentary crew were likely the work of as many as six assailants. Elliot dismissed as not credible the evidence of three eye-witnesses who previously testified to having seen Richard Thompson in the vicinity of the crime scene late on the evening of November 11.

The most recent Witherspoon Commission found that the murders and disappearances were the result of a criminal

---

2 The "33 With a Bullet" letter is reproduced in the Appendices

conspiracy involving officers of the Hampton Council, the Hampton Internal Security Unit, the Central Intelligence Agency of the United States, and Australian operatives in the employ of international crime organisations.

The Witherspoon Commission ordered that Lorraine di Stasio, the former Mayor of Hampton, Wendy Billingsley, the former C.E.O. of the Hampton Tourist Authority, Inspector Nick Ptsouris, Chief of the Hampton Internal Security Unit, and Raymond Gillespie, Hampton Gambling Ombudsman be indicted on charges of having conspired to murder Keiko Morimoto, Penny Donaldson, Michael Tynan, Gillian Chatterton and Christine Marker. The Commission also determined that there was sufficient evidence for di Stasio, Billingsley, Gillespie, and Ptsouris to be indicted on charges of having conspired to murder Richard Thompson.

In stating his final recommendations, Justice Witherspoon expressed the view that, on the basis of the evidence put before his Commission, it was impossible to establish the extent of Richard Thompson's knowledge of or involvement in criminal activity in Hampton.

(ii)

THE PRINCE

RICHARD THOMPSON'S JOURNAL

To those seeing and hearing him, [the prince] should appear a man of compassion, a man of good faith, a man of integrity, a kind and religious man ... Everyone sees what you appear to be, few experience what you really are ...

... it cannot be called prowess to kill fellow citizens, to betray friends, to be treacherous, pitiless, irreligious. These ways can win a prince power but not glory.

—*The Prince,* Niccolo Machiavelli, 1513

The October segment of Richard Thompson's journal almost defines the word controversial. Not since the banning of Phillip Roth's novel *Portnoy's Complaint* have so many Australians held an opinion about a work so few have had the chance to read.

Initially, heated debate surrounded the authenticity of the document. Hampton's Coroner, Helen O'Brien, found it suspicious that Thompson should have commenced a separate volume for the crucial October-November period when all previous volumes of Thompson's journal had spanned entire calendar years.[3] Was the document genuine? What was its author playing at?

The debate at the subsequent Elliot and Witherspoon Inquiries shifted from questions of authorship to questions of authorial intent. How reliable was Thompson as a narrator of his day-to-day experiences? Were his entries sincere or cynical? The pro-Thompsonites hold that the journal proves Thompson's innocence, while their opponents argue that Thompson has skillfully designed a journal to create an alibi for his criminal complicity.

We do know Richard Thompson was bound by his contract with Hampton Council not to speak, act, or write in a manner that might compromise the Killer's methodologies.

As a consequence, many legal and professional minds have scoured this disarmingly modest and removed memoir in the hope of uncovering a key to Thompson's actual opinions. Most of Thompson's intimates insist this cigar is nothing more than a cigar. Others argue their belief that Thompson actually kept a second, frank journal (possibly on disc) which recorded the

---

3   Readers wishing to examine the previous volumes of Thompson's journal are advised to read Miranda Murray's *If Looks Could Kill: The Diaries of Richard Thompson.*

Killer's activities and private thoughts in fine detail. No physical evidence has emerged to support the existence of a second journal. However, both Commissions were keen to emphasise that Thompson wrote all his correspondence on personal computer, and that the discs containing that correspondence have disappeared, presumably removed at the same time Thompson vanished.

Did Thompson use his hand-written journal to construct an elaborate front? His extreme naivety often seems to be at odds with his intelligent self-consciousness. Toying with ambiguity and ambivalence, Thompson frequently meditates on the possibility of constructing an alternative version of himself through a fictional journal. The Elliot and Witherspoon Commissions spent a total of eight months debating just how artful, careless, innocent, or cynical Thompson may have been in his choice of words or subject matter. His every phrase was examined for a subtext, alternative meaning, or pointed shift of tone. Thompson's journal seemed to beg the interpretation of forensic experts, psychiatrists, and literary scholars, and the Commissioners duly sought those interpretations.

Richard Thompson's inelegant prose has become the most scrutinised in modern Australian literature. Yet none of the experts have been able to finally determine Thompson's narrative situation or intent, nor have they been able to interpret his journal in such a way as would establish his guilt or innocence beyond reasonable doubt.

Concentration on legal and ethical matters has tended to overshadow reappraisal of the Killer's character. The most commonly accepted view is that Richard Thompson was well-meaning but ingenuous.

I share the view expressed by Laura Moore in her book *Cannibalism for Beginners*. Though Thompson found persuasive justifications for his actions, he was preoccupied with the impression he made, and his charm acted to mask dishonest and self-aggrandising tendencies. Moore argues that Thompson suffers from an extreme narcissistic disorder—his self-love in competition with an equally rampant self-loathing.

According to Moore, Thompson also confuses virtuosity—the effective performance of his duties—with virtue, or moral excellence. In the journals we see Thompson attempt to persuade himself that he is an author, and his 'authorisation' entitles him to dispose of minor characters at will. If the killings were intended to unite the Hampton community, they also provided a means by which Thompson could set himself apart from his fellow citizens. I am inclined to regard this distancing process as a measure of Thompson's unconscious contempt for those who chose to trust and revere him.

The journalist Michael Phillips claims that he once asked Thompson whether the Killer ought to be excluded from the random method by which martyrs are chosen, to which the Killer responded, 'What purpose is served by treating the shepherd as one of the sheep?'[4] Whether or not Phillips quotes Thompson accurately, the statement is consistent with the Thompson that we encounter in this volume. The final installment of his journal reveals a character whose interests and ambitions are more aristocratic than democratic. Thompson constructs himself as a non-elected head of state; The Prince who bestows favour or disfavour. His fatal inability to predict, recognise, or confront the criminality enveloping his office are in large part a consequence of his desire to place himself above the political fray. Hence Thompson's disinclination to challenge expected but unenforceable discretions in his private journal. Thompson is not merely protecting the Killer's secret methodology, he is protecting palace secrets. He celebrates his superior otherness.

---

4   Michael Phillips, "The Dark Shepherd" in Russell/Campbell (ed) *Approximate Life: The Enigma of Richard Thompson*. Miranda Murray disputes the attribution of this statement to Thompson, arguing that it is uncharacteristically arrogant. Murray believes the statement was made by Wendy Billingsley, and that Billingsley was mistakenly presumed to have been quoting Thompson. See intro. to *If Looks Could Kill*.

Clearly, any reading of Thompson's journal must be coloured by knowledge of subsequent events, and my views are at odds with some respected scholars who see Thompson as not merely a folk hero, but a modern literary hero, an author who demonstrates phenomenal wit and honesty. He is often spoken of as someone who seems to be writing against the tradition of the disingenuous, self-serving memoirs so regularly produced by Australian heroes, most notably the heroes of Australian sport.

At least a wider public now has the opportunity to examine the final segment of Thompson's journal and to construct its own version of its author (or authors).

The reader may now ask, Who is this Killer? Are these the meditations of a foolish egotist, a madman, or an heroic visionary? How genuine is this man who seems so obsessed with the possibility of heroic action, and the myths surrounding his own heroic status? Or are these journal entries merely the calculations of a murderer who seeks to veil his crimes by pretending to be a latter-day Camus?

OCTOBER

I want to be away from here, to be in Paris at New Year, eating crepes from corner stalls, able to look at people without having to imagine whether I will hear their last words. To eat pastries and drink wine and move freely without scrutiny. To find a place where I can be outside of myself ... Is it true that the Russian Csar Peter the Great once threw a New Year's Eve party that only ended when all the food and grog ran out in April?

.

According to a radio commentator, the killings are a hoax. This theory has it that the so-called Martyrs have been 'disappeared' to some comfortable foreign outpost where they're sustained by secret bank accounts. I don't understand why people are so determined to fly in the face of reason, why they need to construct these metaphoric heavens and after-lives.

.

Some training as a clown would have been invaluable. During a photo-call at Disney's, the German photographer was dissatisfied with the conventional poses. 'Can I ask you now to—how do you say?—*juggle* the weapons?' I see this man at Yalta with Stalin, Churchill, and Rooseveldt—'If it's not too much to ask, would you mind making for me a human pyramid?' Churchill passes his cigar to an aide as he gets down on all fours ... Then there are the people, and I'm not just talking about tourists, who expect me to speak every known language. Assuming that the Killer must have extraordinarily qualifications, they approach me speaking Greek or Urdu, convinced that I will understand them. Languages and formal qualifications were never mentioned at the interview. The panel already knew that I'd been an English teacher. I do recall Tom Mitchell[5] asking, 'Have you ever had any psychiatric illnesses?' 'Would it help if I had?'

I was surprised that my smartarsery stopped them from pursuing the question. Maybe it didn't matter to the Council that their Killer was a psychopath, so long as he signed autographs, posed for photos, and didn't *look* like a psychopath, all wild-eyed and foaming at the mouth—Jack Nicholson in overdrive.

.

Justine S.[6] has written again saying that she is prepared to offer two million for a 60,000 word memoir. She will send a writer to ghost it if I prefer. She doesn't make clear what kind of autobiography she has in mind. Perhaps she wants a quickie after the fashion of the books written by sporting champions; the usual fake modesty and measured self-denigration—'Did I tell you how me and the boys went out an' got totally ratshit after I'd strangled my old primary school teacher?'—I could betray a few locker-room confidences—'Say, did I tell you the one about the European leader who offered me an honorary doctorate from an esteemed institution if I would supply him with a videotape of one of the killings?' ... *So long as the victim is a young girl, you understand.*'—I could write a memoir full of all that Boys'-Own

---

5   Tom Mitchell, Acting Education Officer, Hampton City Council. Mitchell's older brother, Mark, was killed in particularly dramatic circumstances in the second year of the Festival.

6   Justine Scott of Baird Publishing. In testimony before the Elliot Commission, Scott denied offering Thompson two million dollars for his memoirs. Scott was subsequently convicted of perjury when the letter detailing a two million dollar offer surfaced. She was gaoled for six weeks.

stuff (*The Bumper Boys' Book of Killing*?), about how the job got too much for me, how I wanted to throw in the towel, but somehow managed to hang on in there to make the best killings of my career. Of course, it never does to boast in a sporting autobiography, or to set yourself up as some kind of high achiever. Everything has to be reduced to the natural, to be depicted as something any ordinary bloke could have done if he'd been put in the same position. Sporting memoirs are a guilty pleasure of mine. I read them the same way that academic friends like to read crime fiction, or romantic novels. In a sporting memoir, you'll find more between the lines about what Australians imagine it is to be Australian, or to be heroic, than you'll find in most serious historical or sociological explorations of the national psyche. They always contain the same anti-authoritarian gungho about how an inept administrator tried to deprive the champ of sporting immortality, only for will, guts, and talent to finally surmount these obstructions. The truth is that there is nothing particularly heroic in what I do. Why should I write about it? To what extent should an intelligent man be complicit in the creation of his own myth, or an uncritical addition to the national myth?

.

I once wanted to believe that I was invincible, that I could alter anything through force of will, that I could change the world so that I would be relocated at its heart. This need for invulnerability had less to do with having power to effect change than it had with the desire to feel that I was absolutely necessary. I wanted to believe I had been willed into being for a specific purpose. Then I realised that the essential thing was the part which had been written for me, and that part would annihilate 'Richard Thompson'. I am subservient to the role I play. Beyond that role, I am nothing.[7]

.

A piece of graffiti scrawled on the bakery in Thomas Street:

HOW WOULD YOU RECOGNISE TRUE EVIL?

A radio talkback host once asked me to define true evil, and the only thing that came to mind was beetroot. Beetroot is evil. Not the flavour so much as the combination of that colour and texture. If you want to make the world a happier place, you could start by eradicating beetroot.

.

I'm fat. I've put on two kilos in the past two months, and seven since I took the job. Too many functions, too much wine. I wonder would Hampton tolerate a Killer who didn't match the desired image; an active, youthful man who can be projected positively to the tourist market? A fat, slovenly Killer would look too immoral. A flabby Killer would look like someone who might get pleasure from the act of killing. If you are slim and you've got a good smile, you can sell anything to people educated to buy things sold by happy slim people. All the initial market research indicated that people wouldn't accept a female killer. It violated their expectation that an admirable woman—whatever her achievements in other fields—was one who was still primarily concerned with caring and nurturing. For fairly obvious reasons, it wouldn't have done to choose a black, or someone from an ethnic or religious minority. What is it about the WASP

---

7   Could Thompson, with his acute understanding of irony, really believe this? So much of The Killer's journal suggests a determination to manufacture a heroic myth that transcends subservience to an understood role or function.

male that makes people feel comfortable to see him as a Killer?

.

When I reminded Jane S.[8] she'd promised to have dinner with me, she became nervous and fumbled for excuses; the age difference, how she ought to be studying. None of that seemed to matter when we kissed outside the Gallery after the Kandinsky exhibition. I should have taken her home and ravished her then, when my nostrils were full of her scent, but impulse has never been my strong suit. Everything about this life is premeditated: plots and rehearsals. Jane said she didn't think she could cope with the attention. And I couldn't pretend there wouldn't be attention. As if the press could ignore the Killer's relationship with a sixteen-year old girl. One of the things which attracts me to Jane is how little my notoriety impresses her ... I guess that I've been expecting too much, hoping for a (what do you call it?) 'normal sex life'. This is no 9–5 job, but a weird priesthood. Even if celibacy is not asked or expected of me, how is it possible not to be celibate? Killing someone you were involved with, or had been involved with, would be too much like killing.[9]

.

Millicent Mathews from Kaleidoscope Books called. They are compiling an anthology of stories written by non-literary (illit-

---

8   Jane Stevenson was one of Thompson's few romantic interests during his term as Hampton's Killer. In fact, she was already eighteen years old, and denied having told Thompson she was younger. The psychiatrist Dr Pamela Woodland testified that it would not be inconsistent for a man of Thompson's apparent sexual immaturity to flatter himself by suggesting the power to seduce an under-age girl.

9   Woodland argues that Thompson's resistance to sexual entreaties had less to do with moral strength and integrity than it had with his desire to be seen as a latter-day Ghandi.

erate?) celebrities, and she wants me to contribute. I told her that time-demands would make it impossible to write anything new, but she might be interested in a story that I wrote while I was at university, *Schrodinger Puts Out the Cat*. I shouldn't have spoken without checking to see if I still have a copy of the story. Worse, I now recall what the story was about, and worry it might be too revealing when published in a context where it would be read as a sequence of clues and signifiers to the true nature of the Killer's personality ... The first-person narrator of the story is an inveterate peeping Tom, expert at concealing himself on verandas and balconies. Though he has become disenchanted with the banality of suburban sex, he is unable to rid himself of his voyeuristic habits. Only when he is at home after the event does he masturbate, during an idealised mental reconstruction of the sex he's witnessed. One night, he happens upon an extraordinary couple whose sexual activity takes the form of a bizarre ceremonial display. Circumnavigations, taunts, and teases, accompanied by a recitation of erotic poetry, culminating in a fuck of breathtaking intensity. Excited and beguiled by the strange beauty of their lovemaking, the narrator returns to their balcony night after night, to be further astounded by their inventiveness and orgasmic perfection. Eventually he becomes plagued by the thought that he is no longer an independent witness, that he has become an element in their performance. He thinks it possible that they are not only aware of his presence, but the success of their performance *depends* on his observation and approval. To declare himself would be to risk snapping the thread, but he has to know whether these extravaganzas exist independent of his gaze. Finally, he decides to pay a young man to peer into the lovers' bedroom and report back to him. As the narrator sits in a bar, waiting for this report, he becomes overwhelmed with remorse. What if some kind of inauthenticity should reveal itself to his third party? What if their divine love-making did not touch or impress his agent? Or worse, what if his agent did something to contaminate or terminate this display of sexual pageantry? As I recall, the story concludes with the increasingly drunk narrator trying to decide whether to kill his messenger before or after he reports what he has seen ... Tell me, what would the psychiatric world say when they read of this early fascination with dispassionate killing, with a rehearsed association between killing and alienated sexuality?[10] I think it might be best to search out an essay that I wrote in high school, one of those innocent, ineffectual T.V. parodies that everyone wrote.

.

A word or two must be said about the new toilets at the Gallery of Modern Art. These toilets would flush away an elephant. The power of the torrent is astonishing. You half expect to see honeymooners in anoraks having their photograph taken next to the flush. (Are the Gallery management passing their judgement about the patrons of modern art, their capacity to digest anything?) Still recovering from the violence of this flush, you are unprepared for hand-dryers which char-braise your palms with the ferocity of a dragon snort. Squealing pain. In the cafeteria, you see men with their palms wrapped around glasses of iced water, and you know that, like you, they made the mistake of not using the towels. In this age of superheroes, this convenience is not so much a toilet for men, as a toilet for the Man's Man (designed by Gordon Liddy).

.

---

10 Millicent Mathews testified that Thompson never replied to her request, and no physical evidence of this *Schrodinger* story has been discovered. When arguing the case that Thompson was involved in Hampton's criminal conspiracy, Mark Lipstein suggested that this story is the first evidence of Thompson using a plant. According to Lipstein, Thompson wrote this volume of the journal specifically to invent a hyper-ironic version of himself in order to conceal his criminal intent.

Exactly what is it with these deadshits at the Tourist Authority? They're like zombies, restlessly counter-productive. Now their deadheadedness has given rise to a new promotional idea, HAMPTON: CITY OF DEATH. I had a letter from Wendy Billingsley. Would I support the concept of setting up Catacombs beneath the Sillitoe Reserve? Long underground tunnels would give visitors the chance to view the skeletal remains of The Martyrs. Wendy wouldn't have proposed anything so outrageous if she'd actually visited the Catacombs in Paris. There you see the neatly stacked bones of thousands of ancient Parisiens. Long, tall rows of anonymous skulls and thighbones. You couldn't look at that undifferentiated mortality, the nobles stacked with the peasants, and imagine that anything in life amounted to a hill of beans (or even a hill of bones). And you wonder how those eighteenth century Parisiens would have responded to ad agency fuckwits telling them that Catacombs were the way to go, that a City of Death had enormous tourist potential. 'It may sound sick and morbid to you now, King Louis, but think long term. Visualise the big picture.'

.

Saw HP with his wife J., and their two daughters in Ludstone Street. They seem like the perfect young family now. He is on the board at the brewery, having made his reputation (and fortune!) marketing The Killer's Beer. J. seemed embarrassed by HP's reluctance to speak to me. What she doesn't know is that, in the second year of the Festival, her husband offered me a six-figure sum to make J. one of The Killer's victims. HP stood there scuffing his foot on the footpath, trying not to make eye contact. 'They sure are terrific kids,' I say. 'You should come around for dinner one night,' J offered, 'H is always talking about you.' And I might take her up on that too, just to make the prick squirm ... What joy work would be if I could devote myself to terminating the deserving.

.

Sarah[11] tells me that numerologically I am a seven, and sevens are on an emotional and physical low at the moment. Though I don't subscribe to any of that crap, I *am* on a low. Tracey[12] once described me as an ecstatic pessimist, a self-fulfilling prophet of doom. Maybe my autobiography should detail an intended future. A 200 page list of predictions, desires, and fears: the antithesis of the celebrity listing his or her accomplishments ... The first *prescriptive* autobiography. 'When I least expect to find romance, a door will open to reveal a slim auburn-haired girl whose silky voice ...' etc. I like the idea already. Sometimes I seem to have power over my own destiny the way that I have the power to curtail people's lives. So what prevents me from believing in my freedom to be happy?

.

There is an old song that I can't stop humming, an early single by E.L.O. One of the lines is 'I can't get it out of my head,' but that's not the name of the song,[13] and I'm sure that most of the words I sing have no relation to the original. I need to be careful. On the day that I killed AK, my head was fixed on The Smiths' song 'Big Mouth Strikes Again', and now I can't hear the song without seeing her long red hair dangling beneath the pillow, and her legs kicking till the life was drained from them. Music becomes inextricably associated with strong emotions. *A Clockwork Orange* was like that. Hampton people are amused

---

11 Sarah. Unknown. Possibly Sarah Nixon, the wife of one of Thompson's security guards.

12 Presumably Tracey Harnett, Thompson's lover more than a decade earlier. Harnett had been one of Christine Marker's interview subjects. (See interview 8.)

13 The Electric Light Orchestra song *is* 'Can't Get it Out of My Head'.

that their killer is so fond of alternative music, but what would happen if every song I ever loved became associated with a killing?

.

Wendy B.[14] sent over a videotape of a new Japanese cartoon series, *K for Killer*, apparently based on my activities. Naturally, this animated Killer has Asiatic features, is physically exceptional, is exceptionally polite to children, and has (for English-speaking audiences) a dubbed American accent. 'Remember kids, we're all in this together!' The cartoon Killer seems to possess a telepathic skill which enables him to determine who *deserves* to die. He waits for a crowd to assemble around his newest corpse so that he can deliver a homily. He is a ridiculously authoritative, moral superhero, a man who knows no fear. It's difficult to imagine him being troubled by doubts or dreams.

.

I often wish I wasn't so even-tempered. It's not that I don't feel anger, I have no way of expressing anger that makes my infuriations sound reasonable. I'm certainly not spontaneous. What could be healthier than to express anger when anger is appropriate? The problem is, people have learnt to read my personality. They know how to get right up my nose. Like Andrew Dawson and his smartarse letters. Andrew was in the year ahead of me at Hampton High—a smug, spoilt prick even then, forerunner of the smug Yuppies that virtually strangled Hampton, the middle class who thrived enough to betray their middle class values. Andrew went on to study law, and lives in Sydney, doing remunerative work for the Australian-based multination-

---

14 Wendy Billingsley, Hampton Tourist Commissioner, later charged
    with conspiring to murder Richard Thompson.

als who fuck-up the South Pacific. Neither the nature of his work, nor the fact of his Double Bay mansion, have hindered Andrew's rise within the Labor Party executive, and I'd guess that I've received six letters from Andrew every year since the inception of the Festival. Party letterhead, of course. To begin with, he used to describe me as a grubby parasite, a sexual deviant, and an officer of the economic S.S. But when I refused to bite, he shifted to a more subtle, 'constructive' tack. Why can't I see that my community-conscious rhetoric, and superficial idealism, amounts to an abandonment of *genuine* idealism, that I have not only given (tacit) support to the economic rationalism that's smothering traditional Australian values, I have become the apotheosis of economic rationalist fantasy?—As if fucking hypocrites like Andrew ever did a thing to oppose the sovereignty of economic rationalism within his Party, or in his own life. Did Andrew stand in front of the bulldozers as the guts were ripped out of egalitarianism, the bulldozers that ploughed through everything that once symbolised the (lost) Australian middle class, like the old Southern Stand at the Melbourne Cricket Ground, or our old high school, more to the point? If Hampton now stands at the apex of a money society where the one sacred belief is that there is no such thing as bad money, then the acceptability of that view was made possible by the treachery of the *nominal* socialists, the wolves in their imported suits. It really pisses me off. I'd earn not one tenth what Andrew Dawson does, but I am the class traitor. For caring about people? For caring about the Hampton Community, and the need to act decently according to the wishes of that community? I remember things that fuckwit Andrew with his 'acceptable eight or nine per cent unemployment' would never remember. I remember Hampton before its gentrification, when Hampton was the absolute exemplar of middle class suburban life in Australia. This was before the people who prospered from that life turned on it—their insecurity and spiritual vacuity manifest in the status symbols they bought: the expensive foreign cars, the tasteless mansions. The state schools which had been good enough for them weren't good enough for their own children, weren't *exclusive* enough. A state school education wouldn't tell the world they had money to buy the best that money could buy. I cried when the bulldozers demolished Hampton High. I finally had some notion then of what sacred sites mean to aboriginal people, that it's a sin to desecrate a site of knowledge and initiation. Those sites have an energy which will never dissipate. Even before there was any talk of festivals, I knew that I wanted to retrieve for this community the idea of Community, to remind them of the *need* for Community before the meaning of the concept was entirely buggered by money-cynicism, and status obsession, and exclusivity. It's all very well for fat arsehole poseurs like Andrew Dawson to say that my success has been to rationalise a community of true economic rationalism, a suburb of economic tyrants. He doesn't live among people. He doesn't know what it is to be touched by people, and to be needed by people. His grand sentiments are just the mask worn by The Apparatus. If he knew people, Hampton people, he'd never dare say that the person who finally assassinates Richard Thompson 'will come from Hampton, and the assassin of the Killer will be a true hero of our times.'

·

Every day the task is to recover the meaning of things, to restore the meaning of things, to define and redefine, to make sense, and give sense to things, to battle against the habit of just being, just doing. It's the battle against chaotic meaninglessness, against being overpowered by ripples set in motion by a butterfly fart in Kalimantan ...

·

A lobby group in New York has started a rumour that a disproportionate number of Hampton's victims have been gay, lesbian, or bisexual, and that the Hampton Killing Festival is a front for a right-wing Final Solution. I would have thought these claims were so ludicrous that no one could possibly take them seriously, but the phones haven't stopped ringing. 'Why do you kill gays?' 'Are all Australians violent fuckin' homophobes?' 'Did your daddy wupp you when you wuz a boy?' (Definitely not whipped, *whupped*!) 'Are you a latent homosexual?' I wanted to answer that I am a closet heterosexual, but the headline would write itself, KILLER FUCKS VICTIMS IN CLOSET.[15] When the Council decided against having an anonymous Killer, it hoped everything would be up-front, that their openness would counteract innuendo and rumour of this kind. Now I find that having made no secret of my identity, I have new secret identities fabricated for me every week. If I were to open my memoir with the line, 'My parents brought me up on a diet of human flesh ...', (a show-stopper of an opening line, admittedly) half the population of the planet would turn to their friends and say, 'There, it was obvious all along he was a cannibal.' The more truthful you seek to be, the more people will suspect that you are concealing something.

·

Maybe there is only a finite number of gazes or perceptual dispositions, sixteen or eighteen, like camera settings, and all your thoughts, memories and perceptions are connected by these possible ways of experiencing the world.

---

15   These observations provoked extended debate at the Elliot Commission, with at least three psychiatrists prepared to argue the case for overstrenuous (Freudian) denial, suggesting that Thompson was precisely what he what he was denying, a latent homosexual and a homophobe. Witherspoon later rejected this as a 'convoluted attempt to establish a psychopathology for Thompson which has no basis in hard evidence'.

.

They sicken me, the Virginia Woolfs and Kafkas who kept the most exquisite, closely observed journals for years. Never a weak sentence. Months of astute, microscopic observations to complement their mastery of tone and narrative situation. In their journals, even the most mundane predicament was full of possibility and insinuation. Here I am, an authorised killer, a man who has ended the lives of more than thirty individuals, and yet I would be incapable of describing what it is that I do, even if discretion allowed me to. I can say nothing, write nothing that places my methods at risk. Yet a Woolf or a Kafka, faced with the same limitations, would still find a way to state the essential. They'd create a metaphoric world. You would know from the unsaids, the scrupulously chosen verbs, tenses, and clauses, what it is to exercise a unique sanction, to be the banal face of horror, the repossession man. Every night, they would compose a string of terrific sentences, assembling the ingredients which would one day become a perfect work of art. For whom does a diarist write? Do I write for myself, thirty years hence, a jaded ex-killer retired to a country estate in Ireland? Do I address myself to the burglar who hopes to sell this diary to a German magazine? Or do I speak to something much more abstract, Posterity? I write because I want to explore the limits of what I can and can't write, to find a way beyond the prohibitions and limitations that come with being a living legend made legendary by death.

.

Favourite Foods (as requested by *The Hampton Bugle*)

Suishi
Fried eggs on (burnt-ish) buttered toast.
Muesli (with yoghurt)

Crisp roast duckling in plum sauce.
Swiss chocolate, and Belgian chocolate truffles.
Grilled barramundi.
Jelly babies, snakes, killer pythons, milk bottles etc
Mushroom risotto
Steamed broccoli
Bacon and avocado bagels

In the past week, I've received 246 items of mail. That's more than average, but correspondence tends to increase as the Festival approaches. At least two-thirds is requests for autographs or photographs. Generally, there will be four or five requests for a souvenir from one of the Martyrs. There are invitations to openings, to private parties, approaches for product endorsements, and political endorsements, and requests for charitable appearances; fete openings, hospital visits, even 'Could you sing at our karaoke night?' (What do you think, the Talking Heads' number *Psycho Killer*?) There was a request to appear in a charity cricket match for cancer research, 'Husbands versus The Bachelors '... The World Wildlife Fund wanted to know if I could help out with their new Giant Panda breeding program. I'm not so sure that their efforts on behalf of endangered species would necessarily benefit from an association with a notorious hired killer. Still, I sent them a poem written while I was at high school.

The Black and White Rag

All the forms of propaganda
Invoke a world
Of black and white
Just like a panda.
(And who doesn't like a panda?)

> Monochromal cuddly cute
> They spend their days on bamboo shoots
> Till the last shoot's been shot,
> Then pandas can curl up in the cot
> Just like a cuddly toy
> (And who doesn't like ... etc?)[16]

I get bundles of mail from women who want to sleep with me, saying God has decreed we should sleep together. Letters from women who want to save me. (Probably by sleeping with me.) Every week for the past two years, one young man from Auckland, has sent me a sealed plastic bag containing his semen. Well, I assume the semen is his. He and his friends may take a collection ...[17] This week, I received seven death threats, four copies of the Bible, and an album of photos taken in Belsen immediately after the liberation. I am being prayed for. Yet, I'm also told to be wary of a French-speaking assassin hired by the Vatican. One father wrote that he would be grateful if I could give his fifteen-year old son work experience. 'He is strong, discreet, and thorough.' (I should recommend him to my Auckland correspondent!) I am always receiving gratuitous psychiatric advice.—I should tell them that my desire to kill is a consequence of my daddy 'wupping' me when I was a boy. It wouldn't annoy me so much if these psychiatrists were asking for information to help them learn from my experiences. (One Indian doctor did ask whether I'd ever had 'an unwarranted erection' while strangling or smothering a victim? What on earth does a *warranted* erection look like, and how could an erection be 'warranted' in those circumstances?) Mostly, I'm assailed with

---

16 The World Wildlife Fund denied having received this poem. Thompson was notoriously slow in dealing with correspondence. WWF now intend to use the poem in campaign advertising.

17 In her testimony before the Elliot Commission, Thompson's personal secretary Astrid de Groot denied having seen these semen donations. She was later charged with conspiring to murder Thompson.

learnedness, surmise and arrogance. *What you really want is ...
You are suppressing your essential need to ... You suffer from the delusion that you can kill with impunity.* Not that all the experts oppose my chosen profession. Dr Stella Bronowski of Maryland tells me that she has nearly completed her study *Killing as Catharsis* ... On the one hand, I am a model citizen, on the other, I am a model psychopath ... I am asked to help with homework projects in Budapest. I receive suggested methods for future killings—some of them remarkably ingenious. I receive recipes for cakes and casseroles, business propositions, dozens of begging letters. Sometimes I feel like I have my head stuck through the centre of a target, and I'm being pounded with wet sponges ...'If you don't mind me saying so, you should dress better. Blacks and whites make you look so pallid and drained. You need bright colours.'

.

I should write this book. I've been sleepwalking for too long. A disorganised pursuit like journal writing fails to clarify things. You pose the question, and then avoid the difficulty of seeking to answer it. A structure would force me to attend to the matters I have avoided in these pages ... *Why did I back out of killing X?* Was it, as I persuaded myself, that there would be no opportune moment, (when my job is to contrive opportune moments) or was it cowardice: that I feared the consequences? A dutiful Killer must be prepared to die carrying out the duties of the office. It's one thing to rationalise my position by saying that I am under constant threat from enemies, assassins and psychopaths, I have a duty to defend the integrity of my position. Not all threats are overt. The public is told that my parents and family live outside of Hampton because I cannot be compromised in terms of my choice of victim. They have not been told that my family lives in exile, with changed appearances and identities, in order to save my office from the threat of blackmail by organised crime. I believe in the Festival, and the critical importance of my agency, but in ideal terms Hampton is only the barest approximation of the Utopian society it presents to the public gaze. Only the most naive person subscribes to the notion of absolute purity, that you can dissociate yourself entirely from the vast, corrupt forces which surround you, that you can build a Utopian civilisation on an island in the middle of a cess pit.[18] Every reality is a flawed approximation of the ideas which brought it into being. I like the notion of approximation. To approximate is to assert your inability to arrive at the Truth. You fashion a poetry that hovers in the vicinity of the truth. I remember the director Louis Malle speaking of film-making as a sequence of broad approximations that are gradually refined, and brought into the concentrated focus of a central narrative. But identity is only like that when it takes the form of the false identity celebrated in autobiography. You can't assemble identity like a film, eliminating entire scenes and performances, pretending that what has been cut, whether it be one frame or five hundred, never existed. Identity is messier than orthodox documentary can allow for. Only in fiction do you get the most accurate approximations of true identity. If I were to write my memoirs most truthfully, they would take the form of an expressionistic fiction. Just as Kafka places his clerks in overwhelming situations which indicate their true relation to the cosmos, I would need to unveil the essence of my identity by presenting myself as a man who *imagines* that he has been

---

18 Along with many readers, I find this remark so staggeringly ironic that it is difficult to imagine that Thompson made it innocently. Dr Pamela Woodland asked, 'Is it possible for a remark to be too innocent to be innocent?'

hired to kill seven residents of a suburb every year.[19] To simply proclaim that you are, in reality, just such a Killer is immediately delimiting. It brings to mind something Borges wrote: all classification implies falsification. Classification smooths over difference and contradiction. Being the Killer is not my identity, it isn't what I am, it is something that I move towards and away from in a kind of elliptical orbit. I am an array of possibilities which can't necessary be expressed by, or embraced by, what I do or what I've done. I like the line in one of Hal Hartley's films, 'I'm bad at my job on purpose. If I was any better at it, I might become what I do for a living.'[20] Killing people for a good reason, to sustain a community, is not nearly so odious as being identified as The Killer.

.

A series of wrong numbers, all pathetic types asking 'Is that Leggy ex-Model?' 'Mate, do I *sound* like a leggy ex-model?' There must be a misprinted phone number in an ad for Adult Services. I find it fascinating to imagine the kind of man who would get fired-up at the thought of someone so indefinite as 'leggy ex-model'. (Why did she retire? How ex is ex, and what exactly did she model?) People often ask what frightens me most, and I can never find a good answer at the time. I must remember to mention phrases with numbers in them: 'the wrong

---

19 These meditations were the source of prolonged debate before both
    Elliot and Witherspoon. On the one hand, Thompson's self-conscious
    manipulation of identity was seen as connivance—throwing up
    screens of irony and hyper self-awareness. On the other, the passage
    was interpreted as an innocent attempt by a man in the throes of an
    identity crisis to determine who he is, and what he might become.
    Witherspoon observed that Thompson, in his pursuit of personal
    truths, sometimes muddied *the* Truth. He argued that it is Thompson's
    remarkable honesty which makes him so exceptionally unreliable.

20 The Hartley film alluded to is *The Theory of Achievement*.

number', 'Your number is up'... I don't know why, but they chill me. And this was well before I became Fate's bingo caller. Something about numbers. A friend once told me there are villages in Africa where they don't have streets or street names, and the houses aren't numbered according to their location or physical proximity, but according to when they were built. So you are looking for someone who lives in 127, and you know that it was the house built after 126, but it's way on the other side of town, nestled between 5 and 37. The locals aren't the slightest bit fazed by this. They read Kafka for the jokes. (Did I ever mention that I bought my first personal computer from a salesman whose name appeared on the docket as 'Joseph K.'? Franz has gone hi-tech.) After learning about these numbered villages, I had disturbed sleep for weeks. 'Mate, we have your number.' 'Richard Thompson, your days are numbered.'

.

'Warning! Warning! Danger, Will Robinson!' ... Daphne Emerson from Amnesty International called to advise that the Hampton Festival of Killing would be the subject of a television documentary co-produced by Amnesty and Channel 4. Their choice of Christine Marker as writer-director is surprising. Though she has been a vocal critic of military dictatorships in South-East Asia and the Americas, as a rule she writes quirky short fiction. I've read one of Marker's collections, *Days Without Violence*, and I'd be surprised if she doesn't regard this film as research for a future novel. Of course, Amnesty's involvement makes the film's slant predictable. (I should purchase a pair of plastic vampire fangs.) As always in these affairs, if you choose not to participate, you'll get shot down from a distance, (like a member of the Royal Family). On the other hand, you can offer to speak to them and get shot down at close range. A skilled film-maker can edit anything to support a thesis. If, while being filmed, I chose to justify my actions by using an argument that

I've used previously (and persuasively), they will collage all previous versions of the statement to show that my argument is too well rehearsed, therefore dubious or insincere. It wouldn't be in the film-maker's interests to show that I am well liked and admired. Still, I have a politician's ego, and I enjoy making claims for the importance of my office. What's more, I look forward to meeting Christine Marker. I could ask her to sign her book. If the photo on the back cover is anything to go by, Christine's an attractive woman. She looks a little like Francesca ... I suppose it's inevitable that she will ask me to remember Francesca.[21]

.

I had it wrong. It seems that I am already the subject of a documentary. The producers have been contacting old friends who live outside of Hampton. Tracey called last night to say that she would be speaking to them. I told her that I supposed she would relish the opportunity to drop another bucket on me. When she said, 'No, but I'll answer their questions truthfully,' I felt like asking what she—of all people—would know of the truth. I resisted. Tracey's quite capable of wounding me without provoking her further.

.

To judge from the things said and written about me, I am most admired for my decisiveness. People want to believe that I am an

---

21 Francesca Morricone, a former intimate of Thompson, disappeared
    while travelling in Denmark and was presumed murdered. Francesca later appeared before Witherspoon, to claim that she faked her
    disappearance before taking up residence in London. This strategy
    was her means of breaking with the obsessed Thompson. Thompson had ignored her previous attempts to terminate their friendship.
    Morricone's surprise testimony before the Witherspoon Commission
    discredited an earlier attempt to link Francesca's disappearance with
    that of Christine Marker.

assertive person. The converse is closer to the truth. I believe I was chosen to be the Killer because I was thought to be a compliant, anxious man who would choose to honour his commitment to his employer, even if conflicts of interest arose. Killing is no job for the impulsive or reckless. Far from being a law unto himself, the Killer's actions are more regulated, more scrutinised than any member of this society. I have power only in so far as I am empowered. (I think that I should begin to practice the minimalist waves and hand gestures favoured by the Royal Family.)[22]

·

I remember Mrs Dallas, my English teacher at Hampton High, taking issue with a fiction I wrote about the staff's involvement with Satanism, arguing that it's possible to have too much imagination ... She said that, while it's proper to venerate the Shakespeares and Tolstoys, it's also worth remembering that the people who do the most terrible things are often those with the most fertile imaginations.—'There are times when you'll need to rein in your fantasies.' Though I take Mrs D's point, I do see a paradox in what she was saying. I'm not sure whether it takes a stupendous imagination or a feeble one to think you could live at peace, or be happy, after performing a terrible premeditated act. When John Hinckley Jr. thought that he could win Jodie Foster's heart by assassinating President Reagan, was Hinckley's imagination depleted or over-charged? (Could a man accept the task of killing seven individuals a year purely to impress former girlfriends, or to stick it up the people who said he'd never amount to anything?) And you can apply this paradox of imagination to the larger-scale Utopian dreams. Was the Soviet Union—born from the notion that you could create a happy, truly egalitarian society, (and from accepting the

---

22 For the second time in three entries Thompson draws a link between himself and royalty, lending weight to the view that the Killer had unconsciously adopted the mindset of an aristocrat.

idea that you can disregard or change human nature)—a consequence of too little imagination, or too much imagination? From experience, I can split the critics of Hampton's Festival into two roughly-equal camps. There are those who insist that the Festival, and the Hampton Community shaped by the Festival, is an anti-Christian, socialist abomination. Yet just as many critics argue that the Festival is a predictable development in the brutish history of capitalism. I can only say that I wouldn't kill anyone if the people of Hampton didn't wish me to kill. And someone else would surely do it if I didn't. I do know that I haven't the imagination to picture a world where an absolute moral code pertains, a world free of mists, or patches of grey.

.

King of the kids. No sooner had I finished officiating at the opening of the new child care centre than I was at the primary school being introduced to a class of seven year olds. As fortune had it, I hadn't killed any of their parents. Most of them had been doing projects on the Killer for the past fortnight. One boy was under something of a misapprehension, clearly fuelled by his father. 'Why did you kill my rabbit?... My dad said you came to kill my bunny because we couldn't have a dog and a rabbit.' The teacher tried to help out. 'Mr Thompson's a kind man, Danny. He never kills animals.' 'But he *killed* Thaddeus! He broke his neck!' Eventually, Mrs Ingstrom managed to persuade Danny that I hadn't killed Thaddeus. But Danny knew *someone* had wasted his bunny, and the idea that the Killer isn't responsible for all killings is confusing to kids who think Santa is responsible for all Christmas presents. During question time, some wanted to be individually reassured that I wouldn't harm their pets. (Their parents they couldn't care less about ... Once a kid made me promise I wouldn't kill Bart and Lisa Simpson.) They tend to ask the same questions: Have you ever buried someone alive? Do you ever eat people after you kill them? Have you met Batman and Superman? Couldn't you just blow up a bus and take five years holiday? What subjects do you have to be good at to become the Killer? Does your mum know you kill people? Did your parents tell you that killing people was wrong when you were a kid? Do you ever just hurt people and not kill them?... We sat in the same classroom where I was taught by Miss Hogan in grade one. Back then we didn't seem to worry so much. During recess, the boys played War, America versus the Germans. (Never Australia versus the Japanese.) Whiteboards have replaced the old blackboards, and the big television room—where the entire school crammed in to watch Armstrong walk on the moon—has become the computer room. The old desks have gone, but there's a smell that never goes away, the smell of sawdust over vomit. Which brings to mind my favourite question: Do you clean up after you kill someone, or does your mum do it for you?

·

Why do I deny things, choose the most pessimistic interpretation? Even to the extent that I was reluctant to report what Christine said when I was stating the terms and conditions for filming in the house. 'I'd love to know what your bedroom looks like.' Ordinarily, I'd laugh-off such obvious innuendo, but my extreme guardedness in this instance must have been unmistakable to her. I am a person who over-reads, who feels assailed by a barrage of possible sub-texts.[23] I decide what she means is that a person's most private room reveals a lot about their true

---

23 Several expert witnesses who testified before Elliot and Witherspoon interpreted these utterances as a specific invitation to read the journal for its sub-texts and allusions. According to this analysis, Thompson was producing a calculated text which would mask or confuse his real (criminal) motives. Witherspoon demurred, stating the passage only indicated that Thompson was preoccupied with self-analysis to the point of obsession.

nature, and the Killer's bedroom would be of special interest. Is he messy or meticulous? Sloppy or obsessive? Why do I not want to believe the possibility that Christine may be expressing—albeit in a public, jokified form—her desire to become more intimately acquainted with the bedroom's resident? Why are my lusts so terrifying? I have always been overwhelmed by the strength of my desires, and do everything within my power to suppress them, to see any hope of their realisation as a cruel trick played by an overactive imagination. If only there were a way to cut through the poetry and inexactness of human communication, to ascertain what was meant, exactly. (We killers are so fond of final arbitrations—The Definite.)

.

It must be difficult to be a man. To be firm and decisive, to always know exactly what you want, and to be sure in the pursuit of it, inflamed by fragrances and suggested curves, to be willing to betray anyone or anything—family, sacred beliefs and ideals— for just a few minutes with your dick inside something wet and womanly, to be as one with other men, part-beast yet authoritative, to be always testing the boundaries of violation, to be able to presume that the magic wand in your trousers will be the final persuasion, that its potent maleness will necessarily do someone a favour, to firmly believe that you know what a woman wants, to know what she needs, and to know how to withhold feeling and emotion till that moment when your sex can be revealed like a rabbit hidden up a sleave, to be a man able to divide women into two groups: those to be disregarded except for their labours, and those who deserve to be fucked, and then to define yourself by your ticked-off conquests, by your capacity to aggress, to aggressively initiate and fulfill the manly functions, and to exclude those women who would threaten this capacity or question its worth, to be powerfully unpredictable, predictably powerful, cocksure yet wary, wary of women, to be on a collision course with your wariness of women, to bluff until you believe your own bluff. The difficulty of inhabiting a mad, pinball reality, a pinball sexuality. So much easier to be a Killer.

.

I'm convinced that there are two types of people in the world: those who want to know how the television works, and those who don't want to know. The people who don't want to know aren't fussed that laws, rules, structures and explanations exist. They might even find it consoling to know that things they don't want to know *can* be known. But the people who don't want to know relish the *idea* of magic, the idea that television exists as pure wonderment. They want to believe in magical forces, and miraculous fusions and inspirations. Scientific knowledge is too rational, too available, too democratic. They need a magician.

.

After hearing rumours that the producer of the Amnesty/Channel 4 documentary intends to use 'Docu-drama recreations' of specific killings, I called Lorraine di, telling her she should make it known that any unauthorised dramatisation of a killing would violate The Festival Act, and would necessitate legal action. Though Lorraine was conscious of how a 'factional' presentation might misrepresent or damage the Festival, she pointed out that any legal threat we made could only be bluff. If Hampton went to court to point out the discrepancies between the dramatic recreations of specific killings and the true circumstances of those killings, it would be forced to make public information germane to gambling interests ... How would it ever be possible to tell the truth of what I do when so many conflicting interests govern and appropriate my actions? Any truthful dramatic recreation of Hampton's Killer would depict him as a plasticine figure, a Gumby, artfully shaped and reshaped for every circumstance.

·

Once again voted one of the ten worst dressed men in Australia. What can I do? I used to like the jackets and windcheaters with the 'K' insignia, but then the Tourist Commission began marketing them on a large scale, and it seemed tacky for the tourist attraction to dress like the tourists. Of course, the people at the bureau would be delighted if I wore a hooded black cloak and carried a scythe. Postcard sales would go through the roof. I spent most of one year in an elegant black suit—'People don't come all this way to have their photo taken with a bank manager!' Now, in jeans, sneakers, and t-shirts, I'm a dag, I'm an international fashion disaster. I know I shouldn't be sensitive about it, but I've always had a neurotic desire to please everyone. The next time someone's described as dressed to kill, I'm going to drop the biggest bucket. Why aren't the people who are supposedly 'dressed to kill' dressed like me?—Maybe attack is the best form of defence. I could recommend a Fashion is Murder week to the Council, or dash off a coffee table volume, *Dressing to Kill*, full of comfortable *apres homicide* wear. It would make a nice change, to be able to speak as an authority.

·

In my dream I am walking rapidly along a narrow laneway, defined on either side by tall hedging. The sensation is that of being confined in a maze, though I can see a tiny opening in the distance. Yet my progress takes me no closer to this opening. I am anxious, always looking back over my shoulder. Behind me, the two rows of hedge meet at the horizon. I can hear a roaring noise in the distance which may be the sea. Other than that, there is only the sky to suggest a world beyond the corridor of hedge. As I run and stumble towards the ever-distant opening, I begin to repeat the same word, a confusion between breathing and voice, a word like 'instrument', or perhaps, 'experiment'. Whatever the word, it seems to me that I am uttering a secret shame, a taboo.[24]

.

S. says that I'm a Killer because I lacked the discipline to learn a musical instrument, that being a guitar hero would've given me a better opportunity to express just whatever it is I need to. As much as I love music, I'm no musician. I'm a singer with no range. The Killer doesn't have to be brilliant night after night. He can hit as many false notes as he likes, he can be as flatulent as he likes, so long as he is efficient the seven times when his efficiency is required. He chooses his moment. As a twelve or thirteen year old, I would've killed to be Cat Stevens or Ian Anderson. (And if they'd killed to be me, they would've *been* me ...) Christine said she wanted to become a singer, but her father forbade it.[25] She went to art school in London to study graphic design, but always knew that she wanted to write and make films. She laughs when I tell her she looks different to the author photo on the back of *Days Without Violence.* 'Older and less attractive,' she jokes. I don't know what it is about her that makes me think of Francesca, but I warm to her as someone I know, and trust, rather than the inter-

24 'A heavy-handed plant' opined forensic psychiatrist Professor Nigel
    Browne in his testimony before Witherspoon. Browne argued that the
    account of this dream suggests an author who knows enough about
    dream theory and analysis to remain ambiguous, but not enough to be
    subtle. According to Professor Browne, 'the dream smacks of cynical
    contrivance', though Browne was reluctant to speculate on Thompson's
    possible motives.

25 This exchange may have taken place during a non-transcripted interview
    in late-October. Many of Thompson's earlier journals are time-specific,
    and the absence of dates in this volume aroused skepticism. The Hamp-
    ton Coroner Helen O'Brien regarded the lack of exact dates as evidence
    of a possible inauthenticity. She argued that Thompson's imprecision
    with time is convenient in that it neutralises the possibility of factual
    contradiction, and does not allow us to speculate on the context in which
    a particular entry may have been written. Several witnesses expressed
    surprise that Thompson found time to write at such length.

viewer whose job is to character-assassinate me. I would speak of her more in terms of loveliness than beauty. When she finishes laughing, she beams till her broad smile gradually dissipates. (Who was that KAOS agent in *Get Smart*? Melvic The Smiling Killer … I will need to watch Christine—when I am not so busy looking at her!) She is not particularly dictatorial with her crew. Her cameraman Michael tends to dominate the arrangement of things. I made it clear to him that I was unwilling to take part in a stylised documentary, they would have to follow what suited me. It's too easy for skilled practitioner to make you look like an arsehole or an imbecile with their low-angles and wide angles and fish-eyes. (They'll do this anyway, but that doesn't mean I shouldn't try to circumvent or obstruct their strategies.) They intend a game of cat and mouse, where the most confronting questions will be withheld till they think I am off guard or vulnerable. Hence this game of flattery and counter-flattery. The camera pans along my bookshelves, examines the titles in my video collection, the framed Munch print on the wall, the dishes in the sink. *Do you have any photographs of your parents or family?* Not for the camera. *Do you keep photographs of your victims?* No. But there are many images of them in the Martyrs' Museum. *Can we film you there?* No … Christine is surprised that I have read her stories, but I won't let her know what I think of her work till she has given some indication of the slant of her documentary. I'm surprised to find she speaks English like a speech and drama teacher, yet a second party has been credited with translating *Days Without Violence* from the original French.[26] She *could* have been a singer. There is melody in her voice. Perhaps she hopes I will reveal money as my uppermost concern. Or, she would like me to *think* this is her angle, that I am to be portrayed as a simple mercenary. I will credit her researchers with having more perception than that.

---

26 On the title page of *Days Without Violence,* credit for the English translation is attributed to Carlotta Valdes. It is highly likely that Carlotta Valdes is a pseudonym adopted by Marker when translating her own text.

·

You fumble along, hoping you do more good than harm. Hampton's Killer doesn't know his final place in history any more than Richard Nixon does. Or Margaret Thatcher, or Bob Hawke. As much as you'd like to oppose the description, you're a gambler. (Hold onto your tickets, there's a protest in the Posterity Handicap: second placed Killer versus the winning favourite, Wisdom of Hindsight.) The last thing I expected when I took on this job was that I'd become the Prince of Punt. No one in my family gambled. It wasn't that the Thompsons were particularly wowserish or frugal.

I was brought up to believe the only money that meant anything, the only money worth having, was money derived from honest toil—the old fashioned values of the WASP middle class. Back in the sixties, as I was growing up, there was nothing glamorous about gambling. Gambling was the last refuge of the lowly and desperate. For me, gambling was the horses, and the unshaven men who sat at their Laminex-topped tables on Saturday arvo, ears glued to the fourth from Caulfield, making pen-marks on sheets of hieroglyphed newspaper, and pouring glasses of beer from brown bottles. Gambling and alcoholism were inextricably linked in my imagination, a sad conjunction of too hopeful hopelessness. These jaundiced views must have been formed by the bottle-drives. When I was a kid in scouts, the local scout troop used to raise money by collecting bottles. You'd dash around Hampton carting hessian bags full of clinking glass out to utes, or cars with trailers. We were little kids in scarves and baggy shorts sifting through tall stacks of brown bottles, all covered in webs, and snails and slaters. The unshaven man with the Caulfield races blaring from his transistor directed you behind his shed to a mountain of alcoholic refuse. By the end of the day, the scum dribbling through the hessian bags left your uniform stinking of stale beer. We were innocent intruders, confident we were doing these unshaven men a favour, quite unaware that we had access to saleable information. We could have compiled an alcoholic map of Hampton and sold it off to employers and insurers for a lot more than we got for the glass. Insurance companies would have paid a fortune for a detailed map of Hampton's alcoholics. That culture—the drinking and the gambling—was foreign to my experience at home, and I looked down on those people. Open expression of moral superiority was socially acceptable in the sixties. Now, your moral judgements have to be concealed within statements about diet, fitness and health. If you'd told me in the 1960s that gambling would be elevated to a form of civic duty, that gambling would one day form the economic foundation of this society, I wouldn't have believed it possible. It would have been like agreeing to bathe in a trough of stale beer every Saturday for the rest of your life ... I dunno. Is it possible to be a fatalist and not believe in luck? I'm not sure that I understand what luck is. Is bad luck finding yourself next in line for Martyrdom, or last in line? Was it only good luck that the bouncer's arm came down behind my back to signal a full house when The Cure played the tiny Armadale Hotel in 1980? That arm had to come down somewhere. In the general run of things, you are lucky because you are not unlucky. Take that poor bloke in the newspaper (urban myth disguised as news?), the Greek scuba diver found burnt to death in a forest fire. There he is, minding his own business, swimming a metre deep in the blue sea, when some sort of plane picks him up in a water scoop and dumps him on a forest fire. I mean, what happens inside the poor bastard's head? Is he thinking, My number is up? He's trapped up there with all that water, fish, seaweed and shit. Is Barber's *Adagio for Strings* playing on his personal soundtrack? If it's luck, it's a filthy bit of luck. Totally fucked. But I don't see how you can *ride* luck, or *make* your own luck, or that certain individuals are graced in terms of luck. You could be like George Zanotti, the guy who won a couple of million betting that a male between 20 and 30 would be the next Hamptonian martyred the week David Miller was killed. Is George lucky because he had an instance of good luck, that he won a fortune he didn't earn? Is he lucky thanks to his stars, or because he touched a Chinaman? Or is he lucky because he experienced the *absence* of bad luck, that he didn't fall off the ladder and become quadriplegic, that he didn't become charcoal inside his wetsuit? This is a hopeless fucking world of might and maybe and possible and probable … On Tuesday, it will be two years since Jenny Fitzpatrick died. She was 29 and had a massive brain haemorrhage. What Jenny never knew was that she was so nearly the fourth Martyr. And had she been killed, she would have been Hampton's last Martyr. It was a near thing. For all intents and purposes, Jenny looked like a normal girl. Her family believed she was normal, and never accepted that the brain injuries she'd copped in a cycling accident had left her intellectually bereft. Maybe they ought to have signed documents to have Jenny exempted from the social contract, but they didn't. Not because they thought her dispensable. They didn't want people to regard her as deficient or different. They wanted her to be accepted as a full member of the community. Jenny would accompany her father to his office, sit at a desk opposite his, receive a full salary, and present like the elegant young solicitor I'd been given to believe she was. Was it a stroke of luck that a friend told me about the local solicitor and his vacant mascot the day before Jenny was to be martyred? That would have been the end of the Festival. The thought still chills me. You can imagine the outcry about euthanasia and eugenics and final solutions. Lucky? Who can say whether Jenny was lucky to get those three extra years? Or whether Christine Nelson, (who then became the fourth Martyr) was uncommonly unlucky?…

You just fumble along, hoping you do more good than harm, needing to believe that, but would you bet your life on it?

·

I've been thinking of Christine. She left a lipstick impression on one of my coffee mugs, and I can't bring myself to clean it off. In my thoughts of her, I find it difficult to separate her from Francesca, yet I may be the only person in the world to see this likeness. I am unable to articulate the nature of the similarity, (Can a person be said to have a tone or ambience?) or the reason for my inclination to see this similarity. I'm surprised to find I have a powerful desire for Christine, because she is quite far removed from my favoured physical type. I'm also frightened by what friends and former friends may have said to her. Of course, Tracey will tell her that I am impotent and pathetic. I can wear that. But what if she speaks to Catherine?[27] What if Catherine should tell the world what she never found the courage to tell me to my face: that she never had any powerful or intimate feeling for me, that my strange sense of involvement/intimacy with her was just extravagant fantasy? As a perceptive writer, Christine will note my habit of fixation. She will predict the likelihood that I will become obsessed with her and will use artful seduction to draw me into revelations which may damage myself or this office. I'm sure she despises my profession. I will need to be contrary to her expectations, to anticipate her moves, and to be surprising. She may be Catholic. She may have an overriding desire to have me renounce my work on film. Her position may turn out to be as vulnerable as my own.

·

It feels good to be scheming again, to lose myself in the arrangements for the next dispensation. Once the wheels are set in motion, I become immersed in the details, all the things which need to be attended to. People will tell me that I am distracted, far away.

---

27 Catherine O'Shaunessy was one of Thompson's long-term obsessions, pre-dating his term as Hampton's Killer. Like Francesca Morricone, O'Shaunessy tired of Richard Thompson's fixation, and broke off their friendship. Ironically, she also ended up living in London, less than 500 metres from Francesca. She is now a Professor of Forensic Pathology at the City University.

I relish this immersal. Suddenly the world seems still and quiet, and I can shift the pieces back and forth as I choose. Unlike the political assassin, the Killer has no need to get caught up in motives or emotions ... When I started, I thought it would be best if I took on the robot's mind-set, but I discovered, paradoxically, that it's humanity which makes the program possible. Humanity and intuition enable me to anticipate irregularities and caprice. I told one interviewer that the Killer needs to be a poet. You are not dealing with method so much as the logic of dance. To be part of the dance, you have to make yourself inseparable from the rhythm, feeling the subtle shifts of density, the distance between sounds. When you have planned, plotted and rehearsed to the extent that you can give yourself over to irrational forces, the Martyr will choose him or herself. They beckon you. When I am scheming, a power surges through me so I never doubt that what I am doing is of the utmost importance, that I am a traffic cop at the crossroads of history. My identity and my actions are as one. I was wrong in my attitude to the Hartley quote. I do my job well precisely because I *hope to* become what I do. I swell. I extend. I surpass myself.

.

Wherever you go, you see the essential wisdom of Hitchcock's *Vertigo*, desire fashions reality. The Truth is that particular arrangement of facts which most readily conforms to our understanding of what the truth *should* be (as we need understand it to be). To those who need the Killer to be a flawless hero, he is faultless, exemplary. To those who reject the Killer's function, he is someone who lives in the margins, a shadowy Michael Jackson figure.

.

An invitation to S's fancy dress party—'Come as your favourite fictional character.' I'm tempted to go as Humpty Dumpty. For me, Humpty signifies the fragility of knowledge, the inevitability of subversion, and the problem of continuous, integral identity. If HD could be pieced together again, would he still be an egg? Can any of our actions or our errors be entirely undone?... If I could get a costume, I might go as Bullwinkle the Moose. Bullwinkle isn't so much a favourite fictional character as he is a role model. He's fabulously stoic, feckless but imperturbable. When confronted with the results of his ignorance or misplaced confidence, Bullwinkle is ever-resilient, always finding the courage to forge onwards. Rosi Braidotti once said of Sartre that he had the courage of his contradictions, and Bullwinkle has that in buckets. It's the right sort of courage, I think, the undaunted commitment to commitment for its own sake. When Rocky's voice of reason tells Bullwinkle, 'that trick will never work', Bullwinkle doesn't even pause to consider the possibility of failure, 'This time for sure!'

·

Still more requests to prepare an autobiography, or to assist an authorised biography ... I dunno. I feel as if I've begun to stalk myself. I'm constricted by the consciousness of who I am, and what I am doing. The exercise could liberate me, or it could undo me entirely. Last night, I tried to read Francesca's letters. I hadn't even considered reading them since they were returned by the police. And they are still too painful, the way that she would double-guess me, and take the piss out of my so-obsessive letter writing. The first one that I opened was her *Ten Year Prospectus of Richard's Letters to Francesca ....*

> **July 10, 2003:** *Will write to Francesca to complain that she has not written since May. Will point out one or two recent political happenings. Will tell a funny (perhaps invented) tale about a brush-tail possum ...* **July 14, 2003:** *Will complain to Francesca that her letter of July 8th did not tackle the matters raised in my letter of*

> *July 3rd. Will make one or two banal observations about the Melbourne winter. Will assert the absolute truth of a previously told story about an eccentric film society based in a (fabricated) Melbourne cafe, Travis Bickle's.*[28]

Her letters destroy me. I can't imagine reading them again without pain, nor can I imagine releasing them for the perusal of a biographer. But to rid myself of them, to actually destroy them, would be to initiate something more profoundly destructive.

.

How will Christine pursue the Francesca connection? What if she should discover more than I already know myself?

.

Woken at five this morning by a phenomenal roll of thunder, and was unable to return to sleep. Very black thoughts. I've been plagued by the notion that I have chased-off or alienated everyone I have loved, having chosen a path which would inevitably alienate them. I couldn't settle to read anything, not even to re-read an old favourite like Gogol. Picked out Machiavelli, but didn't open it, my mind immediately racing off to the furious argument Yuri and I had about *The Prince* on Oslo railway station.[29] Yuri insisted a non-smoker should always carry a cigarette lighter in order to maximise his chances to meet women. I could scarcely imagine anything more transparently immoral. (Immorally transparent?) Yuri considers Machiavelli to be an *advocate* of end justifies the means transactions. I prefer to see Machiavelli as a

---

28 Francesca Morricone destroyed most of the letters she received from Thompson, and no evidence of this letter remains.

29 Yuri Dobrolyubov, a school friend of Thompson, now working as a photographer in northern Italy.

bemused analyst of historical realities. If The Killer was 'accused' of being Machiavellian, I should say the accusation implied that I had an acute understanding of human nature.[30] And I do see everything so clearly ... *except* when I become part of the picture, when emotion starts to cloud reason. But my reason's never been so cloudy that I'd carry a cigarette lighter.

.

I can't deny it. Control is important to me. I hate the possibility of accidents, of senseless events, that a horse could stumble over an embankment and land on top of your car, that someone you love could be snatched away by a sudden bolt of electricity. My work permits the illusion of control. I have strategies, schedules. My task is clearly defined, and there is little to be confused or misinterpreted. Which is as well because I can be overwhelmed by ambiguity. I am unable to read subtexts or body language or ulterior motives because I *over-read* them, see contradictory messages in every communication. Fear and desire confuse everything. Nothing unsaid is obvious to me, unambiguous to me, and I am terrified of responding to phantoms, of being lured into making an inappropriate declaration. Yet I am too conscious of my own subtexts, and fear that my body language will betray me, that the messages I give out will be so monstrously obvious that my desires are stripped naked, exposed for all to see on illuminated billboards high above Hampton Street.

.

---

30 Thompson appears to confuse his own position of authority and responsibility with that of the imaginary (Machiavellian) adviser. Hampton's Killer is not a consultant or departmental head, he *is* the maestro, the Prince. Thompson's confused attempts to relate Machiavelli to his moral outlook complements his failure to recognise his own aristocratic ambitions.

To tell everything. How wonderful to set it all out ... It wouldn't need to be the standard kill and tell memoir, it could be a fiction, an elaborate satire, a bizarre expressionistic confection. It would be too simple to set about demolishing the Killer myths by contesting the standard assertions. Far better to ridicule the myth-making process by combining unbelievable truths with extravagant lies so that finally the reader is left dizzied by the imagined *possibility* of truth. How wonderful it would be to perpetrate a grand hoax: to write my own unauthorised biography of the Killer. I've been allowing myself to be rendered inert by the narrowness of my thinking, by the tired distinction between fiction and non-fiction. Where is the autobiography that is less preposterous than the most grotesque invention? Why not fake a journal such as this? Why not fake a book of correspondence between the Killer and some horrendous, imprisoned mass murderer? I could prepare a fake manifesto written by an invented adversary, a demented copy-cat.[31] Only by learning about lying, and deceit, about the nature of calculated untruths, can you begin to approach the truth—to realise one's true self in words. I must speak to Justine about this unauthorised biography (better, *The Unauthorised Autobiography of Richard X—Killer*). Should I mention these literary ambitions to Christine? I wouldn't presume to trust her, but I could trust her to understand.

---

31 In the opinion of Professor Nigel Browne, this section is the most contentious in Thompson's journal. It virtually dares the reader to interpret the journal as a hoax, or manipulative fabrication. Elliott earlier found that Thompson's prediction of an invented adversary—anticipating the murder of Keiko Morimoto by a psychopathic copycat—was sufficient to prove that Thompson was alert to the conspiracy to murder Morimoto, if not an active collaborator. Conversely, Witherspoon argued that a person capable of gaining access to Thompson's security codes could have accessed to his journals. Thompson's privately expressed fears and speculations could have been used to manufacture a pretext that would implicate him in the murders of Morimoto and Christine Marker's film crew.

.

Always a surprising new fact to shatter your favourite illusions ... Is it true that Humpty Dumpty didn't actually begin life as an egg but as an ineffective vehicle used in attacking fortresses in the English Civil War? (If television covered the Dumpty Incident, how many times would they have replayed that fall?... 'Look closely on the left side of the screen, and you can see that he's lost it ... *right there.*')

I sometimes think my life is the biography of Humpty Dumpty written by D.H. Lawrence: fine intentions and dark, dark impulses, a personality too fragile to survive in a world of violent passions.

.

Nearer the event, time expands and contracts all at once.

I've hardly given a moment's thought to next week's speech. Once, I hoped these lectures would become a kind of personal declaration, but I am so inarticulate, and whatever I propose to communicate is crushed by the monotony of my speaking voice. Initially, The Council wanted me to speak in a way that de-mystified the Killer's function, but just now I feel a powerful attraction to mystique.

.

Is it only an insane selfishness that allows me to think of the Killer as some kind of utterly selfless dignitary?[32]

.

---

32 I number among the scholars who believe that this is the closest Thompson gets to genuine self-perception. Because of the statement's force of truth, he feels constrained to express it as mock self-deprecation.

I have been invited to Buenos Aires to address an international forum on cruelty. Are the organisers being ironic? I hate cruelty. I wouldn't wish to torture a torturer. Cruelty is superstition. The logic of cruelty says that there is a finite amount of evil in the world, and the more evil you inflict on others, the less evil will remain to be inflicted on you. Of course, the opposite is true. Cruelty is a muscle. The magnifying glass you held above the unsuspecting ant gave you some idea of what it would be like to be a malevolent God. But finally you are forced to concede that belief in the possibility of a truly evil God is as cruel as any cruelty you could inflict. Your earth shifts in relation to the sun, and your magnifying glass is always double-sided.

.

Christine, a deep red blouse to match her lips. The vibrancy of her eyes. She wants to know about the Angela Kaufmann grubbiness. This is a ruse, a subtext surely. Under her intense gaze, I feel like the ant beneath the magnifying glass, fried by a concentrated beam of light ... I remember the humid evening I declared my love to Francesca, knowing that she would have to turn me down. Neither of us looking up, in case we caught each other's eyes. A racket of birds outside. Swallowed up by concentrated time. When I spoke to Francesca then, I felt as if I was trying to communicate to someone on a faraway star ... How can you appear before a camera, appear candid, without being seduced by the foolishness that people will hear you and understand what you mean? Why can I not just tell everything?

.

People are so thoughtful. In this morning's mail, a type-written quote on a long strip of paper, a statement made by the character Luzhin in *Crime and Punishment* (should I confess that I haven't read *Crime and Punishment?*[33]): 'There's a limit to everything ... An economic theory is not the equivalent to an incitement to murder.'... I couldn't disagree with that, but the citizens of Hampton are no slaves to economic theory. If Hampton has a lesson to offer the world, it is that economics must be subordinate to the will to associate, that economic prosperity is the natural *bi-product* of social cohesion rather than the route to social cohesion. A society prospers by keeping vital the tenets of association. My anonymous correspondent should worry about dictatorial regimes which engage in 'social cleansing' for the sake of their tourist industries, about the politicians who have streetkids 'disappeared' by death squads so that the beaches of Rio are safe for wealthy foreigners. I'd be the first to abandon Hampton if Hampton and its Festival moved outside the control of Hampton's citizens ...

.

Everything about life is incomplete, unfinished business. How many times will I have the same dream? I am at school, about to do my final exam, when I discover that I am about to be examined in a subject that I haven't studied ... geography or mathematics ... I feel powerless like this, knowing that if I were to become sick now, or incapacitated in some way, the year's plans would collapse. That's the danger of working with such small margins of error. If an intended Martyr does something spon-

---

33 The copy of *Crime and Punishment* found in Thompson's bookcase was thick with marginal notes in Thompson's own hand. Either Thompson is lying about not having read the book, or he read it (and failed to note having read it) between the time of this entry and the murder of Morimoto. Testimony before the Elliott Commission argued that this omission of itself suggested a character sufficiently erratic to have been involved in the murder. Nevertheless, as Witherspoon would emphasise, Thompson did not cast himself in the role of Raskolnikov. Though he may have known of a plot to murder the prostitute Keiko Morimoto, he had an iron-clad alibi. (He was being interviewed by Christine Marker at the time of the killing.)

taneous or unpredictable, forgets an appointment or an obligation, six months of research can go out the window. And that leads to those terrifying moments when things are out of control, when you have to make a decision on the spot, when the success of the enterprise is nothing more than an outrageous gamble. A real murderer would feel exhilaration when the gamble pays off, from getting away with it. I almost shut down with terror.

·

It's been years since I've felt such a fierce desire to drink myself legless. I need to construct and fabricate, to insulate myself from Christine's inquisitions. Or else, I should get thoroughly tanked and confide in her, unburden myself totally. That's probably the wrong word, when it would be more like a Swiftian 'unburthening'—the cosmic clearout, the grand evacuation. This morning's horoscope was no help.

> GEMINI: *In a period when you would welcome even a suggestion of what your future is to be, unfortunately you may have to endure a little longer a sense of uncertainty.*

I'm being menaced by love-hunger, and by a future which never seems to draw any closer. There must be someone with whom I could experience a mutuality of need and desire. If I was fully attentive, I could see her approach, *feel* her approach, backward through time. The future will reach back to caress me, to tell me, 'Here, this is Necessity, take her, she needs you, and you alone can love her.' Does the future have this power to reach backwards, to reshape the constellations which direct love to those in need of love?—I'm prattling again. Avoiding work that needs to be done. But I want to be away from here, to be in Paris at New Year, eating crepes ... Yes, you've heard it all before.

Sometimes at night I hear the tinkle of the old milk cart, and the clip-clopping of the horse that used to round the Passchendaele Street bend in the early hours of the morning. It's not a conscious act of remembering so much as an involuntary memory-flash. The sound is *there*. I am hearing something real. In the same way, I sometimes hear the school bell, and the sound of kids playing on the High School oval, though the school's been gone many years now. Why is it that the old Hampton won't leave me? The rattle of coins in the big silver tin left out for the bread man, (Can you imagine leaving money sitting in a public place?) the smell of the butcher shop, the floods caused by blocked stormwater drains, the neurotically neat Anglophile gardens with their gnomes, the red rattler trains with compartments divided into Smoking and No Smoking, the man opening the old gates at the Hampton Street level crossing, the WC Fields films screened at the scout hall, and the sight of people *walking*—walking as people seldom walk now when every home must have at least two cars, and when all shopping must be done in one stop. Hampton was a meat and three veg suburb, a fish and chips on a Friday night suburb. This was Hampton long before the pizzerias, and video rental shops. People asked after your mother and father, confident you belonged to a family they knew. They went to church on Sunday, and the religious education teachers at school could presume that all decent people did go to church on Sunday. Hampton was still full of the old people then, the Great War veterans, or their widows, who lived on the estate built for soldiers returning from the Great War; Favril Street, Amiens Street, Rouen Street, Passchendaele Street ... If you drank alcohol in Hampton, you drank beer from tall brown bottles. Hampton people didn't drink wine. Very few of them could afford spirits ... If you could have all that back again, the old Hampton, the childhood tugging at your mother's apron strings, you probably wouldn't want it. It would all seem so unendurably dull now. Naive. Yet it seems crucial to me that it was there, and that I am here to vouch for it, to know there were people who cared about Hampton, people who loved it dearly for all its suburban tediousness, and that it disappeared despite their affection ... What am I resisting? Change? Maturity? Corruption?... I am a hoarder of possessions and associations, memories and scraps which say I once inhabited a world that is lost forever. As much as I try to possess or reconstruct the past, it evaporates, little by little. What would it be to totally dispossess yourself of these emotions, to erase these scraps of meaning? Is the Killer a dispenser, or a repossessor? Or is he finally no different to anyone else, a helpless pawn of Time?...

.

If everything is predetermined, the future heads towards you at the same speed you head towards it, and your registration of time is the experienced sequence of collisions which are more or less inevitable, more or less fatal.

.

The speech was a fiasco. An underprepared rehash of the things I'd said a million times before. I'd intended to speak about self-sacrifice, using something I heard the other day. Apparently there is an animal in North Africa, the naked mole rat, which burrows under the ground, serving a queen (Can you imagine her pride, *I'm Queen of The Mole Rats!*), and within the mole rat community there is a special task-force of these worker mole rats whose function is to sacrifice themselves if the colony is threatened. Whether this suicidal activity is behavioural or genetic doesn't really concern me, the future of naked mole rat society depends on these (occasional) acts of heroic self-sacrifice. The problem with using this in the speech was that I was still a little cloudy on how the whole thing works, and how I could work it into my narrative without having some smartarse conclude that all the heroic self-sacrifice of Hampton's citizenry had only led to this moment where the Martyrs would be likened to naked mole rats.

.

A job done, without fuss or complication,[34] but I feel strange, as if I'm about to have the rug pulled out from under me.

I've just finished reading Toni Morrison's *Beloved*, and I'm full of omens, auguries and tomorrows. This morning, I was standing over the kitchen sink, making a cup of coffee, when I looked into the backyard and saw three ducks fly past, no more than two metres off the ground. What could it mean, a rare sighting of ducks in Hampton? 'Three ducks at dawn, Killer be warned.'[35]

.

A letter from Dad. It's rare that he comments on my duties, or anything to do with the Festival, (He loathes my trade[36]) but he is adamant I should confront the Council and force them to state

---

34 An allusion to the killing of Marie Donkersloot on October 30th.

35 The Elliot and Witherspoon Commissions spent a considerable amount of time debating the apparent over-pointedness, or sign-posting in Thompson's journal. So much of what Thompson writes seems to anticipate his fate.

36 For security reasons, the Hampton Council financed the expatriation of Thompson's immediate family. The then secret location has since been revealed to be Vancouver.

an attitude with regard to my proposal.[37] He believes the Council's failure to respond represents a threat to my autonomy, that their loyalty may be frail. I have tended to view their silence as a demarcation, as part of a desire to delineate powers. I have supposed they would fear the possibility of the Killer using his profile to usurp power. Still, I have never acted disloyally in my dealings with the Council, and some response is required as a measure of their continued good faith. I didn't expect them to immediately accept my proposal, merely that it would provoke a necessary debate on the long-term outlook for the Festival. Dad sees the Council chopping me off at the knees ... Is there a subtext to this? Maybe Dad isn't talking about the Festival at all, but using this matter to insinuate my treachery to my parents. Despite the material comforts of their situation, they see themselves in exile, cut off from their country, their friends, and their youngest son. (Was that my objective all along, to use the terms and conditions of the role as a necessary wedge, as an excuse not to make peace with them? Tracey once told the press that my parents were the first casualties of the Festival, and they deserve a place of honour in the Shrine of The Martyrs.)

·

37 According to Thompson's father, Thompson submitted a 10 page proposal which argued that the killings should stop after the 50th killing. Thompson believed that the continuing tourism and investments would be sufficient to maintain a prosperous Hampton community, and that the end of killings would free Hampton of the pressures caused by gambling and the boycotts imposed by governments who disapproved of the Festival. No trace of this proposal has been found. Witherspoon argued that the Council would have seen such a proposal as a threat Thompson would withdraw his services if they failed to comply, and feared he might thereafter act as a subversive or oppositional force. Such an implied threat could have been sufficient to motivate a conspiracy to incriminate and/or dispose of Thompson.

Christine was on the phone this evening, needing to be reminded of the protocols ...[38] I haven't mentioned that I spoke to her briefly before the speech, while they were setting up at the back of the auditorium. I don't recall what we discussed, only that she stood so close, nearly on my toes, invading my personal space, as the Californians would say. What should I make of this—myopia or intimacy? Her colleagues looked uneasy, part of the plan perhaps. I was disconcerted, yet I tried to claim the warmth of her, to inhale her scent. She hardly wastes a word. Her eyes touch you with the caress of a geisha.

.

In red paint on the wall of the cinema, and in black on the wall of the library, and in bill posters pasted to construction sites and power poles,

COMING SOON, 33 WITH A BULLET

Wendy suggests that it's a band or a new theatre work. You have to admire their thoroughness. An unofficial festival, a shadow Hampton, is gathering around the official ceremonies and events. Society is always straining at the limits, testing its boundaries.

.

Just for the moment, things are quiet and time is mine. I watched *The Return of Martin Guerre* on video this afternoon. A wonderful film which details a fiction that becomes more real, more necessary than authenticity itself. The people need to believe in the fake Martin Guerre. Truth is an investment, and truth-seek-

---

38 According to tradition, the Killer was expected to stay out of the public gaze during the week-long mourning period that followed each killing.

ers ride the roulette wheel of belief. *Martin Guerre* is about the process of creating a true fiction: persuasion, seduction, confrontation, believability, utility. Memories, dreams and fantasies are like little Martin Guerres running around inside your head, and, if you heartily believe they are real, you *make* them real, you breathe reality into them. Reality can be redefined to accommodate them ... If I were to write a fake version of this journal, or to present this version (or a version more real than this one) as a fabricated journal, I might be able to communicate a truth which wouldn't be tainted by the weight of *the* Truth. Would Christine act as my front, as a fabricated 'ghost' writer or editor? What game could be more wildly exotic than a Killer turned fabulist who imagines a (real) French novelist as the proxy author of an authentic memoir that pretends to be fake? There would be so many masks, screens and mediated meanings that even the most banal observation would be impossibly loaded and reverberant. But there is the bind. Can a killer who is not a fiction writer hope to imagine how an experienced French novelist would imagine and present the day-to-day thoughts of a killer, The Killer who is contractually forbidden from writing about the very acts that make his story worth telling?

·

When I got back from the Council offices, the red light was flashing on my answering machine: Mary, very distressed, her voice at first unrecognisable, calling to say that Ray had been killed, stabbed to death in central London.[39] I couldn't get back to her, so I called her mother. Apparently they'd been to see a Pirandello in the West End. A vagrant approached them. Mary nodded him away, but Ray stopped to give him a coin. Suddenly he was being stabbed, no warning, a frenzy of blows to his chest. He died right there on the street. For nothing. People all about. Mrs

---

39 Identities unknown, possibly former teaching colleagues.

D said that Mary is inconsolable. They'd set themselves up, were going to start a family soon, do all the things they'd put on hold … Everything's fucked. London is totally fucked now, worse than New York, because you prepare yourself for the madness when you go to New York, you associate that kind of insanity with people squeezed out of the American Dream, but, I dunno, the lines of propriety have always been so clearly drawn in England, and now, when people are forced across the line, it's like all deals are off. It's as though you have to be crazy in order to make yourself visible. That's always been my worst fear for society here, the final collapse of compassionate values, the rise of the view that one class of people is expendable … You empty out the institutions, you pull away the safety nets, you drain the charity from people's hearts, and you have nothing but cruel hopelessness and disorder, an anarchy that doesn't even respect the idea of anarchy. It's … I dunno. Can you restore values to a society that's abandoned every value but monetary ones? The old values were only ever there to protect the interests of the privileged in the first place. How do you decide what really matters?… Believe in something, anything. In God? Maybe just the possibility of God. Something, if only the importance of believing in a thing itself and not its economic bi-product … Poor Ray. What could I ever say that would be of any consolation to Mary?

JOURNAL ENDS

The multi-billion dollar industry surrounding Hampton's Killer shows no sign of easing. Barely a week passes without Richard Thompson being 'sighted' enjoying the high life in some remote part of the globe. Often, these sightings have Thompson in the company of a woman who resembles the film-maker Christine Marker.

In the meantime, anonymous informants describe the circumstances of Thompson and Marker's deaths. Graves where Thompson and Marker are said to be buried are exhumed. Any unidentified male corpse found in Australia is presumed to be Thompson until proven otherwise. High circulation magazines delight in featuring bizarre stories: I WAS THE PLASTIC SURGEON WHO CHANGED RICHARD THOMPSON'S FACE, and I WAS THE J. P. WHO MARRIED CHRISTINE TO THE KILLER.

This need for circus notwithstanding, arguments regarding the moral justifications for the defunct Hampton Festival continue to rage. Though monuments dedicated to the Killer are frequently vandalised, Thompson's supporters remain loyal. Each year on June 3, large crowds gather in Hampton to celebrate Thompson's birthday.

The author, Miranda Murray, argues that the absent Killer has become what the diarist Richard Thompson wanted to become, lost among the endless possible versions of himself, everything yet nothing. The Killer has come to embody a reverberant fantasy of hope and disillusionment.[40] I hold a contrary view that Thompson represents nothing more than the selfish pursuit of fame at any price. Had he been a hero worthy of the myth he sought to promote, Thompson would have offered himself as a sacrifice to match the sacrifices he expected from his loyal subjects. Upon discovering the Festival's corruption, a true Prince would have killed himself to restore meaning to the

---

40 Murray, *If Looks Could Kill.*

heroic dedication of the Martyrs. Thompson's journals indicate that the social contract administered by the Killer was always subservient to Thompson's immediate personal agenda.

Thompson desired something beyond mere authority. He craved anointment. We know that he was bitterly disappointed by his failure to persuade the Council to support an annual ceremony where the community would symbolically bequeath to the Killer his entitlement to kill. Thompson's attraction to ritual connects with his notion of a 'weird priesthood' in a more perverse way than the Killer might have imagined.

Some psychiatrists interpret Thompson's project as an Oedipal adventure. In Heather O'Donnell's monumental work, *Packing Death: Where Fear is The Killer*, the author argues that Thompson's failure to differentiate between the restored Hampton he yearns for, and the radically altered Hampton all about him, mirrors his failure to acknowledge that his crucial desire is not to restore the Hampton of his lost childhood, but to fashion a renovated womb: a palace of undifferentiated affection designed to celebrate the Prince's sexual fidelity to his mother, The Queen.

Hampton was Thompson's Motherland in every sense of the term.

Thompson's family have been understandably reluctant to engage in discussion or analysis of the Killer's activities. They are certain he was murdered as part of an attempt to obscure the criminal conspiracies operating at the heart of Hampton's Killing Festival. Turning their back on Hampton and its rampant commercialism, his parents erected a small memorial in the cemetery at Kerang, the country town where Richard was born. Perhaps their true feelings about their son's misadventures are expressed by the strangely ambiguous inscription:

RICHARD THOMPSON

1960 –

our beloved son

missing in Utopia

(iii)

APPENDICES

APPENDIX 1
THE HAMPTON MARTYRS

In April this year, after prolonged public debate, a decision was made to represent Keiko Morimoto, Penny Donaldson, Gillian Chatterton, Michael Tynan, and Christine Marker in the Main Gallery of Hampton's Shrine of The Martyrs. As yet, no agreement has been reached on a proposal to represent Richard Thompson in the Shrine.

YEAR 1
1. CATHY SINCLAIR, 28, unmarried, teacher, crossbow.
2. DAVIS SUMP, 67, unmarried, invalid pensioner, lethal injection.
3. NICK ERMANOS, 25, married, father of one, bank teller, lethal injection.
4. CHRISTINE NELSON, 44, married, mother of six, shop assistant, crossbow.
5. NOEL TARPEY, 54, married, father of four, casino manager, drowned.
6. FRANK HAJNCL, 37, married, father of two, sports administrator, poisoned.
7. DESPINA MERLOT, 17, unmarried, student, poisoned.

YEAR 2
8. MICHAEL BENSON, 23, unmarried, manager of the band Approximate Life, hanged.
9. & 10. TRAN AND JESSICA NGUYEN, 36 and 33, parents of two, hotel managers, poisoned.
11. MARGARET FARRELLY, 49, unmarried, dental technician, drowned.

12. MARK MITCHELL, 44, married, father of five, greengrocer, fed to sharks.

13. DAVID MILLER, 28, unmarried, solicitor, crossbow.

14. PETER METHERALL, 64, unmarried, manager of construction company, crossbow.

YEAR 3

15. JOHNNY BILLINGSLEY, 40, divorced, father of two, local government administrator, poisoned.

16. GAIL WILLIAMS, 39, married, mother of five, gift shop manager, smothered.

17. CAROL MIFSUD, 48, divorced, mother of two, architect, lethal injection.

18. KAREN PETERSON, 31, unmarried, public relations consultant, electrocuted.

19. ROBERT ADAMS, 38, unmarried, writer/composer, hanged.

20. ANGELA KAUFMANN, 15, unmarried, student, smothered

21. GUNTER FASSBINDER, 86, widowed, father of six, retired magician, smothered.

YEAR 4

22. BERYL CHUNG, 53, married, mother of three, librarian, cause of death unknown.

23. AMBROSE TATE, 16, unmarried, student, pushed from roof.

24. CLIFF TULSE, 29, divorced, no children, circus performer, sabotaged trapeze.

25. SANDY OLUFSEN, 19, unmarried, university student, drowned.

26. LEONIE RICHARDSON, 61, unmarried, school principal, lethal injection.

27. SAM PASQUALIDIS, 46, unmarried, father of two, bottle shop manager, pushed from cliff.

28. COLLEEN FENELEY, 53, widowed, mother of six, hair dresser, crossbow.

YEAR 5

29. JACK GODDARD, 59, divorced, father of two, builder, lethal injection.

30. FRANCES KING, 52, married, mother of three, real estate agent, crossbow.

31. JULIE AHMAD, 25, unmarried, mother of one, designer, smothered.

32. JIM FITZGERALD, 58, unmarried, artist, crossbow.

33. MARTIN O'BRIEN, 33, unmarried, importer, lethal injection.

34. MARIE DONKERSLOOT, 41, married, mother of two, general practitioner, crossbow.

ALSO

KEIKO MORIMOTO, 23, unmarried, exotic dancer, murdered.

PENNY DONALDSON, 34, unmarried, sound technician, murdered.

MICHAEL TYNAN, 43, married, father of two, cameraman, murdered.

GILLIAN CHATTERTON, 24, divorced, no children, researcher, murdered.

CHRISTINE MARKER, 35, unmarried, author/film-maker, presumed murdered.

APPENDIX 2
THE LETTERS

On November 9, Richard Thompson received an anonymous, typewritten letter from a person who appeared to be claiming responsibility for the murder of Keiko Morimoto. Thompson immediately forwarded the letter to Inspector Nick Ptsouris. In the weeks following Thompson's disappearance, the letter's author, '33 With a Bullet' emerged as the prime suspect for Hampton's spate of murders and disappearances.

The letter suggested a madman determined to compete with Hampton's Killer. Yet forensic evidence at the Coronial inquest pointed in a different direction. Expert witnesses testified that the copycat murderer's letter had been produced on Richard Thompson's bubble-jet printer. The Coroner, Helen O'Brien, opined that Thompson and '33 With a Bullet' were one in the same. She argued that Thompson had fabricated a psychopathic adversary in order to conceal his own part in the conspiracy to murder Keiko Morimoto.

Though unable to identify the letter's author, Elliot and Witherspoon were reluctant to accept Thompson's involvement in its production, stating their view that the letter was almost certainly the work of the same person or persons who used Thompson's codes following Morimoto's murder.

Thompson's resignation letter of the following day did not surface for three years. In her testimony before the Coroner and Elliot, Lorraine di Stasio denied knowledge of such a document. A private investigator's discovery of this letter proved to be the turning point of the Witherspoon Inquiry.

Why would di Stasio have concealed the existence of the letter if she had not been to determined to implicate Thompson in order to conceal her own guilt? And, if Thompson had possessed knowledge of a conspiracy, why would he have concealed that knowledge to (a presumed co-conspirator) di Stasio? Witherspoon judged that Thompson's letter of resignation prompted di Stasio to have Thompson silenced.

Di Stasio would later claim that she lied about the existence of the letter because the proposal to which Thompson refers had been to involve the Council in secret gambling measures which would have freed Hampton of the need for further killings. Unable to produce Thompson's proposal, di Stasio claimed that a private investigator must have destroyed it at the same time Thompson's letter of resignation was found. No copy of the proposal Thompson put to Hampton Council has ever come to light, and speculation about the nature of Thompson's proposal continues to be fiercely debated.

MR WORTHLESS-SHIT KILLER,

Let me tell you about passion, because what you know about passion could be written in big letters on an arrow-head. Killing's a game for warm-blooded cunts, not for reptiles with calculators and expense accounts.

You don't know shit, Killer.

Because you don't know shit, you're not worth shit, you're just a fuckhead whose never known the thrill of killing for killing's sake. Real killing's like a bungey-jump, you're just way out there. You don't want a soft landing. You don't want your motion to be stopped. You just want to kill again and keep killing till the rope snaps. You want to plunge hard-dicked into the crowd with one final shriek like a kamikaze's Tora Tora because when you're on the razor's edge, you've got to <u>live</u> at the edge, you can't just pretend, politely deleting decent people when your Hampton's so full of its pimps and whores and fuck-monkeys. You don't know shit.

Sure, there going to call me a copy-cat, because this place has no imagination, but I'm not <u>copying</u> you ... I'm not a mirror held up to show you what you are and what you've done, I'm the mirror that shows what you're <u>not</u>, I'm the mirror that reflects your miserable fucking lack of substance. Where is the Killer with blood in his veins and cum in his balls? Where is the Killer who thrives on challenge and competition? You think you're so civilised, the epitome of epitomies, but this civilisation of yours is just an orchestrated surrender to death, a castrated surrender to death, a veneer to hide everything that's venereal—the monkey-fuckers, and the monkeys who dance for the organ-grinder and all the whores who grind the organ-grinders' organs. You haven't <u>seen</u> anything. You haven't <u>been</u> anything. You're just vapour pretending to be cloud. Where's your pride, Killer?

It's not in your dick, that's for sure. All you are is the control that propagates control. You can't even imagine what it is to be what you could be. I'm the crisis of your imagination, the trap door in your worst case scenario. It's got to be better to die in flames than live in chains. You're not worth shit, Mr Worthless-Shit Killer, and I intend to show you that you're not worth shit.

Oh my, look at this mess you've made, a whore-girl swimming in a whore-girl's blood. You could have kept the streets clean. Now the killing monopoly is done. The Festival of Killing is Dead. LONG LIVE THE FESTIVAL OF DEATH!!!

COMING SOON, 33 WITH A BULLET

Lorraine di Stasio
<u>Mayor, Hampton</u>

Dear Lorraine,

As I indicated by phone this morning, I wish to resign from my position as of the above date. I believe that my contract with Hampton Council has been invalidated by the Council's failure to secure my premises, and to secure the integrity of my business dealings. Please feel free to contact my lawyer Petra Knopf at Bardon & Briedis.

I'm sorry it has come to this. I have always performed my duties to the utmost of my abilities, and acted in good faith with regard to the Council, and the interest of the people of Hampton. Up until the murder of Keiko Morimoto, and the violation of my codes, I was confident that the Council was concerned to protect my interests and the on-going prosperity of the Festival.

I have been foolish and naive. I ought to have acted more firmly when the Council failed to address the proposal I submitted in June. I now see that I should have been concerned by the increasing number of 'non-Hampton' people elected to the Council, and taken into the Council's employ. And I ought to have been concerned that inexperienced business managers would lack the capacity to handle a Festival which had grown far beyond our wildest hopes.

I am hurt and confused. Why do I now feel such a strong inclination to believe in rumours, even the far-fetched (?) rumours: that the Council has been working in cahoots with foreign intelligence agencies, that the Council has been acting as an intermediary in arms deals? I also suspect this 33 With a Bullet character is a fiction, a psychopath of convenience. A third-rate Dennis Hopper impersonator. Whose interests would this fabrication serve? How could a person so erratic as this man purports to be gain access to the codes and channels without drawing attention to his activities? And why was the 'Coming Soon, 33 With a Bullet' graffiti allowed to linger on the walls of public buildings? (The Council has always made a big issue out of zero tolerance.) Like Oswald, this man has been *allowed* to be conspicuously conspicuous.

I want no part in murderous challenges. I have lost the desire to carry out my duties, and I have lost confidence in the role of the Killer. I am now of the opinion that the Festival has been irreparably corrupted.

To begin with, I believed the Festival would restore the former Hampton, a place where people knew each other, and cared about the future of the community. What's more, that Hampton would be restored as a place where community was considered to be valuable in itself. I always thought that the gambling was intended to act as a cushion until tourism was firmly established, rather than the be all and end all it has become.

If my only concern was that everyone wasn't pulling in the same direction, I'd be the first to initiate a re-commitment to the Festival and what it was meant to stand for. I now doubt that it was ever possible for everyone to pull in the same direction. This Morimoto tragedy was inevitable.

While acting as the Killer, I have always lived under threat, so I am not unaware that I place myself in further jeopardy by resigning at this time. I trust that you will respect my reasons and accept my resignation in good faith.

Yours Sincerely
[signed **Richard Thompson**]

Crucial documents related to Hampton's Festival still continue to surface at regular intervals.

This volume was just about to be sent to the printers when a previously unexamined letter sent by Christine Marker to her sister Isabelle in Montparnasse was 'discovered'.

Scholars were alerted to the existence of this letter when Isabelle Marker, a journalist, requested its return following the final report of the Witherspoon Commission. As it transpired, neither Elliot nor Witherspoon considered the document. The letter, written in French and untranslated, had been mislaid among papers forwarded to the original Coronial Inquest.

Christine Marker's letter gives us a particularly intimate view of her feelings about Thompson and the Festival, and it appears to settle the question of whether Marker could have (willingly) absconded with Hampton's Killer. Her letter also suggests that the central concern of Marker's documentary would have been to connect Hampton's Festival with dominant cultural trends in Australian/Western Capitalist society.

The translation which appears here has been provided by Miranda Murray.

November 4th

My Very Dear Isabelle,

I'm so sorry, I should have written long before this. Your wonderful letter arrived three weeks ago. I could pretend that work got the better of me, but time is a concertina here, it opens and folds according to need. My time has been more occupied with the thought of work than the actual demands of work …

[Two pages where Christine comments on personal matters raised in Isabelle's letter have been omitted at the request of Isabelle Marker.]

… I am beginning to get some idea of the shape this film might take. Certain themes recur and intersect. Before we came here, I thought that so much of the Festival—the possibility of rationalising a killing spree such as this—must hinge on the Killer's personality. Now I find my position shifting. The Killer, although he is a fascinating case, is no anomaly or psychiatric phenomenon. He's the insecure product of an insecure society. Thompson is a passionless man who wants to present himself as an archetypal Australian hero, the lone surfer riding a wave of social redefinition. He needs to keep reiterating this position in order to maintain belief in it. But the Killer is far from alone in his emotional frailty. Intellectual life here is so marginalised that intellectuals habitually take defensive positions and refuse themselves the vulnerability of passion. When reluctant intellectuals toy with fire, they have no intuition for the dangers of misdirected passion.

Thompson is an Australian Godzilla. Kind, half-apologetic, a powerhouse of good intentions, but at every turn he crushes a building or tramples a schoolbus ... Or King Kong. (Have I become Fay Wray to his King Kong?) He's attracted to me, but he's far too clumsy to act on his attraction. The crew find it ridiculous, with the Killer striving to be impressive, to be a serious minded socio-political theorist. Michael wants me to seduce him. A Mata Hari could see him expose the underside of his personality. The man's intriguing but totally undesirable. Too short, too indefinite. Who would want to kiss a man with such bulbous gums? And he still puzzles me. How can an obviously intelligent man become so far removed from his emotions that he can divorce himself from the horror of his responsibility for the murders? (The word murder is a taboo here.)

Thompson persists in arguing that he is a knight trying to defend the threatened values of community. The opposite is closer to the truth. He so deeply laments the way Hampton changed in the years prior to the Festival, the loss of everything associated with the community he grew up in, that he is now acting to speed the destruction of the avaricious Hampton, this new Babylon. By accelerating Hampton's destruction, he hopes to salvage and restore the sanctity of his memories of a Hampton childhood. In this respect, Thompson is less the disinterested agent carrying out official policy than he is a rogue Catcher in the Rye figure—Holden Caulfield with a crossbow. The Killer imagines he is saving citizens from Life's failure to honour its promise of ecstasy, and he extrapolates a sense of purpose and worth from his own disillusionment.

The Killer's exaggerated disillusionment and sense of failure seems typical of a culture which defines itself by its failure to realise American dreams, by its inability to replicate an impossible Hollywood version of American reality.

And neither are his victims the selfless heroes they make themselves out to be. Hampton's martyrs are not the Burghers of Calais, surrendering themselves to the enemy in the hope of ending an interminable siege. What Mark Twain said is true, 'Martyrdom covers a multitude of sins.' Many of the people I speak to express a fervent desire to be martyred. But few of them impress as people who are determined to enrich their community through altruistic sacrifice. Martyrdom promises to release them from their habitual greed, from the guilty knowledge that they have grown fat gorging on the flesh of their martyred neighbours. And it's not only the martyrs who are devoured. Most analysts neglect the anonymous victims of related exploitation, the children of the gambling addicted and the commercially obsessed. So much in Australia centres on sports and gambling and alcohol, and there are some perverse understandings of what truly noble action involves.

Hampton is no paradise. It's cosy in its tastelessness. If Los Vegas represents Hell on Earth, Hampton is an antechamber en route to Purgatory. There is action, but what excitement or buzz there is here is so artificial. Dollar-driven cynicism motivates everything related to the Festival. The real joy is to escape Melbourne. You need to get right out of the city, two or three hours away, down to the southern ocean where a spectacular road winds along sheer cliffs. With Hampton performing its mourning rituals, Michael rented a Japanese sedan, and we escaped for the weekend, taking our picnic to Apollo Bay. Apollo Bay is a fabulous crescent of white sand surrounded by steep green hills. A million kilometers from Hampton's neon hyperbole. The quiet coastal villages with their fabulous beaches are symbols of the egalitarianism Australians habitually venerate but reject in practice: a simple richness of existence which excludes no one. And that's it, precisely. Anything which isn't exclusive is worthless. If something can't be sold and packaged by advertising firms, if it can't be commodified, it can't have value.

It was unseasonably warm at the coast. The sand was fine and hot under our feet, and it was like being a kid again. We volleyed Gillian's beachball, drank wine, stuffed ourselves with chicken and salads, and waved away insects, all feeling so famously anonymous behind our sunglasses. The water was still too cold to swim, but the sun was hot. Children shrieked as they ran between the sand dunes, fishing boats bobbed about on the horizon, and wisps of breeze fluttered off the ocean. Perfect. We stayed at a guesthouse in the hills, and woke to birdsong: magpies, parrots, and currawongs, and then an awesome electrical storm with breakfast which soon gave way to a clear, cool day.

I would've chosen anything but to drive back to Hampton then. To spend a month walking the hills and forests and beaches. On the western fringe of the city, a huge bridge, the West Gate curves through the sky above the Maribyrnong River. You see the orange of the setting sun reflect off the glass towers which make up central Melbourne, and you can look out across the water towards Hampton to the south-east. I aimed my video-camera at the sky above Hampton then, hoping to see a flaming Killer tumble from the heavens and plummet into the bay.

Some dreams are more likely to be realised than others. I still hope to see you in Strasbourg—with Henri—at Christmas. You mustn't be too hard on Henri. He's just a man, and I've seen many worse. Selfish as he is, he would at least know the difference between self-interest and nobility. Take care, my darling.

All My Love,
C.

APPENDIX 3
'SOCIETY'

There was huge excitement among Festival scholars when an 'unfinished work of fiction' was found among Richard Thompson's papers.

Investigators were originally hopeful this narrative might be a straight transcription of a meeting between the Killer and a psychiatrist, and much of the legal interest in the work vanished when it was determined that, in all probability, 'Society' was an ironic tease written by Thompson, possibly intended for circulation as a hoax.

We cannot know whether Thompson considered the piece finished. Although there are no major alterations to the typed section, the short final section is written in felt-tipped pen, and several lines have been crossed out and corrected.

In my biography of Thompson, I refer to the piece as Thompson's 'Loaded Mirror'. We find the author using fiction to explore darker impulses than he allows to surface in his journal. He wishes to locate himself at various intersections of his imagination.

Clearly, Thompson enjoys the self-conscious play of the *doppel-doppelganger* he constructs, and delights in toying with the reader's good faith. However, we should be wary about dismissing 'Society' as a practical joke and nothing more. Thompson's Journal presents a man who is obsessed with the problems of continuous identity and the possibility of genuine heroism. Who can say that Thompson is not sincere when presenting his personality as a composite of the story's principal characters?

Once again, Miranda Murray is probably closest to the mark when she describes Thompson's 'amateurish metafiction' as 'an act of sadistic self-abuse' and 'the grubby underside of the cult of heroic individualism.'[41]

Perhaps the text is best read as the artist's portrait of himself as Humpty reassembled by Picasso.

------

41 Murray, *If Looks Could Kill*

SOCIETY

You have trouble expressing your emotions ...

Mmm. Maybe that's the Protestant family thing. We're not big on demonstration. I've always had the feeling that if I lost control, I'd lose it completely, like one of those Jekyll-Hyde psychopaths. I could be another Dwayne Herschel.

Dwayne Herschel?

You haven't heard about him? (PAUSE) That surprises me ... Herschel was first-class scary shit. I should tell you about him. He's a big part of the whole picture.

He's someone you knew, this man Herschel?

(LAUGHTER) Not exactly. We met, but you knew Herschel like you knew next week's lotto numbers. His head was a random behaviour generator ... All this stuff goes way back to when I started at uni. I'd never even seen a university till I fronted as an undergraduate, and I didn't have a clue what went on in universities. I knew that it wasn't socially acceptable to look overwhelmed. You had to look cool and indifferent. But everyone else seemed to know each other, and to know where they were going. I knew no-one at all. The best bet was to join every club in sight: the Civilisation Society, the Cricket Appreciation Society, the Friends of Unnatural Llamas ... I joined them all. To be honest, I can't recall joining the Dwayne Herschel Society. It wasn't the kind of club you signed your way into. Membership was by invitation from the President, a bod named James Dickson, who I wouldn't have known from shit. The Dwayne was the big film society on campus, and I knew nothing about films then. I probably lied to James while I was drunk. There was a lot of cheap cask wine about. Mostly I avoid bullshit, but when I first started drinking, I used to tell people that Stanley Kubrick was mum's brother, and Uncle Stan had given her a 'stained glass' window made out of off-cuts from *2001*.

Had he?

It's such an unlikely detail that no-one ever questions it. If you're going to bullshit, your details have to be too weird to have been invented … Anyway, this *2001* story must have impressed James … He was odd. Universities are full of borderline people, but James was Big League strange. Not that he looked crazy. He looked conservative: square-jawed, short hair, briefcase … He could've been President of the Young Liberals. And he had this thing with his top lip when he smiled, a self-conscious thing. He was embarrassed about the bulbous pink gums which masked his upper teeth.

He was President of this Society?

James pretty much *was* the Dwayne Herschel Society. At first, I was too green to know what people meant when they called The Dwayne a haven for loopheads. 'Loophead' might be an affectionate nickname for a cinephile, but these guys were bona fide headcases. The whole atmosphere of The Dwayne suggested a piss-take, or a private joke.

You were going to tell me who Herschel is …

Yes, but it's complicated, because I can't speak about Herschel without thinking of James, and how both of them were so touched, and how attractive madness is to mad people … (PAUSE) You can smile, that's all right, I do see the irony. My fascination with madness is why I stuck with the society for so long. They were all so bizarre and marginal, I thought I'd found a place where I belonged … Anyway, Herschel … The story told to new members was that Dwayne Herschel was a convicted triple-murderer who'd been sentenced to the electric chair in Texas. Herschel was a film buff, and he'd gone to the cinema, sometime in the early-sixties, to see a screening of *The Manchurian Candidate*. Great film. Turns out that Herschel got pissed-off by three kids who gabbed whenever there wasn't any dialogue. He was polite. He told them to be quiet, and when they wouldn't quieten down, he pulled out his handgun and shot them dead.

As you do ...

Exactly. The man was a role model ... It was the sort of mythological hero crap beloved by the student clubs. You didn't take Herschel any more seriously than you took the Unnatural Llamas' claim that Ralph the Wonderllama would rise to crush unbelievers in 1984. Everyone thought James had invented Dwayne Herschel, a bullshit story full of details just unlikely enough to be convincing. The name for a start. Dwayne, a classic redneck name, and Herschel, the astronomer who discovered Uranus. The name had a poetic beauty ... So when James stood up at meetings and declared that the essence of the Dwayne Herschel Society was civility, propriety and order, people would fall about, saying, How dry is this bloke? James would sneak up behind you at a DHS turn and say, Remember this, Richard, the Dwayne's more than just a film society, it's a model society, a prescription for decency and culture. Herschel's sacrifice reminds us that it's our responsibility as artists and art lovers to give order to a disordered universe. We have to impose order where we meet resistance ... It was an inverted morality tale.

But James wasn't kidding?

He was deadly serious. But we *thought* that he was kidding, that he'd created a game of affected eccentricity. And that game was already wearing thin with some people when I joined the society. Factions were forming. Yet people never questioned the view that The Dwayne was meant to be a sophisticated joke.

So how did you find out that James was off the deep end?

Well, like I say, there were factions. A lot of members had gathered around a girl named Amber McKenzie, and she and James loathed each other.

I knew there'd be a serpent.

Yeah, serpents and apples. You're well ahead of the game ... Amber was no ordinary girl. She had gorgeous red hair, and a sing-songish cartoon voice that killed me. She was legendary for a prank she pulled when she was the projectionist at a city cinema. They used to screen a slide before the feature, *Ladies Remember: The Only Safe Place for your Handbag is on your Lap*. Amber created her own version of the slide, *Ladies Remember: The Only Safe Place for your Lap is Under your Handbag*. She showed it fifty times before some humourless old bat complained to management ... The thing about Amber is that she radiated sex. She was a carefree girl. She loved sex, and she loved dope. She was always sucking the lungs out of a bong.

Did you have sex with her?

No. I would've liked to. She was a hornbag. She stuck her tongue in my ear at a party once. I was too drunk to follow up.

But James wasn't attracted to Amber?

He probably was, but he knew she was a rival. Before Amber cranked up the heat, the Dwayne was a hidey-hole for intellectuals who lacked the social skills to become nervous academics. Most of them came from the Theoretical Expressionist crowd, a bunch of pseuds who used to hang around in Brunswick cafes like Travis Bickle's. At Bickle's there a strange green light which made one poseur pretty much indistinguishable from another, and these guys would drink short blacks while they brooded over critiques which lionised unwatchable films ... Terribly intense. And it's not as if you'd ever see them at the cinema.

Dwaynies never went to see films. The society's constitution described it as a *post-cinematic* film society. No films were screened at meetings. The Dwayne presumed its members had already seen enough films to recreate the history of film if need be. The Theoretical Expressionists used to boast that they were shaping a new reality with the force of ideas. They kidded themselves something chronic. Their herd was unheard of outside the ivory paddock.

So where did you fit in?

I liked the weirdness. And the abstractness ... James used to organise seminars about *critical viewing circumstances*, where members spent hours debating what constituted the ideal seat in a cinema, the forms of courtesy to be expected from cinema patrons, whether you should see films before or after a meal ... There was one memorable debate whether members should abstain from sex during the Melbourne Film Festival fortnight ... Unbelievably abstract. None of us went to the Film Festival, and celibacy wasn't a matter of choice for most of us anyway ... But even social retards are vulnerable to the persuasions of sex. They still want to be seduced. The DHS was eighty per cent male, and flirtation and seduction enabled Amber to get a power base. Up until she arrived on the scene, everything had always been so sanitised and theoretical. Though The Dwayne used to pride itself on social redefinition and intellectual subversion, really it was just a safe place to celebrate the fear of human contact.

Until all the boys decided they wanted to fuck Amber ...

Absolutely. And it's hard to explain why. By the usual standards ... How do you express this 'correctly'?... Amber's shapeliness was extreme. I don't know whether you'd call her plump or voluptuous ... Whatever, she had a rare gift when it came to flirting. Even the most reserved Dwaynies would gravitate to her. James could see that too. Every time Amber dampened her lips, the society slipped a little further from his control. So it turned into a crude bun-fight. Each criticised the other's views in the same terms: that they were using the cinema as a vehicle for ideological indulgence. James championed *ideated actualisation*, or *theoretically imposed order*, while Amber played the sensualist. She was after a more satisfying, mystically insightful disorder. Amber used to say that cinematic art exists as *a mood horizon*, that it's an attitude you move toward, or locate yourself in relation to. She'd say that the duty of art was to render chaos in a way which made it *emotionally* comprehensible.

And people bought this shit?

Well, yes. It was complicated and hilarious. It was the hippie versus the Nazi, and the hippie was full of wild ideas. Amber wanted members to be wired with electrodes to test their intuitive response to pornography. She wanted the society to invite film-makers to meetings so theory could inform practice. At one meeting, she confessed to playing recordings of dialogue from Marguerite Duras films while she masturbated.

It's a wonder James didn't arrange to have her killed.

He would have if he hadn't wanted to fuck her too. But James would never admit to himself that he could be slave to something so common as desire. I mean, if James hadn't been attracted to Amber, he would've expelled her from the society long before she started threatening his authority ... From the very beginning, Amber enjoyed demeaning James. He was a soft target. He was the classic name-dropper, and he loved big-noting to new members ... I remember being in a group with him and Amber when James began telling someone how he'd once sat next to the French actress Sandrine Bonnaire during a publicity trip to Melbourne. He said Sandrine smiled at him and invited him to join her for a glass of champagne. Before he could accept, she was shepherded away by the members of the French trade delegation. The way James told it, this was a poignant tale of lost opportunity. And I was inclined to sympathise, but Amber just came out and called James a liar, saying he couldn't make eye-contact with a beautiful woman let alone score with a French starlet. It was horrible. James thought The Dwayne was his society, but he knew that unless he did something dramatic, he'd end up losing the Presidency to Amber. That's when he played his Joker.

The Joker?

Herschel ... The thing James had over us was that we were all members of the Dwayne Herschel Society. We were all there thinking Herschel was a myth, that Herschel's existence had nothing to do with our pretentious club. It turns out that not only was there a Dwayne Herschel, but James had been corresponding with him ...

I thought you said Herschel was executed?

He was sentenced to go to the chair, but his sentence had been commuted to life. After twenty years inside, Herschel was out on parole ...

This is going to get ugly, isn't it?

Yes, but not in the way you imagine ... Herschel had been out for three years. Even before the Amber business blew up, James had been in contact with him, trying to arrange for him to come out and speak to the Society. Herschel was keen enough, but for reasons known only to themselves, Australian Immigration has a mind-set against convicted triple-murderers. So the pair devised a game of bluff and distortion. Dwayne Herschel changed his name to Norman Bates ...

Psycho*!*

Absolutely ... James told authorities he was producing a feature, and needed an American actor named Norman Bates. He then used a connection inside Actor's Equity to write a letter saying Bates had been employed with Equity's knowledge and approval ... I never would have imagined James had that much daring. At the time, we knew nothing about it, only that James had arranged an extraordinary meeting at which Dwayne Herschel himself would be the special guest speaker ...

Which no-one took seriously ...

Of course not. But we were curious to see what James was up to. It was obvious to everyone that James was losing control of the society. And he was being so earnest. He'd hired a hall. He'd contacted all the past members of the DHS. He had HERSCHEL IS COMING t-shirts printed. The whole bit ... So, we gathered in the hall. There were three, maybe four hundred of us, and James was sitting down the front in his penguin suit, beaming. With him he had this thin, grey-haired man. Bad teeth. Checked shirt, Levis. He certainly looked Texan enough. And James stood before the gathering and said what an honour it was to finally introduce Dwayne Herschel in the flesh. He said Mr Herschel had been out of gaol for three years, and it had been the greatest moment of his life when he learned that a film society had been created to honour his memory.

But you thought this Herschel was a fake?

Oh sure. We figured it was a big hoax, and James was doing tremendously well. He was so sincere. Finally, when Herschel got up to speak, we entered the spirit of the thing, and gave him a huge standing ovation. The man had tears streaming down his face. Whenever he tried to speak, he had to pull back from the microphone and compose himself. Herschel must have been very confused. We were responding how he'd want us to respond, but we were laughing too. He was probably thinking Australians have a weird way of expressing emotion ... What James was thinking, I don't know.

So when did people realise this really was Herschel?

Only gradually. He started speaking with a perfect Texas accent, and we enjoyed what we thought was a measured comic performance. He told us how flattered he was, and how a man sometimes has to travel a long way to be appreciated, and the honour of having strangers in Melbourne name their society after him had sustained him through his darkest hours. He said he loved us, in the way that Americans are prone to tell you they love you, and then he said it was important that we should understand the true nature of freedom, because people had lost track of freedom in America, that what Americans meant by freedom was only the freedom to consume and exploit. Herschel described himself as a defender of cultural freedom, and said how shocked he was by the way pornographers and sleaze merchants had been able to use the U.S. Constitution to protect their trade ... He was *so* serious! We were waiting for the jokes, thinking, this is way subtle. Then Herschel said that one day he'd turned on a television chat show and he saw this band of n——s ...

N———s?

Mmm ... That one had the crowd drawing its breath, because the DHS was always politically correct. No Dwaynie would have dared joke about n——s, or calling people n——s. And here was this fifty year old man saying that he'd seen this band of 'n——r rap singers' on television singing about rape, arse-fucking and pussy-splitting, and that the studio audience had one by one told the show's compere they didn't like what the band was singing, but they defended their right to sing it ...

Very American.

Oh yeah ... And Herschel said that if freedom to celebrate rape and sodomy and sexual violence was what the founding fathers had in mind when they protected freedom of speech, then America should have listened to its founding mothers.

A fair point.

Sure. But it was a struggle to follow Herschel's argument, because we were waiting for the jokes, and there he was hitting us with n———s-this, arse-fucking that ... Well *ass*-fucking, actually. It was very disconcerting ... That was when we began to twig, because the more he got into it, the more rabid he got. He said he wouldn't have hesitated to blow away them n———s, just like he blew away the punks who'd denied his right to enjoy *The Manchurian Candidate*. He was shouting, *I told 'em they was being impolite, but they was just trash. They couldn't give a brown shit. I'd do it again right now, because you can't let people get away with that. Bad manners is a virus. If folks show they don't want to be part of a society, or they threaten the meaning of that association, you have to require them to desist under threat of forcible dissociation ...*

Forcible dissociation ... He meant killing them?

Yes ... And just in case we missed the point, he pulled a gun out from under his belt, and swung it around over his head ...

Oh!

It's a great way to get a crowd's attention ... This guy was right off the fuckin' planet. He said that by shooting someone you show 'em you're serious ... Here Dwayne was, praising our society because we'd given him the moral strength to go on with life, and we society members were all there shitting ourselves, thinking, Holy Fuck, the Dwayne Herschel Society is going to be massacred by Dwayne Herschel! We're going to be annihilated by our own myth.

Which is an extreme antidote to pretentiousness.

Tooright ... Dwayne finishes his speech. Total silence. Except for James of course. He was approaching the microphone, applauding, telling Herschel he knew we'd all like to take this opportunity to thank Mr Herschel personally ... It was at that moment we realised we'd missed the obvious, that James had been fucked in the head from Day One. We knew then that James actually *believed* in his theories of civility, propriety and consideration. I'd always thought his ideas were a hoot, and that he knew they were a hoot.

But Herschel didn't kill anyone?

I don't know why. Maybe we satisfied his standards of courtesy ... Anyway, someone dobbed him in. He was arrested, and the police held him for a month before he was deported back to Texas. He got eighteen months for parole violations ... When I said he didn't kill anyone, he did kill off James' presidency.

And the Dwayne Herschel Society ...

Not at first, no ... It should have, but the notoriety increased interest for awhile. There were new people clambering to become members, and Amber had the ammunition she needed to take over.

They should have changed the name to the Norman Bates Society ...

Or the Charles Manson Society. Especially once the drugs came into it ... Amber changed the place beyond recognition. She supplied *enhanced viewing opportunities* to the members, and soon the DHS members began to refer to themselves as *post-theoretical expressionists*, or even *narco-cineastic expressionists* ... It was too much for me. I can't do dope. I get bronchitis. And it was never my dream to be a narco-cineastic expressionist ...

And too much for James ...

Everything was too much for James. He was in deep legal shit with the Herschel-Bates thing. The police wanted to charge him with conspiracy. So James cleared off ... But being a fugitive didn't stop him sending letters to Amber saying she'd subverted his hopes to make the Dwayne a model of civilised association, and how she'd debased everything ... It hardly mattered, the writing was on the wall. There was so much bullshit going on, and finally Amber got the society caught up in a drug bust. People said James ratted on her, but he wasn't even in the country as it turned out. He'd been arrested overseas.

He'd gone to join forces with Herschel?

That might have been logical, but we're talking about a man who was divorced from logic by this stage. James had been humiliated. Herschel's appearance was meant to be his crowning triumph, and it turned into a scandal ... No one heard anything from him for a couple of years. Then midway through last year a friend sent me a newspaper clipping which reported his arrest in Paris.

For shooting someone in the cinema.

You're so symmetrical!... But there *is* an element of symmetry here ... Police said James had been stalking the actress Sandrine Bonnaire, that he'd made plans to abduct her. Apparently he'd written hundreds of letters telling her how decent and civilised she was, and how the two of them together could be the founders of a model society ... He and Sandrine Bonnaire were going to correct the forces damaging the world ...

That's what comes from seeing too many films ... He was prepared to sacrifice himself for the sake of narrative closure.

Yeah, I guess ... I've never thought of it that way.

[The narrative continues in Thompson's handwriting]

It's an irrational way to act ... Doing something insane, something that's bound to have negative results, in order to maintain the illusion of control ... The only way James could feel certain that he was master of his own fate was to master his own downfall.

But James wouldn't see it that way. For him, it's a pure form of heroism. James would say his heroism will be recognised by history, by posterity …

And how do you feel about it?

How do you mean?

Well, you started telling this story to illustrate your fear of losing control, that if you loosened control you might become an erratic, impulsive character like Herschel … Which one are you, Dwayne, or a control-freak like James?

Neither. I was trying to explain that I was terrified of being like them, of becoming like them …

But you are them, aren't you?

No. You're being cute … These are people I know, they're not cyphers …

… Herschel, the dangerously self-righteous man who is willing to kill for the sake of an impossible order, for an unattainable decency, and James, the local hero, the lynchpin of a utopian society, but unable to deal with the realities of living socially. James is so fearful of his own passions, of his sexual desires, he has to deify and idealise Sandrine in order to suppress his darkest impulses, the animal desire for Amber which threatens his whole sense of self … It's easier for James to play at being an heroic martyr than to face his own fears. The fear of impotence, the fear of his own virility …

You want everything to be so neat …

I want everything to be so neat!

It's different …

Is it?

You want to organise it all into a single story where everything fits into place … And you're square-pegging round holes. You can't stand the idea it might all be mysterious and enigmatic and unruly, that there isn't some greater design waiting to be discovered ... I'm not a composite.

Then why did you tell this story?

To describe the impulses I fear, the people that I might become like ...

And what have you become?

I can't answer that. You only want me to say what you want me to say ...

But what you do ... Your duties ... The control you have over things. Would you say that you are in control, or hopelessly out of control?

I believe in what I'm doing.

Do you?

What do you want me to say?... That I'm out of control? That I'm completely deluded?

No ... I want you to say what you've been trying to say, but this time without the killers, the control freaks and the weird societies ... I want you to tell me who you are.

1995

3

DUCKNESS

LETTERS TO CATHERINE AND MIRANDA

FEBRUARY, 1979–JULY, 1997

The great question of the twentieth (century) is the co-existence of different concepts of time.

—*Sunless,* Chris Marker

Things don't seem to happen in sequence. Everything is about relationship, ebbing and flowing together. It becomes unreal to talk about before and after: you can't say that this happened before that happened

—'*Quantum Physics and Motherhood*', Danah Zohar

DUCKNESS

And he seemed to become more Australian and apathetic each week. The great indifference, the darkness of the fern-world, upon his mind. Then spurts of energy, spurts of sudden violent desire, spurts of gambling excitement. But the mind in a kind of twilight sleep.

D. H. Lawrence *Kangaroo*

Rebecca in The House of Eggs

When she wasn't reading or thinking about the novel she ought to be writing, Rebecca sat in the lounge and contemplated the dust. She was thinking about the dust when her father called out from his bedroom.

Are my eggs ready?

No, I haven't cooked them yet, I was hoping you'd died.

Rebecca timed his pause: one, two, three ...

Not fried, *poached*, her father yelled.

This place is held together by the dust, she thought. And it's only dust that's holding him together. If I dusted him, no one could prove it was murder.

Rebecca considered these possibilities, but knew she lacked the will. The thought of dusting overwhelmed her.

The one room in the house not ruled by dust was the kitchen. The kitchen was ruled by grease. Rebecca picked up the frying pan, tilting it to spread a barely fluid layer of fat. She lit the gas beneath the pan, broke two eggs on the rim, and watched the contents dive into the crackling fat.

I'm frying you some eggs, she yelled.

Poached! I want poached! came the reply.

I'll poach some in my spit if you like ... One, two, three ...

Don't break the yokes!

Rebecca watched the egg whites crisp at the edges. A cloud of greasy vapour rose out of the pan. Opening the window above the sink, she saw a silver train rumble past on its way to Hampton station. When the train cleared her view, Rebecca could see across to the red brick wall on the other side of the tracks. Many years ago, vandals with white paint had daubed NO FUTURE on the wall.

Those old-style punks with their English influences had long since given way to American-style graffiti gangs. Brats in baseball caps will soon be down to paint over that, Rebecca thought. They'll paint it over with the swirly New York graffiti that only the artists and their mates can read. The new gangs couldn't give a shit there's no future. The pseudo-Americans will spray the punks and their anarchy into non-existence.

Rebecca picked up the egg-flipper, drove the metal tip into the egg-yokes, and watched the yellow dribble across the bubbling white.

Sorry, dad, the yokes broke, Rebecca yelled.

Waiting on Godot

Dad's terminal, her brother Trevor had said.

At the time, Rebecca understood this to mean that her father was terminally ill, that he was on the verge of death. She took three months leave from teaching, believing that someone should be there to see him out.

Yes, Dad's Terminal, Rebecca thought, as she pulled a dusty paperback from one of the bookshelves in the lounge. What Trevor really meant, she now realised, was that I should live here in Dad's Terminal, that I should dedicate my life to his dust.

Rebecca remembered standing before her Year 12 English class to explain that she was taking three months compassionate leave. She would be back, she promised, well before their exams.

But Miss Parker, George Soutanis complained, your dad's gotta die sooner or later. If we fail English, our lives are fucked.

Denise Sutton, who hardly ever said anything, said, It's probably not even true your dad's dying. You're probably taking a trip to the Greek islands.

If only she had escaped to Naxos or Meskos.

When three months passed, Rebecca chose to resign, and promised herself she would write a book while caring for her father. She intended to write a grand tale of risk and adventure, a novel which rehearsed in fine detail the life she would lead when her father died.

But her father didn't die, and Rebecca seldom addressed an empty page. She was often forced to consider the possibility that she had taken on the nursing role as a deliberate distraction. Her invalid father was an excuse not to challenge her fear of sexual involvements, or her fear of failing to achieve a great literary ambition.

Four years passed. Four years attending to a man who ate little other than eggs, toast, chipped potatoes and sausages. He never once praised her efforts, and she learnt to measure time in the frying, scrambling and poaching of his eggs.

Give these pillows a bashing, will you? There's a lumpity bit boggling my coccyx.

Speak English! That pig-Irish drivel gives me the shits!

But Rebecca's anger was wasted on the apparently healthy man in the blue and white pinstriped pyjamas. She thumped his pillows, propped him up, and tried not to notice the perspiration rings expanding under his arms. And always when she was at the peak of some unspoken exasperation, he would ask about her work-in-progress.

How goes the novel?

The novel ! How could I write in this place? It's impossible to work here.

No, you're right, he'd say, Australia is impossible now. Australians blame everything that's gone wrong on the Yanks, but we still crawl to them, and beg them to set things right. It's impossible to work here.

Finally, Rebecca turned her attention to the paperback she had selected. She slapped the book against her thigh to shift the dust, determined not to let it intimidate her. The novel was *Women in Love* by D.H. Lawrence. Inside the front cover was the biro inscription,

> Rebecca Parker
> Year 12
> Hampton High
> Tel. 98-5977

The Virgin and The Duck Hunter

Rebecca was seventeen, and in her final year at High School, when she first read *Women in Love*. She considered that she had been opened up by D. H. Lawrence. After reading Lawrence, she looked at the football heroes who were lusted after by the other girls in her class, and she was unable to imagine how they could excite love, the real passionate love she yearned for.

Lawrence breathed emotion. He wasn't frightened of excesses, or contradictions, or confusions or repetitions. Lawrence wasn't distant like the other authors she knew. He wrote like someone who'd got his hands dirty.

Rebecca consumed *Women in Love* in one long sitting, and read *The Rainbow* the next weekend. For class that Monday, she prepared seven foolscap pages of notes.

Her teacher, Mr Longreach, was an informal, charismatic type. The girls in his class would speculate whether Mr Longreach wore underpants beneath his tight, faded-blue jeans.

The consensus had it that he didn't wear underpants. Instead of sitting on a chair behind his desk, Mr Longreach liked to sit on the desk, with one foot drawn up onto the table surface, so he leaned slightly to one side.

Rebecca could still picture Mr Longreach as he appeared that Monday, his copy of *Women in Love* held up to the class. He asked who hadn't finished reading the novel, and the usual stragglers put up their hands. The teacher sent them to the library.

Someone asked, maybe it was Frank Sheehan, why the class had to study *Women in Love*. Whoever it was told Mr Longreach that *Women in Love* was a bucket of shit.

Rebecca thought she saw Longreach's crotch bulge slightly at that moment. He took on a serious expression. Yes, I'm sad to say that *Women in Love* by D. H. Lawrence, is a piece of wet, overrated crap.

Rebecca, in her distress, saw the football boys enjoy this immensely.

Can anyone tell me what the D.H. in D. H. Lawrence stands for? Mr Longreach asked.

Rebecca might have suggested Dark Hedonist, but Simon Burton got in first with Dick Head. Mr Longreach called this a good try, before pointing out that dickhead was one word not two. He'd gone on to say that he had the misfortune to study D.H. Lawrence at university. He and his colleagues used to refer to Lawrence as the Duck Hunter, owing to an idiosyncrasy of his prose.

Even pretentious droners like T.S. Eliot never droned on like Lawrence, Longreach told the class. Lawrence isn't a writer. Lawrence is a jackhammer. The teacher chose as his example the way Lawrence used the words 'dark', and 'darkness'.

Rebecca remembered asking if that wasn't to do with sexual apprehensiveness, but her teacher said it would have been all right to use the words in that fashion once or twice, Lawrence didn't know when to stop.

Longreach asked the class if they knew how many times Lawrence used the words dark, darkening, and darkness in *Women in Love*.

Two hundred and fifteen times! he said. I've counted them! The world drowned in darkness, the magnetic darkness, the potent darkness, the innermost dark marrow of the body, the voluptuous resonance of darkness, the waves of darkness, the suave loins of darkness.

Mr Longreach told the class Lawrence was a fraud, ridiculous and irrational. Rebecca was still furious she hadn't been able to counter then as she would now, that passion *is* irrational, fierce and ridiculous.

The teacher went on to tell the class that he and his mates had parodied Lawrence's excesses by substituting the word 'duck' wherever 'dark' appeared. They called themselves the Duck Hunters, the assassins of pretentiousness.

Everything begins to slide off into the duckness, Mr Longreach went on, delighting in his own legend, into the great stormy duckness above the great duck void. You are met with a profound duckness, a fire of the chill night breaking constantly onto the pure duckness, the unknown duckness.

Rebecca watched her teacher recite all two-hundred-and-fifteen known instances of duck and duckness, and was consumed with simultaneous fury and embarrassment. She begged the bell to ring, feeling slightly ashamed that her emotional virginity had been given up to the man now lampooned as a duck hunter.

She remembered Longreach's dumb-arrogant comments at the bottom of the essay she wrote on *Women in Love*.

> *Naive, impressionable girls are always sucked in by Lawrence. You must learn to combat pomposity by taking the mickey, Rebecca. You need to explore your inner duckness.*

Now, when Rebecca returned to the opening lines of *Women in Love*, she did so determined to reclaim the darkness for Lawrence, David Herbert Lawrence, the man who knew more about passion or conviction than any man or duck hunter she'd known in Melbourne.

A Duckness Embraces Professor Sharp

Rebecca recalled the day her brother Trevor was appointed Professor of Australian Literature at the University. After rushing out to buy a set of polo-necked jumpers and matching jackets, he saw a hair consultant, and exchanged his black-rimmed glasses for contact lenses. Trevor then asked Rebecca if he should trade in his ancient motorcycle for something more in keeping with his new office.

Trevor would zoom through the southern suburbs of Melbourne on his Triumph, wearing a long red scarf that trailed in the wind. Rebecca told him to keep the bike, that it would help him to retain the common touch, but she really hoped Trevor would be intercepted by the police and booked for not wearing a helmet. She wanted to see her brother brought down a notch or two.

Trevor was a clever man, devious enough to overcome his lack of imagination or insight by reading the inclination of the wind. He had the knack of discovering a crucial piece of dirt which could be held over an empowering agent.

Once a fortnight, Trevor roared up the driveway. He always claimed he was visiting his father, and he would leave a stack of books for his father to read, but Trevor rarely entered his father's room.

He would place a stack of books on the table in the lounge, telling Rebecca, When did this place last have a good dusting?

You'll be buried by this filth, Trevor once told her. You need to trade this crypt for some invigoration. A good shagging would do you no harm.

Rebecca wanted to say, You condemned me to this, so don't come goose-stepping in here telling me what I need, though the idea of a good shagging appealed to her. What she actually said was, It's *my* life. She knew that if she hit Trevor, he would use that against her when the moment suited him.

Rebecca, could you scramble me some eggs? a voice called from down the corridor.

She will in a few minutes, dad, Trevor replied.

Rebecca turned her back on her brother but he refused to notice.

If you tidied this place up, you'd see things differently. You might even get to work on that novel.

When she turned, Trevor was flicking through her paperback copy of *Women in Love*.

It's reading this crap that makes you overwrought, he observed.

Rebecca was used to Trevor ridiculing her taste in fiction. So, what masterworks of Australian literature are you teaching these days? she asked.

Masterworks went out with Leavis, Trevor said. We take seminars in sporting autobiography, narrative structure in television soap opera, advertising strategies in women's magazines, and the role of the duck in Michael Leunig's cartoons. We've got a fabulous seminar which compares notions of optimism and free will in Australian horoscopes with their American counterparts. None of these kids want to read novels, least of all Australian novels. We've passed the time when you can have an elite hierarchizing the worth of things according to elite values. We analyse the forms and genres the public chooses to consume. We take ordinary values seriously.

Rebecca felt like she had missed something. This was Trevor, who had spent seven years writing an unpublished thesis on sexual metaphor in Shakespeare, claiming to champion the interests of the common Australian.

But where will the leaders come from? she asked. Who is

going to create values, and question values, if you've got the brightest students in the country convinced their best bet is reading French theorists in translation and gazing up their own arse? We need universities to be creating an audience for original thought, for writers and critics who can offer alternative versions of Australian society, and future societies, not just using Gallic hocus-pocus to rationalize the way things are.

You've got us wrong, Trevor said. The doctors in the English Department don't prescribe. We don't exclude or belittle.

No, and you don't take responsibility either.

Trevor stayed for a cup of tea, as he usually did. He said Rebecca could go back to teaching and still care for their father, so long as she organised her time properly. If she were a true writer, she would have written her book already.

Rebecca watched from the window as Trevor kick-started his Triumph, revving it long enough to annoy her neighbours. When he finally moved off, Rebecca waited to see the last of the light cutting a path through Trevor's duckness.

Trevor's bike could still be heard in the distance, shifting gear in South Road, when Rebecca called to her father, Do you want me to scramble some eggs?

An omelette.

An omelette then, Rebecca yelled.

When she opened the window to the cool night air, Rebecca heard voices from the other side of the railway line. The brats with their spray cans had arrived. She was so pleased with the accuracy of her forecast that for a moment she didn't hear the other voice, the voice filling her head with phrases which were forming themselves into complete sentences. At first, she tried to organise the words in her head, but soon she realised there would be too many to recall. She put aside her mixing bowl and reached for a pen.

An hour passed.

Ignoring bellows from her father, Rebecca sat to read the paragraphs that she had written. She knew it wasn't masterly prose, but it was the beginning of a story she would have to complete.

It was Professor Sharp's fashion to address the shiest female students in his tutorial when asking questions which related to the use of vulgarisms or euphemism in a literary text.

What do you make of the word 'wick' in this context? he asked the crimson-cheeked Anna.

Stella, perhaps you could tell the class what this word 'coynte' refers to?

When Stella dissolved into tears, the Professor spoke without sympathy, I don't think that's necessary. We're adults here.

Professor Sharp was a strangely contradictory man. Though he delighted in telling embarrassed young women that coyntes were cunts, and that a fetching woman is one who makes a man come, he was steadfast in his contempt for modern female writers who punctuated their fiction with immodest description or the language of the streets.

For several years, he kept displayed in his classroom a photocopy of a review in which he assailed a young novelist for showing no more skill than the harlot's capacity to talk dirty, and he made clear his opinion that her preoccupation with unconventional sex was an outrage to public decency. Her novel was unfit to be classed as literature.

The subsequent fame of this writer did nothing to undermine the Professor's confidence in his judgement. In fact, nothing unnerved Professor Sharp until he came into contact with a second-year student named Catherine O'Shaunessy.

Catherine was an outwardly shy, round-shouldered blonde. She had exactly the kind of prettiness which ordinarily attracted the Professor's interest. During the first tutorial of the year, Professor Sharp would sound-out his new students with a passage of poetry, and he chose to ask Catherine what the word 'quaint' meant.

Catherine ran her finger beneath the line on the photocopied handout. She looked at the phrase for a moment, before removing her glasses to look Professor Sharp in the eye.

You might not realise this, Catherine told the Professor, but the combination of your bald head and a polo-necked jumper makes you look exactly like a penis with ears.

As her father continued to bellow about his omelette, Rebecca scribbled a title above her story. The first thing which came to mind was 'Modern Education', but she quickly discarded this to replace it with a title that always made her smile whenever she considered the work in progress, 'The Duckness Embraces Professor Sharp'.

1991

DIDO

Now I'm older, I can see that my life has been blessed with advantages. If you lined up all the people who'd ever lived on this planet, 999 in a thousand would choose to swap places with me. The dead ones especially. My problem is that I was never taught to appreciate the wonderful objects and opportunities I was given, or to recognise my generally advantaged situation in life.

It always comes down to love. My parents mistook gifts, expensive schools, and clothes for genuine affection. I'm not saying it's their fault I grew up to be the person I am, or they failed to care about the kind of person I became. Despite their wealth, my parents are fine people. They must have wanted their only son to mature into a man with a true appreciation of life and his place in it. Even now, they still seek to remedy the situation. They feel guilty they never gave me enough time. Through Miss Murray, my parents hope to give me the time they hadn't the time to give.

Governesses are rare in Melbourne, and I would venture to suggest that I am the only thirty-seven-year-old man in this city who has his own governess. Which isn't to mock the situation. I am learning to become less cynical and more appreciative. I may prove to be the forerunner of a new breed: wealthy, emotionally-immature men who have their practical and moral concerns managed by a well-qualified intermediary.

Miss Miranda Murray (I'm forbidden to call her Mazzy) is an extremely well-qualified young woman. Her mother is a Tetley, of tea fame, and her father has a seat in the House of Lords. The Murray family own a fine home in Woodstock, and are related to the Churchills by marriage. After attending finishing school in Zurich, Miss Murray took a three-year course in domestic instruction at the prestigious Fothergill College in South London, returning the following year to write her Honours dissertation, 'A Systematic Approach to Late-Adolescent Hygiene', since published as *The Enemy Between The Folds*. As dux of her year, Miss Murray was destined for a well remunerated position in one of the Arab states until my mother approached her with a challenge no ambitious governess could refuse.

Though she is a slender, softly-spoken twenty-three year old, with a complexion typical of the English gentry, an easy smile, and the prettiest strawberry-blonde hair, only a fool would take Miss Murray lightly. She is sufficiently studied in her craft to command respect. When Miss Murray demands that I tidy my papers under threat of no pudding, I hustle. When she refuses me permission to see Cassandra Bartlett, on account of Cassie's uncouth telephone manner, I accept that her judgement, though harsh, constitutes my own best interest. But you mustn't imagine our relationship is all instruction and interdiction. My governess is well-schooled in the science of fun.

Where my parents believe they erred by not giving enough of their time, Miss Murray gives me nothing but time. My days are now broken up into regular, bite-sized chunks: drawing lessons, music lessons, music appreciation, riding, physical instruction, exercise, free-reading, literature, speech, philosophy and argument. I can't imagine what I did with my time before Miss Murray arrived to organise it.

We discuss John Stuart Mill and Spinoza as if the future of the Australian Tourist Industry or professional golf depended on it. She slaps the back of my hand if I get lazy with my chords. She tempts me with old-fashioned foods like crusty homemade pies, and Yorkshire puddings. Miss Murray's potato gems are a delicacy beyond compare.

If the sun's out, we sit under the big liquid amber while she reads aloud from her favourite novels: *The Mill on The Floss*, *The Mayor of Casterbridge*, or *Emma*. On occasion, she will invite me to take her from behind as she reads. She is a great one for combining pleasures, and for choosing the right patter to stir my blood.

You might raise my skirt and take me roughly while I read from Chapter Four.

Naturally, I accept her gentle invitations, though neither of us pretend this is what my parents had in mind when they took the delicious Miss M into their employ. I dare say they wanted her to dissuade their son from dabbling with the stockmarket, or cocaine, or combinations of both. And indeed, she has succeeded in tempering the advance of my vices. I no longer gamble at the casino, or drink to excess, or spend long evenings slouched alone in front of the television. In fact, the television is always off now, to serve as a dark mirrored screen in case I need to see her reflected, naked above me, swivelling and grinding, managing me to a nicety. Doling out a serve of sticky pudding, as she so fetchingly refers to it.

I mustn't convey the impression that I always buckle to my parents' wishes, or bark at Miss Murray's command. I will not cease to be my own man merely because a governess administers my time and reports back to my parents. Sometimes, I find it necessary to make a statement to that effect.

As we sit side by side at the keyboard, I seize Miss Murray's wrist, and direct her hand to the beast in my trousers. This is the game she calls 'putting a collar on the dolphin.'

Richard, I shouldn't need to remind you that there is a time for games, and a time for practice, and it ill serves us to confuse the two.

The dolphin's very sad without his collar, Mazzy.

Miss Murray. If you continue to address me by my Christian name, I shall have to report back to your mother. I'll tell her you've made impertinent requests for gratification.

In which case, I'll inform the Fothergill College council that their most esteemed graduate accedes to the sexual demands of children in her charge. What would that do for your career, Miss M?

Opening my fly, she runs a finger down one side of the agitated mammal.

Richard, you are trying to extort sexual favours from me.

It's extortion only if you believe it is, Miss Murray.

But mostly I do as she wishes because I could wish for nothing more. I like her best when she kisses me hungrily on the lips and calls me the young master, or when she is angry and threatens corporal punishment.

Curiously enough, her anger reminds me most of my maternal grandmother. It fell to Omar, an energetic woman in her early sixties, to care for me while my parents scoured the deserts of north-western Kenya in search of ancient bones. Though I loved Omar fiercely, I felt her love most urgently when I provoked her anger. I would choose exactly the right moment to throw a tantrum in a supermarket aisle. It might have been about something so trivial as her refusal to buy me a White Knight, or a Bertie Beetle. I would shriek and wail.

Richard, if you don't stop this minute, you'll get Dido when we get home!

How I adored Omar's threats of Dido. The very word Dido was a thing of intricate beauty, more poetic enticement than a punishment to recoil from.

This Dido so often proved to be a wooden spoon whacked hard at the back of my fat thighs, a physically ambivalent experience which combined excruciation and exhilaration. (At other times, I'd be allowed to lick cake mix off this same wooden spoon.)

I remember my beloved Omar red-faced, stretched beyond reason to this senseless violence, the spoon in motion, and the mess of sound and emotion that was Dido incarnate.

Dido meant something different to Omar than it did to me. Dido was the reward I would get for being less than I could be. I'm telling you Richard, stop it this minute or you'll get Dido!

Dido was a credit voucher in the shop of things to come.

Maybe Miss Murray is the Dido I'd been promised. Her destiny is to take me to the other side of Dido, that dark place where punishment and reward are indistinguishable.

Yet I fear Miss M won't stay. She's too professional to say so, but she hates the dusty north winds, and yearns for winter snow. Sitting in front of the broad dresser in her bedroom, she vigorously applies moisturisers and lotions, rubbing them into her hands, and deep into her perfect cheeks. Sometimes, she lets me smother my lips in rum 'n' raisin lip balm, and we kiss till her lips say enough. But one day those lips will say Enough is enough, and Miranda will head back to a leafy corner of the Cotswolds.

On Sunday evening, she sits at the big table and writes her weekly report. My Shostakovich is coming along, I am generally tidy, mostly well-mannered, but still given to moments of selfishness. I need to be more considerate with my pony, Warren. My diction shows the benefit of improved breathing and relaxation, and I am developing a more sophisticated understanding of God's role in the dissemination of goodness and evil. I have a fine singing voice, but I need to become more broadminded in my appreciation of literature.

I contest the latter point. This is the pot calling the kettle black. If only Miss M would allow me to read the moderns, or even the so-called post-moderns. I used to read Toni Morrison, David Ireland and James Ellroy before she arrived to regulate my reading. Miss M should broaden her own outlook beyond Tolstoy, Turgenev, and Austen.

But her narrow literary tastes contrast with her adventurousness in the sensual arts. Most notably, she delights in a strange rowboat-like position which bends my intent almost to snapping point, a strange, ineffable verge that might be Dido itself.

Oh baby, she coos. My baby. My baby.

This Dido is nothing compared to the one I will face when Miss M reports to her employers that I have acted disgracefully. She will be forced to tell my parents that I have sabotaged condoms in the hope of securing her governance of my time. Miranda, my darling, please hear my confession. I'm a selfish scoundrel. I will deserve everything I get.

1996

CLOUDY DAYS IN VELESK

To the best of my knowledge, no weather has been forecast for Velesk tomorrow. Nor has weather been anticipated in Velesk these past eight years. For most people, Velesk is no more than a quaint memory. More quaintness than anything—Is it possible to retain the memory of an insinuated city? Maybe these questions are better left to philosophers. But I know that I am not alone in yearning for weather reports which offer metaphysical distraction.

I first heard about Velesk from my friend Christine. Though sceptical, I knew Christine to be a level-headed woman, not given to fantastic speculation. Eight years ago, she was teaching geography and politics at a prestigious girls' school, and she had already published scholarly articles on Australian foreign policy in the Asian region. Due to these interests, Christine made an effort to monitor international news broadcasts. She rarely missed the SBS World News in the evening.

Following local weather predictions, SBS ran a summary of weather in the world's major cities. The international forecasts appeared as a graphic detailing as many as sixteen cities, three or four of which were verbally ... italicized by the newsreader during the ten seconds the graphic appeared on screen. One Thursday evening, eight years ago this week, Christine's attention was seized by the newsreader's reference to a city she had never heard of: *'Ten to twenty-one, and clear in Velesk.'* Her eyes rushed to the graphic. Wedged between forecasts for Tel Aviv and Vienna was:

VELESK Clear 10–21

Thinking it odd that an obscure city was considered prominent enough to be included with New York, London, Mexico City, Buenos Aires and Johannesburg in a list of major cities, Christine went to her comprehensive Gazetteer, expecting that Velesk would prove to be a heavily populated, politically insignificant city in the nether regions of Eurasia, a metropolis of two or three million souls tucked away somewhere between Tadzhikstan and Kazakhstan. But neither the Gazetteer nor the Oxford Atlas mentioned a city named Velesk.

The former Soviet states were highly volatile then, and it was far from unusual for cities to take on new names, or to revert to former names. So Christine wasn't surprised when the reference books let her down. Surely the SBS news department could clarify the situation. Not so. A frazzled producer told her she had no idea where Velesk was, nor could she explain how the city came to be mentioned on the newsreader's autocue, or the accompanying graphic. There had been no mention of Velesk on the producer's running sheet. While the news department suspected a practical joke, they also thought the glitch might prove to be the result of a computer virus. Weather bulletins on the Internet had also mentioned Velesk, which was then, according to their sources, anticipating a clear day, with a maximum of twenty-one, following a minimum of ten.

By next morning, Christine had forgotten the episode. She didn't think to mention it in the staffroom. But scanning a copy of *The Age* during her lunchbreak, she found among the brief weather forecasts for the major cities of the world—this time sandwiched between Valletta and Vienna—

VELESK Clear 10–21

None of Christine's colleagues had heard of the city. The head of the geography department thought Velesk was probably just a misprint for the Russian city of Volsk, a port on the Volga River. However, on that evening's SBS World Weather

Outlook, following Toronto on the graphic listing of major cities, the teacher was once again surprised to see

VELESK Cloudy 12–19

Christine soon realised that she wasn't alone in her curiosity. A brief report on page six of the following day's *Age* indicated that readers had been calling the paper to glean some knowledge of Velesk. With staff unable to explain the unknown metropolis' sudden appearance in international forecasts, the writer echoed the SBS suspicion of a computer virus, or even a hoax, and indicated that *The Age* would omit reference to Velesk in future forecasts until 'Velesk makes itself known to the geo-political community.' Nevertheless, on page 28 of that edition, readers found the same prediction that SBS broadcast the previous evening:

VELESK Cloudy 12–19

It should have already been clear to those interested in the matter that Velesk, having waited so long to present itself to the world, would not be easily disregarded.

Some days after that, around the time Christine first contacted me, commercial news bulletins began to report the mysterious case of a persistently nonexistent city which seemed to be experiencing a succession of cloudy days. The puzzling appearance of Velesk in world weather forecasts had not been confined to SBS or *The Age*. Global information services reported the receipt of summary weather outlooks for a city no one knew anything about. What's more, the enigmatic Velesk resisted all attempts to obliterate or ignore it.

Television producers in Japan and Argentina declared their inability to correct any graphic or autocue reference to Velesk. References to the city would be deleted, only to reappear just as weather information was being broadcast.

The tone of reporting on the Velesk mystery was flippant. Cynics treated the matter as a leg-pull, the technological equivalent of circles in cornfields, and the news audience was expected to deduce that Velesk was a gremlin, or cybermutant. Attempts to solve the problem had somehow bred a form of treatment-resistant offspring. It says something for human need that usually ignored weather forecasts so quickly became cult viewing. And the new cult was not let down:

VELESK Cloudy 12–22

What stole my attention, and captured the imagination of others who knew my fiction—Christine among them—was how closely this peculiar eruption resembled my published fantasies. The mystery could easily have been a story written by me: a tale of theories, speculations, false assumptions and presumed conspiracies. So I wasn't surprised when local literary critics voiced the opinion that this Velesk scenario was a tale of my making.

Choosing to overlook the fact that Velesk was a global mystery, and my media connections didn't extend beyond Melbourne, *The Age* published an article by the cultural studies guru Nick Johnson which emphasised similarities between the appearance of Velesk and events depicted in my story 'Transcendence'.

While flattered to be thought capable of perpetrating a delicate hoax on a large scale, my delight was tempered by confusions which undermined Nick Johnson's argument.

To begin with, Johnson confused 'Transcendence' with another story in the same collection, 'Star Gazing'. In 'Star Gazing', the inhabitants of a large Melbourne-like city open their morning newspapers to find outrageously personalised and telling astrological predictions. These predictions are unique to each reader. The newspaper's management are at a loss to explain the appearance of so many different predictions within the same edition. Naturally, the paper's tabloid opposition howl it down as a dirty stunt, and rush to make imputations about the mental stability of readers who would claim that they are being directly addressed by astrological predictions.

As neither 'Transcendence' nor 'Star Gazing' were stories I wished to hang my hat on, I was slightly embarrassed to field questions from reporters enthused by the Johnson argument. They asked if I was solely responsible for the Veleskan micro-fiction, or part of an international plot. While claiming innocence, I stated my admiration for anyone who could have brought off such an ingenious hoax, if it was a hoax. A dramatic change in the meteorological outlook supplied a convenient diversion:

VELESK Rain 12–18

In the United States, two theories soon gained pre-eminence. The first argued that these Velesk forecasts were coded messages from aliens, the equivalent of saying, *Watch This Space*. The second theory argued an earthbound conspiracy. The forecasts could be read as a series of coded messages transmitted either by a major drug syndicate, a terrorist organisation, or a secret group flexing its muscles to demonstrate a new subversive potential.

Christine knew the mediocrity of my literary output sufficiently well to realise that Velesk, for all the sublime modesty of its existence, was bigger than anything I could imagine. When she saw me dragged into the game, she dropped over with her latest researches.

At that stage, there had been something like nineteen separate weather forecasts for Velesk. Christine fed this data into her computer in the hope of obtaining a geographical fix on the city. Velesk seemed to have a temperate climate. By relating temperature-range and volatility to the one-word forecast, Christine's computer suggested autumn, which then implied that an earthly Velesk must be located in the northern hemisphere. Of course, the computer's deductions presumed that 'tomorrow' in Velesk coincided with a tomorrow somewhere on earth. Depending on the premises you began with, the weather forecasts for Velesk were capable of confirming whatever you wanted to believe about practically anything:

VELESK Clear 10–23

'Clear' suggested a visual depth of field, the opposite of murky. Were the good citizens of Velesk able to *see* their weather, to perceive atmospheric conditions in the way that we perceive them? And what could these degrees mean?

In relative terms, a minimum temperature of ten could be unbearably cool, while a maximum of twenty-three might endanger frail, elderly Veleskans.

Clear—Clear—Clear might be the three oranges on a cosmic poker machine, the signal for an attack, or international political subversion. Cloudy, on the other hand, warned operatives to maintain their stealth. Nothing was concrete. Everything was possible.

A Hobart travel agent achieved notoriety by taking bookings for Veleskan tours, advising prospective clients they should pack to take account of all weather contingencies.

VELESK Cloudy 10–21

Those who weren't terrified of imminent alien invasion joked about the Veleskan obsession with the weather. People made light about the drought in the capital, imagining the Veleskans being forced to sink bores, and apply water restrictions. Just two days of drizzle, and one day of rain in twenty-two. What could 'Rain' mean to Veleskans? An intense continuous downpour, or periodic showers?

On day twenty-four, Christine had a letter published detailing her view that Velesk was situated somewhere between fifty to sixty degrees north of the equator. The city's weather didn't appear to be subject to temperature fluctuations caused by proximity to an ocean, lending weight to her argument that Velesk—whether it had a population of ten, or ten million—was situated somewhere within a 300 kilometre radius of Orsk in the former Soviet Union. The publication of Christine's computer-fix on international news services provoked immediate rebuttal from scientists in Boston, who were 'practically certain' Velesk would be found somewhere between Columbus, Ohio and Baltimore. By contrast, Italian scientists insisted that the coy metropolis was in Belgium.

These 'fixes' inspired treasure seekers and doomsday cultists to descend on the regions specified. While some travellers hoped to find a buried alien spacecraft, others had their hearts set on Noah's ark, or Nazi gold reserves. Others said that they merely wanted to be on site, prepared to receive further instruction.

VELESK Clear 9–23

I particularly recall the senior NASA official who was sacked after stating categorically that the forecasts represented a coded communiqué to an alien who had been stranded on earth. The Velesk weather reports informed the alien of a newly arranged rendezvous with a spacecraft which would transport him back to his planet. On the same day, a prominent French intellectual suggested the mystery was fabricated by NASA to generate a financial boost to the US space budget.

VELESK Clear 10–21

Once dragged into the debate, (my publishers were thrilled by the surge in sales) my 'expert' views continued to be sought by television companies desperate to keep the game in motion. Ratings figures were higher than they had been since the early days of colour television. A climate of heightened anxiety sparked a retailing boom, and the public couldn't get enough Velesk. Any new observation, with just a slight shift of emphasis, was apt to be seized upon, igniting an outbreak of theories and counter-theories. I argued that people were taking the matter too literally, or too metaphorically, and the truth lay somewhere in between these extreme depictions of Veleskan reality. The forecasts needed to be subjected to a more lateral analysis.

Velesk was a city which existed only through a capacity to project its future existence. Though we knew something about Veleskan expectations for the immediate meteorological future, we knew nothing about the accuracy of these forecasts, or how these anticipated futures merged with the present. We couldn't know what the weather had actually *been* in Velesk, or if it made sense to speak of Velesk existing in the present.

I was convinced of the pointlessness of searching for Velesk as a geographical location. Our only concrete knowledge of Velesk was as a temporal site, or projected site. Our failure to locate it was a problem related to our idea of time.

If Velesk proved to be a city on a planet in a distant universe, it made no sense to speak of a Veleskan tomorrow, or 'forecast', in the same way that we might speak of tomorrow in Paris. It is always problematic enough to speak of now, a *now* that exists simultaneously in both Melbourne and Gdansk, let alone drag intergalaxial *thens* into the equation.

The Veleskan forecasts were as much about the meaning and possibility of tomorrow as they were about a single, unambiguous tomorrow which would happen, inevitably, within the terms of tomorrow as we ordinarily understand it. For all we knew, these Veleskan tomorrows might have been ten days ago, or ten million years ago. To suggest that cunning Veleskans had specifically targeted this civilisation for the purposes of instruction, or even a practical joke, was just a little *earthocentric*. It was the psychological equivalent of the scientific thinking Galileo swept out the door.

VELESK   Rain 12–18

In a widely published article, I proposed two theories. The first argued that Velesk was indeed a city on earth, and that Veleskans were employing this microscopic assertion of existence as a means to reach back to us from the future. The forecasts could then be seen as a form of quiet reassurance, a confirmation that there would be a future worth living. The future would be worth living because the people of the future cared enough about their fellow creatures to worry about ancestral anxieties. The Veleskans of tomorrow didn't wish to unsettle us with powerful demonstrations, or to interfere with our situation in a way which might radically alter the course of history. The forecasts were a message left on an answering machine by Godot. *There is a tomorrow worth waiting for. Things will become clearer.*

VELESK   Clear 8–18

I favoured a second theory, not because it was more verifiable than others, merely because it endorsed my own system of belief. Put simply, I hold that time—by which I mean chronological time, the orderly succession of pasts, presents and futures—is an illusion. I believe that all history belongs to a single, indivisible moment, a moment of pure finitude which is, paradoxically, pure infinitude. *The eternal.* Our sense of direct, or progressive movement through time, of one event causing or determining its successor, merely suggests the physical limit of our capacity to perceive and comprehend 'external' experience. Any sense of ordered succession through time describes the extent of our power to engage with the universe, rather than indicate defining laws which pertain to the universe itself.

This theory has it that all the events in history exist contemporaneously—the Battle of Agincourt alongside the crucifixion of Jesus Christ. Furthermore, that all *possible* events, every possible course of history, exist within this single eternal moment.

Once in awhile, our perception broadens to allow a hint of these parallel realities. Hence *deja vu*. Hence Velesk. Cloudy, tantalising, erotic Velesk.

The beauty of these Veleskan theories and speculations was that none could be disproved. All were equally credible, equally incredible. The unfathomable city was mysteriously egalitarian in concept, and indiscreetly mysterious in fact. The thirty-seventh and final forecast read:

VELESK Cloudy 12–19

When the forecasts ceased (bar fabrications and hoaxes soon established as such), the Doomsday crowd expected the worst. But the worst was nothing more than the absence of further data in an already information-saturated world. Psychiatrists complained about a need to treat vast numbers of patients grieving this sudden loss of *beyond*. In truth, these psychiatric opportunists were encouraging people to feel that loss. Velesk had been excellent for business, and psychiatrists were among those who felt its loss most fervently.

I watched the forecasts and waited. Everyone did for a time. But gradually we came to accept that Velesk had no further need of our attention. Or else, we'd exhausted our need for Velesk. The enigmatic city became the lost city, a presumed-dead civilisation whose death could not be verified. Or maybe Velesk went into hibernation, and will one day erupt back into existence like an inverted Pompeii.

Eight years can pass in a day. Oddnesses, however extreme, manage to be accommodated, or even forgotten. There will certainly be anniversary reflections on the curious phenomenon of Velesk, but these will be of the same order as anniversary rehearsals of the Moonlanding, or the Kennedy assassinations. Maybe I am wrong to believe that Velesk is stranger or more compelling than a maritime disaster, or Pol Pot. Strangeness is as relative as time.

I suppose I should get together with Christine, to reminisce about our brief moment in the spotlight, and old times in Velesk. She was right. Not even in my wildest imaginings could I have invented modest, weather-fixated Velesk. Only a genius could give shape to its rare clouds, or describe the unique elusiveness of Veleskan tomorrows.

1996

STEVE WAUGH

(OR THE FIVE MINUTES BETWEEN 3:35 AND 3:30)

If she calls by four, I'll still have time to thaw out the veal, and we can have that with carrots, broccoli and potatoes.

If the phone rings in the next five minutes, it will be her, but if it rings after that, it will be mum or Fabulous.

If Fabulous calls before I turn on the radio, Australia will be bowled out before tea, Warne won't have enough runs to play with, and the West Indies will win just after lunch on the last day.

If I turn on the radio and Steve Waugh is in, Australia will collapse and be all out before stumps, but if either of the not out batsmen is 27, Australia will win.

If she calls after five, we'll just have to buy take-away, because there's no point thawing out a good piece of veal and having it go to waste because she's late, or already eaten without having the courtesy to tell me.

If the repair people quote more than $120 for the VCR, I'll knock them back and get Fabulous to have a look at it, but if they say it's fucked, I'll write a letter to the manufacturer telling them it's only two weeks out of warranty.

If I get through two more papers before three thirty-five, I'll check the scores, and if I turn on the radio and Steve Waugh is already out, I'll turn off the radio and not listen again till after tea, but if I turn on the radio and Steve Waugh is in, but not on strike, I'll keep listening till tea or till Steve Waugh is out.

If the manufacturer refuses to come good, I'll threaten them with Consumer Affairs, or threaten to contact the Minister for Consumer Affairs.

If Steve Waugh is already out and I have to turn off the radio, I'll take a stroll down to the newsagent, and if the book is reviewed in *ABR*, or in one of the monthlies, Ian Healy will make fifty and Australia will win the Test, but if they win the Test on the back of Ian Healy's fifty, they'll lose the series.

If she calls after six, I'll tell her to bring home take-away, tell her that she can't expect me to cook for her if she won't let me know what she intends to do.

If the phone rings in the next thirty-five minutes, I won't answer, unless it rings five times before four, in which case I'll answer the fifth call.

If I turn on the radio and Steve Waugh hits the first ball I hear described for four, a close relative will die before Christmas.

If Fabulous drops over before five, I'll tell him that she's been giving me the shits and I'm moving out.

If she comes in after seven and doesn't mention this bloke by name in the first five minutes, that'll mean she wants to fuck him.

If I ask her what this bloke means to her and she lies, or says he doesn't mean anything to her, that'll mean she's been fucking him without telling me, but if she tells me that she's been fucking him but wants to stay here in the house, I'll tell her she can stay so long as she never brings him to the house, but if she brings him to the house I'm going, because she can't expect me to stay if she won't respect my sensitivities.

If I turn on the radio and Steve Waugh gets out to the first ball I hear described, that'll mean she wants me to piss off.

If the repair people call to say they can do the VCR for $120, but I'll have to wait another week for them to get in a part, that'll mean she wants me to stay.

If the phone rings in the next half hour, I'll only answer the third call, and if it's Fabulous or mum, she won't come in to-night, and she won't call me.

If she comes back drunk and tells me she's been out pissing-on with him, I'll tell her how I actually feel about her, that I've al-ways loved her, even if she tries to make me shut up about it.

If I turn on the radio and Steve Waugh is still in but gets run out between tea and stumps, Australia will win the series.

If she comes home with him, if she brings him back here ... if she actually brings him back here with her tonight, I don't know what I'll do.

1996

THE IMPERMANENCE OF THINGS

A person with an excellent memory and a powerful imagination has no excuse for being bored. When all else fails, there is always time-travel. Life, as Kundera once noted, is elsewhere.

A person with an excellent memory and a powerful imagination will enjoy imagining potential boredom situations, situations which challenge the memory and imagination to alleviate the onset of boredom. The greatest challenge for that person is to imagine the condition of boredom itself, without looking beyond to its alleviation, without unintentionally activating the means of alleviation. The time machine is always fuelled and ready for motion. The greatest threat to the imaginative, memory-retentive time-traveller comes not from an obstructed passage through time but the prospect of avalanche, the danger that one might be overwhelmed by the consciousness of time itself.

Anxiety is the mortal enemy of the time traveller. A time traveller can use memory to conjure pain so acute that the prospect of pain *is* real pain. The form of anxiety which plagues the time traveller is not fear of a specific event, or an apprehensiveness related to pain or deprivation, but the elevated consciousness of compressed time. *Everything is now.* Within the machine, within the path of the machine's motion, everything is immediate.

If I do not remember being a passenger in a train delayed by a snowdrift outside Stockholm, I imagine the situation so vividly that it becomes indistinguishable from genuine memory, or the memory of a dream.

My fellow passengers groan when the Swedish conductor advises that we may be delayed for eight or nine hours. They are unable to face the terrible prospect of being alone with themselves for even so short a time. Most will experience this delay not as a disruption to their journey, but as a threat to the motion of the planet. They live for sensation, for a sense of motion, if only for that most illusory progress, the sense of an orderly progression through time. Denied sensation, left at the mercy of their intellectual or emotional resources, they are at risk of perishing from boredom. But the time-traveller receives any delay or postponement as an opportunity. Empty time is a canvas waiting to be caked thick with coloured pigments.

To lust is also to list. When the definitive text is written on time-travellers, the author will note a common need to express intensity, or concentrated temporal engagement, in the form of lists. A time-traveller controls time by reordering it, by ridiculing the foolishness of perceived chronologies. Delayed by a snowdrift outside Stockholm, the time-traveller will happily open his or her suitcase to produce a notebook which owes its presence in the case to just such a contingency. An empty notebook is a list willing itself into existence.

In this Snowdrift Notebook, I have written, or imagine myself having written, that, as of March 25th, 1996, I am 13,079 days old, and my immediate desire is to compile a list of *The 100 Happiest Days*.

Even for a seasoned time-traveller, this is a major challenge. One's happiest moments do not necessarily belong to the happiest days. Nor do the happiest days automatically number among the most momentous, since the momentousness of an event does not always reveal itself at the moment of event, but within subsequent consideration of the moment. Momentousness is apt to shift with re-consideration and redefinition.

Equally, the time-traveller plagued with an overdeveloped consciousness of time is more conscious than anyone that perceived joy will always be betrayed by a poignancy intrinsic to happiness. The very tenuousness of the happy moment implies the assertion of lost happiness. Any list of *The 100 Happiest Days* will not simply be the reclamation of those periods of insistent pleasure, but a list of one hundred lost happinesses. Not even the time-traveller's skill at making the absent immediate can distort or annihilate the consciousness that one is travelling through an Empire of Poignancy.

To simply transcribe my list of *The 100 Happiest Days* from the Swedish notebook I had in front of me, or imagine I once had in front of me, would serve little purpose. The list is a long succession of dates. These dates are shuffled, crossed-out, and rearranged. Double-ended arrows indicate shifts and replacements which I once thought ought to be made. Each date corresponds to a day luminous within my memory, or my imagined memory. An exact transcription of such a list would make as much sense as a move-by-move description of a chess match to someone unfamiliar with the rules of chess, or the abbreviations used to describe the moves.

For instance, June 28th, 1995, and May 28th, 1995 vie for the top position on my hierarchical list of happy days. One is crossed out to be replaced by the other, only for a double-ended arrow to indicate the provisional reinstatement of June 28th as the ascendant day among those 13,079 days of variable happiness. (How does one compare an exquisitely happy day of little 'event' with a brilliant day full of happy events?)

No simple reading of my denotations will summon the *intensity* of my engagement in the process. In order to classify the happiness of a given day, you need to recover that happiness by re-experiencing it, to become as one with the temporal milieu: all the complex emotional, physical, and historical contexts which erupted into experiences of pure, sustained happiness.

You might look at the date June 28th, 1995 and see it as no more than an arbitrary division of time within a logical continuum. If you accessed a newspaper library, you could list a number of significant events which took place on that day, or were reported on that day, or were expected to occur on that day. Your own diary may well record an entry for June 28th, 1995 which details business meetings, personal encounters, or even the result of a football match. (Highly unlikely, it was a Wednesday.) For the time-traveller, a date does more than signify a point within so-called objective time or history, it is a doorway.

Still, my failure to tidy or finalise the list betrays the increasing sense of frustration I had with this Happiness list, and this dissatisfaction, or imagined dissatisfaction, must pertain to the use of dates as signifiers of happy days. My personal happiness, the purity or intensity of my emotional or sexual exhilaration, did not make that *date* happy. Any heightened consciousness of time, of the peculiarly fluid experience of time that comes with time-travel, can only accentuate discontent with these sign-posts to the illusory presence of objective time.

It is meaningless to speak of time divisible into equal segments, as if all encounters with time take place according to the same rules and the same understanding of the rules. None of us inhabit the present for more than a moment, let alone inhabit the *same* present. The very dates which make a list possible or coherent intrude upon the (inviolably subjective) happiness to which those dates are supposed to refer. Making this list was the equivalent of signing my happiest days over to a calendar manufacturer. My moments of indescribable joy may as well have been appended to a glossy shot of Thomas Hardy's Dorset, or a naked female bodybuilder.

Examining this list notebook, I see that I abandoned, or imagine I see abandoned, the precision of a hierarchy which was to be my list of *The 100 Happiest Days*. That list is set aside in favour of a non-hierarchical listing of happy moments. I might have imagined then that these acts of recollection would constitute a more intellectual or goal-directed activity than time-travel ordinarily permits. Considering this second list from a distance, it appears to be unusually targeted. Yet, there is also a truth, a genuine immersal, that makes the list trans-portive. It not only maps a specific journey through time which pertains to the original journey or imagined journey, it acts to re-direct me through time on an unanticipated return trip.

To recover that moment just before the first kiss, when focus softens and the background begins to swirl, when you might have heard an almost imperceptible crunching of cogs as time drew to a halt.

Those moments as a young child watching the opening credits of Disneyland when you could actually believe that happiness was not an emotional condition but a place.

The hot-pink kite ducking and diving against the blue of an immeasurably blue sky.

Those moments when time was nearly bursting at the seams, when the regulation hour after dinner had passed, when the glare was so intense you could barely open your eyes, the sand so hot beneath your feet that you had to run, the parched air full of salt and rotten seaweed and squealing children's voices, when there was no more exciting prospect in the world than the sensation of thrusting your head through the breaking waves, locks of salty wet hair clinging to the back of your neck.

Moments when reality bewilders desire: Catherine O'Shaunessy enters the crowded lecture theatre and appears to be searching for someone, and you are shocked by a realisation that the student she is searching for among all these students is you.

Always those moments near the completion of an ordeal you'd dreaded for months in advance—an examination, or a speech, or a task which threatened to expose your inadequacy—when you realise the worst is over, and that soon you'll be in a hot bath, or sipping a glass of red wine, and the dark clouds over your appointment diary will be gone.

Those time-stretched, slow-motion moments when all your despair at global conflict and famine is erased by the half-forward in the red and black guernsey who snatches the ball off the top of the pack and storms into goal, his fist punching the air even before the ball clears the umpire's head, when you feel a seizure at that place in your chest where coronary occlusion is indistinguishable from ecstasy.

In the train to Sandringham, reading Gogol's Dead Souls, where in spite of your acute self-consciousness you begin to laugh hysterically, and just for once don't give a fuck if everyone looks at you.

And those moments in the car with your high school friends when it is unquestionable that you've landed among the most brilliant, exuberant people on earth, and you can switch on the car radio confident that the first song you hear will be your favourite song.

That feeling when it all clicks, when everything falls into place perfectly, and you see, you know, exactly what The Author was getting at and why things were arranged in a certain order, when you appreciate the possibility of an essential order.

That moment when, after weeks of having photographs taken, arranging mail to be redirected, repeated visits to the bank, calls to the travel agent, persuading someone to mind the dog, collecting the passport, doing financial calculations, finalising hotel arrangements, buying the new suitcase, visiting the old relatives who might die in your absence, having injections, attending farewell parties, making checklists, packing, repacking, redrafting the will, booking the taxi, queuing at the check-in, and bundling your luggage into the overhead locker ... That precise, perfect moment when your arse hits the seat and you can begin to embrace the idea that your journey might be more pleasure than ordeal.

Did I ever intend to list one hundred of these moments, or make a totally comprehensive list?...

Something is seizing me. We passengers on the train delayed by a snowdrift somewhere between Stockholm and the ferry to Denmark are advised that we are to be transferred onto a series of coaches. *I remember this now.* If I recall this coach transfer, I recall it as the time-traveller who finds his re-entry point in the form of a ridiculous, minimalist German pop song, *Da Da Da* which an old lady on the coach insists that we all sing along to. I am singing. I can hear my slightly flat, but not unenthusiastic voice among a ragtag choir of voices. This is a moment reclaimed from time in its entirety. Should I classify it according to a happiness ratio or expectation? I am in a coach driving along a highway somewhere in Sweden. It is snowing, and I am singing *Da Da Da.* Inside my case is a list of happiest moments which might yet become more poignant through my failure to complete it. Someone passes me a crumbling Danish pastry. I am singing *Da Da Da*. If it were in my power to take you with me, to share that pastry with you, I would. But you have no place in this journey because your notion of happiness, your idea of the possibility of happiness, does not depend on you being there. And that man with the raucous Australian voice two or three seats behind me. *I remember him now*. Steve Hair, a road-train driver from Catherine in the Northern Territory. Half-man, half-amphetamine. Steve is the one who will wake me from a deep sleep inside a warm railway carriage aboard the ferry to Denmark. He will pick me up and carry me to the deck so that I can feel the snowflakes on my cheek. 'Snow! Isn't it fuckin' great?… Mate, we're in Scandinavia, and it's fuckin' snowing!' The raucous voice several seats behind me belongs to a man who will introduce himself to me as Steve Hair. I am on a coach driving along a frozen highway in Sweden. I am singing *Da Da Da*. I am travelling through time, deep into the Empire of Impermanence. I will never be bored.

1996

FORK MAN

Though most insults lose their impact through overuse, one or two vulgarities still manage to deliver, and we have a duty to be careful when using them. Terms like dag and dickhead have become endearments, but you can still trigger a brawl by calling someone a deadshit or a fuckwit. I mention this only to assure you that I have fully considered my duty to the language before making the following declaration: Gavin McGibbon is a turd.

You won't remember my name, but you may remember me as the so-called 'Fork Man'. I was a human interest story, the unlikely survivor of the flash floods at Narraya.

The whole thing was incredibly dumb. I didn't know that country at all. The river rose so quickly there was no time to get away, not even to climb back up to the main road. I was swept through the gorge by a wall of water, powerless in the current. I can't recall seeing the tree, so maybe I smashed against the trunk. I must have grabbed hold of it instinctively. I don't remember climbing to the knotted branch. Most likely I just rose with the level of the water. But I felt safe there in the fork, even when the water was tugging at my knees. I felt confident that if I stayed there everything would be all right. When the flood receded after a day or so, I was fifteen metres up with no way of getting down. I thought I was in the fork six days at most, and didn't believe the rescuers when they told me it was twelve. I'd been thinking about things, daydreaming, having quite a good time. The more thirsty and hungry I got, the weirder the dreams.

I thought it must have been the weird hallucinations that interested the television people. Well, who knows what I was thinking? I behaved like an idiot. Vivien Johnson told me they wanted to make a film of my time up the tree, and it was going to be like Beckett, Australian Beckett. Even when they paid me the twenty thousand, and their researcher spent just an hour chatting on the phone, I still believed they were interested in my experiences and the film was going to be arty and challenging like Beckett.

The agreement I signed was seven pages long. I'm an intelligent person, and I've read plenty of documents, but I should have asked to have the contract's sub-clauses clarified. I expect people to act in good faith, and trusted I was dealing with folk who wouldn't exploit the ambiguities of an oddly phrased agreement.

One stipulation was that I would be expected to fully co-operate with pre-production research. I took that to mean that I would be required to offer any help the scriptwriter deemed necessary. As it happened, I never met the writer. Yet Vivien Johnson stressed this full co-operation clause when she informed me that Gavin McGibbon was going to spend a week living with me. She said Gavin would be playing my part in the film, and he needed to observe me at close range to enable him to get into the character.

Gavin is taller than I am. Quite a bit taller, and more muscular. He'd spent time in a gym. I couldn't think of one respect in which Gavin and I were alike. And when his name was first mentioned, I hadn't heard of him. The producers told me he was a highly respected dramatic actor, that he'd been nominated for a Logie. Television critics might have told me that Gavin had been the heart-throb in two early-evening soaps. When I mentioned his name to friends who knew his work, they said, Oh ... he's the last person I would have expected.

Speaking to Gavin on the phone, I warned him about the lack of room in my flat. He said he didn't need much room, and

I'd hardly notice him, before arriving at the front door with just two suitcases, video equipment, a full length mirror, and an exercise bike.

Gavin said he was excited to meet me. Getting this role, playing me in the telemovie, was going to be his big break. He told me that when he read the script, he thought the part had been written for him.

Say that again.
Say *what* again?
What you just said …
Why?
It's really interesting the way you crush your vowels. It's how you position your tongue.

Even when I cooked for both of us, Gavin never ate with me. At least, not in the usual sense of eating with someone. He video-taped me eating. After I finished, Gavin sat in front of the monitor and tried to mimic the way I had eaten. Gavin said that, thanks to his training at the Institute of Dramatic Art, he would only take three days to have my eating habits down pat.

But Gavin, I didn't eat anything while I was up the tree. I practically starved to death. The whole thing about my story is that I didn't eat.

But you eat in the flashbacks. You recall every meal you've eaten in perfect detail … Besides, I'm not trying to mimic you. This is about entering your psyche. By the end of this week, you should be able to confront me with an experience you've never had, and I'll handle it exactly the same way you would.

That's great. Just now, I'm confronted with your dishes, which is something I've never encountered before. How do you think I should handle it?

My money says you'll get angry. That's good. I need to see what you're like when you're passionate.

I didn't like the way Harriet was so excited about meeting Gavin. And she shouldn't have said that Gavin was too much of a hunk to take my part. When I told her Gavin was just a dumb soapie star pretending to be Robert de Niro, she called me a cultural snob. What could be dumber than getting caught fifteen metres up a tree for twelve days? The hardest thing for Gavin would be to convince the audience that an intelligent man wouldn't have found some way to get down.

When Gavin told me he needed to meet Janine, that he needed to see how Janine and I interacted, I couldn't think what he meant. Then it struck me that the scriptwriter must have turned Harriet into Janine. And I couldn't wait to tell her that her hunk Gavin was now making a film about a stranded man who spends two weeks fantasising about the terribly desirable Janine.

If I walked down the street to get a paper, Gavin came with me, trying to copy the way I walked. When I noticed him getting rounder at the shoulders, and beginning to slouch, I pushed out my chest and pressed my shoulders back, but I couldn't sustain it.

When people recognised Gavin in the street and spoke to him, he would reply as he imagined I would, an embarrassed smile and a mumbled greeting, with eyes turned downward.

I could have said, For Chrissake, Gav, stop it, it's giving me the shits, but Gavin would have looked at me with sponge-eyes and committed my anger to memory.

One time, I came out of the shower to find him sitting on the couch next to Harriet, asking if she could remember the first time we kissed, and she told him that she hadn't enjoyed it, because when I stuck my tongue in, it tasted of onion.

She'd always told me it was the most perfect kiss she'd ever had.

You don't like your parents very much.

Whaddaya mean? I love my parents.

The way you speak to them on the phone. It's like a business call.

We're very reserved. That doesn't mean we don't love each other.

But you know they don't approve of Janine.

Harriet!... My parents love Harriet. They think she's great.

Your mother told you she was a tart.

She *what*? Who told you that? Did Harriet say that?... It's bullshit! My mother wouldn't say anything like that.

No? What about when you told your mum about the abortion?

The *what*? What fucking abortion? Harriet's never had an abortion, and if she'd had one, I certainly wouldn't tell my mother about it ... Where the fuck have you been getting this crap?

Gavin told me he hadn't brought the script with him because he had already committed it to memory. Gavin didn't tell me lawyers had instructed him not to show me the script or to divulge details. When Gavin told me that he thought the script had been written for him, he neglected to mention that he'd paid someone to write it for him. Gavin never once let on that he was the film's executive producer.

You don't eat well, do you?

Gavin, fuck off!

You need more fruit, more fibre ...

Gavin!

And you should get your eyes tested. Have you noticed the way you squint?

Twenty-thousand dollars sounds like a lot of money. You can think of a lot of things to do with twenty-thousand dollars. If someone offers you twenty grand without asking for much in return, you are inclined to accept their offer.

But there are circumstances in which twenty-thousand dollars doesn't seem like a lot of money, and in those circumstances you begin to question the kind of things which can be given monetary value, and the highly relative meaning of a term like 'lot'. It's possible for a lot to be a lot and still not be nearly enough.

Gavin began to answer the phone as me, and conduct conversations where he would make decisions and offer opinions on my behalf. That didn't matter so much if he was speaking with someone who had called to speak to him, or to the producers of the telemovie, but I was infuriated to find him arranging dinner with Harriet and asking if Gavin could come along.

Gav, if you want to have dinner with my girlfriend, you ask her out as Gavin, but don't ask her out as me. And don't have me asking if you can tag along, because I wouldn't want you there, all right?

It's O.K. She didn't know it wasn't you.

Bullshit!

I've mastered your voice. I've caught the negative way you think. She thought it was you. And she sounded like she was really keen for Gavin to come along.

Look, if you and Harriet want to fuck, you should fuck, but leave me out of it.

Well, I don't think I could ... I mean, I'd need to watch the two of you fucking before I could fuck her the way you would.

Gavin ... I wasn't serious.

But it would help. I think it's a good idea.

I told Gavin that my innermost fears were private, that they were my business.

No your fears are my business ... That's if you want an accurate portrayal. Maybe you're not ready for that.

Gavin, I don't mean to be hurtful or negative, but you *can't* do it. You're nothing like me. You're a talentless moron.

You're beginning to see yourself through me.

Bullshit!

And you're scared of confronting things that have always terrified you ...

Gavin ...

When you were a kid, you were disgusted by handicapped people, weren't you? And that old coat of yours, you think wearing it keeps you safe from bad people and acts of God ...

Fuck off!

Weeks later, Harriet told me she and Gavin slept together. A strange moment. I would have expected to be homicidal or suicidal if I discovered that Harriet had been unfaithful. I was surprised to find myself numb. It was a numbness that I took for indifference, and Harriet saw it that way too, turning on me, saying it proved I never really loved her. Because I was unable to confront my deepest fears, I was incapable of real love.

Hey, wait a second. It was you who slept with that big dumb fuck!

It was no big deal. I don't care about Gavin. He said it would help him to understand you better if we slept together, and I thought it might help me to understand you better.

How very understanding! It must have been a great therapeutic experience!

As a matter of fact, I didn't enjoy it. He gave a very technical performance ...

You let Gavin fuck you!

No, I didn't. I wish I had let Gavin fuck me. I wish Gavin had wanted to be Gavin when he fucked me. As it was, I couldn't really tell the difference.

I've heard a lot of stories—probably apocryphal—about the American actor Dennis Hopper coming to Australia to play the bushranger, Mad Dog Morgan. Hopper was a student of 'the method', and got into a role by trying to become the man he played. Even when he wasn't on set, he would stay in character. Anyway, the stories have it that bushranger Dennis ran amok through southern New South Wales, holding up tourist buses at gunpoint. The producers had permanent brainache trying to keep him out of gaol.

Method actors tend to have an underdeveloped sense of irony, and this deficiency allows them to plough on regardless.

When I found Gavin practising my signature in my chequebook, he wasn't even embarrassed.

It's close, but I haven't quite got it. You press so hard.

That's it, Gav, you've gone too far!

Hey, do that again, that thing you just did with your lip …

I'm gathering your stuff, and I'm dumping it out on the street.

It's like a twitch … I can use that.

Gavin, I'm gathering your stuff, and I'm dumping it in the street.

This might be a good time for you to hit me. I think you want to.

I moved toward the guest bedroom, doing my very best to stay calm. Gavin, I'm dumping your stuff in the street.

Gavin looked at me, and repeated what I'd said with exactly the same intonations. Then he tried it again, this time slightly altering his emphasis on the word 'dumping'.

Bit by bit, I gathered his stuff and dumped it in the street.

I once spent twelve days sitting in the fork of a tree, frightened I would starve to death, remembering everything which had ever happened to me, sucking rainwater off leaves, fantasising about Harriet, and rehearsing the wonderful reunions that would follow my rescue. Reality, dream, fear and hallucination all meshed together like a perfect work of art. My sister Maggie said Gavin was the price I had to pay for not treasuring the integrity of a unique experience. Maggie told me I lacked strength of character.

Harriet was invited to the preview screening, but she'd already moved to Canberra. And I would have declined the invitation too, if the producers hadn't sent the limousine to fetch me. I tried to avoid Gavin, and the publicist berated me for refusing to have my photograph taken with him. It made no difference. They took photos of us individually, then tricked them together, so the entertainment magazines could run photos of Gavin and I with our arms around each other at the preview of 'the film tipped to make hunky Gavin McGibbon a superstar'.

Gavin was already behaving like one. He arrived with his glamorous new girlfriend, Liz Mitchell, who, as coincidence had it, was the film's scriptwriter. Liz told reporters she always had it in the back of her mind that she would do something with Gavin.

I drank too much wine, and sat with my family, trying to conceal my despair as the ninety-five minute travesty flickered away on the big screen ... The great turd camped in the fork of a tree, his head flooding with puerile thoughts I'd never had, nourishing himself with the memory of sentimental moments I'd never experienced.

When the film ended, there was a long silence. Then, unaccountably, an intense volley of applause. I was staggered. How could people embrace this tripe? Even tough critics were on their feet screaming for Gavin, and Gavin rose to acknowledge them with a wave and a smile. I heard a voice from behind me say, This will be the making of him. He could be anything that boy.

When the applause died down, my mother turned to me and said she was sorry they'd changed my story and made such an awful movie.

It's all cliché, I said. It's total crap.

Yes. But he was wonderful.

Who was?

Gavin ... He had you down pat. Even the twitch ... He was the dead spit.

It's funny. I'd often used that phrase, but I'd never really thought about it, where it comes from, and what it actually means. Of course, mum's use of it—to suggest indistinguishability—was treacherous and inappropriate, the exact opposite of what I thought. But I liked it anyway, and decided I'd use it myself ... The dead spit. Yes, Gavin was the dead spit.

1996

AN EVENING WITH BOO RADLEY

Irony's a bitch sometimes. You meet a girl, and almost at that instant, you make up your mind. You decide that she's attractive, or funny, or bossy, or dull, or worth sleeping with. And because you insist on doing this, you make godawful mistakes, though you seldom get to know how stupid these misjudgements were. But every once in a while, your hasty imperceptiveness returns to club you over the head.

I read in this morning's paper that Shelley Thorsen won the Tony for Best Actress on Broadway. The report describes her one-woman show, *An Evening With Boo Radley*, as a *'tour de force'*. After rereading this report several times, there can be no doubt. This is the same Shelley who once tried to abduct me in Montparnasse. Sweet, funny, fucked-in-the-head Shelley turns out to be the most famous woman I've met, and, if you discount two negligible Australian Prime Ministers, the most famous person full stop. Shelley has clout. The thing is—and this is the pointy end of the irony—when I met Shelley Thorsen in Paris, she was just a rich kid fool enough to confuse me with a British film star.

If you've got to be alone in a big city, then Paris might be the best place to be, but I hadn't intended to be by myself that Christmas. The way I'd planned things, Paris was to be a weapon of seduction.

Though crazy about the film publicist, Amber, I kept fucking-up just when she was at the point of surrender. I'd botched things so often that only a big gesture could restore the balance. So I took out a loan and bought two air tickets to Paris, booking a month's accommodation at the enticingly named Tim Hotel on the Rue d'Arivee. Paris would be cultural lubricant, an incitement to vital fluid exchange.

I'd planned to spring this on Amber at a decisive moment. We'd be watching *The Umbrellas of Cherbourg* on video, I'd make a subtle reference to spending Christmas in the city of love, and the evening would end in a hot, slippery entanglement. (Amber is a voluptuous redhead, and I had been hanging out for entangled slipperiness since our first meeting.)

I can't recall how advanced my preparations were. A quiet video evening at her place had been arranged, but I hadn't yet rented *The Umbrellas of Cherbourg*. (One look at Catherine Deneuve's wallpaper sends women crazy with desire.) Maybe I'd begun to check use-by dates on my condoms. Then Amber called. I spoke rapidly like someone who had a night of amorous exploration in mind. There was a longish pause. Amber told me that her mother had died.

Her family came from all over the place for the funeral. Given the suddenness—her mother was just fifty—Amber coped pretty well. I told myself that a Christmas in Paris would be good for her, but I'd better hold off mentioning the tickets for a couple of weeks.

As it happens, I didn't tell Amber about the tickets. So far as she's concerned, there never was a month of romance, not even in prospect. I hadn't seen her for a couple of days, and when I got back to my flat, there was a message on the answering machine. Amber had called from Pretoria. She'd made an impulsive decision to spend Christmas in South Africa with her brother, who was a diplomat there. If she could find work, she would stay on.

Given the choice between spending the summer moping in Melbourne, or rugging-up to mope in Paris, I chose Paris.

Like I said earlier, if you have to be alone in a big city, Paris is the best place to be. Galleries and museums, fabulous bookshops and cemeteries. The patisseries are wonderful, the cheese is brilliant, and the wine is red. (With the refund from Amber's ticket, I found myself drinking better wine than I might have otherwise.) And there are the cinemas. Paris is a cinephile's heaven. You can guarantee that every film you've ever wanted to see will be showing somewhere in Paris.

So it was hardly the most miserable time of my life: walking, drinking, depleting the French stockpile of almond croissants, viewing the German Expressionists at the Tokyo Palace, and The Universe of Borges at The Biblioteque Nationale. And every night after dinner, when it was too cold to walk, a couple of films. Sure, I wanted Amber snuggled on the other side of my expensive double-bed, but a Cassavettes retrospective was reasonable consolation for a man who gets off on film.

The only really bad time was Christmas Day. I walked, and stuffed myself full of pastries and cake. Though wanting to eat a proper holiday feast, I couldn't warm to the idea of dining by myself when so many Parisien families were out celebrating. By evening, I was in need of comedy, and *Harold and Maude*, with its toe-tapping Cat Stevens soundtrack has never failed me. Paris being Paris, *Harold and Maude* was showing near the Sorbonne.

And I did feel much better to be laughing at Bud Cort's multiple fake suicides, and Ruth Gordon's eccentric driving, sharing my laughter with a hundred people on a chilly Christmas night. It took my mind off Amber and the torrid sex I might have been enjoying.

When out the front of the cinema, wrapping a scarf around my neck in preparation for the stroll back to Tim Hotel, a tall, pretty girl approached me, camera in hand. Her voice soon gave her away as an American.

It would really mean a lot to me if you would take my photograph.

Sure. Not a problem.

And just my saying, Sure. Not a problem, sent this girl into paroxysms of delight.

Oh, I love your voice. It's so charming.

Already I sensed that things were out of whack: the

disproportionate enthusiasm, the too-rapid assessment of my vocal charm. But this was a drop-dead gorgeous girl, slender with auburn hair, a fabulous smile, the whole package. And she spoke a near-approximation of English, unlike the beauties who had recently turned my head. I certainly wasn't going to crush her desire to have me take her photograph outside one of Paris' least memorable cinemas. I might have imagined she was an American college girl whose vacation project was to have her photograph taken in front of every cinema in Europe, which would be enough to make her exactly my sort of girl.

When I asked her to pose so the composition would be balanced by a string of Christmas lights in the street behind her, the American brushed off my artfulness. She smiled a strange, automatic smile, I pressed the shutter button on the Polaroid, and my job was done. Then she ran to throw her arms around my shoulders and kiss me.

Oh, you're so fabulous. I've loved everything you've done. You've no idea what this means to me.

I had no idea what this meant to her.

Inviting me back to her apartment for a drink, she apologized for not having introduced herself.

Excuse me, I'm at an advantage, I know who you are, but you don't know me. I'm Shelley. My apartment's a couple of blocks from here.

Of course, I had to go with Shelley if only to find out who the fuck she thought I was. Blessed with chameleonic features, I've been taken for a local in Scotland, Germany, France, and Italy. Some say I look Jewish. But this was more specific. She had someone in mind, and I was intrigued. I won't pretend that sex wasn't a part of it. She was a fabulous looking girl, and I was open to the idea of trading fluids with her. But I'm not an opportunist when it comes to sex. I'm quite fussy really. I don't have to believe I'm in love with the girl, but I need to feel that nothing I know would *preclude* my falling in love with her. That's why I didn't tell Shelley straight out, Hey, I think you're confusing me for someone. I knew I wouldn't want to go with her if the error was too outrageous.

Had I known that Shelley thought I was the actor Hugh Grant I would have been extremely worried.

I expected that Shelley's apartment would be the typical one-bedroom dive in the student quarter. Not so. A full-time security guard received her in the foyer. An antique lift took us up to the fourth floor. Shelley's apartment was tastefully lavish. Ultra-modern. Her kitchen adjoined a massive living room. Beautifully framed Chagall and Miro prints on the walls. A television set slightly larger than Dr Who's Tardis. The whole deal must have cost a fortune.

Well, I said, this is fantastic. I had you marked down as a student.

Did you really?... I'm not a student. But this isn't mine. It belongs to my parents. They're in Chicago mostly, so they let me have this place while I'm rehearsing.

Rehearsing?

Oh, you don't want to know about that, she said, handing me a glass of red wine.

I must have said something like, Mmm, y-yes, please tell me about it, because whatever I mumbled made her go off like a porn actress in the final reel.

Say that again! *Please*! Say it just like you said it then.

Tell me about it.

No, *with the stuttering*. It's that thing you do in *Bitter Moon*. I saw *Bitter Moon* four times. I'm your biggest fan.

I think you're mistaking me for ...

There's no need to be shy. I'm not going to kidnap you or anything.

Until then, the thought of abduction hadn't crossed my mind.

That's a weird fucking film, *Bitter Moon*, she said. Polanski's an odd man ... Did he ever speak to you about Charles Manson?

Shelley thumped the pillows next to where she was sitting on the sofa. Come and sit here. I've got so many things to ask you.

I'm a film buff, and I'd seen *Bitter Moon* not long before. I hated it. Peter Coyote's close to Julian Sands and Richard Dreyfus on my list of Box Office Poison. I could picture the affectedly indecisive Home Counties actor that Shelley was confusing me for, but I couldn't remember his name. (All this was well before *Four Weddings and a Funeral*, and the blow-job in the back of the car.) I knew that he and I looked nothing alike. His accent was Oxbridge, and mine was conspicuously Melbourne-nasal. The only thing we might have had in common was an inability to look attractive women in the eye when speaking to them.

No, Polanski's never spoken about Manson to me, I told Shelley. I don't think it's something he likes to dwell on.

Her hand was rubbing my thigh, and my thigh was enjoying it more than my head wanted it to.

You're going to be *so* famous. I can tell. I have a gift for predicting the future.

Predicting that Shelley's hand would soon be inside my Levis, I thought I should change the subject on behalf of the actor she was confusing me for, so he didn't get a reputation for being easy.

What are you rehearsing?

Do you really want to know?

Sure.

This succeeded in removing her hand. She wouldn't be able to talk about her work while groping me.

It's an epic one-woman show. Very expensive. It goes for five-and-a-half hours without an interval.

If I weren't so keen to stay in character, I might have exclaimed, *Five-and-a-half hours without an interval! You're fucking kidding!* I opted for a polite, That must be exhausting.

Have you seen the film *To Kill a Mockingbird*?

Sure. Gregory Peck. Robert Duvall. It's a classic.

That's what I'm doing.

You're doing a one-woman stage version of *To Kill a*

Mockingbird?

No. Not a stage version. I'm telling the film ... Just me. No props. No costumes. No music. I'm recreating the emotional experience of the film.

I had a premonition then that wasn't about my fame as a British actor in Hollywood, or getting sucked-off on the back seat of a car. I took a discreet look at my watch. It was 12:45. My premonition had to do with a five-and-a-half hour show without intervals. A show which had a PATRONS MUST PISS AND SHIT BEFORE ENTRY sign on the door. This was the show about to unfold before my eyes.

And I should head-off your informed curiosity, because it's exactly the question that was puzzling me, How can a film which runs for two hours become a five-and-a-half hour performance?

Well, it wasn't a this-then-that account of the plot an excited twelve-year-old might relate. Shelley did it all, *became* everything. Not only did she do the voices and describe the actions and interactions, she did the music and sound affects and described the cross-cutting and the camera moves and shot-sizes, while offering an elegant, ironic commentary on what the characters might have thought they were doing, or would have preferred to be doing.

In *The Purple Rose of Cairo*, a character leaves the screen to enter Mia Farrow's life, but Shelley dragged you up through her imaginary screen so you could smell Walter Cunningham's syrup as he poured a half-jug over his meat and greens. You felt the panic as Jem's trousers snagged on the barbed wire. I became oblivious to Shelley's performance. That was the brilliance of the thing. I never sat back and said, By Christ, that's the best Gregory Peck I've ever seen, how could a woman so perfectly capture the resonance of Peck's voice?, because I was seized by the immediacy of events, too much a part of things. And I can't tell you how good her Gregory Peck was. But everyone was equally good. You felt the heat of the courtroom, and trembled before Ewell's evil bigotry. Shelley's *piece de resistance* was the Mad Dog scene.

One moment Shelley is the dog hopping and bopping at the end of the street, the next she's the maid Calpurnia herding Scout and Jem through the front door. Cal calls Atticus, and Atticus drives over with his colleague, Hec. Of course, no one thinks Atticus can do anything practical—he's a lawyer, a man of learning—but Hec passes Atticus the rifle. Atticus twitches around, slowly getting a sight of the target. The mad dog's still rolling and lurching towards him. Atticus throws away his glasses.

Bang!

The dog drops dead. Perfect fucking shot. The Finch kids are disbelieving, mouths wide open. Shelley's Atticus tries awfully hard not to be smug about this.

'Don't go near that dog, d'ya understand? He's just as dangerous dead as alive.'

But it's Shelley's Hec who offers Jem and Scout a picture of the world before their world began, telling them what they never knew, that their daddy was the best shot this side of the Mississippi.

The mad dog sure the fuck knows that. Dead and foamy-mouthed on the gravel. Any attempt to relate this, to communicate the kaleidoscopic brilliance of Shelley's world, is bound to fail. It should never be permissible for a writer to tell you that you had to be there, but you had to be there. I heard the shots, the violins, I was spat on and snatched away by evil men, I sweated and trembled. Shelley was electrifying.

When it came to those final scenes, when Scout gets introduced to poor Boo Radley, the hero who has just saved her brother's life, I was blubbering away in front of enchantress Shelley. Poor Boo playing possum behind the bedroom door.

'Hey, Boo.'

Atticus always the well-mannered host.

'Miss Jean-Louise, Mr *Arthur* Radley ... I believe he already knows you.'

The sweep of violins. A final voice-over above the montage of wide streets and images of Atticus' perfect fatherdom, all full of the lost Eden we once had, and the knowledge of serpents and redeemers. Closing titles.

Shelley was standing in front of me, entirely spent. I was sitting in front of her, every emotion drained from me. Inconceivable as it might have seemed just then, I was in Shelley's apartment in Paris. The old south had vanished. Five-and-a-half hours had passed.

Shelley, that …

No, it wasn't. I didn't get Tom and Mayella. Mayella's generally my best turn, but I couldn't get her tonight … Would you like a drink or something, Hugh? Maybe we should just go to bed. The sun will be up soon.

A drink would be great.

I'm thinking, Hugh? Hugh? *Hugh Grant*! That's right. She thinks I'm Hugh Grant. Somewhere amid all the Scout-this, and Yer a nigger-lover, Mr Finch-thats, I managed to forget that a relatively unknown actor inspired this whole astonishing performance.

And this same Hugh Grant would now expected to give a performance of his own. If I'd given in to the call of my trousers, I'd have fucked Shelley underneath her Christmas tree—she was beautiful beyond belief—but there was an Atticus Finch inside my head offering sage advice. *Richard, when I was a boy, my daddy told me something I've never forgotten. He said, Son, you can sleep with all the cheerleaders you like, have a threesome with your teacher and the blackboard monitor, only son, it's a sin*, a sin before God, *to sleep with someone who thinks you're Hugh Grant.*

I had time to think these things because after making me a stiff gin and tonic, Shelley disappeared into another room. I just knew that she'd come back in a transparent negligee, and all Atticus' wisdom would be forgotten. Trying to convince myself, you can't fuck this girl. It would be dead wrong. She's just given the most devastating stage performance since Booth shot

Lincoln, but someone that nutty couldn't walk the streets without being mugged by squirrels.

I did my best to picture Amber in South Africa. I tried to persuade myself that I owed Amber fidelity. However fierce the internal debate, if my host had returned in anything vaguely transparent, the Don't Jump on Shelley lobby would have been vanquished.

Ten, maybe fifteen minutes passed. When Shelley returned, she was clothed as she had been when she departed, but she was carrying a large photo album, the type with tissue-paper dividers. She was still very excited.

I'm thrilled you liked my show. And I'm even more thrilled to put your photograph in my album.

I hadn't looked at the Polaroid when it developed, and wasn't that keen to examine it now. Shelley, for all her strangeness, was a remarkably handsome woman, and my snapshot didn't flatter her. I was shocked to discover that her album was full of similar, hastily snapped photographs. All had Shelley as their subject.

They're all photographs of you.

Yes, but yours is special to me, Hugh. I'm going to give it a page to itself.

You really should let photographers take more time. None of these shots do you justice.

Oh! No, they're not meant to. That's not the point. It's a kind of private joke. It wouldn't matter if I wasn't in them, but me being the subject unifies the deal.

Which is?

She turned a page to show me the first photograph. It was taken in the street at night. Shelley's smile looks forced. She's too close to the flash.

Do you know who took that photograph, Hugh?

Having no idea how Hugh Grant would answer, I wasn't game to speculate.

Woody Allen.

Bullshit!

That's what everyone says, but it's true! I was in a side street near the Pompidou Centre. I'd just finished photographing something. And this man came around the corner. It was Woody. Well, I lifted my camera, a reflex thing, my one chance to take Woody's photograph, and the poor man ... He was like a vampire shown a crucifix. He had an arm up over his eyes, saying, No. No. *Please.*

Well, I apologized. I didn't know what had come over me. And Woody was gracious about it. So I asked him a favour, whether he'd take *my* photograph, so that I'd know I had a photograph taken by Woody Allen. And he joked about whether he could be trusted with my camera, but there it is. A Portrait of the Artist as a Young Woman by Woody Allen.

That's amazing! But what are all these? I asked. She had maybe ninety of these snaps in her album.

That's the weird thing. After that, my camera was a magnet for famous people. I only need to walk at night, and, *voila!*

She began to point at snaps.

Boris Becker took that ... That was Beatrice Dalle. I was worried about asking her because she looks so unhinged, but she thought it was hilarious. Most famous people think it's the funniest thing. They're all so relieved someone's not trying to photograph them ... That was Charles Aznavour, and that was Milan Kundera. That was Mick Jagger, that was Barbara Walters, and that one there was Naomi Wolf ... Let me see that one ... That was Liv Ullmann, I think ... Where's my favourite?

She turned over several pages.

There!

It was a picture of Shelley in the street at night, just as all the others were Shelley in the street at night.

Who do you think took that?

Margaret Thatcher?

You're close!... *Mikhail Gorbachev!* He was *so* nice. He wanted me to take a photograph of him, or to have another man take a photograph of us together, but I refused. I have this sense of purity. If I let people who aren't famous take my photograph, the camera would cease to be enchanted.

My heart sank then. By allowing myself to be mistaken for Hugh Grant, I'd risked the enchantment of Shelley's Polaroid.

It took just a moment for a more cynical thought to cross my mind.

Shelley, you'd be surprised how few people ask me to take their photographs. Not many people recognise me, especially in Paris.

Now maybe. But I just know you'll be more famous than William Hurt ... Y'know, only three people have ever refused me: Francois Mitterand, William Hurt and Sandrine Bonnaire.

Being a cinema buff, I knew who Sandrine was, but not many would.

Well, maybe it wasn't Sandrine Bonnaire, I said. Are you sure you weren't confusing her for someone else?

If I'd abducted Shelley's mother, and roasted her on an open fire, I couldn't have prompted a more outraged response.

What the fuck's that meant to mean?

Only, well, you know, that you might see someone and think it's Sandrine Bonnaire, and they might just be someone who looks a bit like them. In the dark.

Hey!... If you're going to call me a liar, call me one straight to my face. Tell me this photograph wasn't taken by Woody Allen, that it could have been taken by any fucking idiot in the street. That this snap wasn't taken by Sting, that it was just another 45 year old Englishman who smelled like Sting ...

Shelley ripped the Sting photograph out of the album, and hurled it across the room.

You might be a charming actor, Hugh, I know that you'll be famous, but you can't call me a liar. You've got no fucking right. I'm going to be more famous than you.

One day, someone just like me will ask me to take their photograph.

I couldn't argue with the logic of that.

Look, I'm sorry Shelley. It's late. You're tired after doing the show. I think I should go back to my hotel.

You're *dumping* me! I do my show for you, make you drinks, and show you my collection. Then you call me a liar, and dump me, just like that. Well, I don't need your photograph, Hugh. I'm the only fucking American who knows who you are, and now I don't give a shit.

Shelley ripped the photograph I'd taken. It seemed to me that she was doing something profane, something I regretted. Maybe I regretted it more than she would later.

You don't mean that, I said, putting my hands on her shoulders to calm her down. You're tired. You misunderstood me, Shelley. Of course you wouldn't have confused someone who wasn't William Hurt for William Hurt. That's not what I meant.

You're right, I am tired. Stay with me, Hugh. Make love to me.

Skimpy negligees work better than psychotic episodes when it comes to persuading me to act against my better judgement.

No, I have to go. We'll see each other again. I promise.

You're just saying that.

Tonight. I'll meet you outside the entrance to Luxembourg Metro. Seven. No, eight. Eight outside Luxembourg.

Tonight at eight.

Shelley kissed me tenderly on the lips, but I couldn't wait to hear her door shut behind me, to get down the stairs, and out into the real world. If I could have eradicated sexual desire at that moment, I might have. I felt like a true enemy of the people.

And Shelley looked so lovely, standing there in her doorway. All shagged-out, insane longing.

Tonight. Don't be late.... And Hugh, *je t'aime*.

It was nearly nine. Outside, Parisiens were bustling past in the sleeting rain. An old man walking toward me hit the edge of a dog turd with his heel, and skidded three metres, but kept his feet heroically. I might have liked to grab his collar and interrogate him. Do you think I look the slightest fucking bit like Hugh Grant? I refrained. The old turd-surfer had better things to do.

And so did I. I slept like a baby.

Maybe this story should end with a warm southern voice-over, with a woman who sounds like *To Kill a Mockingbird*'s narrator saying something to restore gentleness to my tale. You already know I had no intention of waiting for Shelley outside the Metro entrance. I felt bad about it, but she was waiting for someone famous, or someone who was on the verge of becoming famous, which is exactly what Hugh Grant did, probably thanks to Shelley's voodoo Polaroid.

I wandered around Paris by myself for another week, avoiding the cinema, desperately hoping I wouldn't run into Shelley, but still fantasizing about the great sex we might have had if she hadn't forced me to make an adverse judgement about her sanity. I told myself I would have been taking advantage of her, that it was morally indefensible. For me to have slept with a poor touched soul who thought that I was a British actor ... well, a decent, heroic man like Atticus Finch wouldn't do that. It would've been like fucking a mockingbird.

Around the time Shelley would have been waiting outside Luxembourg Metro, I was in a cafe writing a letter to Amber in South Africa. I told Amber I wanted to marry her. I was going to write plays. They would be famous plays, I was sure of it. All I needed was her love, and an ounce of good fortune, a lucky break.

I didn't marry Amber. I never heard from her again. She shacked up with a journalist in Kenya. Although I have written plays, no one will produce them. I have no connections, no famous theatrical figure to champion them. Of course, Shelley once might have.

Could Shelley have loved me if I wasn't British? Could she have looked me in the eyes and said, Richard, *je t'aime*? She has her Tony now. She's as famous as anyone needs to be. No one who wanted to be someone would refuse an invitation to sleep with her. Everyone will want to take her photograph.

1996

CRIMINAL HISTORY

I. Protection

Life is full of character-building experiences, and topping my list of these is Acting Sergeant Ross Headlam. It's hard to say what sort of person Ross started out as, but police work hadn't been kind to him. Most days, he gave the impression he'd woken up chin-deep in a bath full of snot and expected his fortunes to slide.

I don't dislike coppers. I worked with plenty of them. A copper can seem like a reasonable person when you're talking about football or grog, or when they're describing their past acts of heroism, but only a fool would engage a copper in discussion about the future of society. No one confused Ross with a reasonable human being, and no one ever sought his views on the future. You didn't need to.

My desk was two metres away from the desk where Ross spent the first two hours of each shift reading the newspaper and muttering to himself. Over a period of weeks, I began to see this meditation as his process of extrapolating the general from the particular. Ross never passed comments about individual news stories, or photographs, or comic-strips, he'd just gather it all up and add it to the pot his psyche was stewing. Finally, sentences began to form.

You can't tell me that computerisation is a step forward.

Or, You know what smog is, Timmy?

You weren't expected to answer this question. Your duty was to be silent while Ross defined smog.

It's nuthin' to do with exhaust fumes or that crap. Smog is the product of human negativity.

Usually after such an utterance, Ross closed his newspaper and vanished to the toilet for an hour. His concentration was intense.

One morning, I saw Ross gaze at the horoscope page for seventy minutes. His phone rang twice but he didn't answer.

You know what the future is, Timmy?... It's the sum of all possible threats. The future is a dark storm of heinousness waiting to break.

After a meeting with the Commissioner and his senior advisers, Acting Sergeant Ross Headlam returned to the office, and approached my desk carrying a dozen bottles of liquid paper and a mission statement.

Timmy, my boy, you have acquired new duties.

And what might they be, Ross?

Your new job is to protect our protectors from themselves. These might look like white-out bottles, but they're the clerical version of the morning-after pill. They offer post-hoc contraception to history's innocents.

2. The Bat Phone

Back in 1987, with economic rationalism still in its infancy, the world was full of undemanding clerical jobs in large government offices, sheltered workshops where the confused could catch their breath on the way to wherever they were meant to be going. As a failed teacher who dreamt of becoming a writer, I spent twelve months working as a clerk in the Information Bureau of the Victorian Police Department.

A large staff of shift-working public servants did the dogwork for the uniformed police who ran the office. Mostly, the clerks answered telephone and telex enquiries, and supplied criminal records information to officers in cars, stations, or the major squads. There were several positions of slightly greater responsibility. One involved the administration of the Bat Phone.

Only the authorised Bat Phone operator was permitted to give out information requested via that phone. These information requests came from agencies entitled to receive confidential criminal records information: bodies such as the Federal Police, Prison Release, Customs, or the National Crime Authority. Any breakdown in strict procedure—a failure to check an authority code—might result in highly sensitive information falling into the hands of felons, or corrupt officials.

Having shunned responsibility, I had no ambition to take on the Bat Phone. The microscopic increase in pay was no incentive. Given the choice, I would have preferred to engage in basic duties which required little thought, automatic tasks that left space for fruitful daydreaming. I was not given the choice.

When Dale, the evening shift Bat Phone operator, was forced to take extended sick leave, Ross Headlam deemed that I was the only person sufficiently discreet and trustworthy to replace him. I might have been flattered by that judgement if I hadn't perceived a certain irony.

Discretion had never been my predecessor's forte. A dedicated member of the Collingwood Cheer Squad, the catty Dale spent most of his time assessing and discussing the physical attributes of Collingwood footballers, especially the tightness of their shorts, and the sheen of their robust thighs. Dale often boasted that he'd slept with two of these gods, an indiscretion which wouldn't have threatened his wellbeing if he hadn't been foolish enough to name these men in front of police who moved in football circles. Dale's workmates were told only that he'd need twelve months to recover from an unfortunate accident.

Answering the Bat Phone was not the only duty assigned to the Bat Phone operator. During quiet times, you were expected to crosscheck work returned from the typists, and to organize searches for missing files. None of this threatened to compromise my personal values. However, my second month in the job coincided with a new directive from the most senior police officials. Ross Headlam returned from a meeting carrying a dozen bottles of liquid paper, and placed them on my desk.

I had a new duty. My task was to protect serving police officers from their worst literary instincts.

So began my career as a Stalinist reviser of criminal history.

3. Additional Particulars

Midway through the 1980s, the Victorian government began to extend the provisions of the Freedom of Information Act. As these extensions became more pervasive, senior police grew nervous about the possibility of public access to Information Bureau documents.

One grey area of the new legislation, so far as it related to the mounds of documents held at the Bureau, involved gratuitous police judgements and predictions concerning the character, behaviour, and future criminality of recorded criminals.

Victorian police were as unfond of paperwork as they were of criminals. Officers were inclined to offer highly unflattering opinions of convicted offenders in the 'Additional Particulars' section of the Antecedent Form, otherwise known as a Two-Ten. The senior executives of the department were concerned that public access to these forms would leave the department and individual officers open to writs for libel and defamation, or to charges of sexual and racial discrimination. And officers didn't always stop at offering their opinions about the criminal subject of their report. They often made adverse comments about family members, relationships, nationalities, organisations, living conditions, and life-styles.

My task was to save as much information as might prove valuable, but to obliterate any remarks that might conceivably cost the department (and the Victorian taxpayer) big money.

To describe an offender as 'vile and disgusting' might be within the bounds of legal acceptability, but not so his innocent de facto wife, and, since this information was hardly crucial in either instance, both remarks could be whited-out. 'Her record suggests that she is an inveterate offender' could remain, likewise, 'Her record suggests that she is likely to commit further offences', and 'Her record suggests that she will continue to come under police attention'. But 'Her long record indicates that she will continue to offend' was too risky and required obliteration.

These speculations on the probability of future offence presented the greatest threat to the financial wellbeing of the writer. It was not in an officer's interests to be publicly exposed as the author of a prediction like 'this filth will continue to predate', no matter how soundly based according to principles of inductive reasoning. So you slathered on the whiteout.

But at another level, I began to become fascinated with the police officers' implied view of time, history, and human evolution.

You could hardly fail to recognise that their casual speculations about human nature and the possibility of ordered society would make a fruitful area of study for criminologists or psychologists in as much as these unguarded observations began to suggest a collective police psyche. In my experience with the liquid paper bottle, the essential characteristics of this psyche were: a jaundiced or deterministic view of human nature, intense cynicism and pessimism, and a tendency for racial and class stereotyping.

Strike 'human vermin'.

Strike 'typically hopeless abo'.

Strike 'noxious little pillow biter'.

According to this generalised psyche, anyone who had been convicted of an offence, or anyone who had been *caught* offending once, was, almost without fail, someone who had long been engaged in undetected felonious activity. His or her status as a 'criminal' would, by definition, demonstrate an inclination to the pursuit of crime.

These predictions indicated a police force which envisaged an entropical future where perceived inevitabilities governed the breakdown of social order. Offenders and offences would breed and multiply. When called upon to speculate about the future in the form of the collected individuals who would shape and inform it, the average police officer imagined a less than brave new world.

I slathered on whiteout, conscious I was doing a snow job on a version of the future. But I couldn't be sure whether my liberal doses of liquid paper were removing or manufacturing the preconditions for zero visibility.

I did know the worst thing that could happen to me, both as a clerk, and a hopeful citizen of the third millenium, was to imagine myself into the future that police imagined: a world of predetermined violation and indecency, a world of escalating chaos and genetically-programmed malfeasance.

4. A Society Based On Competition

Ross Headlam only became animated when he collected money. Apart from reading the paper, crapping, and offering haiku on concepts which needed redefining, his main task was to organise raffles, the football-tipping competition, the Tattslotto syndicates, and any other competition which took his fancy. When Ross approached with a folder in his hand, you knew the speediest way to get rid of him was to reach into your pocket and cough up the required cash.

How much am I up for this time?

Two bucks.

What's the prize?

Two hundred ... The rest goes towards the Christmas Party.

And what do I do?

You've got to guess the Christian name of the first criminal— charged, not cautioned—born in the 1980s.

Jesus, Ross! That'd make him seven now. Half the staff here will leave before you pay out.

No way, Timmy. We'll have one in the next month or two. A little thief, or an arsonist. You mark my words.

Yeah, O.K ... I'll take Jason.

Taken.

Shane.

Nah, mate. Shane's gone.

Brad or Brett?... I'll go for Brett.

Brett it is. Good luck.

That was the last I expected to hear of Ross' Criminal Prodigy competition during my time in the office. Yet, true to his intuition, just three weeks later a winner was announced.

As it happened, the hot favourites Jason and Shane were rolled by a Mark, born in April, 1980. Bernie Peperkamp pocketed the two hundred dollars.

Hey, Ross. This kid, Mark, what's he up for?

Guess.

Shop-lifting?

Worse than that.

Drug abuse and car theft?

Worse.

Worse than drugs and car theft! He's seven, fer Chrissake!

Rape, and aggravated sexual assault.

Nah, you're kidding me.

Little brat held a screwdriver to a kid's neck while his ten-year-old brother fucked him up the arse.

No way! You're bullshitting.

That's the future, Timmy. It's coming soon to a suburb near you.

5. Criminal Science

We're all capable of living down to our lowest opinion of ourselves. I think criminals are better off not being able to read their police files. And not just because many of the things said about them, their families, and friends are highly speculative and ill-informed. If it were possible for a criminal to read his or her own file as a disinterested observer might, they would probably decide they didn't amount to much. They would see themselves as expendable citizenry.

I happen to subscribe to the view of an essential human nature. We don't really change much from what we start out as. Certain conditions will invariably, perhaps automatically, activate predisposed drives. Which isn't to say that I'm sold on the science of predicting criminal behaviour. Who can say which of those many essential drives were most essential till they've been brought into effect? For a science to rightly call itself a science, it must have a strong predictive capacity. Criminologists have always displayed their greatest expertise when invited to be wise after the event.

Immediately after the second War, the British penal system bought into criminology as a predictive science. Juvenile offenders, even those who had committed relatively petty crimes, were subjected to exhaustive psychological profiling in the belief that intense scrutiny might lead to an accurate forecast of future outcomes. But there is a difficulty with this. Even the criminally disposed have a myriad of criminal potentials.

As a fourteen-year-old in Borstal, Ronald Biggs told an expert in adolescent psychiatry that he often masturbated. This admission led the expert to predict young Ronnie would likely come to police attention as a sex offender. And maybe if Biggs had been a less successful robber, his thoughts would have turned to this second avenue of criminality. But the so-called scientific approach to antisocial behaviours would seem to tell us less about potential sex-offenders and train robbers than it does about a once-prevalent distaste for masturbation.

Cardinal Newman's famous credo about the child at seven being a blueprint of the adult to come probably holds, but how do we estimate which of many different traits will come to the fore, or become dominant?

At age seven, my ambition was to write television scripts. I dreamed of writing episodes of my favourite show, *The Man From UNCLE*, a popular American spy spoof which then screened on Channel 7 at eight-thirty on Thursday nights. That was the sacred hour of the week for me.

The Man From UNCLE was pretty much dead and buried by the time I was ten, but by age 28 I found myself writing sketch comedy for a highly successful television show (the title, *Fast Forward*, is itself ironic in this context) which went to air on Channel 7 at eight-thirty on Thursday nights.

Was any of this inevitable? It certainly wouldn't have seemed so fifteen months earlier when I was slopping whiteout on indiscreet speculations and predictions.

Had I known that all was predestined, that I was genetically-programmed to write television scripts which would air on Channel 7 at eight-thirty on Thursday nights, I might have saved myself years of unnecessary worry. One of the times when I was most worried about where life might be heading was sitting at a desk opposite Acting Sergeant Ross Headlam, shaking my liquid paper bottles so their precious contents wouldn't go dry and crusty.

6. History as A Piece of Work

After reviewing so many documents in so many files, you began to get an appreciation of the police officer as historian. They were authors of a hidden history, fashioning a sub-cultural version of the culture for a privileged readership of (presumed) shared values.

With so many contributors to this history over a prolonged stretch of time, I was surprised that my attention could be drawn to the style of individual authors. Certain themes and motifs would recur with sufficient frequency to convey a picture of a distant police officer. One historian who comes to mind is Senior Constable Davis.

In the Additional Particulars section of four Two-Tens relating to four separate (male) offenders, Senior Constable Davis opined that the offender would never completely reject the criminal way of life unless he 'distanced himself from the piece of work sharing his bedroom'.

I took 'piece of work sharing his bedroom' to come within the terms of my guidelines for erasure, and applied the liquid paper in all four instances, but not without a thought for Senior Constable Davis. I imagined him thawing a frozen dinner while he contemplated all the pieces of work that could bring a man undone in this city, thankful that he'd been able to distance himself from the piece of work who had so nearly warped his soul.

7. The Sunrise Clause

Not once in my experience did a police officer completing the Additional Particulars section of the Two–Ten offer the opinion that the subject would certainly not offend again, that in spite of past crimes he would choose to marry a nice girl and live in a white house with his wife, three children and a cocker spaniel, that he might decide to write perceptive books which offered useful insights into his own past, and criminality *per se*: that his future life, and the lives of many others he would meet, had probably been informed and enriched by his brush with infraction.

8. A Crime of Convenience

However much I might have wanted to protect those who protect us from themselves, I hadn't been a police officer, and I would never be entirely privy to the workings of the law enforcer's psyche. Once, I made the mistake of asking Ross to speculate on those who committed Melbourne's notorious, unsolved, Great Bookie Robbery.

We'll never know who did that. They might as well close the file.

But what if the same gang struck again and left new clues?

If that mob strikes again, they won't leave clues.

Those blokes are criminal masterminds.

They're *what!*... You mean they got lucky. They silenced the right witnesses, and struck a bunch of detectives who didn't ask the right people the right questions, or didn't want to ask the right questions.

Luck had nothing to do with it, Timmy. It was all in the planning, their meticulous attention to detail. Those blokes are geniuses. They had every right to be confident they'd never get caught. That was a brazen daylight robbery. You've gotta respect blokes who could pull off something like that.

Through Ross, I began to grasp a key tenet of police psychology: The Myth of The Criminal Mastermind. The Criminal Mastermind is to frustrated police what alien abduction is to the spiritually confused.

According to this myth, the imbeciles, deadheads, and psychotics who uniformly grace police records are balanced by an undetectable circle of Criminal Masterminds: criminals the police are powerless to apprehend.

The Criminal Mastermind is the criminal who cannot be caught, *by definition*. Nothing could convince police who subscribe to this myth that a deadhead could get lucky, that an imbecile could evade detection, that a psychotic would not ultimately give himself away. Nothing could persuade such a police officer that the concept of criminal masterminds is a rationalization of the inadequacies of law enforcement, that it's a mythology of convenience.

9. God

Because all history is ultimately the history of provisional knowledge, ignorance, and irony, we shouldn't be too harsh on the Senior Constable who wrote of one sixteen-year-old offender:

> This boy operates under a mistaken belief that he
> is something special because his two brothers play
> League football, but you can rest assured that he'll
> never amount to anything more than a legend in his
> own mind.

After some consideration, I decided to save this prediction for posterity. The brash young offender in question was already in the process of becoming the footballer who would be universally revered as 'God'.

10. Pushing Eternity Uphill

During the four and a half months I spent as the Bat Phone operator, I obliterated several thousand dangerously contentious predictions, estimations, and opinions. Though I knew this would not be my life's mission, that I would return to full-time study the following year, I never really warmed to the task. I might have preferred to see the officer-authors forced to take responsibility for their frank judgements. And, at another level, I felt part of me being eroded. I needed to balance these erasures and eradications with a creative act.

When Ross was in the toilet, or collecting money, I began to manufacture history.

I opened a new file, and fabricated a detailed criminal history for a nonexistent arch criminal named M. Meursault. In keeping with his atheistic, antisocial outlook, M. Meursault had no Christian name as such, but sometimes passed under the aliases of The Stranger, or Sisyphus.

Found guilty of Crimes against God, and an Aggravated Assault on Metaphysics, M. Meursault had been sentenced to 'push eternity uphill'. His was a file I would slip quietly among the tens of thousands of authentic files. It was a file that would never be accessed, and what justice there was in Meursault's obscure punishment would never be seen to be done.

In the process of creating M. Meursault, I began to see my editorial task in a new light. Just as Camus said of Sisyphus that we need to imagine him happy, that we should imagine Sisyphus as a man who would find a way to relish his eternal punishment, I tried to imagine myself as someone who was engaged in constructing a more hopeful, optimistic world. My liquid paper didn't only come to the defence of those who ought to have known better, I saw it having a magical, liberating effect on the criminal recipients of my godlike largesse.

As thrice-convicted burglar X moves between the supermarket and his run-down station wagon, he feels unaccountably lighter. He smiles at a stranger, the first time he has done so since he was a young boy. He smiles with no thought of reciprocation or profit. X will never understand that this aberrant behaviour coincides with my obliteration of the statement 'will certainly continue to re-offend'. He is about to begin again, to become the author of his own history. If he needs a title for that volume, I would suggest it be called *The Remote Possibility of Happiness*.

1996

STILL LIFE WITH LAMINGTONS

From the cafe, I could see Jack standing with an old man at the end of the pier. They were pointing at the ferry timetables, and you couldn't tell whether they were arguing or joking. First Jack shook his head, then the old man shook his head. Finally, Jack put his hand on the old man's shoulder and headed up the pier, calling out to me as he neared the cafe.

'You can see why this place was the home of philosophy. It's totally fucked.'

'No ferries?'

'Oh yeah, there are ferries. But no direct trips from here to Meskos. The old bloke reckons the only way you can get to Meskos is to take the Trykos ferry. But even that stops at six islands before it gets there. And the ferry from Trykos to Meskos only runs every third day ... Where's the logic? Meskos is twenty times the size of the other islands—you can practically swim to it from here—but there's no fuckin' ferry.'

'Mate, these people are very thingy about Meskos. After Perseus escaped the minotaur, he was going to meet up with his betrothed on Trykos, but the sirens tricked him into swimming to Meskos where Demosthenes had him emasculated and sold into Trojan slavery. You couldn't get anyone here to take a direct ferry to Meskos.'

Jack belted back the last of his red wine and looked me in the eye.

'You just made that up.'

'Well, sure. What do you want me to say? Of course, there's no ferry. This place is fourth world.'

We were quiet for a while after that. My brother and I had been travelling for sixty hours. Neither of us had slept or shaved.

It was impossible to understand why it might take another two days to reach an island just four kilometres off the coast.

'We'll have to pay one of the fishermen.'

'Yeah. Fuck it.'

I held up my empty glass to see whether Jack wanted another.

'Dick, you don't have to go through with this if you don't want to. Mum and dad wouldn't hold it against you. You could say there wasn't a ferry, that the signs weren't auspicious.'

'Nah, we've come this far. And I'm curious.'

'Well, this isn't a book you can close when the story bores you. It might be your last chance to back out.'

I could hear someone dropping coins into the jukebox and hitting buttons to make their selection. I might have expected to hear Nana Mouskouri, or some drug-soaked rembetika, but the song was 'Love Will Tear Us Apart' by Joy Division. Jack was right. The signs weren't auspicious.

There was a time when I was suspended in time like a mosquito in jelly. I was so panicked about the future that the present ceased to exist. Trying to save myself, I shut off all emotional engagement with the world.

Is it really possible to love someone too much, or is that an excuse invented by the lover who failed to love well enough?

I loved Miranda so much I couldn't stand the thought that she might not always love me. The most minute conflict or misunderstanding became the portent of a disaster to come. So I shut off my emotions and sent her away, panic disguised as cool decisiveness. When I finally realised what I had done, it was too late to remedy the situation.

Time, Mirandaless time, existed only to be obliterated.

Convincing myself that hard work was good for the soul, I worked with a furious intensity. I needed to be so far inside time that time would cease to have meaning, would cease to correspond with the world beyond my desk. I wrote, and wrote, and re-wrote. And when I paused to look up from the desk, two years had passed without me being aware of their passing. Worse, Miranda was still gone.

It was only when I reacquainted myself with banal, commonsense time that the crying started. I was 37 years old.

It's excruciating to be bailed out of a psychiatric hospital by your elderly parents, to have your emotional life dragged into a public domain, to find yourself on the receiving end of so much warmth and sound advice.

'What you should do is find yourself a nice girl and get married,' my mother told me.

'Thanks, Mum, you're right. Tomorrow ... No. Tomorrow's Good Friday. I'll marry a nice girl straight after the holidays.'

Just because everyone had been so patient with me didn't mean I'd abandoned the right to be sarcastic. Other than doctors, nurses and shop assistants, I hadn't spoken to a woman I didn't know for more than three years. Talk of lifelong partnership was just a little abstract. But Mum refused to be put off.

'Look, Richard, you can be unhappy if you want to. But that's different from choosing unhappiness as a way of life. Some people decide to be unhappy because they're frightened of feeling lost when they're happy.'

'You've sold me, Mum. I'm getting married. Go out and buy yourself a new dress.'

'I'm serious. You have a lot of love to give someone.'

'I'm overflowing with eligibility, but I don't see women beating a path to the door.'

'You should meet Elizabeth Colley. Elizabeth is a beautiful girl.'

'Who is Elizabeth Colley?'

'Max and Gwen's daughter.'

'Mum, Max and Gwen live in Greece.'

'I'll show you her photograph. Gwen sent a photo with her letter last Christmas.'

Mum rummaged through a drawer in the kitchen and returned with a photograph of the thirty-two-year-old Elizabeth

Colley. A man's idea of a beautiful woman seldom coincides with his mother's idea of the same, but I had to admit that Elizabeth Colley met my mother's description: serene and lovely, with a soft, shy smile, and glorious long red hair.

'Nice try Mum, but you can't tell me that someone who looks like her has spent her life waiting to meet a dickhead like me.'

There is one thing I should make clear at this point. I never considered that I was involving myself in an arranged marriage. I didn't think of it like that. I would have recoiled at the suggestion.

If you ever visit Meskos, don't forget your sunglasses. Blinding light bounces off white stone buildings packed onto the steep hills which rise above the port. According to my guidebook, Meskos is the largest and most populous island in its group, but I couldn't say what people do to earn a living. The fishermen play cards in the cafes, and the locals make no effort to sell the island as a travel destination. Many less attractive islands do substantial tourist business.

My father said that intelligence agencies use the island for satellite tracking and information gathering. While there's no shortage of high antennas and dishes on Meskos, we never met other foreigners, let alone CIA types. And I don't recall seeing an area where entry was restricted. The islanders seemed prosperous and happy. The presence of two Australians didn't seem to bother them.

Everyone knew the Colleys. Max and Gwen had lived there forty years. Max had been one of the two doctors on the island till he retired seven years earlier. Being six foot six and Australian would have been enough to make him stand out even without all his quirks.

Kind locals stopped to explain the route to the Colley house. They drew maps in the dirt. They told us that it was much too far to carry suitcases. Island people often have a distorted sense of scale. Gwen's letter told us they lived a mile and a half from the port, but the hills were steep enough to keep you honest.

'How will we know which house is his?' Jack asked Dad.

'Oh, I'm pretty sure you'll know where you are when you get to the Colley's house.'

Which was true, but we were almost led astray. Nearing a crossroad, we encountered two exquisite girls: dark hair, tight black fashion jeans, luminous blouses. They couldn't have been older than twenty, and neither would have looked out of place in a Chapel Street boutique. They smiled at us, and their eyes sparkled with all the right sorts of incitement.

'Will we see you at the disco tonight?' the girl in the hot pink blouse asked. 'Good music. Hash. Whatever you want.'

Seeing Jack wanting to say yes—having momentarily forgotten he was a married man, and, for the purposes of this venture, my chaperone—I spoke for him.

'Sounds great. But it depends ... Do you know Elizabeth Colley?'

I could hear them both giggling as they walked away.

'Holy shit!' Jack said, looking back over his shoulder, determined not to miss a wiggle. 'Whoo! We've come to the right place!'

The Colley house could not have been other than the Colley house.

A fence of unpainted wooden railings enclosed a large bushy block. The garden was dense with eucalypts and flowering gums which nearly obscured a weatherboard dwelling with a slanting roof of red corrugated iron. Surrounding the house on all sides was a broad veranda. Television aerial on one side, tall mast with an Australian flag fluttering on the other.

An attractive cooking smell wafted out of the house, and I could hear the moan of the north wind as it passed through the wires of a Hills Hoist in the backyard.

Dad met Max Colley in 1945. They were young doctors with the occupying forces in Japan. Even though the two men are the same age, it's fair to say that Dad hero-worships Max. Max was a brilliant footballer and a potential Wimbledon champ. If you speak to people who knew Max the sportsman, they always tell you, Max Colley could have been anything.

My father's Japanese experiences saw him veer towards the peace movement and left-of-centre politics, but Max headed in the other direction. I've never understood how people can maintain friendships with ideological opponents, but Dad managed to stay in touch with Max as he went first to Washington then back to Korea. Dad rejects the idea that his friend worked for the CIA, believing The Company would have had Max spend more time in Australia if he had been an operative.

As it happens, Max did spend long periods of time in Australia during the 1950s, just as the Cold War was shifting into top gear. The scrapbook shows Uncle Max hitting up with Lew Hoad and Ken Rosewall. Dad reckons that if Max was CIA his mission would have been to nobble that pair.

During a return visit, Dad introduced Max to one of Mum's schoolfriends, a nurse named Gwen Lester, and the couple got married after a whirlwind romance. According to Dad, Max had the idea that he and Gwen would take medical expertise into the third world, but they only got as far as the Greek islands before falling in love with Meskos.

To my knowledge, Max and Gwen have left Meskos just once since 1958, returning to Australia in the mid-sixties to finalise Elizabeth's adoption. When they found they were unable to have children, Mum used her connections to stitch up a deal. Even on that trip, Max and Gwen breezed in and out of Melbourne. They signed the papers, had their baby daughter christened in the Scots' church, and left on the next boat. Though Jack and I attended Elizabeth's christening, neither of us recall it. Which is a pity, because it was a social event. The new Prime Minister Harold Holt was there. Apparently, Holt offered Max a major diplomatic posting, but Max declined. He said his work on Meskos meant everything to him. If you speak to people who knew conservative politics in the fifties and sixties, they always tell you, Max Colley could have been anything.

'Bugger me with a stick, wouldya look at these two!.... You, you're just the image of yer old man ... Come in, come in. You lads must be scroted. It's a bloody long haul from Melbourne ... Don't know where Gwen and Lizzie have got to. Sit tight and I'll fetch a beer.'

My hand was still throbbing from Max's grip. He was the most energetic 75 year old I've met. A bald, Herculean giant, part-Chips Rafferty, part-Monsieur Hulot, trying to leave the room in two different directions at once.

Jack was examining the damage to his own hand. 'Did Max ask if we were 'scroted'?'

In the distance, we heard Max calling his wife and daughter, to no response. Every time Max moved, he sent vibrations through the large house.

'Gwen, Lizzie! Get out here, we've been invaded by young bronzed gods.'

I'd never been referred to as a bronzed god. Jack has a definite bronze about him. I'm closer to Transylvanian aristocracy.

Max's voice bellowed from the kitchen, 'Richmond Bitter all right for you blokes?'

We raised eyebrows in perfect sync, and Jack called back, 'Yeah, no worries.'

'*Richmond Bitter?*'

'I don't reckon they've brewed the stuff since '62,' Jack said. 'We might be in for a treat.'

'In for a treat' was a phrase Jack used whenever unusual punishments were in the offing.

More crashing from another room, 'Orr, bugger it!'

I'd seen houses much like the Colleys' house before, back when my family used to visit elderly relatives in northern

Victoria. Polished floorboards, a massive living room lined with bookcases filled with old hardbacks. Big cabinets of crystal and Wedgwood. Old reclining chairs covered in red vinyl. Framed black and white photos of dead family members, and a large colour-tinted photograph of the Queen. The same image used to hang on the wall at Hampton Primary. A big piano in one corner, a television covered with a blue towel in the other.

Finally, traces of conversations from a distant room.

'Where have you been? The boys are here. I've been trying to rustle up some grub.'

When Max returned, he was balancing a tray holding three massive cans of Richmond Bitter. The cans were made of ancient steel, and the quantity of beer they contained was measured in fluid ounces. Max then used a can-opener to rip the tops off dog-food style.

'I don't expect you boys'll be fussed about glasses. Gwen will be with us in a jiff. Young Liz has gone to tizz herself up.'

We raised cans to acknowledge Max, but the cans were so heavy you needed both hands, and they were frighteningly cold. They must have spent thirty-five years huddled in a refrigerator, waiting for this moment of consummation.

'I save the Richmond for special occasions … Tell me if it isn't the best drop you've ever knocked back.'

To me it tasted like beer that had spent thirty-five years in a steel can. Jack's the connoisseur, but his pupils were spinning out of control. That might have been three days without sleep as much as the grog. And we'd shared a cone with the fisherman who brought us over to the island. Maybe the whole Meskos experience was hallucination: the local girls, Max's folk museum, everything.

Seeing Jack had flaked, Max moved forward to address me earnestly.

'Bet you can't wait to see our Lizzie. She's not very worldly, but she's a pearl. 'Course, we should have fixed her up with an Australian lad years ago, but her mum and I couldn't handle the thought of being without her. She's a bonzer lass. She's talked of nothing but you coming since we got your mum's letter.'

Jack heard none of this. The beer demolished him. Maturity had increased the alcohol content, and I was fighting to hold my eyelids open.

Finally, Gwen appeared. Though seventy or thereabouts, Gwen was a tall, elegant woman, quite striking. She was carrying a tray of plates piled high with scones and pikelets.

A little flustered, Gwen introduced herself to Jack, without noticing his coma. She'd start a sentence but fail to finish it. Not for the first time, I was told I was the dead spit of my father.

'You'll have to excuse Elizabeth. She'll be with us in a minute,' Gwen said. 'You took us by surprise.'

Though flagging badly, I did my best with the food mountain. Max quizzed me about the Essendon football team, and the current state of Australian tennis, while Gwen wanted to know about my family. Jack contributed no more than the occasional splurt.

'Eat those scones while they're hot. Scones that can't melt butter are poison.'

I hadn't eaten fresh scones since the invention of the microwave oven, and these were sensational, but my head was swimming. While Max disappeared to fetch more beer, I tried to explain to Gwen that Jack and I were experiencing critical sleep deficit. While doing so, I knocked a saucer off the coffee table, and the clatter on the floorboards sent a cat scurrying from under the couch, momentarily shaking Jack from his hibernation.

As I apologised, Max returned with the beer, and following close behind him, carrying a tray loaded with cupcakes and lamingtons, was his daughter.

Elizabeth Colley was even more lovely in the flesh than the photograph I had seen. She wore a white blouse, a tartan skirt of green and blue to just above the knee, and dark blue stockings. She was tall, with high cheeks, a pretty mouth, long waves of magnificent red hair, and her soft, pale skin looked like it had never seen the sun.

When Max introduced Elizabeth, I shook her hand and said it was a pleasure to meet her. She said nothing in reply, but released a serene half-smile which sent a flush through her cheeks.

'Make sure you try one of Lizzie's lamingtons. You won't find better on Meskos.'

Since no one else was eating, I took it as my duty to eat three lamingtons while Max and Gwen nattered about the grand days of sea travel, and the silent Elizabeth measured my reactions. With each lamington, I tried to be more enthusiastic than I had been previously. And they were top-drawer lamingtons: freshly desiccated coconut, dark chocolate, and much fresher cake than a lamington-eater has a right to expect. But my pupils were doing three-sixties, and somewhere between the third lamington and the second cupcake, I joined my brother in unconsciousness.

During the days which followed, Jack made himself scarce by wandering down to the port. Though he said this was to give Elizabeth and I the chance to be alone together, he meant to escape the stupendous quantities of food produced in the Colley kitchen.

The sight of Elizabeth made my heart quiver, but getting her to stay still or say something required more skill than I possessed. Every time I contrived a situation where we shared the same space, Max would wander in to abduct me.

Even in retirement, Max lived a vigorously active life, and insisted I play tennis with him. Tennis is not my game. I have no serve, and my backhand's so feeble I have to switch grips and play left-handed forehands. Still a formidable player, Max's game was made all the more daunting by the peculiarities of his home court.

Max's tennis court is one of the twentieth century's finest examples of arsehole architecture, with everything designed to protect Max's invincibility.

I should have guessed something was up when Max unveiled a home rule decreeing that ends would not be changed. Owing to his need to hear the phone, the end closest to the house belonged to him. Naturally, his end was beautifully shaded, while I found myself looking directly into the sun. What's more, the red gravel surface, rolled smooth as a freeway on Max's side of the net, was strewn with large stones on mine. Not immediately apparent to the trusting eye was an M.C. Escher technique used to mark the lines. Perspective had been artfully distorted so that Max's opponents defended an area fifty per cent larger than his. While Max rarely had to move for anything, I needed to sprint ten seconds to cover the baseline. Cruellest of all was a wicked camber which always directed the ball away from my lunging racquet. Max's opponents were asked to defend a very large, lumpy car bonnet.

I might be a lousy player, but I'm proud and competitive. I didn't intend to be humiliated by a man I wanted to impress. Max couldn't have cared less about my humiliation. He talked the whole match through, knowing I was too breathless to respond.

'You'll have to work on that backhand, Richard. I used to hit up with Rosewall. Kenny had a bugger of a good backhand.'

A top-spun lob came straight out of the sun and hit me above the right ear.

'I might have given Kenny and Lew a run for their money in my prime. But those lads were lucky to have their prime after the War.'

When a wicked smash hit a large stone and kicked away at a right angle, Max showed no obvious sign of embarrassment or sympathy.

'If you ask me, Australians have an unfair advantage. It might even be genetic. Look at Ron Clarke, Murray Rose, and Dawn Fraser.'

A drop volley looped over a net that seemed fifty metres

away, and my legs were jelly. I was too gutted to wave a handkerchief in surrender.

'More likely it's the outdoor life. Australian youngsters don't wait for someone to entertain them. They're always swimming or kicking a ball. You never see that with these lads on Meskos. If it's not the plonk, it's drugs and loud music. And most of the girls are just painted trollops ... Excuse the French, but what else can you say?... They're out to all hours, and their parents don't care. If unmarried girls had abortions in Australia like they do here on Meskos, there'd be a scandal. Church leaders would cry out, and there'd be a Royal Commission. But it could never get like that there, because Australian parents care about their children. They teach them self-discipline, and family values. Here, all the kids get taught is how to expect something for nothing.'

A perfectly dinked backhand landed on the line and scooted down the hill. Before I could get to the net to shake hands, Max said, 'What say we make it best of five?'

'I'm not going to lie to you, Richard. Gwen and I will miss Liz terribly. But you two will want to have children, and Australia's the only place for that ... Things have changed here. There used to be a local culture. Now, it might as well be America. People only seem to care about gambling and getting smashed. We've done our best to make sure Lizzie hasn't been contaminated by that. I like to think we've brought her up to be a fine young lady.'

A forehand volley at the net hit me square in the testicles. It was all I could do not to vomit.

'Hey, take care of those! You might have my grandsons swimming in there!'

I had a feeling that Max's grandsons and I were caught in a strong rip.

Dinner had to be postponed half an hour owing to Jack's late return from the village. I knew instantly that he was stoned, and hoped this fact would elude our hosts. The task of tucking in his serviette brought on an uncontrollable burst of giggling.

'This is one of Elizabeth's specialities,' Gwen announced. 'I hope you boys like mock chicken casserole.'

'*Mock* chicken,' Jack said. '*Mock* chicken.'

I kicked Jack's leg under the table.

'Mmm, it's delicious,' I said.

'Strong flavour. You must grain-feed the chooks here,' Jack added.

'Your dad and I used to go out shooting in the Mallee,' Max said.

Before he got any further, Jack hammered his fork on the table, feigning indignation. 'Max, I hope you're not impugning my father as a *mock* chicken hunter ...'

'*Jack* ...'

'Did he mock, or did he hunt?'

'It's an old-fashioned way of saying rabbit, Jack,' I explained.

Jack stopped as if shot. Generally he made a point of not eating cuddly things.

'You're a fabulous cook, Elizabeth,' I said, trying to draw her into the conversation.

'Lizzie knows Mrs Beeton backwards,' Gwen answered.

'We'd all like to know Mrs B. backwards,' Jack said, this time to the obvious annoyance of Max, who knew crudity when he heard it.

'You seem to be having a lot of fun down in the village, Jack.'

'They have a wild social scene in town,' Jack said. 'Do you get down there much, Liz?'

'No, she doesn't,' her father answered. 'The young blokes down there might seem like fun, but they're hopeless bludgers. Pack of bodgies the lot of them.'

'*Bodgies*,' Jack repeated.

Elizabeth was removing our plates.

'What's for pud, Lizzie?' Max asked.

'Lizzie's made a beautiful jam rolypoly,' Gwen said.

'Sounds fantastic, but I couldn't eat another thing,' I said.

'Lizzie's gone to some trouble,' Max said. 'Never slight a girl who takes trouble with her rolypoly.'

I had the top bunk, Jack had the bottom. Even in our thirties, he pulled rank.

'Jack, you can't come here stoned.'

'Can't you speed things up with Liz? We've got to get out of here. These people don't know about cholesterol. I'm shitting whipped cream.'

'If she's not with Gwen in the kitchen, Max is dragging me off to discuss Arthur Calwell and Frank Sedgman. Max thinks the whole thing is a *fait accompli.*'

'Then get her back home, and start making babies.'

'Jack, I haven't heard her speak except to say, 'Would you like more cream with that?''

'Hey, when a girl looks like her, that's all she needs to say.'

'She's dead stunning, but I can't see her being a riot in the cot. She'd belong to the lie back and think of Canberra school.'

'Bullshit! Conservative girls are always best value once they're wound up.'

'I dunno.'

'Dick, find out, pronto. We can't stay here forever. Not with the mock scones and chooks. You're makin' a fuckin' mockery of courtship.'

When I finally heard Elizabeth's voice, it was her singing voice.

After Sunday roast, Max insisted that we sing around the piano. Lizzie sang with a sweetness that was touching. She knew all the old Irish and Australian folksongs, but nothing written since Richie Benaud was a boy.

'Why don't you sing us something, Richard?'

'I can't sing.'

'Since when does that matter?'

As it happens, I love singing, but I have no voice. So I sang a nervous, flat rendition of a Matt Johnson song. The sub-conscious mind is a tricky bastard. I sung the first song which came to mind, and only when I began to sing the chorus did I realise its strange appropriateness. It came over as a declaration of intent. '*This is the day your life will surely change. This is the day when things fall into place.*'

I saw Elizabeth watching me, running her teeth over her lower lip. I wanted to grab her and kiss her.

'That was lovely,' Gwen said. 'Richard deserves a treat.'

Elizabeth scurried off to retrieve a massive pavlova, the whipped cream packed with banana and passionfruit. While she was gone, Max tidied away her sheet music. He was desperately sad.

'She's a bonzer girl that one. You'll take good care of her, won't you Dick?'

'I'm sure he will,' Gwen added.

Elizabeth's pavlova was an item of such delicacy and brilliance that I might have proposed marriage on the spot. A woman who can master a large meringue crust is capable of anything.

Eventually, Gwen left to take a nap, and Max dragged a reluctant Jack onto the tennis court, leaving Elizabeth and I alone in the sitting room. While I examined the bookshelves, she worked on a patchwork quilt.

'Do you have a favourite writer, Liz?'

'Jane Austen and Tolstoy are my favourites, but mostly I read Australian authors.'

'Yeah? Who do you like?'

'Barbara Baynton, Eleanor Dark, Kenneth Slessor.

'How about *modern* Australian writers?'

'I like some George Johnston ... *My Brother Jack* is good.'

'You should read Beverley Farmer. She's written beautiful stories about a young Australian woman living in Greece.'

'Greece doesn't really interest me. It's only Australia I know about.'

'Things have changed since Max and Gwen last saw

Australia.'

'Not nearly as much as they've changed here. It makes you dizzy. You wonder if people actually believe in anything, if there's anything worth holding onto. Australians would never be so negative about the future. They're much more hopeful. No one on Meskos hopes for anything more than money.'

'So did you and young Lizzie have a chat about things?'

Max stripped the top off another tube while Jack went upstairs to die.

'I should show you the studio.'

When Max retired from medical practice, he took up painting. He warned me beforehand that he was a beginner, telling me I shouldn't be too harsh in my judgement. He was still trying to clarify his artistic vision.

To be honest, I was shocked. I'd expected fey traditionalism, or landscapes, but Max had a vigorous expressionistic technique, not so pared back as de Kooning, but broad, powerful brush-strokes and abrasive colours.

'These are really wild, Max.'

'Wild, yes, that's probably the right word. I'd like them to be wilder, angrier.'

I'm no critic, but Max was a better artist than he gave himself credit for. Although he described most of his works as preliminary studies, they looked like finished paintings.

This is my favourite, he said. 'Evil Begets Evil'.

Two naked males appeared to be locked in a fight to the death.

'It's a tag-team wresting match. That's Doc Evatt, and that's B.A. Santamaria. Santamaria's trying to tag Frank McManus in the blue corner, but Doc is pulling him back ... Hard times, Dick. If the Commos or the Micks had got their way, Australia would have been buggered. Thank Christ big Bob held the show together with some common bloody sense. Australians must wish Ming was still running the show.'

'Some do ... Do you keep track of what's going on in Australia, Max?'

'You don't get a lot of Australian news here ... Not enough to get the full picture. To me, the worst thing was changing the currency. How could the Libs countenance a treachery like that? It was one thing to go decimal, but changing the names ... What was wrong with pounds, shillings and pence?... Don't get me wrong. I love the Yanks. They won us the War, but we don't have to live like them. We're lucky our Lizzie's a pounds and shillings girl.'

'How do you mean?'

'Elizabeth was born on February 13th, 1966. Made it by a day ... It would have been nice if she'd been born while RG was running the show, but Ming was top man when she was conceived, and that's the main thing.'

I could offer no sensible response to this. I suddenly had the terrible idea that Liz might be Ming's love child, that Menzies was literally the top man when she was conceived.

'Stick with me for a tick, I've got a portrait of RG and Dame Patty here somewhere.'

Max flicked his way through a pile of canvasses stacked against the wall. I was worried that Menzies and Dame Patty might be depicted in a nude tag-team wrestling match.

'You know, I'm not sure I could go back now. Dollars. Taxes on petrol. Pro tennis ... Still, I've heard this young bloke Howard is top-shelf. He's not the kind of man who'd let the bodgies intimidate him.'

I had peculiar dreams where I made brief trips back home to check my answering machine and collect the mail. The only items waiting for me were carefully boxed cakes posted by Elizabeth. Magnificent productions: Strawberry Cream Torte, and Raspberry Temptation. Lizzie's cakes ought to have been photographed, they deserved immortalisation, but they were inedible. Her cream hadn't travelled well.

Three weeks passed. Jack and I lost the need to use belts. Life with the Colleys was like the revenge of Margaret Fulton. Nothing slowed the lamington production line: honey-coated lamingtons, cherry ripe lamingtons, rocky road lamingtons.

Between the lamingtons, there were tarts and dumplings, pies and pastries. Yorkshire puddings. Casseroles by the trough-full. While Jack and I began to resemble constipated Sumo wrestlers, the Colleys remained slender and elegant. Either they had rapid metabolisms, or they were secretly bulimic.

Jack and I were never permitted to carry a dish or enter the kitchen. This secrecy about the kitchen led us to imagine a room like Dr. Who's Tardis, a larder that cheated space and time. Where did the fresh bananas and strawberries come from? Where was the silo holding the Colley's stockpile of desiccated coconut? You wouldn't dare open the freezer for fear that you'd find Heather McKay or Norm O'Neill being cryogenically preserved.

Jack let out a tremendous fart which sent a shudder through the bunkbeds.

Mate, you've got to bring matters to a head. We're cooking up a dental emergency. I want to see my kids again before I die.

I tried to imagine what Elizabeth might be thinking, what she was hoping, and whether I corresponded to the man she'd always longed for. I tried to picture what it would be like to live with her in Melbourne, and how such a sheltered woman might react to a city so different to anything within her experience. Though she'd been taught at home, Liz was bright and capable. But she'd been brought up to become a wife, and wives were no longer the kind of wives that Elizabeth had trained to become.

Could such a woman be deprogrammed, or *want* to be deprogrammed? Did she dream of making scones for rugged firefighters, or surf lifesavers? Maybe she dreamt of moving among a crowd of sophisticates who sipped sherry and discussed Eleanor Dark and A.D. Hope. How would I know if she'd have the patience or desire to deal with someone who'd been so fucked in the head as I had been?

Elizabeth Colley was highly desirable, more attractive than she knew. She was also inscrutable.

'Do you swim, Richard?'

I'd been reading *The Tree of Man*. Elizabeth was sewing. Never before had she initiated conversation.

'I love the water, but I'm not a strong swimmer.'

'Are there beaches near home?'

'There are terrific beaches at Sandringham and Black Rock, and there are fabulous ocean beaches an hour's drive away.'

I might have mentioned sharks, freezing water, ozone depletion, and skin cancer, all my usual fears, but we were on a roll.

'You can't swim on the beaches here. The islanders get drunk and swim naked.'

I could picture Elizabeth swimming naked, red hair sweeping toward a magnificent bare arse, her long legs spreading and closing. The erotic charge of it left me giddy enough to joke.

'I'm too shy to swim naked. I like to keep my tatts where people can't see them.'

Elizabeth was scandalised. 'You don't really have tattoos? Only sailors and convicts have them.'

'No. I hate tatts. They're gauche … But I do have a silver stud through my clitoris.'

I waited for a smile, or a scowl, but there was neither.

'What's a clitoris?'

My parents never liked the girls I brought home, but they did their best. While they wanted me to find a girl who would devote herself to supporting me, I was always attracted to brilliant women like Miranda Murray, women with loads of ambition and character, women who were practically certain to discard me in the course of time.

Even though I'd brought it on myself, Mum and Dad hated

to see me hurt. They would have been thrilled if I'd come home with a pretty, old-fashioned girl like Elizabeth Colley, a young woman who had been educated to value pleasantness above all else.

But my parents have absorbed enough modern influences to agree with me on one matter—I'm talking about implicit agreement here, it's definitely not the kind of thing we discuss. They would both accept that an intelligent, thirty-two-year-old woman on the verge of entering married life should have a better than fair idea what a clitoris is.

If I wanted to back out, I now had an excuse. But I didn't know what I wanted. Neither did I know what Elizabeth wanted. I thought I knew what she expected me to want.

I've spent most of my adult life cultivating a low-level of expectation, a level of underachievement I could easily live down to. The people who knew me expected little from me, and I generally chose to do no more than they expected.

Gwen Colley had little to say on most issues. Cooking, sweeping, sewing, and stretching Max's canvasses seemed to be her life. I found it hard to picture her as the same woman who kept regular correspondence with my mother for forty years. But it was Gwen who finally hit the pedal.

'I think Lizzie's expecting you to speak to her, Richard. You mustn't wait for her to lead the way with these things. Elizabeth's not as shy as you might think, but she does have a strict sense of propriety and etiquette.'

I understood all this to mean that Elizabeth was waiting for me to propose a married future in Australia, and such an arrangement had Max and Gwen's blessing.

I went to the bathroom to brush my teeth, bumping into my bloated brother as I left.

'Dick, see if you can't have her packed and ready to leave by Friday.'

I found Elizabeth sitting at the piano playing Beethoven.

When she saw me enter, she smiled sweetly, and stopped playing.

'You didn't have to stop.'

'Oh, I already know the rest.'

'Look, Liz, let's not beat around the bush. You must find this as awkward as I do. When Mum showed me your photo, I was pretty certain you were my sort of girl. Then your folks made it clear you were interested to meet me. Well ... I like you a lot, Liz. You're a beautiful woman. A bloke'd be crazy or gay not to be attracted to you ... I won't pretend that this is what romance is all about. I'm never going to be wealthy or famous. I'm ordinary as they come. But I'm honest. You're a sensible girl from a fine family. If you'd like to, I think we could make a go of it.'

'Oh, Richard.'

Believing this to be a so-grateful, prelude-to-tears 'Oh, Richard', I went on, hoping to spare Lizzie's embarrassment as much as anything else.

'The financial side of things will work out. I could go back to writing for television till we're on track. Though you don't have any qualifications or experience, you're intelligent and personable, and Max has great connections. We could fudge a Greek *c.v.* and no one would be the wiser.'

'Oh, Richard. I'm so sorry.'

'*Sorry?*... You don't want to come back to Australia with me?'

'You're a very nice fellow, but ...'

'Look, you don't have to be in love with me, Liz. I used to be a romantic, but I don't trust that stuff now. Love is a muscle. If there's respect, trust, and good will ... I mean, these arrangements often work famously, because people are determined to make them work.'

'It's just ... You're not the kind of man I expected you to be.'

'Oh ... What kind of man were you hoping for?'

'I expected you to be more ... I don't know. More vigorous. More certain of yourself. Fearless and optimistic. You're good looking. You're kind. You're obviously quite clever. But you're open to some strange ideas. You're very, susceptible, I think ... I expected you to be more Australian.'

Susceptible? Yes, a fair cop. Susceptible to vibrant ideas. Novelty. Pretty women, always. To stillness, but a stillness that precedes motion. I am much too susceptible.

There's no direct ferry from Meskos to the Greek mainland. That hardly seemed to matter on the return journey.

Jack tried to comfort me, but seeing I didn't need comforting, he sought the company of a pretty Viennese art student who offered him some Turkish hash. She told Jack that the CIA used Meskos as a drug clearing-house for southern Europe.

As they stood at the rear of the ferry, giggling and exchanging conspiracy theories, Meskos slowly disappeared into the late-afternoon haze. I held my arms open to a faint cooling breeze, much like a primary school kid pretending to be a tree swaying in the wind, and almost as happy. I was going somewhere.

When I got back to Australia, I would do all the things I'd never seriously thought about doing. Heroin. Group sex. I might even give golf a try. I was middle-aged and single. Maybe I'd always be single. But I was young enough—vibrantly young—and growing younger by the minute.

1997

ACKNOWLEDGEMENTS

Having lived in the same Melbourne suburb for almost sixty years, I am passionately attached to Hampton. Ghosts reside in every street and on every corner. I can't begin to imagine the sense of attachment or belonging you would have if your ancestors had roamed the same spaces for one thousand generations. I offer my respect to the traditional owners, the Boon Wurrung People of the Kulin Nation. Their lands were never ceded.

A portion of this book was written with the generous support of a Developing Writers grant from the Literary Board of the Australia Council.

Many thanks to Peter Mathews for championing this project, and to Matt Rubinstein at Ligature for investing in it and making it happen. I have long dreamed of having the three volumes united in the way I originally intended.

So many teachers, mentors, editors, family members and friends contributed to the writing of these fictions, and most are acknowledged in the original publications. Special thanks to Sophie Cunningham, Patrick Gallagher, Annette Barlow, Polly Croke and April Murdoch at Allen and Unwin for their valued contributions, and their belief in this project. I am also indebted to Lars Ahlstrom, Lizzie Eves and John McDonagh for championing *The Prince*.

My thanks to Ann Valos and Buddy for their assistance, love and support during the assembly of this version.

I would particularly wish to acknowledge the kindness, good humour, and inspiration supplied by my dear friend Mia Tolhurst (1977–2013), and to express gratitude to two wonderful parents, Marjory Richards (1921–2019) and Alistair Richards (1919–2018). It is to the memory of those three that I humbly dedicate this volume.